THE OLD WHEEL

THE ADVENTURES OF HOLLOWAY HOLMES

BOOK 2

GREGORY ASHE

H&B

Published by Hodgkin & Blount
https://www.hodgkinandblount.com/
contact@hodgkinandblount.com

Published 2023
Printed in the United States of America

Version 1.03

Trade Paperback ISBN: 978-1-63621-059-9
eBook ISBN: 978-1-63621-058-2

The conversation, which had roamed in a desultory, spasmodic fashion from golf clubs to the causes of the change in the obliquity of the ecliptic, came round at last to the question of atavism and hereditary aptitudes. The point under discussion was, how far any singular gift in an individual was due to his ancestry and how far to his own early training.

— "The Adventure of the Greek Interpreter," Sir Arthur Conan Doyle

Any truth is better than indefinite doubt.

— "The Adventure of the Yellow Face," Sir Arthur Conan Doyle

The old wheel turns.

— *The Valley of Fear*, Sir Arthur Conan Doyle

Chapter 1

I Forgot

"How to Break Up," the title of the article on my phone said, "and Still Be a Gentleman."

"First thing you've got to remember," Dad said, "is go easy."

I barely heard him. One of the advantages of having a smartphone again—thank you, Jesus—was that I had access to, you know, everything. At least, most of the time that was an advantage. Times like this? When I'd spent the last four days reading articles titled "The No-Bullshit Break-Up" and "Be a Man and Do It" and even, kind of confusingly, "In Pursuit of the Carbon-Neutral Break-Up: Yes, It's Possible"? No, not much of an advantage. Not an advantage at all, really.

Dad jabbed me in the knee with an Allen wrench.

"Ow!"

He gave me a level look. People say Dad and I look alike, although I only see it in our jaws, our mouths, maybe a little around our eyes. His hair is gray and buzzed (not like mine), and his skin is closer to bronze (I'm more of a dark olive), and he's built strong (so far, undetermined, but I think I'll end up somewhere between him and Mom). He tried to jab me with the wrench again, and I stepped out of reach. "Phone away." He waved the Allen wrench at the old mountain bike—technically his, although I was the only one who used it anymore. "I'm teaching you how to do this, buddy. I'm not doing it for you."

Sighing, I pocketed the phone. "How to Break Up and Still Be a Gentleman" had sounded like a lot of bullshit anyway.

Dad pressed the Allen wrench into my hand and pointed to the bike. It sat upside down on the cold concrete slab of the maintenance garage. The nice thing about working at the Walker School (one of the nice things, although to be honest, there weren't a ton) was that Dad had this huge, heated garage. In December, though, with the glass-block windows frosted over and the wind off Timp screaming against the cinderblock shell, it wasn't exactly warm. The ceiling heater rattled overhead, struggling to keep up, and the smell of hot dust mixed with the odor of two-stroke engine oil. But it was a hell of a lot better than doing this kind of work outside.

"Step one, get the lower forks off."

So, I went to work, and for a pair of quiet minutes, I didn't have to think about anything except disassembling the suspension fork. Dad wheeled over an oil-stained office chair and sat; he was doing so much better since we'd gotten health insurance and he could get all his prescriptions and take them consistently, but he still got tired easily, and his balance got funny sometimes. Almost a year and a half later, we were still dealing with the effects of the car crash and the traumatic brain injury. I guess that's why they call them *long-term symptoms*.

"Did you ever break up with Mom?" I asked.

The question popped out before I realized I had formed it in my head. My face heated, and I kept my eyes on the bike as I tugged the lower forks loose. Dad rolled closer, and the sound of the casters on the concrete kept time with the heater's faint rattle.

"Put these on." Dad passed me a pair of nitrile gloves. Then he handed me a tiny screwdriver. "We're improvising here, so you're going to be careful. See those foam rings? You're going to get them out—and you're going to do it without damaging the seals underneath, understand?" He sat back, and his hands curled around the armrests. "And no, I never broke up with your mother. She probably thought about breaking up with me a time or two."

I nodded and kept my gaze on the bike. It probably would have been easier with a specialized tool, but it wasn't terribly difficult getting the foam rings out with the screwdriver. They were dark with oil and dirt, and they left smears on the gloves.

"Any reason you're asking?" Dad said in what I'd started to recognize as his I'm-so-carefully-neutral-I-could-be-Switzerland voice.

I shook my head.

The furnace rattled. The wind snaked against the walls of the garage. I turned the foam rings over in my hand and finally couldn't stall any longer and looked up at Dad.

He had his Switzerland face on. "Get the rubbing alcohol and a tub — we should replace those, but for today, we're going to clean them up as best we can."

So, I jogged over to the workbench, found the rubbing alcohol and an empty plastic tub, and carried it back over to the bike. I poured in enough alcohol to cover the pads, but when I went to strip off the gloves, Dad shook his head.

The chair creaked when he rocked slightly. "Do you miss her? That's a dumb question; I know you miss her. But...did something happen?"

"No."

The chair creaked again. "You happened to be wondering if I ever broke up with your mom?"

"I guess."

He rubbed a hand over his hair, and it made a soft sound.

"How do you know if something is serious?" I blurted this question like the last one. I heard myself, and I made a firm decision to get a lobotomy. "Like, if you should stick it out when you have a rough patch, or if that means you're not, you know, supposed to be together?"

Dad was silent for a long time. "Did you get her pregnant?"

"Dad!"

"Did you?"

"No!"

"Are you using condoms? Because I don't care if she tells you she's on birth control—you use a condom every time."

I blew out a breath and fished one of the foam pads out of the alcohol. "Jack."

"Yes, oh my God. Can we please stop talking about this?"

He didn't say anything to that, which was kind of an answer. He sat there, staring at me, legs spread, hands tight around the arms of the chair. I squeezed the pads to get the oil out, rinsed, and repeated.

Finally, he said, "That's enough."

He stood and walked over to the utility sink. His first few steps were unsteady, but then he evened out. Water ran. When he came back, he had a bucket and a sponge. He worked the sponge around in the soapy water, and then, using the chair for balance, got down on his knees and started to clean the bike's frame.

"I'm supposed to be doing that," I said.

"You're sixteen, buddy." His voice was softer, and he kept his eyes on the sponge. "Why are you worried about sticking it out?"

"I don't know."

He moved the sponge in slow, careful swipes, and clumps of dirt fell away. Muddy water ran down to the concrete slab, and trickles of it curled inward along his wrist.

"It's just—" I hooked my arms around my knees. "There's a lot going on right now. And, I don't know." There wasn't a good way to tell my dad that I was feeling a little conflicted because of a gray-eyed boy who had made it painfully clear that he had no interest in me. "I don't know."

He paused, the sponge halfway up the bike's frame. "Do you like her?"

"This is the worst conversation of my life."

That got a tiny smile out of him, and he started scrubbing again.

"I don't know," I said. "Yes, I mean, obviously. Ariana is great. But sometimes I think maybe I—I rushed into this."

Dad made a noise that could have meant anything.

"What?" I asked.

He shook his head.

"Come on."

"Nothing." He smiled and tossed the sponge in the bucket. "I remember what it's like to be sixteen. You think you have to dip your wick into everything."

"Dad!"

He laughed. "It's not like you're the first teenage boy in the history of the world, buddy."

"That's not—it's not like that."

"Ok."

"It's not."

"I said ok, son. If you say that's not what it is, I believe you." One knee cracked when he got to his feet. "You like her, right?"

I groaned, but when he waited, I nodded.

"Well, why don't you see what happens? Take her to that dance. Winter—what is it?"

I squinted a dirty look up at him. "You know it's Wintersmash. And it's not a dance. And I can't go; it's invite only."

Dad frowned at that. "I'm sure you'll get an invitation."

Responding to that—telling him the truth—would only hurt him, so I didn't say anything.

After a moment, Dad cleared his throat. "It doesn't have to be the Winter thing. I'm just saying slow down. You feel like you rushed into this? Well, as an outside observer, I'm telling you I think you're rushing again. You've been dating—what? A couple of months?"

"But we've been hanging out longer than that."

"Well, it's a free country. You can break up with her whenever you want. But this is your first serious relationship; why don't you give it a little time and see how it develops?"

I thought about that. Then I looked up at Dad. "Do you like her?"

"It doesn't matter what I think."

I made a face.

"I like her," he said with a laugh. "She's good for you."

I made a different face.

Dad tried to flick me with a shop towel he pulled from his back pocket, and I barely dodged in time.

After that, it was easier to work than to talk. Everything Dad said had made sense. It had been—well, it had been what I'd been hoping he'd say, actually. And now he'd said it, and I hadn't died of embarrassment, and somehow…somehow I felt worse. Because what I wanted to say was, *But it doesn't feel right*. Or maybe, *But what if there's someone else, and even though I don't have a shot with him, I feel totally different when I'm around him?* Or maybe, if I were going to get agonizingly specific, *I know what love feels like, and this isn't it*. But, of course, all of those things were a fuck-ton scarier to say out loud, and sometimes, Jack Moreno was a coward.

With Dad watching to make sure I did it right, I replaced the rings, oiled them, and ran suspension grease around the inside of the upper forks. I was reaching for the lower forks when he said, "Run home and wash up. I'll finish here."

"I'll do it."

"You're going to be late." This time, he did get me with the towel, and even through my jeans, it stung. He grinned when I yelped. "Ass on fire, buddy. Run."

He was exaggerating; I had plenty of time before Holmes came over to help me study, and even if I were late, he wouldn't mind. Well, he would because he had this uncanny clockwork precision to everything he did, but he was nice enough that he wouldn't say anything. Going back to school had been awesome, an opportunity I'd never thought I'd get, but it had also meant coming face to face with the reality that teachers, unlike YouTube videos and Wikipedia articles, actually expected you to do something with what you were learning, and sometimes that was a hell of a lot harder than remembering the odd bit of internet trivia.

Outside, the Wasatch Mountains were blisteringly white with snow—so much snow that even at night, the canyon seemed bright. It furred the bare branches of scrub oaks and aspens, and it glazed the dark green of the pines. The wind bit at my ears and stole my breath in long steaming coils as I jogged home. It wasn't far from the maintenance building, but I thought maybe Dad was right, and I should have worn a coat.

I let myself into the cottage—we didn't bother locking the doors, not all the way on the ass-end of Timp—and turned on the lights. It was warm, which was one good thing you could say about it. It wasn't falling down;

that was another. It was small, and when you first stepped inside, the thing you noticed was the smell from the three-quarters fridge, like something was burning. But it was ours, at least, as long as Dad stayed on at Walker, and that was enough.

I kicked off my Nikes by the door and was hopping toward the bathroom, peeling off my socks, when a knock startled me.

When I opened the door, Holmes was standing there. There's no good way to describe him: you start with one piece, like his eyes the color of starlight, and then you have to talk about the perfection of cheekbone, mouth, jaw, and then you're on to his neck, the breadth of his shoulders fanning out as he turned, the curve and line of arm until you reach that one knobby knuckle. The whole reason people started carving sculptures was because of guys like Holmes, where everything about him had the look of cold-chiseled perfection. He was wearing his usual getup: a wool driving coat, a pale oxford, dark chinos, chukkas wet with snow. He was gripping his school bag, and when he saw me, his hands relaxed. I noticed things like that with him; I liked noticing things like that, liked what they said.

"You left your socks on the floor," he said.

I shut the door behind him.

"Your dad has asked you several times not to leave them in the common areas of the house."

"Hi, H."

"It's eleven degrees outside. You shouldn't be barefoot in the winter."

"How was your day?"

He studied me, eyes like mercury beads. "My day was normal."

"You can do better than that."

Grimacing, Holmes passed me his bag and began working his way out of his coat. "I ate turkey sausage and scrambled eggs for breakfast. And I had a protein shake."

"But you didn't eat dinner."

"I had the protein shake late in the afternoon."

"That doesn't count."

"It most certainly does."

"Uh huh. One good thing?"

"I learned about a useful backdoor on a popular brand of doorbell camera, and I completed all my schoolwork."

"And one bad thing?"

"I already told you about the turkey sausage."

"Oh my God, ladies and gentlemen. A joke."

Holmes yanked the bag back. "You're a bad influence. We're beginning with chemistry tonight."

"No, please, I'll give you anything you want."

You couldn't tell, but Holmes ate this stuff up like candy. At least, that's what I chose to believe.

"I'll tell you where I hid the Nazi codebook. You can have my firstborn!"

"Your firstborn would doubtless leave socks everywhere."

"H!"

"Your room—"

"My room is fine! And for the record, I don't want to catch you sneaking in there to clean up again. If you find your present, I'm not going to give it to you. It's supposed to be a surprise."

You had to learn to read the microexpressions: the subtleties of mouth and eyes. He pretended to be busy hanging up his coat.

"If we are going to continue our arrangement—" H began.

The knock at the door stopped him. He glanced at me.

I shrugged and opened the door.

Ariana stood there. She looked cute. Scratch that. She looked fantastic, done up in a belted jumper dress that showed off her legs—and her curves—with her hair in perfect curls and boots she knew I liked on her. She smiled at me, gave Holmes a curious look, and leaned in. I kissed her automatically.

"Ready?" She glanced at me in my work clothes and bare feet and smiled uncertainly. "What's up? Are we still on for dinner?"

Dinner, my brain said.

"No, yeah, I just—"

Holmes ripped his coat from the hook. "It's my fault," he said, the words clipped and emotionless. "I'm sorry for keeping him."

"H, wait. I forgot—"

But he plunged out into the night, and the door clicked shut behind him.

Chapter 2

On the Outside

"Look," I said. "Do you want them or not?"

His name was Travis something, and he was one of those short, chubby kids who hadn't really hit puberty yet. He'd said he wanted Roblox Robux cards, the physical ones that included an exclusive virtual item, and so I'd gone to Target, Walmart, and finally Best Buy, burning up half a Saturday to get them for him.

He made a face, staring at the gift cards.

Thursday morning, with the air so cold it felt like glass and the sky clear and the sun still coming up behind the mountains, I could pretend I wasn't thinking about last night. On the quad outside Walker Hall, where I had most of my classes, kids walked hurriedly—most of them headed for Walker, but others going to the science building, or the athletic center, or making a late dash to the dining hall, or, if they had study time, the library or their residence.

"Fine," I said, moving to pocket the gift cards. "I'll return them."

"No, no. I'll take it. But—can you do one fifty?"

"Two hundred." Double the face value, but—for a kid trapped at Walker—the only way he could get them. "Yes or no?"

"Yes, yes." He whipped out his phone. "I can make the transfer in crypto, but I understand if you want me to run it through a cash app instead."

I stared at him. "Cash. We agreed on cash."

"Ok, cash app—"

"No. Not cash app. Cash. You pay me in cash."

Travis squinted at me. "Uh, it's an app."

"Never mind," I said, jamming the gift cards into my backpack. "Forget it."

Travis wailed in outrage, but I slung my backpack onto my shoulder and started across the quad.

Cash was king; that was the bottom line for me—and, by extension, for dad. A lot had changed for us over the last two months: Dad had started getting the care he needed, and that meant he could work regularly, and I was back in school. But healthcare now didn't take care of the bills—medical and otherwise—that had piled up after the accident, and even though Dad handled most of the calls from collectors, I knew we were still in serious trouble. Add to that my own growing expenses, such as a new phone, clothes for school, and having a girlfriend who had the totally reasonable expectation that every once in a while, I could actually take her out and do something fun, and I was starting to think I needed a full-time job. Especially when dicks-for-brains like Travis tried to pay me in crypto.

I sauntered through the crowd, smiling, nodding, keeping my eyes open for my regulars. Jimmy caught my eye, turned red, and looked away. Ryan frowned and gave a tiny shake of his head. Kai turned away from me, rucking up her backpack like that would make her invisible. Other Walker students took a different approach. Jessica gave me a huge smile and waved, but when I started toward her, she said something to the group of girls she was with, and they burst out laughing. I changed course, heading for Tevan and Brock and their little knot of meatheads; Tevan whooped and pumped his fist in the air, and Brock cupped his hands around his mouth and shouted, "What up, Abercrombie?"

It was the kind of fine-tuned assholery that kids perfected. None of it was enough that you could point it out. Nothing you could slap a label on. The stupid nickname came closest—Dad had bought me the hoodie from Abercrombie last Christmas, when we'd had no fucking money at all, and for him, it was the best shit ever because it had been cool when he'd been a kid. Trust the Walker kids to find a way to turn it into an insult.

"Fuck them." The voice came from behind me, and I turned. Dawson McKee had dark hair and deep eyes, a kind of rugged masculinity that was attractive without being handsome. He had his hands in his pockets, and he glanced at Tevan and Brock as he said, "Bunch of 'roided-up ball-less fucks."

"At least they're not playing the janitor card yet."

"Too soon. When they think people are forgetting, they'll remind them."

I thought about Ryan's tiny shake of the head, how Kai had rucked her backpack up, the way Jessica's smile had dissolved into laughter when I tried to approach. "Yeah, I don't think anybody's going to forget my dad shovels their shit. Or that I used to do it too."

Dawson shrugged. "Probably not."

In September, I'd caught Dawson and Aston—two of Walker's social elite, members of the clique of hot, rich boys I called the Boy Band—in a compromising moment. Later, I'd seen a video that had confirmed my suspicions. Dawson had given me a few significant looks over the intervening weeks, and the message had been clear. He was giving me one of them now.

I grinned. "What?"

"You know what."

"Gosh, golly."

A tiny smile lifted the corner of Dawson's mouth. Quietly, he said, "You're cute."

My grin got bigger.

"I want something," Dawson said in that same low voice.

I burst out laughing. When Dawson frowned, I said, "Sorry, it's just— usually people try to be subtle about it."

"Why? You know you're hot. You know I'm into it. And I want something. It doesn't hurt to remind you that, you know, I'm into it."

"What do you want? I can get you that Astroglide, but it's going to take a couple of days. Maybe not until Monday."

"Yeah? Lube, that's the first thing you thought of when I told you I wanted something?"

I rolled my eyes. I rolled them big, for his benefit.

He laughed and inched closer. "Told you you're cute."

The five-minute bell rang, and students began to move toward Walker.

"Time's up."

"Swear to God you won't laugh?"

I put my hand in the air.

"You won't tell anyone?"

"Discretion is my middle name."

Dawson's heavy eyebrows drew together, and he did a quick, sidelong glance to make sure no one was close enough to hear us. "Viagra."

It took me a beat too long. "Oh."

"I'm not having problems, dickweed."

"Dickweed? I thought I was cute."

"It's for fun. You know, to play. But I want the real stuff, none of that fake shit from the gas station."

"Let me see."

He had dark eyes, and they were surprisingly intense as they fixed on me. "What do you mean? You've always got the shit."

That had been true a few months ago. I'd had a falling out with my dealer in Provo, though—if you count Holloway Holmes smashing his head into a truck and, subsequently, beating the shit out of him and his boys as a falling out. Until I found someone closer, I had to drive up to Lehi now, and that meant more time, more gas, and higher prices for everything. On top of that, the new headmaster, Dr. Cluff, was making my life harder than it needed to be: random searches, room checks, the threat of drug tests. "I mean, let me see. If I can get it, how much do you want?"

"What can I get for a hundred bucks?"

The stream of students heading into Walker had thickened, but I spotted a familiar face. To Dawson, I said, "Half up front. I don't do credit anymore."

"Come on; I'm good for it. Have I ever shafted you?"

I smirked.

"Enough with the cute stuff," Dawson growled. "You know I'll pay."

"Half up front, Daw. Sorry."

When I turned to go, he grabbed my arm. So low I could barely hear him, he muttered, "I could, uh, find another way to pay you." His tongue touched the corner of his mouth, and he looked nervous—a lot more like a teenage boy, a lot less like the sexy caveman. "I told you, I'm into this whole thing you've got going."

Because I had no idea what to do, I laughed, and I kept laughing as I slipped out of his grip. Dawson's face darkened, and I tried to soften the laugh with a smile, the whole time putting more space between us. Before he could try something else, I turned and plunged into the river of bodies.

Stray elbows and swinging backpacks jostled me as the current carried me forward. My brain wanted to process the fact that Dawson McKee—Dawson McKee of the Boy Band—had just tried to trade sex for Viagra. Which maybe was irony, I guess? But that was a question that could wait until Language Arts. The bigger question was why—why he was so desperate for it, and why he couldn't pay.

I barely caught Hayden before he stepped inside Walker. He stumbled when I tugged on his sleeve, and then he let me pull him to the side, out of the stream of students. He was one of those tall, lanky kids, with big eyes and a pathetic attempt at facial hair. He glanced at the students passing us, but none of them were paying attention.

"Hey," I said, "I got it."

He looked over at the other students again.

"It's the same shit he uses—same dosage, same pharmacy, everything." When he started to turn his head again, I said, "Quit looking, dumbass. Meet me in the bathroom in a minute."

Hayden made a face.

"What?" I asked. "It's legit; I checked it myself. You wanted what Holloway Holmes uses, and I got it."

"Uh, I changed my mind."

"You can't change your mind. I already got it; you already paid half."

"Fine, whatever, you can keep the money, but I don't want it."

I grabbed his coat when he tried to weasel away. "What the fuck?"

"Marcie said it was going to make me—you know, like him."

"What? Smart? Strong? Able to operate on an hour or two of sleep?"

"You know," Hayden said, his voice pitchy, his chest rising and falling rapidly. "A freak."

He pulled free, and I let him go.

When the last student passed through the double doors, I dug my thumbs into the corners of my eyes, swallowed a scream, and kicked Walker's bricks three or four times. Then I headed inside.

I was late, of course. Ms. Albrecht announced the tardy to the whole class. A few kids looked smug, but most of them were too tired this early in the morning to process much of what was going on. I took my seat, and Ms. Albrecht started class.

In a lot of ways, school at Walker was like my old school—you had good teachers and bad ones, students who wanted to clown and students who were natural people-pleasers and students who were uber-diligent and were aiming at the Ivys. Some of the classes were interesting, but most of them were boring as hell. I'd forgotten, in the almost year and a half since I'd been in school, how much time got wasted during the day, and how much instruction was spent on things that I had absolutely no interest in learning. In that sense, I'd take YouTube and Wikipedia over a classroom any day.

There were differences, however. The kids were one—the amount of money they had, for starters. It wasn't the differences you might find in a normal school, with some kids coming from a trailer park and some kids coming from million-dollar homes. Walker was in a different stratosphere; these were kids with parents who only traveled on private planes, who had multiple homes, all of them worth millions of dollars, who had trust funds and estates and, Christ, I don't know, polo horses.

And that much money had a trickle-down effect. The buildings at Walker, including the classrooms, were a far cry from my old school, with its painted cinderblock and drop-ceiling tiles. While it had been clean and relatively new, nobody would have ever mistaken it for anything but a public institution. Walker, on the other hand, looked like somebody had taken Mr. Boddy's mansion straight out of the game Clue and decided to use it for a school. Or Professor Xavier's mansion, if you wanted to go with X-Men. Or maybe Castle Dracula, if you wanted to go goth. The walls had dark wainscotting and old-fashioned plaster, and while the floor was linoleum because of all the snowy students trooping through, the hallways were filled with tables and trinkets and oil paintings and crystal chandeliers.

In the classrooms, the desks and chairs were real wood, none of that particleboard-and-laminate shit. You could tell the stuff was old, too—the kind of smooth, worn look that you can only get with time. Plus, generations of Walker students had carved the usual stuff anywhere it couldn't be seen at a casual glance—names, dicks, the standard swears, plus some new-to-me ones like *nipnubs* and *frotmeister*. The real masterpiece, though, was some sort of hybrid Cleopatra-Sphinx with enormous boobs, which was kind of a tribute to Ms. Albrecht's World History class, I guess. The place always smelled like Murphy oil soap and chalk dust and wet footwear, and I was still fighting several months' worth of conditioning to grab a mop when I saw the tracks these kids were leaving all over the place.

I didn't mind World History, mostly because I didn't mind Ms. Albrecht—she was a petite woman, with a mane of blond hair, and she wore a lot of puffer vests and cute jeans, and if she hadn't been fifty, she probably would have been a babe. On top of all that, she was a decent teacher, although she was, as recently demonstrated, also a hardass. But I couldn't get interested in World History; I didn't care about imperialism, which probably made me a traitor because at some point, way back in the ancestral line, I was some sort of product of imperialism. But it was boring, and so I let my brain go on autopilot, turning pages and passing back worksheets, while I tried to figure out how to solve my money problem.

The problem was liquidity. I'd read all four pages on Wikipedia about liquidity; liquidity was a big deal for someone operating in my particular shitstorm. I'd learned my lesson with Watson earlier that year: never buy on credit. So, as I had with Hayden, and as I'd told Dawson, I wanted cash up front. Half, minimum. But that meant that sometimes—like with Hayden—I got stuck footing the other half until I delivered. And, if the kid turned out to be a little shit like Hayden, I ended up with a prescription vial full of mixed amphetamines and less cash than when I started. Sure, I could sell the addies to Holmes the next time he ran out (which, yes, I felt like shit about, and yes, I continued to do, and yes, was about as fucked-up a situation as there was), but that didn't help me now. I needed cash, not pills—cash I could use to buy Christmas presents for Holmes and Ariana and my dad; cash I could use to pay my phone bill; cash I could slip into the old jelly jar where Dad kept our grocery money, my one way of contributing without him noticing.

"Jack?" Ms. Albrecht said.

I looked up.

She waited.

Nobody laughed, but the movement of bodies, the shift and rustle of clothing, carried an undercurrent of amusement.

"I'm sorry," I said. "I spaced out."

"I asked if you could list the imperialist powers."

"Spain, um, England, the Netherlands."

This time, someone did laugh. It sounded like Brock.

"From the nineteenth century, Jack. We're talking about the nineteenth century."

"Oh." A flush moved into my face, and after a few pounding heartbeats, I shook my head.

"Russia, Italy, Germany, the United States," another voice said. "And Japan."

I made myself not look over. I didn't want to see Aston's smug face. It was bad enough that Dawson's fuck buddy and joint member of the Boy Band was still here, at Walker, after he'd tried to murder Holmes. From what I could tell, he hadn't gotten more than a rap on the wrist—community service, I'd heard. Because his grandfather was a bigwig in the Mormon church, an apostle. And because Aston had cried and told a sob story about how Headmaster Burrows had threatened him into helping. I didn't doubt the last part—Burrows had been scary, and Aston had been desperate to cover up his big secret—but it didn't count for much in my book. Aston had laid a hand on Holmes; that was the end of the story.

"Very good, Aston," Ms. Albrecht said. "Jack, why don't you tell us what you put down for number four?"

I glanced down. My worksheet, which I had diligently filled with scribbles, told me nothing.

"What were some of the driving factors for nineteenth-century imperialism?"

I rubbed my forehead, keeping my hand there as a shield.

Someone whispered something. Brock laughed again.

"Quiet, please," Ms. Albrecht said. "Jack?"

I shrugged and lowered my head.

After a moment, she let out a disappointed breath. "No, Aston," which meant the little shit had raised his hand again. "Axle, go ahead."

Another member of the Boy Band began to speak, and the words buzzed in my head.

When the bell rang, I shoved everything into my backpack and launched out of my seat. Ms. Albrecht called my name, but I kept going, almost knocking over a girl named Juliet in the process. We had ten minutes of passing time, and my next class—Language Arts—was in Walker. The thought of milling around in the halls, while everybody either laughed in my face or pretended I didn't exist, sent me toward the back of the building. I went out to the concrete apron that served as the faculty smoke pad, although everybody pretended there was no smoking at Walker (never mind the sand-filled bucket full of butts or the unmistakable odor of old cigarette smoke).

I shivered, pulled on my coat, and tried not to think about anything. Not class. Not cash. Not an extra thirty addies. Not the Boy Band. Not how fucked up it all was, that I'd been so jealous when I'd been on the outside, and now, it turned out, the inside was so much fucking worse.

I was so busy not thinking and wishing I had a vape that I didn't hear the voices until they were almost on me. They were pitched low, but there was no mistaking the anger. I thought about ducking back inside Walker, and then I thought, Fuck it.

A moment later, Dawson and Aston came around the corner. Dawson's face was red. Aston looked pretty as ever, with his messy blond side part and, even in December, his salon tan, but as I watched, he twisted away from Dawson's grip and said, "Ask Riker."

"I already asked everybody." Dawson reached for him again.

But Aston shoved him. "I said no. Stop!"

"You can't say no to me," Dawson said. He opened his mouth to say something else, and then he saw me. Something twisted his face— frustration, I thought, but also something hotter, what I thought might be rage. He spun away from Aston and stormed back the way they'd come.

Aston half-turned, staring at me. He was breathing hard, and his hands opened and closed at his sides.

"Fuck off," I told him.

He took another breath, a deeper one, like he was bracing himself. Then he walked toward me.

I shouldered off my backpack; I hadn't ever actually gotten to punch Aston, and if he was about to pick a fight, I didn't want my bag messing up my chance to break those perfect teeth.

"I told you to fuck off," I said.

His eyes were tight. His lips pulled back, and a tremor started in his jaw.

"Fine," I said. "I should have done this the first time I saw you back on campus—"

And then I realized he was crying. His shoulders were staring to shake, and he tried to hug himself, but then the tears fell, and he pulled his hands up to wipe his cheeks.

"I need your help," he said. "Please."

Chapter 3

Five Thousand Dollars

You aren't allowed to break a guy's nose while he's crying, so I had no idea what to do. Aston said something unintelligible, crying harder, and then he fell apart completely: hands over his face, shoulders shaking, sobbing.

"Well, shit," I said.

I picked up my backpack and dusted off the snow. I looked around, hiking up the shoulder straps, giving him time. I shoved my hands in my pockets and thought about those lucky sons of bitches who could turn themselves invisible.

He kept crying.

"Come on," I said, "it can't be that bad."

That made him cry harder.

After about five seconds of that, I patted his shoulder. "Hey." That was genius-level Jack Moreno. "Hey, hey."

He scrubbed at his face; his fancy, clear-coat salon nails had been chewed ragged.

"Aston, you've got to take a deep breath. I can't help if you're like this."

He started to hiccup, his whole body quivering between sobs.

I scooped up some snow and threw it in his face.

He stopped crying. The snow glittered in the sunlight, almost prismatic as it melted against his flushed cheeks. He stared out at me from behind the white mask. Outrage widened his eyes.

"Deep breath," I said in a calm voice.

After a few deep breaths, he ran his sleeve over his face, wiping away snowmelt and tears and snot. His eyes and nose and cheeks were red. I thought I detected a fresh trickle.

I hurried to say, "What do you need help with?"

He looked around. We were alone on the smoke pad, but behind Walker, a long parking lot curved away to the west, stretching behind a line of pines to the faculty housing. A few adults were moving toward us—teachers who didn't have early classes, I guessed, although I couldn't recognize them at a distance.

"Follow me," I said.

I no longer had Dad's master set of keys to the campus, but there were spares of the most common ones in the maintenance building, and I'd added a few of those to my personal collection. I let us back into Walker, and then I turned down a side hall. Walker Hall was the original building of the Walker School, and it had been built to impress. Part of that job, it turned out, meant having a number of conference and meeting rooms—where prospective parents could be wined, dined, and reassured that abandoning their difficult children on the back of a mountain was a respectable—nay, an admirable—thing to do. Most of the time these rooms were empty, so I found one and let us inside.

Dark wainscotting. A bowl of wax fruit. An oil painting as big as I was that showed a severe-looking old white guy with his hair in a pompadour. I sat at the table, squirming free of my backpack and coat, and my phone buzzed.

The message was from Holmes: *Where are you? You're late for class.*

As Aston dropped into a seat opposite me, I texted back: *Running late. You didn't answer my question.*

I sent him a kissy-face emoji and locked my phone.

When I looked up, Aston was wiping his cheeks again, but he seemed more in control of himself. He stared at the polished tabletop, and after a few long seconds, he muttered, "Sorry."

"Gee," I said. "You did try to kill my best friend, and you probably would have tried to kill me, and you weaseled out of the consequences completely, but sure, it's nice that you can apologize for, you know, getting a little weepy when you ask for a favor."

His chin came up, and for a moment, he met my eyes. "You think there weren't consequences?"

"Did Mommy and Daddy take away your allowance?"

He cut his eyes away.

"Did Grandpa spank you?"

He made a weird scoffing noise, and I realized it was a laugh. "Grandfather would fucking love that."

"What do you want, Aston?"

He rubbed his face again, massaged his eyes, and for a moment, it looked like we were back at square one. But then, in a trembling voice, he said, "Someone's doing it again."

"Doing what—" But then I caught myself. "Someone's blackmailing you?"

Still rubbing his eyes, he nodded.

A few months before, our former head of security, Olin Campbell, had blackmailed Aston for being gay—which for most people in 2020 wasn't exactly a secret worth dying for. If you were Aston Young, though, descended from a long line of proud, sexually repressed Mormons, and your grandfather was an apostle, which was a big fucking deal, then apparently it was worth keeping quiet.

"Shit," I said. "Who?"

He made that weird, dry rasp of a laugh. "That's kind of the question, right?"

"Hold on, you want me to find out who's blackmailing you? And, what? Stop them?"

"Just find them."

"Then what?"

He dropped his hands; I couldn't see them under the table, but from the way he moved his arms, I guessed he was wringing them. "It'll be taken care of."

For a moment, I didn't know what to say. "But man, like…how? How is this happening to you again?"

A burst of noise—short, brutal laughter with no amusement behind it—and then, "I know, right?"

In the hall outside, a vacuum buzzed to life. It came closer. And then it bumped against the door to the conference room, rattling it in the frame, and both of us jumped. Our eyes met, and I grinned in spite of myself. Aston's smile was exhausted but seemed surprisingly genuine. Maybe this is what the Boy Band was like when they came off stage, I thought. Maybe this is what they were like when they stepped out of the spotlight. Or maybe this was part of the act, too. Holmes thought I was a soft touch.

"Yeah," I said slowly. "Sorry, but no."

"I know I've been a shit—"

"Tried to kill me and H, remember? Listen, I'm sorry. This is a shitty situation, and nobody deserves that. But I've got a lot of my own shit right now, and it doesn't include getting involved in, well, stuff like this."

Aston's throat moved. He wiped his eyes again, but if he was crying, I couldn't see the tears. When he spoke, the strain in his voice was audible as he fought and failed to keep it even. "Please. If my family—if this becomes public." He stopped. He put one hand on the table and stared at it. "Why do you think I'm here? Why do you think they put me here?"

Well, I thought, that's about as fucked up as it gets.

"There are other options." He breathed more heavily, the rest of the words spilling out. "There are camps."

The vacuum bumped away down the hall, the sound growing smaller. Aston still had one hand on the table like it was holding him up. With the other, he ran those clear-coat nails around his mouth, fingers trembling visibly.

"Aston—"

His head snapped up, and his eyes caught mine. "I'll pay you."

Ok, I know. I know it makes me a shitty person—maybe the shittiest kind of person—that I hesitated.

"How much do you want?"

"It's not—"

"Five thousand?"

With five thousand dollars, I could keep the jelly-jar fund stocked through the school year, and I could get a whole new wardrobe, and I could buy something kickass for Holmes and Ariana and yeah, even Dad.

But Aston must have mistaken my shock for a refusal because he said, "Ten thousand?"

The air in the room suddenly seemed too warm. Sweat dampened my underarms.

"Ten thousand is too much," I said, and I hated how hard it was for me to say it. "Five is fine."

"Thank you."

I couldn't help myself; I blurted, "And a bonus, you know, if I do it fast."

"Oh my God, Jack, thank you." A huge, crazy grin slipped out, and he pulled his shirt up to mop at his eyes. "Thank you, thank you, thank you."

"Don't thank me; I haven't found him yet."

"You have no idea—you are fucking fire, man. You have no fucking idea what this means to me. Thank you."

"I've got some conditions."

His head bobbled. "Yeah, of course, absolutely."

"You tell me the truth. I'm not your parents. I'm not your grandparents. I don't care what you stick your dick in, or vice versa. So, you tell me everything; that's the only way we're going to figure out what's going on."

"Sure, yeah."

"We keep this a secret. Have you told Dawson?"

"What? Why?"

I gave him a look.

Face coloring, Aston mumbled, "Oh. Uh, no."

"Then what were you fighting about?"

"What?"

"Outside. Like five minutes ago."

The blank expression lasted a moment longer. Then Aston shook his head. "Fuck, man. I'm so out of it. I haven't slept in, like, two days. He wanted to borrow some money."

I let the silence creep in.

Aston sat up straighter. "No way."

"He tried to buy from me and couldn't pay," I said. "And then he's hitting you up for cash, and all of this happens the same week somebody tries to blackmail you."

"You don't understand; it's not Daw."

I grunted. "You don't tell him anything, understand?" I waited for Aston's nod before continuing: "You don't tell any of the Boy Band. You don't tell the Bloopies. You don't tell your parents or your siblings or your grandparents. You don't write it in your diary. You and I are the only ones who know about this."

He scratched his cheek, and for the first time I noticed the bristles—a couple of days' worth, the stubble of sleepless nights and sleepwalking days. The shadows under his eyes were more visible now, although he'd definitely used concealer—or whatever you used—to make them less noticeable. And the nails, I thought, my attention coming back to his fingers. Chewed down to the quick.

"The Boy Band?" he said.

"You, Dawson, Axle, Riker, Jaxon."

He ran the backs of his fingers over the stubble again, still staring at me. "You have a name for us?"

"Yeah, well, you make it easy."

"Who are the Bloopies? What is a bloopie?"

This was why smart people, like Holmes, didn't shoot their mouths off. "Skye, D'Layne, Remmi, Kaylee, Marielle. The girl version of the Boy Band. We're getting off topic; my point is, don't tell anyone."

Aston's hand stilled on his cheek. He pursed his lips.

I could see the question forming on his face, so before he could ask, I said, "And I get to break your nose."

"What?"

"You hurt H bad. I want payback."

He stared at me. "Are you serious?"

"You're goddamn right I'm serious."

"That's crazy."

"No, Aston. What's crazy is smashing the smartest person on the planet in the head with a lacrosse stick—after he's been shot, by the way—and still somehow managing to have your ass handed to you. You know he could have killed you, right? But he didn't. I would have, but I got busy and then the police showed up and it was too late. So, I want to break your nose. That's the least you deserve."

"Burrows—" But whatever excuse he'd been about to offer, he stopped himself. With a laugh, he shook his head. "Fine. You know, you two are perfect for each other. Pair of fucking psychos: Abercrombie and Supercreep."

I sat forward. I grabbed one of the pieces of fake fruit, an apple, and sat back. I tossed it from one hand to the other. The surface was waxy, and light rolled along the contour of deep, burnished red. The slap of it hitting my palm matched the hard strokes of my heartbeat.

Aston shifted in his seat, looking everywhere but at me. "I'm sorry—"

"If I ever hear that name out of your mouth, I'll tell everybody you're strictly dickly, and I'll make sure they believe it. You can say what you want about me, but he's either Holloway or Holmes to you. And you'd better make sure the rest of your fucking friends watch their mouths when I'm around."

"I didn't mean—I'm tired, and—"

I pitched the apple at him. He caught it, barely, and then he shook the sting out of one hand.

"Let's go," I said.

"Ok, but, like, what are we going to tell people? I guess I can say I walked into a door—"

"Jesus Christ. I'm not going to break your nose right now. We're going to your residence; you're going to show me how the blackmailer contacted you."

Chapter 4
Psychic Staring Effect

Aston lived in Baker House, which was also Holmes's residence, which meant I'd spent a fair bit of time there over the last couple of months. We went through the lobby, past the bulletin board with pictures of the residents and their room numbers and, leftover from last month, paper turkeys and orange letters that said GOBBLE GOBBLE I'M THANKFUL FOR YOU! Holmes, in his picture, was so sullenly impassive that I knew someone had forced him to have the photo taken. I was going to steal it at the end of the school year, and then I was going to put it into one of those Christmas tree ornaments, one of those little decorative frames, and give it to him just to see the look on his face.

On the third floor, Aston let us into his room—a private, of course. If his parents had been worried about, uh, hanky-panky, they should have thought of giving Aston a roommate. It would have made sneaking a boy into his room harder. But then, from what I'd heard—and, occasionally, seen—at Walker, roommates presented all sorts of other opportunities.

The room smelled like fading body spray—the kind that would have been named Jackal or Beast or Roar, the chemically strong kind that seemed to take up permanent residence high in your nose. A U of U flag hung on one wall; a window was centered on another; and the third was taken up by the desk and closet. Blue plaid bedding, a mini fridge with a Taco Bell sticker on the door, the black-and-red gaming chair, the PS5 (which had only come out a month ago), the TV the size of my sofa (which was not a joke)—it all felt like standard Boy Band fare. On the nightstand, he had a tangled charging cord, tissues and lotion (cue mental vomit), a tube of Burt's Bees lip balm, and a clutter of framed four-by-sixes. I moved over to take a look, while Aston closed the door. Behind me, I could hear him shifting his weight from foot to foot. The photos weren't anything special: various configurations of an eyewateringly boring, attractively blond family. The hardass in the black suit and the comb-over had to be the infamous Grandfather. In the back, behind all the other pictures, was a framed photo of the Salt Lake Temple.

"My parents," Aston said. I hadn't heard him come up behind me, and now he was close enough for me to smell the breakfast burrito on his breath. "Bruce and DeeDee. My sister Camdyn. Grandfather. And that's Wendy."

"You don't call her grandma?"

"She's his second wife; they got married last year."

"Jesus. Seems kind of late in the game."

"Yeah, well, being married is a big deal for Mormons. It doesn't look good to stay single."

The last few words held so much packaged bitterness that I glanced over my shoulder. For a moment, something vulnerable and alone showed in Aston's face. Then he frowned and dropped onto the bed.

"Let's see it," I said.

I expected him to reach for his laptop or pull out his phone, but instead, he dragged one of the pillows over to him. He rummaged around inside. Paper crinkled as he pulled it loose. Several sheets, I saw. He held out the topmost, and I raised my hands and shook my head.

"Has anybody else touched it?"

"No, I haven't told anyone."

"You need to keep it somewhere safe. And you need to buy some of those plastic page protectors in case there are fingerprints on it—they sell them in the school store. If this guy sends you another one, don't touch it with your bare hands. Gloves." I gave him a crooked smile. "In a pinch, use a condom. Unlubricated, obvs."

He glared at me, but he laid the page on the bed. I moved closer to examine it. It looked like cheap copy paper, the kind we stocked in the library and the computer lab and the production center, which it probably was. It had been printed landscape. The font didn't look like anything special, but I wasn't exactly an expert on fonts. All caps.

$50,000 OR THEY GO TO YOUR PARENTS.

When I looked over at Aston, he dropped his gaze and mumbled, "Do you have to?"

"It's up to you, I guess."

He drew the remaining pages closer to his chest. Then, cheeks flaming he laid the next one on the bed.

Aston was…athletic. I'd give him that. The picture captured him riding a dick—whose dick, you couldn't see because of the angle of the camera. The most you could tell was that he had dark hair on his legs—no tattoos, no distinguishing marks. Aston's head was thrown back, his hands planted behind him, his thighs bunched with muscle. He was pretty, I decided. And flushed with sex, his dick half-hard between his legs, he was disturbingly hot, which suggested that I was perhaps the worst human ever to live. I recognized the blue-plaid bedding and the splash of red—the U flag on his wall.

"You can turn it over," I said.

He flipped the page without looking at me. He was still for a moment, probably bracing himself. Then he laid out the next one.

The angle was different. Aston was on his hands and knees, jaw dropped, a strand of drool hanging. Red mottled his face, and his eyes were glassy, his pupils blown. High on something, although I couldn't tell what. It might have had something to do with the bottle of poppers someone was holding under his nose, but from his vacant expression, I thought it had to be more than that. A bite mark darkened his collarbone. A hand clamped on his hip. The arm led to a torso with a fair amount of dark hair but lacking adult mass and definition. Whoever had taken this photo, they'd been careful not to capture the second guy's face—or to crop it out, at least.

"Ok," I said.

Aston flipped it over and put his face in his hands.

I moved back to give him some space. "Do you recognize the men?"

"Dawson. In both of them."

"You're sure?"

He dropped his hands so they hung between his knees. His eyes were red again. "It's not like I keep a stable of guys to fuck me on demand."

"How many partners have you had in the last year?"

He wasn't a great liar, but he wasn't terrible either. He paused a little too long, that's all. "One: Daw."

"You want to try that again?"

"Is something wrong with your fucking hearing?"

"Ok."

"And you've got no idea why Dawson might be suddenly hitting you up for money?"

Aston shrugged. "He didn't say."

"Maybe ask him next time. It'd be nice if I could wrap this up fast and earn that bonus."

Lip curling, Aston didn't say anything to that; he didn't have to.

I moved over to the closet. I took the clothes out, which was a monumental effort, and then I removed the hang rod and checked it for anything suspicious—a tiny spy cam would have been awesome, but I found nothing. I ran my hands over the walls, but they were painted cinderblock. There were no secret doors, no blocks that could be removed, no discreet holes.

"What are you doing?" Aston finally asked.

"Do you leave the closet door open?"

"I don't know."

I tried not to sigh. Then I thought of my room, and I wondered if maybe this was what Holmes felt every time he set foot in my room.

"It's open sometimes," Aston said. "I don't know."

"Someone took those pictures of you from inside this room. It would have been nice if they'd had a more permanent setup, but my guess is that they managed to hide the camera in here at some point, and then they removed it later. Put those back."

Aston looked at the heap of clothes. "You took them out."

I put my hands on my hips.

"You should have to put them back," Aston mumbled, but he gathered an armful and lugged the clothes toward the closet.

"Say something about how you're paying me," I said, "and see how that goes."

He stared daggers at me as he gathered up more clothes.

While Aston put the closet back in order, I climbed onto his bed. He didn't have a headboard, which would have been a nice place for a spy cam. The walls looked nice and solid—no obvious places where a camera could have been hidden. I got down, the mattress creaking, and checked his desk. He had a laptop sitting out, and when I opened it, a piece of blue painter's tape covered the built-in webcam.

"Did you do this after you got the blackmail letter?"

Aston gave me a scornful arch of his eyebrows. "The day I got the laptop."

"So nobody could watch you jacking it to your favorite channel of Boyfriend TV. Nice."

"You're gay. Or bi. Or whatever. I've seen you on apps. Why are you being so mean about this?"

"Because I don't like you," I said. "And it's fun."

But it actually hadn't felt all that fun to begin with, and it was less fun after being called out, and even less fun after that comment about the apps. I should have thought about that before. Not that who or what I liked was a secret, but I hadn't exactly been open about it either, and things were different now; I was a student here. I'd turned off the apps when Ariana and I had gotten official, but now I was starting to think I needed to have some quiet, careful conversations with a few of the kids I'd, uh, met up with back in the bad old days.

I moved over to the television because it never hurt to be thorough. I looked it over, and then I inspected the PS5. I had no idea what I was looking for. Maybe one of these days, I'd get lucky.

"I'm careful, you know." When I looked over, Aston shifted his weight. His jaw was set like he hadn't even meant to say that, but more words poured out. "I have to be careful. So fucking careful. About what I say. About my hair. My clothes. My—my voice. Can't sound too faggy in front of Grandfather. It's just—how was I supposed to know Olin was a pervert and had cameras all over campus? And now, in my own room? Sometimes it feels like—" He closed a hand around his neck. Not enough air, I thought. The walls closing in. Like someone's choking you.

I considered saying, *You can't be too careful if you're fucking in public, whether you know there are cameras or not*, but it felt like a low blow. Maybe it was karma, for Aston to get blackmailed twice in such a short amount of time. But he wasn't the only one who suffered the occasional lapse in judgment. I'd done my fair share of stupid stuff; it came from being sixteen and horny every waking minute and finding a minute alone with a cute guy, even if it was in his car, in the middle of the afternoon, parked by the dumpster behind a Deseret Book. Someone from the Mormon bookstore must had trashed a whole shipment of poster-sized religious art prints that day. If I'd ever wondered if I was going to hell, getting a fiver while a million Jesuses stared at me seemed like a clear enough answer.

Instead, I said, "When Olin did this, did he use a note?"

Aston arched his eyebrows again. "No. He came in person. Plugged the flash drive right into that TV and showed me."

"Did you tell your family?"

"Christ, no. I wouldn't be here."

Gee, I thought. "How'd you pay him?"

"He wanted two hundred bucks a month."

I waited.

An alarm clock started going off in the room next to us. Ten seconds. Twenty.

Aston shouted toward the wall, "Kyle, get up!"

"How'd you pay him?" I asked.

"It was two hundred bucks," he said as though that were the answer.

I let that sit for a minute. Then I said, "And you haven't told your family about this?"

He stared at me, eyes wide at, I guessed, my stupidity. After an insultingly long time he said, "No."

"Let's keep it that way for now."

When I turned toward the door, Aston asked, "What are you going to do now?" His voice had risen, all the nerves exposed, the fear out in the open again. "What are you going to tell Sup—Holmes?"

"I told you," I said, glancing over my shoulder as I opened the door. "We're not telling anybody about this. That includes Holmes."

There's a Wikipedia page on the psychic staring effect, which isn't psychic at all it turns out, and the page uses the word *tingling* a disturbing number of times. But there's a section about gaze detection, and it turns out there might be something to that phenomenon of being able to tell when someone's staring at you—that a different part of our brain lights up when we're being stared at directly, and that you can pick up this information in your peripheral vision, subconsciously, without even being aware of it.

A frisson ran down my spine.

Holloway Holmes stood in the hallway staring at me, the cold perfection of his face a sealed book.

Chapter 5

Jonny Evans

"H—" I began. I was still trying to wrap my head around him being there, in the hallway outside Aston's room, when he should have been in class. And, at the same time, a part of me wasn't surprised at all. That part of me simply looked at him and thought, Of course. "What are you—"

He looked past me to Aston, then back to me. His eyes were gray cinders. "You shouldn't skip class; you've got a C in Language Arts."

"Did you follow me?"

"What aren't you going to tell me?"

"Hey, I asked you a question."

He studied me for a moment. Then he stepped forward, and I fell back. Holmes moved into the room, and his eyes scanned everything: me, Aston, the bed, the papers Aston had laid there. When his eyes came back to Aston, he said, "Leave us."

He was sounding distinctly posher. Bad sign.

"It's my room—" Aston began. The words withered, and he scurried out into the hall, pulling the door shut behind him.

Then we were alone. Holmes moved past me to stare at the blackmail letter. He used a handkerchief to turn the photos over, considered each one, and then laid them face down again.

"If you were following me," I said, "that's not cool."

He turned around. It wasn't fast or surprising or sudden, but I took a step back. I caught myself doing it, and I planted my feet and shoved my hands in my pockets and glared back at him.

Somewhere down the hall, a flute trilled off key. This is how I'm going to die, I thought. Murdered by a jilted Holmes while some boner practices the flute.

"I told you I was going to be late to class," I said.

Holmes's pulse beat in his neck.

"Did you ever think maybe I was doing something private? Maybe I didn't want you to know what I was doing?"

He didn't do anything; he stood ramrod straight, hands at his sides, and stared at me.

"I have a right to some privacy sometimes," I said. "Did you think about that? Did you think about the fact that even though we're friends —"

"Are we?"

For a moment, the shock of it was so great that there wasn't anything else. Then the hurt rolled in. "Uh, yeah. Of course."

He took a step, and I completely forgot my resolution to stay put. I backed up, and he kept coming, and I kept backing up until my ass hit the windowsill, and I sat without meaning to. That was even worse, because now Holmes loomed over me. He was so skinny, but it was hard to remember that when I had to crane my neck to look up at him.

"H," I said in a quieter voice, "don't be mad."

"I'm not angry."

Definitely posher. He was bidialectical, and most of the time — probably as camouflage — he sounded American. But with each word he spoke, he slipped deeper into that cultured Englishness, and it was scary and he didn't sound like my Holmes and it was, if I'm being fully honest, hot as hell. This was more of the accent than I'd ever heard at one time together. And I'm sixteen — see above regarding hormones and general stupidity.

"Everything happened fast," I said. "I wasn't —"

He took another step, and I leaned back until I was pressed against the window. The cold of the glass seeped through my clothes. He noticed, of course — he noticed everything. It made him stop, and an expression I couldn't read crossed his face.

"Are you frightened, Jack?" The corner of his mouth twitched. His father had tried to beat that tell out of him, tried to train him not to bite his lip. Watching him as he struggled with the nervous habit, watching him as he tried to do what he'd been trained to do, made me want to track Blackfriar down and put him headfirst into a mulcher. "Are you scared of me?"

Then it clicked. This was Holmes, and Holmes, for all of being a genius and the best, most amazing person I knew, was — well, the polite word was insecure. Not that he didn't have good reason, considering the fuckwads he'd gotten tangled up with in the past.

I stood. It was hard because he'd moved so far into my space that we were almost touching, close enough that someone seeing us through the window might think this was the beginning of an embrace. A kiss. Red warning lights flashed in my head, and I shut that line of thinking down. We were the same height. I could smell the woodsy heat of his body spray or cologne or whatever it was. His hands closed into fists at his sides.

Leaning in, I brought my mouth to his ear and whispered, "Why would I be scared of a skinny-assed white boy like you? Mess with me, and I'm going to give you a wedgie that'll rip your asshole like tissue paper."

I pulled my head back.

Holmes blinked.

"And then I'll give you noogies until you're begging me to stop," I informed him at a more normal volume. "And then, if you're still mad at me, I'll tickle you."

He gave up and bit his lip—not too hard, not the full distress that I'd seen before. His teeth made white crescents. He was trying so hard, the struggle playing itself out in his face until he burst out, "A wedgie couldn't do that to a human being. The mechanics are impossible."

"It happened to Jonny Evans in eighth grade. He was in surgery for, like, a week. They had to make him a new butthole halfway up his crack."

"You're lying." But doubt had crept into his voice.

I shrugged.

"This is a joke."

"Fuck around, boyo, and find out."

I examined his face. Then I gave him a smile. He was doing a Holmes thing, not looking me in the eye, so I moved my head until he was. This was something we'd been working on.

"I lied," Holmes said, but he still wasn't looking me in the eye. "I am angry with you."

"I guessed."

"I don't want to do this right now."

"It's good practice."

"Not when I'm angry."

"Especially when you're angry."

He made a frustrated noise. Then he smiled. The expression was a little stiff; he wasn't used to doing it, and it was another of those things that he was self-conscious about. I'd read about people who get up at two or three in the morning—on vacation, no less, when they're in Hawaii—and then they drive hours and hours, and all of it is to see the sunrise from this one specific spot, and I thought, Come to Utah if you want something worth your time.

"You're such a dork," I told him. "B-plus."

As usual, his face relaxed, and the smile went from gorgeous to perfect. Then it shuttered into a scowl. "You always give me a B-plus."

"Please don't be mad at me."

He hesitated. "Was I really being weird, coming to find you?"

"For you and me, it's not weird. I want you to come find me. Especially if it's some bad guy and he has me tied up with ropes on a train track or something. Although, if it's a hot guy, and he's got me tied up with ropes in a fun way, don't you fucking dare get involved."

Jokes like that used to send Holmes into a rage; now he scowled harder.

"I was being defensive," I said. "I was surprised, and I was embarrassed, and then I got a little angry. That's why I said that stuff. And, for the record, that's why I kept backing away. I was—am—a tiny bit ashamed, so if you could try looking at me with, like, sixty percent less judgment, I'd appreciate it."

Because he was Holmes, he probably calculated the sixty percent, but his face softened.

"If it's someone you don't know well, though," I said, "you should be careful. They might take it the wrong way."

He nodded. Another social detail processed and encoded. We were tutoring each other, I guess, although one of us (me) was definitely getting more out of the bargain.

His voice took on an unfamiliar edge when he said, "Is this what friends do, Jack? Keep secrets like this?"

Down the hall, the off-key flautist struck again. Then someone—a boy with an impressively deep voice—bellowed, "Touch that flute one more fucking time, and I'm going to shove it so far down your throat, you'll be farting scales."

In spite of myself, I grinned, but Holmes didn't; he was still watching me, his face intent, the question hanging between us like the shimmer of a gong. I smoothed out my expression and shook my head. "Nope. It's not what friends do."

"Then why did you do it?"

"Because I'm a piece of shit." Holmes frowned and opened his mouth, but I said, "Because I need money and I'm embarrassed. And because I'm embarrassed I'd help Aston for money—it feels, well, shitty. He hurt you; I should be trying to knock his block off, not helping him. And because I didn't want you to think I was using you for, you know, your big, juicy brain. But mostly it's the embarrassment thing." My neck was hot. My face prickled. "I'm having round two of it right now, by the way."

"Jack, you don't need to feel embarrassed about your financial situation."

"Tell me that the next time Ariana wants to go out and I can't pay for Del Taco."

"Ariana does not care how much money you have." Holmes wrinkled his brow. "Does she?"

"No, she doesn't. But I do. We're getting off topic. I was a piece of shit. I shouldn't have lied to you, and I shouldn't have gotten angry when you found me. I'm sorry, H."

"I'm sorry too."

"Oh yeah? What are you sorry for?"

"I don't know; you told me that's what people say in fights."

I grinned. "Yep, that was perfect."

"You know I'll help you, Jack. With anything." You could only hear the question if you knew him. "That's what friends do."

I nodded. "We still need to figure out that butt-bump secret handshake you promised me."

"I never promised—" He caught himself, folded his arms across his chest, and glared at me. "Tell me what's going on."

As best I could, I laid out what Aston had told me. Holmes examined the papers again. He didn't ask any questions, so when I finished, I said, "To sum up: I know it's fucked up; I'll tell him I changed my mind—"

"Don't be ridiculous. If anything, you should ask for more money." He moved to inspect the closet. "You're sure there aren't any cameras?"

"Not unless they're invisible. Um, H, you're sure you're ok with this? I mean, he tried to kill you, and this is exactly the kind of thing you don't like, people getting close to you for what you're good at."

"It's an interesting problem. And I've been bored. And it's a good way for you to make some money; like Sherlock and John Watson, we're consulting detectives now." He brought his leg up and side-kicked the closet wall. Nothing spectacular happened—not unless you count the visual reminder of that jack-in-the-box ass. The cinderblocks didn't give way, a secret door didn't pop open. He didn't even smash through the wall Robocop style. H made an annoyed noise and went back to his examination. "And I don't think Aston meant anything personal by it."

"Killing you is pretty personal."

He made that same noise again.

"If you don't mind," I said, "I'm going to take it personally. For both of us."

"Whatever you like," Holmes said in a tone like he hadn't actually heard me.

Holmes spent some time examining the rest of the room. He came to a stop next to the TV, and he frowned. Crouching, he lined himself up with the bed. He got on his knees, pressed his cheek to the carpet, and stayed still for a long moment. Then he stood and moved to the door.

He opened it so quickly that Aston, who must have been pressed up against it, started to fall. He caught himself, gave Holmes a nasty look, and tried to play it off. "What—"

"When did you rearrange the furniture?"

"What?"

"The bed. When did you move the bed?"

"I don't know. A couple of weeks ago." Aston glanced at me. "What's going on?"

"H found some dust bunnies. He's going to prosecute you for disorderly bedroom in the first degree."

"The only person on campus who has committed disorderly bedroom in the first degree is currently standing here with us," Holmes said primly, "and he is not Aston Young."

"What the hell, H?"

"I found pizza in your desk drawer."

"They were pizza rolls, big shot, and that could have happened to anyone."

"Anyone who mistook their desk drawer for a repository for bite-sized breaded pizza products."

"Did you come up with that on the fly? The legal definition of a pizza roll, I mean."

A hint of color rose in his face. "It's hardly a legal definition."

"Holy shit, you've been saving that one."

"I was not saving it!"

"You were. You were saving up a zinger. This is the best day of my life. Wait, why were you going through my desk?"

"I do not save zingers. And I needed a pencil, which I thought would be in your desk, not—as you later showed me—in your underwear drawer because, quote, 'you were coming over, so I straightened up.'"

"What are you two talking about?" Aston shouted.

"I had some pencils and loose change on my dresser," I said, "so I just kind of swept them into the top drawer because H has this thing about my bedroom—"

Holmes shook his head. "It's a war crime."

"It's a normal bedroom at normal, messy bedroom levels."

Aston slapped the door. "Hey! You're supposed to be helping me!"

"The second photo—" Holmes reached for the picture, but when I shook my head, he stopped. "—was clearly taken from that side of the bed. That wall is solid; there's nowhere a camera could be hidden. Therefore, some other possibility had to explain it. The television stand is at the right height, and when I inspected the carpet, I found marks that suggested the furniture had been moved recently."

Some of the color bled from Aston's face. He hugged himself, and his voice was shallow when he said, "It was over there. The bed was here; I swapped them because—" He hugged himself tighter. "—because Dawson suggested it."

I glanced at Holmes. "Want to pop next door and see if there's anything interesting in Dawson's room?"

"Obviously." To Aston, he said, "Return to class. I'm going to collect these—"

"No!" Aston interposed himself between Holmes and the papers on the bed. He shook his head.

Holmes looked at me. "If there are fingerprints or other trace evidence, I may be able to lift them."

"He's the client," I said. "If he says no, that's his choice."

"No," Aston said again. "I don't want anybody to—" He stopped and shook his head again.

"Then you may want to find a better hiding spot than—" Holmes frowned and checked me for confirmation. "The pillowcase?"

"Don't show off," I said.

Holmes didn't say anything, but he did look unbearably satisfied with himself.

"What am I supposed to do?" Aston asked. "Should I tell them I'll pay them?"

"Of course not," Holmes said, sounding slightly offended. "Did they give you a way to communicate with them?"

"No, but—"

"Then how would you tell them anything?"

I shook my head and nudged Holmes toward the door. "Don't do anything yet. We'll be in touch."

We left Baker House and went next door to the unfortunately named (at least, for a boys' residence) Woody Hall, where Dawson had his room. One of my keys got us into the building. It was quiet as we climbed the stairs—which made sense, with most of the kids either at class or taking a study hall. When we emerged onto the second floor, a hint of weed hung in the air. It didn't smell like the cheap shit I'd been getting from Lehi, which meant somebody had their own stash. Or, worse, somebody might be trying to horn in on my business. Music was playing too—a steady, thumping beat that grew louder as we got closer to Dawson's room.

"Doesn't anybody in this place go to class?" I asked.

Holmes's face stayed perfectly smooth.

"Stop it," I said.

"I didn't do anything."

"You're calculating my tardies and absences."

"The most distressing one is geometry."

I groaned. "You're not even in my geometry class. I'm always on time. I'm a model student."

"You do realize that you can eat chicken tenders from the dining hall every day, don't you? You're not contractually obligated to stay until you clean out the dining hall."

"This is why I said stop."

"If I were to plot your tardies by time of day, there would be a significant correlation with meals and sleep."

Fortunately by then we'd reached Dawson's room, and I didn't have to throw myself down the trash chute or climb out a window. I took out my keys, saying, "I'm not sure if I have one that will open this—"

But Holmes reached past me, touched the handle, and turned it. The door swung open.

The first thing I saw was naked bodies.

They were mid-fuck, facing us doggy style. Dawson was bottoming, his face flushed and his body shaking as the other man pounded into him. The top wasn't anyone I recognized: maybe my age, maybe a bit older, with almond skin. He had dark hair in a faux hawk, thick eyebrows, lips so full they looked pouty. His stiff nipples looked like bronze.

Dawson let out a strangled squawk, but the top kept drilling.

I opened my mouth to say something—I wasn't sure how you asked, *Who the hell are you?* while also apologizing for walking in on a guy mid-bone, but I was going to give it my best try

Before I could, though, the top noticed us. He straightened, slapped Dawson's ass hard enough that Dawson cried out, and smirked. "Oi, Holloway, want to have a go?"

Chapter 6

Cage Match

Holmes's face was on fire, of course, but he didn't look away from Dawson and his fuck-buddy. He reached over and hit the speaker, and the music cut off.

"Should we—" I whispered, touching Holmes's elbow.

"No," he said at a normal volume. "You can't turn your back on him. Dismount, Paxton. And both of you, cover up."

I'm not sure if anyone, in the history of the world, had been ordered to dismount while balls deep (maybe pony play, the filthy part of my brain suggested), but the top—Paxton, Holmes had called him—took it in stride. His smirk grew, and he swatted Dawson's ass again and said, "Ease up, luv; you heard him."

I wasn't exactly a good person, but I had aspirations of one day being a decent one, so I did my best not to look directly at them as they separated. Holmes seemed to suffer from no such qualms. His face was redder, if that was possible, but he stared fixedly as Dawson wrapped himself in the towel that had been under him and Paxton slid off the bed. That was the point when I gave up on ever being a decent human being because I couldn't help myself. Paxton had some serious equipment. Big, red, angry tackle. And, I mean, good for him, although it was hard not to wonder—

"Jack," Holmes said.

"Right." And then, because I couldn't stop the next word: "Sorry."

Paxton gave me a grin over his shoulder as he pulled up a pair of red briefs; that only made it worse, in some ways, because they fit him perfectly and let the imagination run wild. He straightened, ran a hand through his faux hawk, and considered us. Me, mostly. I'd seen that look on guys and girls before, so it wasn't anything new. The blush lighting me up, though— that was new.

Briefs in place, Paxton padded over to us. Holmes tensed, and I shifted my weight to move forward. Holmes shook his head, so all I did was watch as Paxton kissed his cheek.

It didn't last long: a brush of lips, maybe not even a full second. It seemed to go on forever. Long enough for me to remember the Wikipedia article on World War III—they hadn't listed this situation as a possible cause, so I'd need to edit the page and add it. Einstein had a quote on there, about fighting World War IV with sticks and stones. As Paxton pulled back, I thought maybe I'd run outside and find one. You could fuck somebody up with the right stick.

Holmes, of course, didn't even break Paxton's arm or anything, which was simultaneously disappointing and unbelievable.

"Hello, luv," Paxton said in a different voice—a quiet one, that sounded like it was meant for Holloway alone. "Missed you."

Holmes still held himself rigid. "Move away."

Something I couldn't read crossed Paxton's face, but he stepped back. His gaze returned to me, and a crooked smile pulled at one corner of his mouth. "You're gorgeous, aren't you? But then, Holloway always liked them pretty."

Holmes didn't exactly grab my arm or step in front of me or, you know, brand my ass, but he bristled, and his tone sharpened. "Sit on the bed, Paxton. Keep your hands where I can see them."

Hands raised in surrender, Paxton stepped backward. He sat on the bed—not too close to Dawson, buddy distance, the way you would with a guy if you hadn't been, for example, fucking his brains out a couple of minutes before.

By that point, Dawson seemed to have recovered. His arms were folded tightly across his chest, and his caveman forehead was furrowed. "You can't be in here—"

"Don't speak unless I ask you a question," Holmes said.

Dawson's mouth opened, but he stopped, swallowed, and didn't say anything. Paxton did an exaggerated wince.

"H," I said, "want to tell me what's going on here?"

The color in Holmes's cheeks—those perfect red circles—had only intensified since the kiss, and his pulse hammered in his neck again.

"H," I said again, as gently as I could.

He blinked. Then I watched as that ferocious will took mastery again. It was like watching someone smooth water into stillness by sheer concentration: his breathing slowing, his hands uncurling at his sides, the tension in his jaw easing, and finally, last of all, the color softening in his cheeks. "I'm sorry," he said, and the look he turned on me was a mixture of embarrassment and, I was fairly sure, a hint of fear. Of punishment? Of having lost control? I didn't know exactly, but I knew who had put it there. Another gift from Blackfriar Holmes.

"It's ok," I said, cocking my head at the door. "Maybe we should—"

"No." He let out a slow breath. "No, Jack. We can't. Paxton is...slippery. He cannot be trusted."

"Now that's a bit harsh, innit?" Paxton asked from the bed.

"You've got to help me out," I said. "I can keep an eye on them if you need a minute to, you know..." Pull yourself together wasn't exactly the kind of thing you said to Holloway Holmes, but I didn't have a good alternative.

"I'm fine, Jack. Thank you." Holmes breathed slowly again for a few seconds. "Jack, this is Paxton Adler. Paxton, Jack Moreno."

Paxton winked at me.

"You know each other," I said.

"Well, that's us sorted," Paxton said with a laugh. "You got a smart one, Holloway."

"Yes, we know each other," Holmes said. "He is an...acquaintance of the family."

"He's my cuz."

Holmes shook his head, but he didn't say anything.

When the silence had stretched out long enough, I said, "And he just happens to be here fucking Dawson because...what? Dawson's a cheap piece of ass?"

"Hey!" Dawson said, sitting up, but he shrank down again when Holmes glared at him.

"Excellent question," Holmes said. "What are you doing here, Paxton?"

"It's a school, innit?" Paxton gave us wide-eyed innocence and shrugged. "'Nuff said."

"You're no longer of an age for school."

"I'm a bit slow; takes me longer."

Holmes gave a shockingly nasty laugh. "No, I don't think so."

Paxton leaned back, hands behind him on the mattress. He had a defined chest, a flat stomach, minimal body hair. Groomed, I thought. I put him at twenty, twenty-one. He was still smirking at Holmes, and Holmes's control was fraying again, his chest rising and falling more rapidly, the red in his cheeks darkening.

"Tag me in," I whispered to Holmes.

He looked sidelong at me.

"Wrestling?" I said. "Cage match? You tag out by tagging me in."

"What are you talking about?"

I cocked my head.

After a moment, he hissed a furious breath and nodded.

"That's proper beautiful," Paxton said. "Love that."

"Stop messing with him," I said, turning on him. "I think you might genuinely like him, so knock it off."

"But it's fun, innit? Twisting his tail?"

"Yeah, sure."

Holmes's jaw dropped. "Jack!"

"What? It is." To Paxton, though, I said, "But enough is enough; knock it off."

Paxton studied me; his smile changed caliber—more serious, more authentic, more dangerous. I wasn't sure what it meant.

"What are you doing here?" I asked.

In a very soft voice, his dark eyes unchanging, he said, "Going to school, right?"

Ok, I thought. Message received. I turned to Dawson. "This is why you needed that Viagra?"

He flushed and shot me the bird.

"You want to tell me what's going on?"

Apparently I was less threatening than Holmes—or Dawson had been saving this up for the first question. "What's going on? What's going on? What's going on is a couple of fuckwad freaks broke into my room, which is breaking and entering and trespassing and—and violates my civil rights. And you'd better believe that when I tell the headmaster, she's going to kick you both out and fire your dad and what the fuck are you going to do about that? And then, you know what? Then I'm going to find you, and I'm going to beat the shit out of you. I will fucking kill you, understand?"

Hands on knees, I got to eye level with Dawson. He stared back at me, buzzing with adrenaline. "Here's the deal, Daw. You're upset because we barged in on you, and that's embarrassing. And for a guy like you, maybe it's more embarrassing because we walked in on you taking dick like a champ, although, hey, no reason to be embarrassed about that. Maybe you're embarrassed because you thought this was your secret, and you're afraid we're going to tell someone. And maybe you're still mad at me because I wouldn't sell you that shit on credit. I understand there's a lot going on right now, and that might be making you say things and do things you wouldn't normally say and do. But I'm going to level with you: I don't give two shits. You ever say something like that about my dad again, you ever even come close to threatening him, and we're going to settle it right then. Hear me?"

He dropped his chin, and his eyes cut away.

My heartbeat pounded like a metronome in my ears. "I asked you a question."

He jerked out a nod and mumbled, "Yes."

I stepped back and looked out the window. The sun had climbed higher, and the snow caught like a blaze. When I closed my eyes, the afterimage was a banner of yellow and green. I opened them and turned back to the two on the bed.

"Well, what is it?" Paxton asked. "Not that we mind a visit, especially if you want to stay and play, but you did interrupt us."

"Aston Young is being blackmailed," Holmes said, his gaze settling on Paxton. "I think I have an idea by whom."

Paxton laughed. "Not me, luv."

"No, of course not."

"Do you know anything about this?" I asked Dawson. "The other boy in the pictures is you."

He directed his words to the carpet: "I don't have to talk to you."

I shared a look with Holmes; in his subtle Holmes way, his face mirrored my frustration.

Dawson swiveled toward me, regaining some of the tough-shit aura he usually carried—you know, the days somebody hadn't walked in on him taking it long and deep. "What are you waiting for? Get out."

The tone settled something inside me—everything had been so fucking weird since the moment we stepped into the room, and Holmes still wasn't acting like himself. I didn't know what to do about Paxton or the effect he was having, but I did know how to handle spoiled Walker boys.

"Yeah, I don't think so." I turned in place taking in the room. "See, ordinarily, you'd be in class right now, not getting your ass bred."

Dawson growled and shifted forward on the bed. I couldn't see Holmes, but he must have done something because Dawson shrank back into place. Paxton tried to hide a smile by scratching his chin.

"The whole point was to take a good look, see if we could figure out what was going on, if you'd left anything incriminating."

"Incriminating? Like what?"

"Oh, I don't know. Any blackmail notes you hadn't delivered yet—that'd make my life nice and easy."

"I don't have anything to do with that, so you can leave. Get out." Like he was choking on it, he added, "Please?"

The short exchange had given me a chance to take in the room: the single bed raised on cinderblocks, with its gray comforter and white sheets bunched at the foot; a poster from what I guessed was a graphic novel—something called *Preacher*, and it did look pretty badass; the window frosted over, milky with sunlight; the closet door open so that the mirror faced the bed. So they could watch themselves, I realized with some significant yuck. The closet itself held a single pair of khakis and a few button-downs. Unlike Aston's, there was no clutter of designer jackets and, more important for a boy, sneakers. I crossed to the dresser and opened drawers.

"Hey!" Dawson shouted, and bed springs made their metallic sounds. Then Dawson let out a frightened cry.

"Holloway, stop terrorizing him," Paxton said.

A handful of Volcom t-shirts. A pair of jeans from a brand I didn't recognize. A Vineyard Vines sweatshirt. Nothing cheap, sure. But a lot of empty drawer space as well.

I checked Holmes, who still hadn't moved—what was he doing to terrify Dawson? Maybe he'd show me sometime if I asked—and got down on the floor. The carpet was rough against my cheek.

"Now we're getting somewhere," Paxton said. "Help him get his pants off, Holloway. Pretty boy, hips up a little. You'll enjoy it more."

I gave him the middle finger without looking up, and Paxton laughed.

Then I spotted them: indentations in the carpet, like Holmes had noticed in Aston's room. Only these weren't indentations from rearranging the furniture. This was something that was gone. A TV stand, I guessed. With its own PS5, or whatever the hell Dawson's parents had bought him.

Getting to my feet, I brushed myself off. Holmes's face looked more composed, and he gave a decisive nod.

"Seriously?" I asked. "You already figured it out?"

"I did need the extra time while you examined everything," he said in an apologetic tone.

"Fuck me. This is so fucking unfair."

"Ok, you looked around," Dawson said. His shoulders curved, and he pulled the towel tighter. "Can you go now?"

"Sure," I said. "As soon as you tell us how long someone has been blackmailing you."

Chapter 7

A Fight with a Bush

Paxton broke the silence. "Blackmailing Dawson? For what?"

"Silence," Holmes said.

"For having sex? With me?" Paxton put his arms behind his head. He had nice biceps, great pits, serratus muscles so defined you could play a chord on them. With a laugh, he said, "People should be paying us to watch."

"Yes, you'd love that," Holmes snapped, and the venom was so hot and raw that I looked over at him. The flush was back, and my Holmes—the icy, controlled Holmes—had vanished again. "I told you to be silent."

"Yeah, well, that's the problem, innit, because—"

"Shut up," I told Paxton. "You're egging him on. I don't know why, but my best guess is that you're trying to keep him worked up so he won't look too closely at whatever you're trying to hide. If I have to, I'll take you out of here and keep you somewhere else while H finishes up with Dawson."

Paxton offered me a broad, slanted smile, and I thought on the *Great British Baking Show*, somebody would have called him cheeky. On *Peaky Blinders*, they would have said cheeky bastard. "Go on, luv. Give it a try."

"No one's blackmailing me," Dawson said, his voice wound tight. "So, both of you fuck off—"

"You sold all your clothes. Some of it to those online places that resell designer stuff, but a lot of it on eBay or KSL, I bet. Same thing with the TV, whatever gaming system you had, the TV stand itself. Trust me, I know what it looks like when you've gone through everything you own, trying to figure out how much you can get for it."

"You're making this more difficult than it needs to be," Holmes said, his voice steadier now. "You appeared in the same blackmail pictures as Aston. Your belongings are gone, as Jack pointed out. Why drag this out?"

Paxton leaned over, hooking an arm around Dawson's neck and pulling him close to whisper in his ear. Dawson grimaced and elbowed Paxton away, but he nodded.

"Ok," he said stiffly. "Fine. I'm being blackmailed."

"How did they contact you?" Holmes asked.

"They sent me something. A letter. And pictures."

"Let's see them."

"They're gone, man. I burned them."

Holmes frowned. "That was stupid. How long has it been going on?"

"I don't know. A month."

Holmes didn't look at me, but I thought he was trying to do the same thing I was: build a timeline. We'd uncovered several blackmailers at Walker in September. Those people were gone now, but Walker—an elite private school designed as a holding cell for troubled teens who also happened to have wealthy families—was a perfect spot for a blackmailer to operate. It made sense that someone else would have tried the same trick again. What I found interesting was how quickly it had happened.

"And you've been paying?" Holmes asked.

Dawson nodded.

"How much?"

"A thousand dollars a month."

I frowned, and I caught Paxton staring at me, noticing the expression, before I could smooth it away. A thousand dollars a month wasn't chump change—I mean, I couldn't have come up with it, not unless I sold some seriously good shit. But it was a far cry from the fifty thousand that someone had demanded from Aston.

"Which you've chosen to raise by selling your possessions," Holmes said. "Why didn't you ask your parents?"

"My parents gave me a credit card," Dawson said. "No cash advances; I tried. And big surprise, blackmailers don't take Visa."

Something moved outside: metal rang tinnily, and then there was a clattering thump, and a dark shape zipped past.

I spun toward the frosted glass.

"Fucking hell," Dawson said, sitting up straight.

Paxton laughed.

When I glanced over, Holmes didn't exactly look amused—he was still clearly thinking about committing a few murders—but a hint of something showed around his eyes. "Squirrel," he said. "On the downspout."

"Fuck me," Dawson and I muttered at the same time.

"You didn't answer my question; why wouldn't you tell your parents the situation?"

"In the first place," Dawson said, "because they stuck me in this shithole because they didn't want to deal with my problems."

"And in the second?" I asked.

Dawson gave me the side eye and flicked his chin.

"In the second place?" Holmes prompted in a hard voice.

"They would have made a big deal out of it." Dawson's heavy brows drew together. Each word became stiffer as he added, "They'd ask about Aston."

My giggle was disbelief mixed with nerves. "You're protecting him?"

"The fuck do you care?"

"Are you serious right now? You're so worried about Aston's reputation that you're—you're putting yourself through this? Why? Because you're in love?"

Dawson lurched off the bed. He came toward me, building up speed as he came. Holmes tried to move into his path, but Dawson planted a hand on his chest and shoved him. I could have told him it wouldn't work; Holmes turned the move to his advantage, seizing Dawson's wrist and turning it, applying pressure. Dawson tried to turn, to shake him off, but that only made it worse. Holmes followed Dawson, increasing the pressure, so that Dawson's change of direction ended with Dawson pressed face-first against the wall. He cried out as Holmes increased the pressure on his wrist.

Paxton inched toward the edge of the bed.

"Stay where you are, Paxton," Holmes said without looking back at him. "Or I will let Jack deal with Dawson, and I will handle you myself."

For a moment, Paxton stayed still. Then he said, "Gave me a bit of a stiffy, Holloway. Say it again."

The color in Holmes's cheeks darkened. He didn't respond.

Dawson was panting, the sounds rapid and pained. He tried to shift away, but Holmes wouldn't let him, and he let out a pathetic groan.

"For the record," I said, "I could have taken him."

"Who?" Holmes asked. "Dawson or Paxton?"

"Uh, either."

A grin exploded across Paxton's face. Holmes's face was completely expressionless.

"Seriously?" I asked.

"Is he that bad, bruv?" Paxton asked with a laugh.

Holmes's mouth flattened out. "He once lost a fight with a bush."

"I didn't lose a fight with a bush! My shirt got caught, and—you know what? Fuck all y'all. H, let him go; I know you're not hurting him, but he doesn't like it, and he's upset enough already."

Shaking his head, Holmes released Dawson and stepped back. Dawson clutched at the towel to keep it from falling. He turned, his back to the wall, and touched the arm that Holmes had been holding—running his fingers from wrist to elbow. I watched him, and he looked at the floor and rolled one shoulder.

In a low voice, he said, "It's not—I mean, it's complicated, all right?"

"You mean, you're fucking around behind his back?"

"I mean everything. His family—his fucking grandfather—and yeah, the money, all of it." In a strange voice that I realized was pain, he laughed and said, "We never said we were exclusive."

The furnace kicked on, stirring the air—the smell of the heating system mixing with the room's trapped funk of sex and sweaty bodies. A draft tickled my nape. It teased a lock of Holmes's golden hair.

"You should be talking to Emma," Dawson said in that same crushed voice. "It's got to be her."

"Emma?" Holmes said.

"Emma Whiting." When neither of us responded, Dawson said, "She and Aston used to be together."

"And that's why you think she's behind this?" Holmes asked. "She feels jilted?"

"Fuck no. She's behind this because she's fucking psycho. Do you know she almost killed this guy at her last school? That's why she's here at Walker. Her boyfriend tried to break up with her—no shit, she about beat him to death. As soon as Aston learned that, he broke up with her."

"And told everyone," I said.

Dawson gave another of those one-shouldered shrugs.

"And him?" I asked, cocking my head at Paxton.

Rubbing his jaw, Dawson dropped his head again. "He came on to me in the bathroom. I said fuck it; I have study hall this hour."

"Nice."

"It's not like—we've hung out a few times. I knew he was cool."

"Now that's sweet, innit?" Paxton pushed off the bed. "And that's us sorted, so I'll scarper—"

"No," Holmes said. "You'll come with me and answer my questions."

Paxton stepped into a pair of khakis. He wriggled into a sweater, fixed his faux hawk in the mirror, and pulled on a pair of drivers. "You sure? You and your mate here have got a nice lead. Why don't you track down this girl, Emma, and later, we can get a kebab or a takeaway and catch up—"

"Now, Paxton. Jack, you first, please. Dawson, I suggest you rethink some of the choices you made today. It's obvious that you're lying to some degree; the sooner you decide to tell us the whole truth, the sooner we'll be able to resolve this."

Dawson snugged the towel up an inch and nodded, refusing to look at anyone.

I stepped out into the hall, Paxton behind me, and Holmes followed. We made our way toward the stairs; the sound of video game guns came from farther down the hall, where a door stood open. It sounded like *Call of Duty*, which wasn't exactly my specialty, but I'd played it enough to recognize it. My attention was still half-focused on the question, trying to decide if it really was *Call of Duty*, when Paxton bumped into me. I automatically adjusted my balance, distantly registering a buzz of annoyance that he couldn't walk a straight line. Too late, I realized what was happening.

He hooked my ankle and pulled my foot out from under me. I started to fall. Holmes shouted something, and Paxton grabbed me by the collar and yanked. I flew backward and crashed into Holmes. We both went down in a tangle of limbs. Paxton's footsteps pounded away, and a moment later, the door at the top of the stairs crashed shut behind him.

Chapter 8

Big Boy Feelings

In the first flurried minutes of chasing Paxton, I thought we still had a chance. The immediate aftermath, though, proved me wrong. Paxton was gone by the time we emerged from the building, and Holmes was so angry—with me, for letting Paxton get away, even though he was too kind to say so—that honestly it was a relief when Holmes insisted I go to class while he continued to search for Paxton. (Also, he wasn't wrong: Dad would legit murder me if I had two tardies in one day.)

I went to third period. I ate lunch. It was the usual thing—getting as many of the chicken tenders as my tray could support without breaking, and then pretending to decide where to sit. For a guy like me, with so many options, it was tough. Should I sit with that group of kids who wanted nothing to do with me? Or should I sit with that group of kids who actively despised me? Or maybe with those kids, who were simply too embarrassed to be seen in public with me? Or, joy of joys, I could join the Boy Band and the Bloopies. Walker's shining stars always sat at the same table: five boys, five girls, all of them beautiful and wearing designer labels and laughing and showing each other shit on their phones.

If Holmes came to the dining hall during lunch—which he only did when I could bully him into it, which, to my own credit, I was getting better at—then we sat together at the Island of Misfit Toys. That was the table in the back corner with me, Holmes, a boy in a back brace, and a pair of twin girls who groomed each other in public.

Today, I sat there alone, and I tried not to see it as a sign.

The thing about sitting on your own? You hear more of the conversations around you than you would if you were chatting with friends, or watching stuff on your phone, or thinking up yet another new, creative reason to get your only friend in the world to please for the love of God eat one chicken tender so I'd know he ate something today.

Everybody was talking about Wintersmash. If they were going. Yes, they were going; they got their invitation yesterday. No, they weren't going because somebody was being a bitch. On and on like that. It was basically the only thing anyone talked about, I guess for good reason. We were down to the wire; Wintersmash was tomorrow. I figured my invitation had gotten lost in the mail. Maybe they'd addressed it to Abercrombie.

I limped through my three afternoon classes, managing to make a fool of myself in all three—in geometry, I kept cubing four wrong, even when Mr. Zimmerly asked me to slow down and take a breath and do it slowly; in Team Sports, I botched two sets in a row, and the third time, I got it spiked back into my face; and in Spanish, I apparently managed to say, *I am pregnant*, which Ms. Quezada-Loza took an obvious pleasure in explaining to the class.

When I dragged my sorry—and now, apparently, pregnant—ass out of Walker Hall, Holmes was waiting. The color in his cheeks was from the cold, I decided, and the late winter sun struck highlights in his hair. He had his hands stuffed in the pockets of his wool coat, and his face was unreadable.

"You didn't unfriend me?" I asked when I reached him.

"What?"

"Look, I'm sorry about Paxton. I really am. I should have had my head in the game, and I royally fucked up. I get that you're mad at me; I just want you to know I'm sorry, and it won't happen again."

"Jack, I'm not angry with you. I'm angry with myself. I knew Paxton would make an attempt, and I was unprepared."

"You were unprepared because I was lying on top of you."

"I didn't expect you to stop Paxton. I certainly wouldn't unfriend you because of a miscalculation or a moment of inattention. What brought this on?"

"I don't know. You sent me away—"

"Jack."

"I know, I know." I squinted at him, and then I moved my head to catch his eye. After a moment, he smiled. "B-plus," I told him. "And you're still a dork."

The smile snapped into a line. "You are a dork. And your shoes are untied."

He wouldn't let me go anywhere with them like that, so while I tied them, I asked, "Are you mad?"

"I'm furious."

"I thought so."

"Not with you, Jack. With myself. A Holmes is always in control; I shouldn't have let that situation get out of hand. If I had been focused—" That choice of word, and the way his whole body tightened and he seemed to be trying not to look at me, told me what he meant: If I'd been skating on addies.

"Can you do something for me?" I asked as I stood.

He blinked. Timp's shadows made his eyes so dark they were almost blue.

"I've got this friend, Holloway Holmes, and I don't like people being unkind to him. So, maybe you could cut him some slack this time? Because he's human, and human beings aren't always functioning at one hundred percent precision and efficiency."

"I am Holloway Holmes."

"Uh huh."

After a moment, he moved his hands in his pockets, gathering the coat around himself. He wasn't meeting my eyes again, and when he spoke, his voice was softer. "Jack, it is not that simple."

It is, actually. That's what I wanted to say. But I blew out a long breath, the vapor catching the sun to rise like an aura over Holmes's head, and I didn't say anything.

"Come on," Holmes said. "I found Emma."

We started north, up the canyon. We passed the faculty housing, and we passed the boathouse and the lake, and we kept going, which meant either the athletic center or the activity fields. The shadows got longer, softening the edges of the stone around us, and my breaths tasted like the frozen air and the lake. The ripple of water against the shore kept us company; it would freeze in January, I thought, but it was nice, now, to listen to it.

"We were not romantically involved," Holmes said. The words had his usual controlled, emotionless delivery, but the bursts of vapor between them were sharp. We went another ten feet, snow crunching underfoot, fingers of light and shadow curling along his cheek. "I wanted you to know that."

I nodded.

West, the sun was setting, and the sky was one of those firework sunsets: giant swaths of red and orange, so intensely vibrant that it looked like the world was ending—in a beautiful way, if that makes any sense. You could get glimpses of the valley, brown buildings and brown grass, all of it ant-sized and far away. Another world. We passed under a row of pines, and the smell of the fresh needles and resin and duff that had managed somehow to stay dry.

"He was important to me," Holmes said.

I waited, but I was the one who spoke first. "Do you want to talk about it?"

After a few paces, I looked over. He was biting his lip, the blood scarlet, brighter than anything else in that world of half-tones and shadows.

"Because if you're doing this for me," I said, "you don't have to. I trust you."

"I don't know."

"That's ok."

"I don't want you to misunderstand the nature of our relationship."

"You never boinked. Not once." Holmes's face caught fire, so I grinned and added, "No smushing, smashing, grinding, humping. I bet not even any tongue tangling."

He stopped walking. I'd never seen a white boy literally melt, and I thought about staying to watch, but I smirked, hiked up my backpack, and kept going.

His hurried steps came after me a moment later, and then a handful of snow went down the back of my shirt.

I screamed. Sue me; I'm a human being.

"H!" I danced in place, trying to shake the snow loose, which meant trying to dislodge my backpack and flap my shirt and coat, which meant I looked, I'm pretty sure, like a lunatic. Most of the snow melted before I could get rid of it, so then my back and underwear were wet and freezing. I eventually gave up. "What the actual hell?"

Holmes was watching me, a hint of uncertainty around his eyes. His face had an edge to it: challenge, anger, embarrassment. But the uncertainty told me even he didn't know what this was—throwing down or messing around.

I went with messing around and gave him my best fake scowl. "Payback is a miserable son of a bitch."

The anger and challenge lingered for another moment, but he couldn't hold them. The smile that burst out was raw, untouched, a little rough around the edges. It changed everything about his face: the cold-chiseled perfection became something more, a kind of beauty lit up from within by happiness that he'd tamped down for so long, softening his mouth and eyes and cheekbones until he was almost too good to look at, like I didn't deserve this.

As I scooped to pack a snowball, Holmes sprinted toward the athletic center.

"Yeah, you'd better run!"

I pegged him in the calf, the powder exploding to dust the backs of both legs and his chukkas. He didn't slow or stumble, though, so I ran after him.

He was faster, of course. I mean, he was better at everything. But it was a little embarrassing that he was that much faster.

By the time I reached the athletic center, he had barricaded himself inside the vestibule. The smile had died to a tiny grin, a flicker that played at the corners of his mouth. He was holding the crash bar with both hands, and when I tried to yank the door open, it wouldn't budge.

"There are other doors, motherfucker," I said through the glass.

"You were being rude and ill-mannered, and you were saying inappropriate things, and—and you were teasing."

I pressed my face against the door, flattening my nose against the glass, and Holmes giggled and turned his face into his shoulder for a moment. I almost got the door open then, but even distracted, he was freakishly strong.

"Fine," I said, releasing the door, "here I come, you little weasel."

"Truce!"

I studied him. Then I said in my flattest voice, "Temporary truce."

"Jack!"

"You put snow down my shirt, you little shit. You're not going to get away with that."

"It was payback for what you said!"

I grimaced—I made a big show of it, because Holmes liked things like that, even though he wouldn't come out and say it. Then I said, "Fine. But, you owe me a movie. With popcorn. And a drink. And nachos. And one box of candy."

"Popcorn and a drink. The nachos are bad for you, and you drank the cheese when you thought I wasn't looking."

I burst out laughing. "A movie with popcorn and a drink. Deal."

Warily, Holmes pressed the crash bar. The door inched open.

"I'm going to be frozen. I'm going to be lucky if my ass doesn't freeze off. They had to give Jonny Evans a prosthetic butt because his ass froze off."

"You said they had to make him a new butthole after that wedgie."

"He had a rough life, H."

He had his hands in his pockets again, and in a low voice, he said, "I do not want to be teased about Paxton."

His voice echoed slightly in the vestibule. From beyond the next set of doors came familiar sounds: raised voices, doors opening and shutting, a timer buzzing.

"All right," I said. "But you know, laughing about something, joking about it, even teasing about it—that makes it a little easier to handle. That's one way to deal with stuff that you don't know how to handle."

He didn't look up, but after a moment, he nodded.

"That's how I deal with my impossible good looks," I said.

Holmes shot me a look from under knitted brows.

"I have to laugh about it because it's overwhelming, being this good looking. Some days, I don't know how I live with it."

He tried to slam me in the door, and I was laughing too hard to put up much of a fight.

"You're not supposed to laugh at your own jokes," he finally said, and he left me half-crushed in the vestibule doorway.

I caught up to him in the lobby. Dad had put up the giant Christmas tree, and instrumental Christmas music played over the speakers in the ceiling. A banner on the far wall read, *Happy Holidays!* Holmes led me through the athletic center, past the gyms, where someone was shouting, "Defense! Defense! Defense!" and past a multipurpose room where the Bloopies had gathered to do Pilates, and past the weight room where three-fifths of the Boy Band were making an effort to impress each other, which consisted of racking weights, leaning on weights, looking at their phones, doing maybe one set, and, in general, looking pretty for whoever happened to walk by.

I'd cleaned the wrestling room plenty of times, but I'd never had a class in there. When Holmes and I stepped inside, I wasn't sure what to expect. The floor was covered by mats—for wrestling, obviously—and mirrors lined one wall. Dumbbells were racked to our left, and a much smaller Christmas tree, this one strung with tinsel and paper chains, to our right. The place smelled like sweat and BO and vinyl and chemically pine air freshener.

I recognized the three kids by sight, although I didn't know their names. Two girls and a boy. The first girl wore her black hair in a pixie cut, and her cat-eye glasses looked painfully hipsterish. She had a reddish cast to her umber skin, and she wore a loose-fitting tracksuit. The second girl had long, dark hair; she was petite, where the other girl was statuesque, and she had a golden complexion. The boy was white—the kind of creamy white with ruddy cheeks that said America's Heartland. His blond hair was cropped except for disheveled bangs, and he had a surprisingly sweet beard for a teenager.

The three of them hadn't noticed us yet, and the boy was still talking.

"Not too high, not too high," he was telling the petite girl. "Bring your hands down a little; you want to keep your guard low."

Holmes snorted softly. The girl in the tracksuit, who was observing, made a face that the boy didn't see.

"Ok, good. Now, kick me in the head."

"In the head?" Holmes asked in a scandalized whisper.

I squeezed his shoulder and put a finger to my lips.

"Won't that put Glo off balance?" the tracksuit girl said. "She could aim for the knee and keep her stability."

"Trust me," the boy said. "You always go for the head."

I'd seen Holmes outraged plenty of times—mostly because of things I'd done or said, or occasionally, what he found in the mess of my bedroom (one time it had been a vape, and he'd gone nuclear, but that wasn't as bad as the time he'd found a Pop-Tart in one of my socks)—but it was a whole new kind of pleasure watching him be outraged with other people.

The shorter girl—presumably Glo—threw a few wobbly kicks, each time barely catching herself before she fell.

"What if she kicked him between the legs?" the girl in the tracksuit asked. "She can generate more power, and she'll definitely hurt him."

"Well, yeah," the boy said. "But that's kind of fighting dirty, isn't it?"

"Breathe," I whispered to Holmes. "Your eye is going to pop out."

"Let's say he gets in too close," the boy said. "The kick slows him down, but he keeps coming."

"Because you couldn't generate any power," the girl in the tracksuit said. "Because you were trying to kick him in the head."

The boy ignored this. "If he gets you in a chokehold like this—"

"Why are you grabbing your own neck?" the girl in the tracksuit asked. "I thought in a chokehold, you applied pressure to the back of their skull—"

Holmes had been making an increasingly distressed noise. He took a step, and I tightened my grip on his shoulder, but he shook me off. "I can't," he said in a low voice. "This is a travesty." Then, in a louder voice, he called, "You've done at least eighteen things wrong in the thirty seconds that I've been watching, and four of them could have gotten you killed."

Three heads whipped around. Three sets of eyes stared at us. The boy released the smaller girl, and the three made a triangle. I didn't miss the fact that the girl in the tracksuit took the point, and I didn't think Holmes missed it either.

"Hey, bro, we're in the middle of something—" the boy began.

"You're in the middle of giving terrible advice that might, ultimately, get these girls hurt. Stop now before you embarrass yourself further."

Trailing after him, I gave a wave. "Also, hi. I'm Jack. This is Holloway."

The girl in the tracksuit flicked a look at me, but most of her attention was on Holmes.

"Seriously?" the boy asked. "The Holloway Holmes? Bro, that's so fire. I thought it was you, but we've never, like, talked, so—"

"Be quiet now," Holmes told him.

Shock wiped the boy's face clean. He shut his mouth. Then he grinned and nudged Glo. She just stared at us.

"We reserved this room," the girl in the tracksuit said, "and we're allowed to use it until five-thirty. We'd like some privacy."

"We need to talk to you," Holmes said. "We can either have this conversation here, in front of your friends, where you will most likely find it uncomfortable and embarrassing. Or, you can come with us, and we'll conduct the interview in a more discreet location."

"H," I said quietly, and I tugged on his sleeve as I caught up to him. "Ease up—"

The blond boy's smile had dropped away, and he frowned as he stepped forward. "Hold on, Emma doesn't have to go anywhere with you."

The girl in the tracksuit shook her head. "I'm handling this, Rowe."

"No, this has got to be some kind of misunderstanding. What's going on? Why do you need to talk to Emma?"

"I've told you once to be quiet," Holmes said. "This conversation does not include you. I won't tell you again."

"Hey!" Glo said. "You can't talk to him like that!"

"Dude—" The boy—Rowe, the girl had called him—shrugged. "— Emma's my friend. It kind of does include me, you know?"

Holmes rounded on him, and the boy swallowed. He didn't take a step back, though, which said something about his moral character—or, maybe more likely, his stupidity. Silence opened like a vacuum. From down the hall came the squeak of rubber soles on wood floors and the drumming of a basketball in play.

"I asked you to leave," Emma said into the quiet. "I don't know what you want—"

"You were Aston Young's girlfriend," Holmes said. "True or false?"

Emma stared at him. "I'm not talking about Aston," she finally said. "I don't want to talk to you at all. We're working on something—"

Holmes opened his mouth, and this time, I squeezed his biceps. He glanced over at me, and when I shook my head, he shut his mouth again.

"We got off on the wrong foot," I said with a smile. "Can we start over?"

"No," Emma said. "I want you to leave now." Turning her back on us, she said, "Rowe, show me again how you did that thing with your elbow."

Rowe glanced sidelong at us, his face filling with color.

"Holmes can show you," I said, the words leaving my mouth before I'd thought the idea through.

"We don't need anyone—" Glo began.

"Yeah, um, that'd be all right," Rowe said, the color in his face darkening. "It would be cool to have somebody to spar with. You know, somebody else who's been trained."

"No," Holmes said. "We don't have time—"

"Yep." I caught his arm and angled him toward Rowe and Glo. "You guys have fun, while Emma and I have a chat." I looked a silent question at Emma, and after a moment, she gave a grudging nod.

Holmes had gone still—the kind of stillness I had learned to recognize as his efforts to master tremendous anger.

"Level one," I said quietly. "Hear me?"

"He wants someone trained," Holmes said. "You heard him. He wants someone to spar with."

"Fine. Level zero."

"Jack!"

"I don't trust you; you've got crazy eyes."

Holmes wrested his arm away. "I do not have crazy eyes."

"Level zero, H. Tell me."

"Level two."

"Level zero."

"Level one, as you initially suggested."

I gave him a look.

After a moment, he growled, "Very well," and stalked over to Rowe and Glo.

At Holmes's urging, the three of them moved down the length of the room. Rowe was bouncing on his toes, already grinning again, but Glo had a dubious look on her face.

"Bro, don't you want to take off your coat?" Rowe asked.

"I don't think that will be necessary."

Emma watched them, and then she glanced at me. She wore no makeup, I realized now, and while the cat-eye glasses gave her a hipsterish look, her build under the tracksuit was athletic verging on muscular. Up close, I saw she wore fingerless gloves—another nice hipsterish touch. I wondered who she was trying to fool.

"What was all that about level zero?" she asked.

"Holloway has this crazy idea that I'm no good in a fight."

"Because you once managed to miss a punching bag," Holmes put in.

"I didn't miss it," I said to Emma. "Well, I did. But only because he distracted me. Anyway, he's determined to make a killing machine out of me, so we train every once in a while. I had to make levels because it was embarrassing."

"What's level zero?"

"Still embarrassing, but it doesn't hurt as much."

To my surprise, she smiled. Then, smile fading, she said, "I'm not going to talk about Aston."

"All right."

"I have nothing to say."

"Listen, he's a prick; I get it."

She shook her head.

At the other end of the room, Holmes said, "Let's return to your instruction on the chokehold. I believe you were demonstrating how to escape?"

I sighed and rubbed my eyes.

"Yes, we dated," Emma said abruptly. She was looking at us in the mirrors, so I did too. With that reddish cast to her skin, it was hard to tell if she was blushing, but she folded her arms and shifted her weight and looked like she wanted to step back from me. "It wasn't anything serious. I don't care about Aston; that's why I broke up with him. The whole point of breaking up is so he's not in my life anymore."

"But that's kind of hard at a place like Walker," I said. "I've only been a student a couple of months, but I know how this place works. It's a bubble. And Aston's up there with the Boy Band and the Bloopies, and when he talks shit, it spreads fast."

A clear, startled laugh came from Emma, and a surprisingly devilish grin crossed her face. "The Bloopies? The little mermaid doll toys?"

"They have color-changing tails."

She laughed again, and I smiled; she had a nice laugh, and a nice face, and it would be a shame if she were behind all this stuff.

"Let me guess—Skye and that group."

"Oh yeah."

"And the Boy Band is Aston and his little gang?"

"More or less."

She laughed again. "I love it."

Frantic noises drew my attention. Holmes had Rowe in a chokehold, and the blond boy's face was bright red. He was trying to pry Holmes's arm free, and his heels scraped the mat.

"Hold on," I told Emma. I called across the room, "H!"

Holmes made a face, but he released Rowe. The boy sagged and would have fallen if Holmes hadn't steadied him.

"Level zero?"

"That was level zero," he said without looking at me. "If I'd applied the hold in earnest, he would have passed out from lack of blood to the brain."

Rowe was still hacking for breath, and now Glo was rubbing his back and giving Holmes dirty looks.

"Do you want to try that again?" I asked.

Holmes threw me a furious glare before turning his attention back to Rowe, saying something too quiet for me to hear. Whatever it was, it made Rowe nod—with an unbelievable amount of enthusiasm.

"I'm going to have to go over there eventually," I told Emma. "He's going to make me tan his ass."

She gave me a curious look. "You two aren't exactly what I expected. I've seen you around campus, and everyone hears—" She stopped, touched her face, and broke our gaze.

"Everybody hears the stories about Supercreep and Janitor Boy?" I asked.

"It's like you said: this place is a bubble." She made an effort to look me in the face. "I didn't say everyone believed the stories."

I shrugged. "People can say what they want. Having your whole world turned inside out makes it harder to care about shit like that."

"Yeah," she said, as though speaking to herself. "It does, doesn't it?"

"Go on," Holmes said to Rowe. The blond boy's face was still ruddied, but he was grinning again as Holmes directed him. "Punch me in the face."

"H," I said.

He bristled but didn't respond. Rowe threw a punch that looked almost as bad as one of mine, and Holmes moved out of the way. It was something, watching him. Everyone should have had the chance. To see silk ripple, to watch water part. Rowe threw another jab, but Holmes was already gone.

"Aston told you I beat a boy to death," Emma said. "Because he broke up with me."

"I heard a version of that. Almost to death."

"Look at that," Emma murmured. "He's getting kinder."

"I figure it's bullshit, like the stories about me and H."

Emma shrugged. She took the cat-eye glasses off, folded them, and held them loosely in one hand. Her face was more angular without them, more severe. Striking in a way that it hadn't been before.

"Here's what I was thinking," I said. "Someone's blackmailing Aston, and it's possible you're the one doing it; I mean, you're the ex, and maybe you figured out something about Aston while you were dating, and now you're using it against him."

"Like the fact that he's gay and has sex with Dawson?"

The only sound was Rowe's harsh breathing and the whiff of blows that caught only air.

"Maybe," I said. "Something like that."

Her smile was tight. "The first part was pretty obvious after a while. The second part I didn't figure out until after we broke up."

I sorted questions like a deck of cards and settled on: "How did that make you feel?"

She laughed again, that same light, startled sound. "Relieved. I mean, I feel sorry for him; he's in an impossible situation, and Dawson isn't exactly the kind of partner you'd want to get you through something like that. But relieved, mostly."

"Relieved about what?"

"I'm not blackmailing him. I don't know how I can prove that to you, but I'm not. I don't care about him. I don't need his money. I don't want to punish him or hurt him or destroy him. I want to be left alone." Her gaze slid to Glo and Rowe, and in that quiet tone she'd used earlier, she said, "I want everyone to leave me alone."

I nodded. I couldn't hear Holmes—not his breathing, not his movement on the mat, not even the whisper of his clothes; it sounded like Rowe was shadow-boxing. The music in the hallway changed—Wham!'s "Last Christmas" came on.

Emma made a throwing-up noise. "Every year," she said. "I hate this song."

"Everybody hates this song. They only play it because there's an evil syndicate that promotes it in an attempt to destroy Christmas."

A broad smile crossed her face, and when she glanced at Holmes and back at me, her smile got bigger.

"What?" I asked.

"Nothing," she said, and if anything, the smile got even bigger. "I can kind of see it now."

I didn't know what that meant, so I said, "Maybe you can still help us. Is there somebody who might hate Aston enough to do this? Someone on campus, I mean. A kid he bullied, or another ex, or, uh, a partner."

Her smirk flared and vanished, and she shook her head, but she said, "Maybe."

"Maybe?"

"I don't think it's someone on campus. I mean, Aston is annoying, and he can be a bully—but, like, in passing. He's the center of his own universe; he doesn't have time to actively bully people. He and the—well, you call them the Boy Band—they're jerks, sure, and they might say something mean, but they're not like these afterschool-special bullies whose sole purpose in life is to make other people miserable."

"But it might not be bullying. Someone might just want the money," I said.

"I guess. He hasn't dated anyone else seriously, not that I know. And at the beginning, he's convincing. I don't think any of the girls he's hooked up with would have suspicions. It might be someone else in the Boy Band, or maybe the Bloopies, but I can't think who—they're pretty tight, and they know each other's secrets, some of them. But they're all so self-absorbed, and they're all so...innocent."

"Not exactly the word I'd use to describe them. Trust me, the shit they buy."

"That's not what I mean. Insulated, I guess. Naïve. They don't know anything about the real world. Maybe Aston does because of what happened a couple of months ago, but—I mean, look at him. No consequences. Nothing. He's back at school like it never happened. I don't think any of them know how ugly the world can be, and you have to know that—have a sense of it, anyway—to do something like this."

It was a surprisingly insightful comment. It was also the kind of thing you could only say if you'd seen some of that ugliness yourself.

"But you said maybe," I prompted.

"Have you met his sister?"

"I didn't know he had a sister."

"She's...a lot. She's obsessed with him, actually. Like, she spies on him for their parents. To get him in trouble. She's always showing up, surprising him like she's going to catch him doing something. She talks down to him. She yells at him. He puts up with it; he says they're close, that's all."

"But?"

Emma plucked lint from her sleeve, avoiding my gaze. "I don't know. It's weird. His whole family is weird. You asked who might hate him enough to do this. It's not that she hates him, but…"

I nodded, and I was about to ask another question when the unmistakable thud of a body hitting the floor echoed through the room. When I looked over, Rowe lay flat on his back on the wrestling mat. His face was screwed up in that look of someone who's had the wind knocked out of them. Holmes was straightening, reaching up to check that neat Ivy League cut. I'd been on the receiving end of a hip throw plenty of times over the last few months, and I knew what it looked like—and, more importantly, what it felt like.

"For Christ's sake—" I began.

Rowe flopped over onto his side and made a croaking noise. Glo crouched next to him, her face screwed up with worry, and Rowe let her help him upright. Then I realized the croaking noise was laughter. Beneath the beard, Rowe's flush deepened as he laughed—well, hacked—harder and harder.

"Dude," he finally managed to wheeze. "That was dope!"

I would have given a month of jelly-jar money to have a photo of the look on Holmes's face.

Then Rowe hugged him, and Holmes's body looked like something strung out of steel and cables, his hands already moving to detach Rowe and, most likely, hurl him to the floor again. Or put him in a compliance hold. Or maybe break his neck.

I opened my mouth to explain, but Holmes must have figured it out himself, because he relaxed—well, he went from DEFCON 5 to his ordinary rigidity.

Rowe thumped him on the back a few times before releasing him, still laughing and, now, massaging his ass. "Dude, you clobbered me!"

"You put too much weight on your front foot—"

"Did you see that?" Rowe called over to us. "That was flipping awesome!"

Holmes threw me a look that, on anybody else, I would have called nervous. I gave him a thumbs-up from low at my side, and he relaxed a little more, but confusion still mapped itself across his face.

"You could have gotten hurt," Glo said. She was holding on to Rowe's arm, and for the first time, I noticed how she looked at him. And then I thought about how Emma had looked at the two of them, and I thought about the three of them down here, all by themselves, and I thought, Oh, got it. Glo pulled Rowe around to face her, but she snapped at Holmes, "He might have a concussion!"

"He took the fall surprisingly well—" Holmes began.

At the same time, Rowe said, "I don't have a concussion; I'm fine."

"He's like a puppy," Emma said to me. "I swear, he could fall down a flight of stairs, dust himself off, and ask if we could do it again."

I laughed.

"I've got to fuss over him," Emma said. "You know how it goes."

I watched Holmes, who was straightening his coat and not looking at me—the way little kids try to avoid your gaze if they know they're in trouble. "Yeah," I said. "I know."

Rowe ignored Emma's and Glo's questions, talking a mile a minute at Holmes instead, asking him how he'd done the throw and what he could have done better and if he could show him how to do that chokehold—on and on. Holmes's eyes got wider and wider.

"Come on," I said, touching his arm. His flinch was tiny, but it was there. I ignored it for a moment, checked Emma and Glo with a look, and, in a louder voice, said, "No more roughhousing today, boys. Let's get out of here."

Rowe protested something about another round, but Emma and Glo herded him toward the door, and Holmes and I fell into place a few yards behind them.

"Did you get hurt?" I asked.

Holmes forgot about being guilty long enough to direct an indignant look at me.

Laughing, I shook my head. "On accident, obviously. Maybe you pulled something from throwing that meathead around."

"I'm fine," he said stiffly.

"Are you mad at me?"

This time, his look was searching. "Are you mad at me?"

I snorted.

Something changed in his expression—a hint of the wily Holmes that occasionally surfaced. "You were able to conduct an effective interview because I provided a suitable distraction."

"Uh huh. And you were able to vent all those big boy feelings about losing Paxton and witnessing Rowe's total incompetence."

Circles of color bloomed in Holmes's cheek.

"And you didn't even use one pain compliance hold," I said with a smirk.

His back got ramrod straight.

Laughing again, I squeezed his nape. "Relax. Rowe was right: watching you do that was fucking awesome."

He didn't smile, but his shoulders softened, and the lines around his eyes eased.

When we emerged from the athletic center, Rowe spun around to face us. "You guys, we've got to do that, like, every day. H could teach us, and, like, Jack too, obviously."

"Gee, thanks."

"I mean, that was seriously badass." He wound up for a huge punch. "H, you're fricking fire. You know that, right?"

Holmes darted a look at me. This time, I managed to swallow the laugh. "We'll see; H is pretty busy most of the time. But maybe."

"So, when I did that uppercut," Rowe said, "you barely even moved your head, which means you totally knew it was coming—"

The squeal of tires cut through his words. On the campus road that ran past the athletic center, a truck screeched to a halt—a haze of smoke and the smell of burning rubber drifting up. I had just long enough to process a few basic facts: it was black, it was massive, and it didn't have license plates. Then the window went down, and I caught the glint of blued steel and glass. A scope, my brain suggested.

Holmes, distracted by Rowe, was still turning around.

The shock only lasted a moment, but I knew it had been too long.

Rowe's tackle carried him into Holmes, and then it was like being caught up in some sort of weird scrum-slash-bum rush: the three of us stumbled into the girls, and all of us went down. A gunshot cracked the air a moment later, and then two more came. Something whizzed past me, and there was a weird, soft noise of impact. A fine grit of dirt sprayed the side of my face, and a moment later, my brain told me a bullet had hit the ground inches from me.

An engine roared, and tires squealed again.

It wasn't a thought so much as something at the back of my brain taking over—instinct, maybe, or a genetic predisposition for trouble. I got to my feet and sprinted after the truck. For the first five yards, I narrowed the distance. Then the driver hit the gas, and the truck began to pull ahead.

I tossed my phone sidearm, and it landed in the bed of the truck.

A moment later, the truck was gone—disappearing around the next corner. It had all happened in a matter of a minute, maybe two. Holmes was already jogging toward me, and Emma was helping Rowe and Glo to their feet. There had been no witnesses. No screams. No sirens. If Rowe hadn't been so quick to react, some of us would have died, maybe all of us, and no one would have known until they stumbled across our bodies.

A hand on my arm yanked me around. Holmes's eyes blazed wide and silver, and for a moment, I couldn't think, couldn't say anything. He curled a hand around my neck. He touched my shoulder, my chest. Patting me down, my brain supplied. He's checking for injuries. He's being practical.

And then, as quickly as it had happened, he stepped back. He held his hands out to his sides like he'd been burned. For one long moment, he continued to gaze at me, and I couldn't read what was in his eyes. Then he looked away. Someone else might have missed the shiver—someone who hadn't watched him, studied him as long as I had.

"Are you hurt—"

"Fine." I tried to blunt the adrenaline edge in my voice. "I'm fine, H. Come on; we've got to go after him."

Chapter 9

Mormon Boyz

We left Rowe, Emma, and Glo with instructions to call the police, and then we ran. I wanted to go straight to the cottage, but Holmes insisted on a quick detour to pick up one of his gear bags from his residence hall. When we got to the cottage, Dad wasn't home, but the keys to the Dakota were on the hook by the door. I had Holmes send him a quick message, telling him we were taking the truck and would be back soon, and then we started down the canyon.

While I drove us off campus, Holmes used his own phone to pull up the Find My Device prompt and enter my information. A moment later, he showed me a map, with a pin marking my phone. When the map refreshed, the pin had shifted toward Provo.

"Ok," I said. "Buckle up."

"My seat belt is already buckled," Holmes said.

"Do you do it on purpose?"

"Yes. Seat belts reduce the risk of death for front-seat passengers by up to forty-five percent."

I counted to ten in my head. "Do you ruin every single badass moment for me on purpose? That's what I'm asking you."

"I don't know what you mean."

I shook my head.

"Is saying, 'Buckle up' badass? Because typically teens correlate danger with high social prestige, not safety." In a rush, he added, "Although I think it's admirable that you're safety minded."

"Please stop."

Holmes wasn't smiling, but then, he was carefully keeping his face turned down, and he was such a little weasel sometimes that I couldn't trust the silence.

December in Provo Canyon is, well, about as beautiful as any other time of year. In spring, you see everything coming back to life, and the Provo River runs high from the melt, wildflowers everywhere and the trees in bloom. In summer, you get the cool breezes to break up the heat, and all the shady riffles on the water, and the spray of Bridal Veil Falls like samite spun out into the air. (Samite: a rich silk fabric woven with gold and silver threads—thank you, Mr. Scholz, eighth-grade Language Arts.) In the fall, you got the trees changing color, the scrub oak burning red on the slopes.

In the winter, it was an anatomy of snow and ice and stone. The air was crisper, clearer, and the granite pitch of the canyon walls looked fresh cut, all sharp edges. Ice hung in toothy sheets. But the snow softened everything, giving it a kind of fairy-tale quality, and the green of the pines and the green-blue of the cedars reminded you this place was still alive. When we came around a bend and saw the river, it was slaggy with ice, the slabs breaking up on the rocks and then spinning, trapped.

Following the tracker, we left the canyon and drove into Provo. You could tell where the oldest parts were—most of the homes built around Center Street and then moving east, around Brigham Young University's campus and up into the foothills. But the tracker led us west, across town and toward Utah Lake. The closer we got, the more signs there were of new development. Land in Provo—well, land in Utah generally—had gotten more and more valuable, and people were squeezing homes into every nook and cranny.

When we turned into the neighborhood, you could tell it was new because all the houses looked ten years old: all of them brown stucco with fieldstone accents, street after street of perfect lawns and neatly edged curbs and unblemished asphalt. I slowed the truck and checked the clock. It was a little after five, and between the houses, I could see the sun going down over the lake, turning the water red and orange and cutting out the western mountains like paper dolls. Cars flowed steadily through the neighborhood—everybody was coming home from work, ready for happy dinners with their happy families in Happy Valley.

"Shit," I said. "We couldn't have picked a worse time."

Holmes cocked his head.

"The streets are going to be busy," I said.

"I believe it will be an advantage. Instead of a solitary truck that might be noticed by people who have nothing else to do—"

"Nosy neighbors and snoops," I said.

"—we blend in with the flow of traffic. Children will be inside for dinner. And, as you can see, most of the people returning home are parking in their garages, which means that their attention will not be on the street."

After a moment, I said, "Huh."

Holmes shrugged. "Probably."

I raised my eyebrows.

Coloring slightly, he shifted in his seat. "There is, of course, a higher density of possible witnesses. And since everyone else is inside, our presence outside will be more remarkable."

"You should have stopped while you were ahead."

"It's important to give you a full analysis—"

"H."

He closed his mouth and looked faintly relieved.

We wove our way to the back of the neighborhood, where the houses were built right along the lake. Holmes tapped the window as we passed a house, but when I shifted my foot to the brake, he shook his head. I kept driving.

"Take the next turn, please." I did, and Holmes immediately said, "Park."

This street didn't look any different from the others, but I pulled to the curb and stopped the truck. By twisting around, I could still get a look at the house Holmes had indicated: a ranch, the same brown stucco as everything else, with blinds in every window. There was a light on in one room, and the garage door was down. Well, both garage doors were—it had a third-car garage tacked onto the side. Window wells suggested basement bedrooms. It could have been any other house on the street with the small exception of the blinds.

"You're sure?" I asked.

"That's where your phone is. Or, perhaps more accurately, where it's saying that it is. It's possible, I suppose, that it's been hacked. A minor possibility, but—"

"H."

He nodded and stopped.

"Ok," I said, "what do we do?"

"I have a plan."

"Fuck yeah you do." I gave him a beat, and then I said, "See, that was a badass line, and notice how I'm not stepping all over it?"

Holmes gave me a shockingly dirty look and pulled his gear bag onto his lap. As he spoke, he drew articles from the bag and placed them on the seat between us: dark chinos, an extra pair of chukkas, white button-ups. "Who is perhaps the most invisible person moving in public in Utah?"

"Mail carriers," I said.

He paused. "Besides mail carriers."

"Amazon delivery drivers."

This time, the pause was longer. "Besides—"

"UPS drivers, FedEx drivers."

He was breathing through his nose now.

"Basically anyone with a van or truck and a delivery," I said in what I considered my most helpful tone.

Holmes took several more breaths. "Besides them."

"Well, possibly utility workers, white moms with strollers, white moms without strollers, white ladies in jazzercise outfits—"

"Mormon missionaries," Holmes said. It wasn't quite a shout, but he definitely lost control of his volume at the end, and I had to cover a smirk.

"Oh," I said. Then I looked at the white button-ups and the dark chinos and the extra pair of chukkas and I groaned. "Oh."

"Change," Holmes said.

"Seriously?"

"Yes."

"You're lucky we're the same size. Well, not exactly the same size since I don't have a world-class bubble butt—"

"Jack, quickly."

I won't lie: I swore under my breath. A lot. I toed off my Stan Smiths and wriggled out of my jeans; my boxers were printed with peach emojis, which Holmes stared at for a moment before jerking his head away. He started to unbutton his oxford, his face turned down toward the footwell. I ditched my coat and jacket and shivered since I was now officially bare-assed (aside from the boxers) as I grabbed one of the button-ups and slid into it. The fabric was cold and unbelievably soft—and clearly way more expensive than anything I'd ever owned. I did up the buttons, humped into a pair of the chinos, and pulled on the chukkas.

Meanwhile, Holmes was doing his own changing act, although he only needed to swap out shirts. I'd seen him before in the gym, when he wore those thin tech shirts. But I hadn't seen him with his shirt off, and it was…well, pretty much fucking everything.

He was still slender, but I could tell if he kept going like this, he was going to be a fucking beast when he started adding on mass. Every muscle was defined: the curve of pectorals, the crescent of shoulder, the rise and fall of biceps. What startled me was the little diamond of blond hair at the center of his chest. What startled me more was how dark the hair under his arms was—like smoky honey.

He raised his head as he began doing up the buttons, and I tore my gaze away.

Holmes produced ties, and I made a face and shook my head.

"I'll help you," he said and beckoned me closer. He worked the tie under my collar and began doing all sorts of complicated things with it. His breath was warm in the cold of the truck's cabin, and his hands were sure and steady.

"This isn't going to work," I said. "You're too pretty to be a Mormon missionary."

"There are no rules on attractiveness for Mormons. I'm sure there's a representative distribution."

"Nope, you're way over the line. You could be one of the Mormon Boyz though. That's with a Z."

It was weird how you could tell someone was amused (mildly) by the way he breathed out through his nose.

"They're super porny, by the way. That's why you could pass for one."

His hands stilled.

"I'm sorry," I said after a minute. "I know I shouldn't have said that. I, uh—would you believe me if I said I'm nervous?"

He nodded and resumed work on the tie, but his voice was still stiff when he said, "You have nothing to be nervous about."

"I know, I know. If I get in a fight with a pile of mulch, you'll beat it up for me."

The corner of his mouth crooked, and his eyes flashed up to mine. "Something like that."

He leaned back and smoothed the tie down my chest, and the brush of his fingers was like someone running an electric charge across my skin. He studied me, and whatever he saw brought color into his cheeks again. He looked away, staring out the windshield as he picked up his own tie, and mumbled, "I only need a moment."

We walked down the block, side by side, matching our stride. A white guy with a daddy part and pajama pants opened his door to shout, "Evening, Elders!" but he ducked back inside before we had to do anything more than wave.

At Holmes's direction, when we reached the end of the street, we crossed and worked our way up the other side. It gave us more time to study the house where my phone had ended up. That one light was still shining, and as we came up the street, it went off. A moment later, another light bloomed in another room. Then that one went off too. Then a third light came on, and I could tell this one was near the garage.

"H, I think he's leaving."

Holmes nodded. "Tie your shoe."

"I'm fine—"

"Jack, I'm asking you to stall."

"Oh. Right."

As I bent, though, he added, "In addition, you should always tie your shoelaces. You're liable to trip and hurt yourself."

"Yes, Daddy."

He made a slightly choked noise, and I smirked as I tied my shoes.

A garage door rattled, but before I could raise my head, Holmes whispered, "No." So, I kept my head down and made sure the laces were good and tight the way Daddy liked them. An engine purred, and tires whispered against pavement.

"What are you doing?" I asked.

"Reading my scriptures," Holmes said. And then, in a tone I couldn't decipher, he added, "Like all good Mormon boyz."

"Oh my shit. Did you say it with a Z?"

He did that little amused breath again, and I was starting to wonder if everyone could do that—if you spent enough time together, paid attention, thought about them enough.

"Ok," Holmes said.

I got up, one knee frozen from the pavement, in time to see a red sports car take the next turn.

"Not the truck," I said as Holmes stuffed a Book of Mormon into his gear bag. "Where did you get that?"

"They give them out for free. I believe that was the shooter. White male, late twenties or early thirties. The tracker shows your phone is still at the same location, so it stands to reason that he left the truck and has taken a second vehicle, probably in an attempt to secure an alibi."

"But do you, like, carry it around with you all the time? Just in case you need to pretend to be a Mormon missionary?"

"In this gear bag, yes," Holmes said absently, still studying the house. "Come on."

"What do you mean this one?"

"Jack, we don't know how long he'll be gone. We need to hurry."

He started across the street at a jog, and I followed him. Instead of going to the garage or the front door, though, Holmes cut between houses. On our left, lit windows and the occasional sound of a voice suggested a family. On our right, the shooter's house was dark.

Holmes crouched next to one of the window wells. He lifted the grate, swung a leg over the edge, and climbed down.

"That wasn't locked or anything?" I asked.

"What would be the point of an egress window if the grate were locked?"

I didn't have anything smart to say to that, so I climbed down after him.

At the bottom of the window well, it was a tight fit with the two of us, and every other breath I caught a lungful of that woodsy heat that I associated with Holmes. He dropped the gear bag with a clank, examined the window—a horizontal slider—and frowned. "An inspection will reveal that we've entered here; I don't know if there's anything I can do about that."

"Why?" I asked. "Normally, they've got a latch that turns. If you have a screwdriver, I can jimmy it for you."

He looked at me.

"What? Some of the faculty houses have these, and a couple of times, I've had to fix the latch."

"I was going to use a hacksaw."

"You don't have to cut anything, but actually, a hacksaw might work even better. But instead of sawing through the latch, use the blade to force it up—you know, to make it turn."

Holmes frowned some more. He was still looking at me.

"I thought we were in a hurry."

After a long, hesitating moment, Holmes said, "Thank you."

I grinned. "Glad to be of service."

He hesitated for another heartbeat, as though he weren't sure what to do. Then he changed: his body relaxing, his movements becoming assured and smooth. He produced a tiny hacksaw from the gear bag and slid the blade between the sashes. With a questioning look to me, he wiggled the blade up. I eyed the latch through the window and nodded. Holmes set to work, and millimeter by millimeter, the latch turned. When it popped free, both of us let out our breaths. Holmes pulled on a pair of gloves, passed me another, and slid the window open.

Holding up a hand for me to wait, he slipped through the opening. He made the tiniest amount of noise when his feet connected with the carpet inside, and I swung through the window after him.

I felt the click as my heel came down on something that was definitely not carpet. I started to raise my foot to see what I'd stepped on.

Holmes's fingers bit into my ankle, and I made an exasperated noise.

"Jack," he said, his voice was cold and empty and precise, "do not move. You've stepped on a landmine."

Chapter 10

The Danites

For a moment, all I could feel was the steel plate underfoot. A landmine, Holmes had said. But that didn't make any sense. We were in a home. We were in a nice, suburban house, and we'd come in through the basement window and because I'd made one mistake coming through the window, we were both going to get blown to pieces—

"Take a deep breath," Holmes said in that same empty voice. "I need you to control yourself."

I took a ragged breath. "Why hasn't it—I stepped on it. I felt it click. Why hasn't it…you know?"

"Most likely, it's activated when pressure is removed from the plate. That's why it's important for you to hold still."

The adrenaline hit me then: I started to shake, and sweat broke out on my face and chest and back. The dark made it difficult to tell if it was only my imagination, but my vision seemed skewed, the way it was sometimes after the optometrist dilated my eyes. My leg started to tremble. I could picture my heel bouncing—a staccato rhythm I couldn't control. Tiny stuff now, micro-level stuff, but it was going to get worse, and one time, my heel would come up from the panel enough to trigger it, and my body's sympathetic nervous system would get us killed.

"Jack," Holmes said. "Control yourself."

"I can't!"

His silence was ruinous—a caved-in, swallowed-up nothing for me to fall into.

And then, with those minute inflections that I recognized as Holmes trying his hardest, he said, "It's ok, Jack. You're going to be fine; I've got you."

The ragged laugh that tore out of me was half sob. "Yeah. Ok."

He made a shushing noise. His fingers were like steel around my ankle, but with his free hand, he rubbed my thigh. I was still trembling like crazy; if he let go—

"You have a system you use for breathing," he said. "You taught it to me once, do you remember?"

I made a weird, moaning noise that was kind of a yes, but I managed to say, "You were freaking out."

"Yes. Can you try that breathing exercise for me now?"

The paramedics had made me do it after the accident, and I'd had a lot of practice with it since, the nights when black undertows of panic came for me. I counted my breaths and counted my exhales. After a few rounds of that, I was still trembling, but not with the erratic, uncontrollable spasms that threatened to trigger the mine.

"Good," Holmes said. He flexed his fingers around my ankle once. "I need to turn on the light. That means I'm going to let go of you for a moment."

Panic burbled out in a single sound: "H—"

"I'm not leaving you; I'll be right back."

It wasn't exactly relief that washed through me, but something eased inside me. He was Holloway Holmes; he always kept his word. I couldn't bring myself to say anything, but I nodded, and Holmes must have recognized the movement. His hand loosened around my ankle, and for a moment he waited. When I didn't scream or jerk my foot off the plate, I guess he was satisfied because he sprang up from the floor. He was nothing more than a dark outline as he crossed the room. At the far wall, he hesitated. Then the lights came on.

When he turned back, the iron control in his face couldn't mask a hint of something.

"Oh my God," I whispered. "You thought the light switch was booby-trapped too?"

He took a beat too long to answer. "It was a possibility."

"H!"

"I needed light, and the flashlight in my gear bag wouldn't be enough. The odds of a second trap were low."

I closed my eyes and swallowed and tried not to scream.

His chukkas whispered on the carpet as he came toward me. He knelt, and metal clicked. His gear bag thudded onto the floor.

"Please tell me you know what you're doing," I said.

"Of course."

"Thank God."

Another of those hesitating silences came. "Although I'm not familiar with this exact model."

I squeezed my eyes shut tighter.

There were more sounds: tools clanking in his bag, more of those metallic clicks, and then a soft snick. Holmes probably tried to suppress it, but a relieved breath escaped him.

"It's all right now, Jack." He chafed my calf. "You can step off the plate."

I cracked one eye and squinted down at him.

For some reason, that made him smile, and he nodded.

The whole thing had taken less than ten minutes. It had probably taken less than five. But it felt like five minutes of grabbing a live wire, and now my muscles were locked tight. When I finally worked up the courage to move, it was more like a shuffling limp.

Nothing exploded.

Holmes rose, saying, "We'll have to be careful—"

I got him in a hug and squeezed until he grunted.

"Holy shit," I whispered.

"Jack."

"Holy fucking shit."

"My ribs, Jack."

"You are fucking amazing, do you realize that? Fucking incredible. You are the most—most fire human ever to exist, and I want to have your babies."

He was starting to wriggle, trying to get out of the hug, but a wave of emotion—relief mixed with so many other, stronger things that I didn't have names for—crashed over me, and I pulled him tighter. After a moment, some of the wire and steel in his body relaxed, and one arm looped around my waist. He tried to stroke my back with his other hand, but he was still holding a tool, which slowed him down a bit.

My voice was wet when I finally managed to say, "Are those side cutters in your hand, or are you just happy to see me?"

When he pushed me away, I grunted.

He squatted to pack up his tools, keeping his face turned away, but I didn't miss the red circles in his cheeks or where my tears still glistened on his skin.

"So, uh, for starters," I said, "I'm sorry I almost got us killed."

"I told you to wait," Holmes said. "I didn't tell you that there was an anti-personnel mine waiting beneath the window."

"Right, but somehow you avoided it."

He shrugged. "Habit."

"And second, I was not joking about having your babies. You are seriously the most awesomest human on earth."

"It was a simple trigger mechanism," he said, and he shouldered the gear bag as he stood. His eyes skated to me and then down to the mine: an ugly steel square secured to the floor. "Anyone with the right knowledge could have done it."

"Uh huh. No comment about the babies?"

"You know I don't like that kind of joke."

"Again, not a joke. And no comment about the phrase 'most awesomest'?"

He thought about that, head canted, and finally said, "No."

I couldn't help it; I smiled. A shaky, washed-out, broken-kneed smile. But a real one.

"If you have no objections, I'll go first?"

"No objections, Mr. Holmes."

He watched me again for a moment, like he thought there might have been a joke he missed. Then he started for the door.

After inspecting it, Holmes let us out of the booby-trapped bedroom and into a space that must have been labeled on the floor plan as a family room: a big, high-ceilinged basement room that would have been perfect for a TV and some comfy couches and a pool table. Instead, it had been repurposed as storage space. Steel shelves stood in rows, loaded with cans of Spam and Hormel chili and Vienna sausages and every kind of Campbell's soup you can imagine. Other shelves held paper towels, bottles of Clorox, toilet paper, stacked green-and-white bars of Fels-Naptha. And other shelves held jugs of water, first aid supplies, unopened packages of batteries.

But the biggest area had been given over to guns and ammunition. Their smell hung in the air: steel and solvent and lubricant. Shotguns. Rifles. Handguns. And boxes and boxes of cartridges. One shelf held what were unmistakably claymores, and I thought of the anti-personnel mine I'd stepped on in the empty bedroom.

Holmes and I moved along each row of shelves, and Holmes's face was impossible to read. When we'd finished, he motioned for me to stay, and he went to check the remaining doors. Two opened onto similarly empty bedrooms—I could see that much from where I stood—and a third connected with a bathroom. The fourth led into a utility room that was also crammed with prepper storage.

When Holmes came back, he said, "He's trapped all the egress windows."

"Jesus."

Holmes nodded and led me upstairs.

The browns and tans and desert color palette of the basement continued on the main floor. We emerged into a kitchen with manufactured-stone countertops and stainless-steel appliances. I checked the fridge, where our would-be assassin-slash-prepper had stocked protein shakes and cooked chicken breasts. The freezer was empty except for more chicken breasts. A few scratched nonstick pans were soaking in the sink, and the air smelled like processed meat—Slim Jims, I decided. I felt absurdly validated when I spotted the wrappers in the trash.

The open floor plan stretched into a living room, with a fireplace and a sofa and two armchairs in gray upholstery and simple lines. Someone had positioned an office chair with the other furniture as extra seating. The blinds were down in all the windows, which we'd noticed from the outside. The photos on the wall showed the same large family in different locations.

"Him," I said.

He was one of those white guys with a pink undertone to their skin that no amount of tanning would ever cover up. It was hard to tell in a photo, but I guessed he was close to my and Holmes's height, maybe a little taller, but carrying a lot more mass. His brown hair was buzzed, and he was clean shaven. Nicely and unmistakably tradmasc, but also unmistakably single, in contrast to the paired-up adults. How about that?

Holmes considered the photo and said, "Because he's single?"

"Well, yeah. You can tell a single guy lives here."

"Explain."

"Uh…I mean, the fridge, the furniture, that shit-show in the basement. The windows. Zero decoration. Take your pick. And none of these photos shows a nuclear family; he's got pictures, sure, because otherwise people would wonder, but nothing that shows him with a family of his own."

Holmes seemed to tally all this, and he nodded.

I reached for my phone to take a picture, and then I remembered that I'd thrown it in the back of this guy's truck. "Garage?"

Holmes took the lead again. The garage looked as new as everything else in the house—no oil stains on the concrete slab, tools neatly hung on pegboards. The first spot was empty, and the second held the black truck, and the third-car was currently being occupied by a boat. I climbed into the bed of the truck, fished out my phone, winced at the scratches it had accumulated during the ride, and got down again.

"He has plates now," Holmes said.

I unlocked my phone to take a picture, and then I saw the missed calls from Ariana, the missed texts, the string of messages asking me when I was coming, if I was coming, what happened. More missed calls from Dad, too, but those were less life-fucking.

"Shit," I said under my breath.

"What's wrong?"

Shaking my head, I tapped out a reply to my rightly furious and probably soon-to-be-ex girlfriend: *Sorry, phone died. I totally lost track of time. Can we chill tomorrow?*

The message hung there on the screen. No reply.

After a moment, I closed the messaging app and snapped pictures of the license plates that had been conveniently missing when this guy had tried to kill us.

"Jack?"

"I don't want to talk about it."

The wind off the lake whistled at the garage door.

When Holmes spoke again, his voice was neutral. "The cab is locked. Would you like me to open it?"

"Let's finish looking through the house."

He turned and headed inside without waiting for me.

It was like running a race in slow motion. I caught up to Holmes in the living room, but as soon as I stopped moving, he power-walked his white ass away from me. When I reached the office, where the desk was littered with papers and an old computer made a buzzing noise, he took off again. The hall bathroom. The master bedroom.

I finally cornered him in the master bath, mostly because there were no other doors except the one I was blocking with my body.

Holmes's face was cool indifference. "Where would you like to search?"

"I didn't mean it to sound like that."

"We don't know how much time we have; we should split up."

"I forgot I told Ariana I'd do something with her, and she's pissed at me, and I'm pissed at me, and I didn't mean to take it out on you."

He was still for a moment. For the first time, I noticed the freshly crusted blood on his lip, and I realized he'd been biting it at some point between now and when we'd gotten to the house. Maybe when he'd been disarming a landmine, my brain suggested. Maybe he's freaked out and exhausted and suffering from a serious adrenaline burn too, only you couldn't be bothered to pay attention to stuff like that; you just assumed he'd be fine.

"H, are you ok?"

"Of course."

"No, I mean—"

"You forgot your plans with her yesterday as well."

"Yeah," I said slowly, trying to parse the voltage of his words. "That's one reason I'm pissed at myself."

"You need to correct that. That's not the behavior of a good boyfriend."

I ran a hand through my hair; through the window, even with the blinds down, I could see amber lights dotting the lake.

"You need to show her that you are willing to dedicate your time and attention to her if you want this relationship to be successful."

My vision crossed and doubled. Little amber lights strung like distant beads, and all that dark in between them.

"Yeah," I finally said. Then I looked at him. "H, are you ok?"

The corner of his mouth trembled. "I should have anticipated, located, and disabled his countermeasures. I took an unacceptable risk, entering the way I did, and I put your life in danger. I miscalculated the nature and extent of the risk in this operation, as well as miscalculating the nature and ability of our opponent." He bit his lip, raising fresh blood, but the next words tumbled out of him anyway. "And—and I need my medicine, but I don't think you'll let me."

I nodded slowly. My medicine, I thought. That's one term for it. But all I said was, "How much do you want to take?"

"I typically need sixty milligrams."

I waited.

H cut his eyes away. "In high-pressure situations, I may require more."

I wanted to close my eyes. I wanted to say no. But saying no didn't fix anything; Walker as an institution, with its student body, was proof of that. "Why don't you take two of the thirties, then?"

His gaze came back, roving my face, searching for something. Then he nodded. He produced the bottle like a magic trick, and he held up two of the pills like they were proof of something before dry-swallowing them.

"No more until we talk about it," I said.

He was silent for five seconds. Then ten. And then he said, "Yes."

"I'll search here," I said. "Why don't you take the office?"

He nodded and strode toward me, but when I didn't move out of the doorway, he slowed.

"I don't expect you to analyze and compute and perfectly assess everything, H. Nobody should expect that of you; it's not fair, for starters. You kept me safe, and that's what you promised you'd do. You should be proud of that."

"I expect it of myself," he said quietly. "I must do better."

When I opened my mouth, he gave a terse shake of his head. I slid aside, and a moment later, he was gone.

My search of the bathroom yielded nothing of interest: hair product, deodorant, toothpaste, a toothbrush that seriously needed to be replaced — and that was coming from me. The bedroom didn't offer much more: your basic straight guy clothes, mostly jeans and t-shirts and hoodies, with gym clothes mixed in, and a pair of khakis and a white button-up for church. On the wall, Jesus was walking on water, and I wondered what that did to boners, and then I wondered if maybe that was the whole point.

Things got more interesting when I found the box under the bed. It was hard plastic, and it was locked. When I carried it into Holmes, who was scanning through the papers in the office, he gave it a derisive look and opened it—no joke—with a paperclip.

Inside, there were a lot—and I mean a lot—of butt plugs.

And again, that's coming from me.

"Uh," I said.

"We suspected his proclivities," Holmes said as he turned back to the paperwork.

"We did? I mean, I guess I thought—well, I guess I figured he had some sort of connection to the blackmail. But I thought it was more like, hired gun determined to stop us, not, um, white boy who's super into butt stuff."

Holmes did that amused little breath through his nose again.

"He's got a shit-load—um, pun, maybe?—of poppers, a fleshlight, condoms. Ugh!"

Holmes glanced over. "A men's fitness magazine?"

"A Mormon inspirational men's fitness magazine," I said, grimacing as I held it up by the front cover. "And the pages are stuck together."

"Oh." Which was Holmes speak for *holy fuck.*

"I know we're not supposed to kink shame, but who is this weirdo?"

"I'm not sure it's a kink." Holmes gestured to the pile of paperwork. "His name is Kazen Bates, he's twenty-eight years old, he is employed by his family's construction business and makes a great deal more money than he would being employed by anyone else, which explains the home, the emergency supplies, and in particular, his ability to afford firearms and ammunition."

"And he's Mormon."

"Of a particularly virulent breed." Holmes picked up a pamphlet—a stack of them had been pushed to the back of the desk, and it looked like more were waiting to be folded. The front said *Brethren in Support of the Daughter of Zion*, and then, below, something that looked scriptural: *Shake thyself from the dust; arise, and sit down, O Jerusalem: loose thyself from the bands of thy neck, O captive daughter of Zion.*

"Is that from the Book of Mormon?" I asked.

"Interestingly," Holmes said, "it's from both the Hebrew Bible and the Book of Mormon—that is, if you accept the standard Mormon account."

"Uh huh." I took the pamphlet and opened it and scanned the inside.

It had the usual Mormon talking points: sex before marriage was a sin, homosexuality was a sin, blowjobs were a sin, pornography was a sin. How that applied to inspirational men's fitness magazines, I wasn't sure. There were hints of some lovely vestigial racism—a few choice quotes from Mormon leaders about staying with your own kind, that sort of thing. And, of course, what I'd come to expect, after growing up in the Salt Lake Valley, as the Mormon-men-over-fifty all-consuming preoccupation with Communism, which, outside of *Call of Duty*, didn't seem like much of a threat anymore.

Most of the pamphlet, though, was given over to a screed about homosexuality. The evils of homosexuality. The victims of homosexuality—apparently, the young boys seduced into the lifestyle by older "groomers." It included a few grainy photos of pre-teens who, I guess, were in the process of being lured away by the evils of butt stuff. And it ended with a call to action: *Join us to help our brothers and sisters loose the bands of their necks, that the daughter of Zion may rise!*

When I looked up, Holmes was displaying his phone. "They've got a webpage, a Twitter account, pages on several crowdfunding websites, that kind of thing, and the nickname for members and supporters is the Danites. They describe themselves as a tactical support organization, but reading between the lines of their propaganda, it sounds like they're more paramilitary—the suggestion, of course, is that they conduct raids on LGBTQ centers and shelters, which is why they need money for all those guns. It's difficult to tell from a quick search how much money they currently have—"

"It wouldn't be difficult for me."

Holmes leveled a look at me. "—but the crowdfunding pages show millions of dollars raised."

"You're kidding me." But as soon as I said it, I knew he wasn't. The year I'd gone to high school in Salt Lake, when the Mormon kids got pulled for an hour every day to go to their seminary class and learn how to be better Mormons, I'd picked up some of the basic ideas. And for Mormons, sex was at the top—of pretty much everything, actually. It was the best, purest thing. It was the scariest, most dangerous thing. You shouldn't think about it. It was ok to think about it, but only once you were married. You should never, never, never jack off (oops). And there was scarier stuff too, like it was better to die than be raped. I wondered how that fit into rescuing people from "groomers." Maybe they mercifully shot them in the head.

"So, we've got an ultra-repressed and closeted homo gunning for us while his public persona is, what? Save the whales, only for straight people?"

"Children are groomed by predators, Jack."

"Ok, yeah, I'm not trying to make light of that. But these guys getting together in Utah Valley so they can share a communal wet dream about their guns and killing fags, that's not exactly addressing the problem."

"How would they share a communal wet dream?"

"My point is, what's the connection to Aston?"

"We haven't found one."

"There's a connection," I said. "Trust me. They've been porking, and he decided to make sure Aston kept his secret by blackmailing him. Now he knows we're on to him, and he's trying to stop us."

"That doesn't make any sense. If they'd—"

"Say porking. Please. For my sake."

"—been sexually involved—"

"H!"

"—and his primary goal was to ensure his secret, there wouldn't be any need to involve Dawson or demand money from Aston or hide his identity."

"Maybe his plan is complicated. Maybe his plan has layers."

Holmes's brow wrinkled slightly. "And how would he know we were on to him? We haven't made much progress in this investigation, Jack. We certainly had no idea that someone named Kazen Bates was a person of interest."

"I don't know. But I'm telling you, that's what's going on."

"It is a mistake to theorize—"

"Oh my God, I know, I know, I know." But then I gave him a crooked grin. "If I'm right, though, you have to buy me popcorn at the movies for a year."

"And if I'm right?"

"Who cares? You're always right."

"That hardly seems fair."

"Are we done in here?"

"I haven't examined his laptop."

I moved over to the desk and wiggled the wireless mouse. The laptop woke and displayed a lock screen demanding a PIN.

"Any ideas?"

"Of course," Holmes said. "Move out of my way and keep watch."

So, I got the super important job of standing at the window, parting the blinds with one finger and watching a dark street, while Holmes click-clacked like a maniac on the keyboard.

After three or four minutes, I said, "Is this realistic? Don't those algorithms tell you it can take billions of years even with a four-digit passcode—"

Holmes made a satisfied noise, and when I looked over, the lock screen had changed to the virtual desktop.

"Is it on purpose? Do you wait? Like, you know I'm going to say something dumb, so you're ready, and you wait, and then it looks like cosmic timing or something like that?"

Holmes cocked his head. His pupils had contracted under the Adderall, and the effect made his irises lighten until the gray looked paper thin. "One might say something about the law of averages."

I laughed in spite of myself as I joined him at the laptop. "Ok, that wasn't bad. Your trash talk has gotten way better."

"I read several articles."

"Stop. You ruined it. You're ruining everything."

Another of those little furrows came back as he scowled at me.

For a few minutes, I watched and offered helpful advice while Holmes dug into Kazen Bates's laptop.

At least, I thought it was helpful.

"Jack, please do not tell me 'now open the next one.' I know to open the next one."

"But sometimes you take too long."

He drew a deep breath.

"I won't say anything," I said.

He let out his breath slowly.

"Except, did you try the C drive?"

"It's all on the C drive!"

I pulled my collar up and chewed on it so he wouldn't see my grin. After he'd had a minute to cool down, I said, "Let's see what kind of porn he watches."

A hint of color rose in Holmes's face, and he moved the mouse toward the red X that would close the browser.

"I'm serious," I said. "You can tell a lot about a guy from his porn. Uh, not that I'm suggesting you put that into general practice."

Holmes stared at me.

"I would tell you," I said, "but there's so much spanking it might give you ideas."

His jaw dropped. Literally. Which was kind of amazing.

"Here, click History—" I laid my hand over his to guide the mouse where I wanted it, and I ignored how Holmes tried to slide his hand out from under mine. "—and now we look for—"

Holmes yanked the mouse away and clicked on the most recent item in the list: Gmail.

Kazen was still logged into his account, which made our lives easier, and Holmes spent a while scanning his emails from the last year. He checked the trash and the spam as well, but finally, we had to give up. He had a few emails from his grandmother, correspondence from church, and a lot of stuff from the Danites. The rest was the usual assortment of junk— sales announcements, new product releases, that kind of thing.

Holmes went back to searching the hard drive, and eventually, we found the videos in, well, a folder called Videos. They appeared to be synced to Kazen's phone, and it looked like they downloaded to the laptop automatically. The most recent one had been taken at night—according to the timestamp, a week ago, on the previous Friday. The video had been shot on a phone, I guessed, and from a distance. I'd spent enough time at the Walker School to recognize the back of Baker House. From the way the phone was trained on one of the windows on the third floor, I guessed we were looking at Aston's bedroom. The blinds were down, but you could see a shape moving behind them. Then the light went off in the bedroom.

A man's rapid breathing accompanied the video as he—presumably Kazen—carried the phone, still recording, around to the front of Baker House. Leaves rustled as he crouched behind a boxwood and continued recording the front door. For a moment, nothing happened. And then a figure emerged. He—or she, or they—was dressed in bulky black clothes. My gut said it was a guy, but he had his hood up, and he walked quickly into a thicker patch of shadow. I thought for a moment that the camera lost him, but then he moved again—nothing more than an outline. Then another figure appeared, moving briskly up the walk, carrying a bag that bounced against their leg. In the video, Kazen's heavy breathing accented the slap of footsteps.

The second figure joined the first. And then one of them spoke—the first one, I thought. The one who had come out of Aston's room. I recognized Paxton's voice—albeit with an unfamiliar edge.

"Is that for me, luv? You didn't need to come. Or were you afraid you'd miss the show?"

The second figure passed over the bag and said something the camera didn't pick up.

In that same, hard voice Paxton answered, "Spoze I am. Spoze I've got a right to be angry. You didn't tell me everything."

The other figure said something else.

"I'll do what you wanted," Paxton said, turning. "And it'll work. But you didn't say—"

The shadowed figure muttered something too quiet to hear, and Paxton's head snapped toward Kazen. It was disorienting; for a moment, with Paxton staring into the camera, it felt like he was looking at me. Then Paxton sprinted toward Kazen's hiding spot—no shouts, no alarm, just focused, furious intent. The camera jostled as Kazen startled. He turned, branches rustling and snapping, and ran. The camera dropped to his side, and then there was only darkness, the sound of heavy breathing, racing steps. A moment later, the video cut off.

"Well," I said, fighting the dryness in my throat. "Shit."

Chapter 11

Hamburger Helper Helper

I tried to talk about what we'd seen in the video—about what it meant to see Paxton coming out of Aston's residence, about watching him get paid off (at least, I assumed that's what was happening). It seemed pretty cut and dried to me: Paxton was behind the blackmail. We didn't know who else was involved, who had paid him, but at least we had something.

No matter what I tried, though, Holmes refused to engage with me. He needed to think, he said. Which was code, I thought, for moping about Paxton. So, I let him think. I let him think for the whole fucking drive home.

When we got back to the cottage, I was already turning into the carport when I saw a familiar silver Impala parked down the road.

"Shit," I said and shifted into reverse.

But it was too late. The cottage's side door opened, and Dad stepped out, backlit by the warm yellow glow. His shoulders were locked, his hands on his hips, and he had a way of holding his head that I'd seen on myself a time or two.

"Your father looks angry," Holmes said.

"Huh," I said. "What makes you say that?"

"His posture, primarily, although—"

"H."

He was silent for a moment. "Oh."

I shifted into drive, eased the truck under the carport, and killed the engine.

"Do you think you could kill me painlessly?" I asked. "Like, snap my neck, and I'd be dead before I know it?"

"Jack."

"Is that kind of thing even possible?"

Holmes canted his head and watched me.

"Asking for a friend," I told him.

"Your father is waiting."

"Yeah," I said as I kneed the door open. "I didn't think so."

As I made my way to the door, I forced myself to meet my dad's eyes. "Hey."

He held out his hand.

I sighed and gave him the truck keys. When I tried to slip past, he shifted his weight to block me.

When we worked outside all day, especially cold days, like clearing snow or digging up a busted pipe that had to be fixed right then, that kind of thing, and the wind came down the canyon nonstop, it could burn the skin on your face—leave it hot and glowing, the way a sunburn did.

"I am not going to do this again," Dad said in a low voice. "I am not going to have the police showing up at my house, scaring me to death because I don't know where my son is and he won't answer his phone."

"My battery died."

He nodded. "So, you're going to lie to me."

"The battery—" I stopped. I remembered the fucking parental app he'd installed.

"Go inside." Something hardened in his voice, and I couldn't read what I saw on his face. "Your friend, too. And what happened to your clothes?"

Instead of answering, I glanced over my shoulder and beckoned to Holmes, who was lingering at the end of the carport. We trooped inside.

At night, with the blinds closed and the lights on, usually the cottage was cozy. Sure, the furniture was totally mismatched, but we'd held on to some good pieces from Salt Lake, and the secondhand stuff was comfortable. It was warm—although, since my entire face felt like a dumpster fire, that wasn't as much of a comfort as it usually was. But most of all, it was safe. This was our place, mine and Dad's.

It wasn't cozy tonight.

Detective Rivera, one of the Utah County Sheriff's Department's finest and my personal law-enforcement nemesis (if he could still be a nemesis after he bought me McDonald's), was sitting on the sofa, sending a message on his phone. He was short but muscular, and you could tell he'd been a wrestler in high school, maybe college too, because he had one cauliflower ear. He was still paying too much for the skin fade he wore spiked up in front; he would have been better off buying a new suit to replace the gray one he was wearing. When he looked up, I forgot about the suit. I kind of forgot how to breathe.

"Jack," he said. "Long time no see."

A few months before, Rivera had done his damnedest to prove first that I'd killed Sarah Watson, and then that Dad had. He'd arrested Dad, and he'd made my life hell—including siccing DCFS on me. After we'd caught the killer, though, he'd turned out to be a semi-decent human being. Mostly.

"Where's Yazzie?" I asked.

"Detective Yazzie," Dad said from where he stood blocking the door, arms across his chest, channeling his inner prison guard. "She didn't want to wait for you two stooges."

"You guys sit down," Rivera said. "We need to talk."

So, Holmes and I sat—Holmes on the sofa, me on the coffee table. I guess I could have taken Dad's recliner since he was too busy sending me nonverbal messages like *Your life is over*, but that felt like throwing jet fuel on an already seriously fucked fire.

"Want to tell me what's going on?" Rivera asked.

Holmes didn't look at me. He didn't squirm on the sofa. He didn't move at all except to breathe, his hands on his knees, his back straight. But I knew, in that moment, what was going to happen as clearly as if he'd held a cue card for me. He was going to handle it, and I was supposed to let him.

In that coldly controlled voice, he said, "You're referring to the gunman who fired on our group of friends?"

"That's one of the things I'm interested in."

"I assume you already took statements from Emma, Rowe, and Glo, but Jack and I will be happy to—"

Rivera shook his head, and Holmes stopped. Outside, branches creaked as the wind picked up again, and pinecones hailed onto the carport's aluminum awning.

"Holloway," Rivera said. "Jack. I think you're both smart, and you're both competent, and you both have a God-given talent for getting yourself neck-deep in trouble without even turning around. I also think I've earned a little trust from you." He looked at me, and I thought of the night he'd spent at the hospital, the day he'd spent shuttling me around, making sure I had food and a place to sleep while we waited for Dad to be released—all so that I wouldn't have to get put into the DCFS system. I couldn't meet his eyes. He continued, "A gunman doesn't drive onto campus, especially not the Walker School, and randomly fire on a group of students. Especially when that group happens to include the two of you. Don't give me a line about school shooters. Don't give me a line at all, if you can help it. I want to know what's going on, and why the kids at this school aren't safe, and what we can do about it."

"And if you don't tell him," Dad said, "your ass is grass."

"We don't know," Holmes said.

Dad made a disgusted noise. "Jack."

I couldn't help it; I looked at Holmes, who was still watching Rivera. His profile was glacial and unreadable. Finally, I said, "We don't know."

"What kind of game do you think you're playing?" Dad asked. "This is serious; you could have been killed."

"I know it's serious!" I couldn't help it—my voice rose into a shout. "I'm the one who got shot at, remember?"

"Don't raise your voice."

"You left the scene of a crime."

"We freaked out, ok? Is that what you want to hear?"

"Someone was shooting at you!"

The juxtaposition of what I'd been through that day—with Aston, with Dawson, with Paxton, with Kazen; hell, for that matter, with a fucking landmine—and the questioning, the badgering, the condescending reminders, like I was a child, it threatened to overwhelm me. And then it was like something snapped, and I heard myself like it was somebody else talking.

"I don't know. I can't figure it out." I surged up from the coffee table. Rivera was looking at me. Dad was looking at me. Holmes was looking at me. Tears surged up, and it was mostly luck that I was able to talk through them. "What do you think? Is there anything in the last couple of years that could explain why I ran the fuck away after almost getting killed?"

"Jack, hold on," Dad said.

But I plunged down the hallway and into my bedroom. I slammed the door behind me, stumbled through the mess of clothes on the floor, and collapsed on the bed. I'd forgotten the lights, but that didn't matter—the room was tiny, and aside from the desk and my bed, there wasn't much in the way of furniture.

Ok, I thought. The thing with the door wasn't cool.

And then I started crying—huge, ragged sobs as my body curled around my pillow. Whatever was moving through me, it was so vast that it felt tidal: a crushing weight that poured out of me, mostly in the form of tears and snot, and then, when it pulled back, nothing.

When I'd calmed down enough that I could hear something besides myself, the house was silent. I mopped my face with the pillow. I squinted burning eyes up at the darkness. It had all come at once: the aftermath of being shot at, of stepping on a landmine, of thinking twice in one day that I was going to die and there was nothing I could do about it. Maybe it had all hit me harder than I'd realized. Maybe, I thought with a smile up at the ceiling. I'd stuffed it all in the same box where I kept the rest of my shit, in that place where I still dreamed about the car accident, about running and leaving my parents to die because I was sure a man with a gun was coming for me. It was something Dad and I didn't talk about—probably because in all those good parenting books, they recommend not reminding your son that his total failure as a human being led directly to his mother's death. And as it turned out, that box of shit was getting pretty full without any help from Dad. Even opening it for a peek could apparently send me into a complete meltdown.

A few months before, with Holmes, I thought I'd made some progress—in the Jack-Moreno-is-a-chickenshit area, anyway. When it had come down to it, I'd stayed. For Holmes, I'd stood my ground. And yes, the rational part of my brain knew that today, Holmes and I hadn't really run away, although the fear had been real. Apparently the human brain has a remarkable capacity for making you feel guilty and shitty and generally worthless all because of one mistake, for years and years. Mine did, anyway.

Why hadn't we told Rivera the truth? Well, I knew why I hadn't; with Holmes, the reasons weren't as clear, although I imagine he'd run through the same logic chain as I had. If we told Rivera we had followed the shooter, entered his home, and identified him as Kazen Bates, closeted psychopath who owned at least one tentacle dildo, well, that would raise some questions. And while Rivera would probably like some help tagging Kazen, there were at least two problems with that. One, we'd broken the law getting into Kazen's house and going through his stuff, and while Rivera apparently no longer thought I was a murderer, I was pretty sure he still had the occasional wet dream about throwing me in jail. Just for a year or two, to help me shape up.

The other problem was bigger. If we told Rivera about Kazen, Rivera would ask more questions. And those questions would lead to Aston being blackmailed. And then Rivera would want to know why I was helping Aston after, oh, a little thing like Aston trying to beat Holmes's brains in with a lacrosse stick in September. And then it would all come out: the favors I did, the deals, what I bought and sold. Yes, they'd found some zannies in the house when they'd searched it in September. Yes, there had been some talk about me dealing. But you'd be amazed what people are willing to overlook when you help solve several murders, and anyway, my concern here wasn't Rivera.

No, my concern was that the new headmaster, Dr. Cluff, would find out. She was a no-nonsense kind of lady. She was coming in on the heels of a major scandal, to put it mildly, and her whole job was to clean up Walker and make it look like a nice, safe, attractive prison-house for rich kids who were inconveniencing their families. If she found out I was dealing, I'd be expelled. And, worse, Dad would be fired. No more cottage. No more health insurance. No more job security because we'd twisted the collective arm of the Board of Trustees.

For the first time, I realized how stupid I'd been over the last couple of months, risking everything we'd managed to cobble together in the aftermath of the accident for—what? A few hundred dollars every month in the jelly jar? A new phone because I had to have the one with two cameras? Clothes that I was sure would finally make me fit in, only they never made any difference? Jesus Christ. I wiped my eyes, still staring up at the ceiling. How dumb are you?

I had a vague, half-formed resolution to stop all of it—to sell the little I had left in my stash, and then call it quits. I couldn't deny a pang; right now, the only reason anybody except Holmes talked to me was because they needed something, and I could get it for them. But risking this fragile stability wasn't worth it. I mean, hell, they needed me. I was basically still staff. It's not like they'd invited me to Wintersmash.

The knock at the door made me swipe at my face and clear my throat. "Come in."

Light from the hallway silhouetted Dad. "You ok, buddy?"

"Yeah."

He was silent for a moment. Then he stepped into the room, closed the door, and crossed to the bed. He stumbled a few times, nickel-and-dime swears escaping him as he tripped on clothes. Finally, though, he reached me, and he sat on the edge of the mattress.

"So, what?" I asked. "Is he arresting me for obstruction of justice?"

"Uh, no," Dad said, and his tone was strange—almost amused. "He asked if he could get you a sandwich."

"A sandwich?"

"I don't know."

"Why would he get me a sandwich?"

Dad laughed softly, and after a moment I laughed too.

The silence sharpened to a point. In an unbearably kind voice, Dad said, "Jack—"

"I'm fine. Honest. I don't need to talk to anyone. I don't—I don't need anything, I guess. I don't need a sandwich."

But this time, Dad didn't laugh.

"I just—it was a lot today."

"I'm sure it was."

The next moment, and the next, and the one after that—they took on a new edge. I rolled to face the wall.

"I won't force you to see someone," Dad finally said. "But I'm worried, Jack. What if next time, you run and you don't have a friend with you? What if you can't take care of yourself because you're upset, and it means you make a mistake?"

"I'll be fine."

"Not to mention you don't have a driver's license, which don't think I've forgotten. You're an amazing human being, and you're the best son anyone's ever had, and God knows you've been through more than what some people deal with in their whole lives. But nobody's made of steel."

I shrugged.

His tone became unreadable again. "I've been thinking about talking to someone."

I flopped onto my back again to look up at him.

"Now that we have insurance," he said.

He was nothing more than a shape in the darkness. I thought about the nights he stayed up watching TV. I thought about all those nights alone.

"Oh no," he said with that same soft laugh. "Wipe that look off your face, my son. I don't need you worrying about me; it's my job to worry about you. I'm telling you that because I hope it'll help you realize that there's nothing wrong with, I don't know, talking to someone. With needing a little help."

"I'm fine, Dad. I promise. It was—I mean, it's not like I get shot at every day, you know?"

He was silent so long that I thought it was coming again, another of those homing missiles of kindness and compassion, and this one would be too much and blow my self-control to hell. But all he said was, "Your friend is still here, if you want to see him."

"H?"

"Detective Rivera said he'd be happy to talk to you later. He left after finishing his conversation with your friend."

"But H is still here?"

"That boy—" Dad stopped. "It was like trying to get a very polite boulder to move. 'Yes, sir. No, sir. I'd prefer to wait for Jack, Mr. Moreno.'"

I groaned. "He's such a nerd."

"You're still in trouble for taking the truck without asking, and for driving with only your permit, and more importantly, for lying. We have each other, Jack. That's all, in the whole world. We have to be able to trust each other."

I blinked through the sting in my eyes and nodded.

"But your friend can stay for a little while," Dad said.

My throat was tight. "Thanks."

I thought he smiled in the dark. "I'd have to get a backhoe otherwise."

"Thanks, Dad. Thank you."

"Until eight."

I half sat up. "Eight?"

"Eight," he said firmly. "Give me a hug."

So, I sat up the rest of the way and gave him a hug, and if he noticed I was still crying a little, he didn't say anything. He hugged me until I let go, and then he ruffled my hair and eased himself up from the bed. A couple of sweaters and loose sneakers tried to take him down on his way out, and when he got to the door, he opened it and said, "And pick up your room, please. This is turning into a biohazard." Down the hall, he said, "Go on in."

Holmes said, "Thank you, Mr. Moreno," and his steps came toward my room.

I scooted to the edge of the mattress and sat there, pulling off Holmes's borrowed chukkas. A moment, later, Holmes appeared in the doorway. He studied me from the doorway.

"See?" I said. "I'm totally fine. No schizo break. No psychotic episodes. Only a hysterical meltdown."

"A psychotic episode does not entail—" He stopped and bit the corner of his mouth; his lip was raw from him worrying it.

"I'm fine. I didn't expect—I don't know, it just hit me."

Holmes nodded.

"Thanks for, you know, waiting."

"You're my friend."

I cocked him a smile and rolled my eyes.

After a quick glance out into the hall, Holmes eased the door shut— quietly, so that my dad wouldn't hear the latch catching. "Jack, Emma didn't tell Rivera why we approached her. She said we had joined them for their self-defense practice."

"Huh." I started to unbutton the oxford. "Why?"

Holmes was trying not to look at me, but his eyes kept sliding back. "That's an excellent question."

After shucking the oxford, I undid the waistband of the chinos. "She didn't want Rivera to know about the blackmail."

"Jack, you have to wait—"

"You already saw me in my boxers once today." I kicked free of the chinos and padded around the room, trying to find something to wear. "And you've seen me buckass before."

Cheeks red, Holmes faced the door. Then he folded his arms. Then he curved his shoulders.

"Maybe she doesn't want Rivera to know about it because she's involved." I snagged a pair of cutoff sweats and hiked them up. "I mean, she was believable when she told me she wanted to be left alone, but maybe she's a really good liar." I found a Stream Queens tee and a hoodie, wriggled into them, and said, "Ok, I'm decent."

Holmes cast a single, burning look over his shoulder. "Socks."

"Seriously?"

"Socks, Jack."

I found a pair of socks and pulled them on. "What do you think?"

"I think that it's unusual for someone to lie to the police unless they have something to hide. And I think it's even more unusual if they've been the target of attempted murder."

"Ok. So, she goes back on the list of suspects."

"You should wear pants in the winter."

"I almost got blown up today. And shot. That means I can wear shorts."

"What logic—"

"Do you want to wear shorts? You can borrow a pair."

His face caught fire again. "No."

"All right then; we're both happy."

Holmes looked distinctly unhappy about my choice of—bottom? That sounded weirdly sexual. My choice of shorts, I guess. But he didn't press the issue, and when Dad called, "Sous chef, you're up," we trudged out to the kitchen.

"Since I got shot at today—" I tried.

"No," Dad said and slid an onion, knife, and cutting board toward me.

I sighed. "It was worth a try."

"I'd be happy to help, Mr. Moreno," Holmes said.

"Thank you, but it's Jack's responsibility—"

"Dad, H wants to help. He'd feel more comfortable helping. Right, H? And, I mean, he's a guest, and I've had such a hard day."

"No—" Dad tried again.

But Holmes had already taken the knife and was trimming the onion. His movements were as precise and controlled as anything else he did.

Dad gave me a look. And then, in case I'd missed the nonverbal *your ass is toast*, he looked at Holmes and then back at me.

"Great," I said. "I'll let you guys get to work. Anybody want a beer?"

"Funny," Dad said and elbowed me away from the fridge.

I dropped onto the couch and took out my phone. Dad had a basketball game on—BYU at San Diego State—and combined with the chopping and sizzling and occasional quietly exchanged word, it made for pleasant background noise. I messaged Ariana a couple of times, but she didn't reply, so I gave up and started down the various internet rabbit holes that were always waiting for me.

In the time that I'd been out of school, I'd tried—with more or less effort, at various points—to make sure I was still learning. Not falling too far behind kids my age. Not getting stupid. And two big parts of that had been YouTube, which had videos on everything, and Wikipedia, which had articles on everything.

I liked reading the article of the day on Wikipedia, even though sometimes they were stubs and sometimes they were way too long and a lot of the time, they were super boring. But they made me think about things I'd never thought about before, and I figured that had to be good for something. Today's was about Mount Takahe, which was—I learned—a shield volcano in Antarctica. It had parasitic vents (ok, I admit, I had to click that one because the name was too good), and the volcano's name referred to a flightless bird (a takahe, which apparently lives in New Zealand).

Oh, parasitic vents? Not as cool as they sounded.

I'd followed the link to the takahe, which was wild—Europeans thought it was extinct because they could only find fossils of it, but then they found a few birds, and then the birds died and they thought it was really extinct, and then, a lot later, they found them again. Oh, and then one of the two subspecies did go extinct. So, you know.

When the conversation began in the kitchen, I pricked up my ears. I couldn't help it.

"How are your classes going?" my dad asked over the sizzle of ground beef in the frying pan.

"Very well, thank you," Holmes said.

"And how's your family?"

"Very well, thank you."

"And how are you adjusting to Walker?"

"Very well, thank you."

"He gets stuck in a loop sometimes," I called without looking up from my phone. "Ask him why In-N-Out is better than Burgers Supreme."

Over the top of my phone, I didn't miss my dad and Holmes giving me identically scary glares.

A lull opened, and the sounds of the basketball game filtered in. Then Holmes said, "I'm very grateful I met Jack, Mr. Moreno. He is a good friend."

"I'm glad to hear that," my dad said.

"If I'm not mistaken, you may have some reservations about our friendship because of the events that transpired today and, of course, in light of everything that happened in September."

"Well," Dad began.

"I'd like to offer you my personal assurance that nothing will happen to Jack."

It was kind of nice seeing it happen to someone else, when they clearly had no idea how to respond to the stuff that came out of Holmes's mouth.

"While my own resources are limited," Holmes said into the void, "I promise you they are fully dedicated to keeping Jack safe."

"That's nice," Dad mumbled. In a louder voice, he said, "Jack, did you talk to Ariana?" At the same volume, he said to Holmes, "You've met Ariana, haven't you? She's a great girl. She's fantastic. Jack did good."

"I understand this conversation may be uncomfortable because the topic is sensitive," Holmes said, "but it's important to me that you know that I value Jack's safety as much as you do."

"Thank you," Dad said, and the cringe was so epic that I actually squirmed down into the sofa cushions, grinning and pulling up my phone to hide my face. "These days," Dad said in that same cringiest voice, "I'm more worried about Jack failing chemistry."

I was still jackassing around, laughing at the two of them, and so I realized what had happened too late.

"I'm excellent at chemistry," Holmes said.

"No," I said, trying to sit up and finding myself swamped in the cushions.

"Oh yeah?" Dad said, and for the first time in their history, he looked at Holmes with interest.

"No," I said. The cushions were still sucking me down. "He's terrible at chemistry. He doesn't even know an atom from a—a—a—from a quark."

Dad and Holmes gave me identical disparaging looks.

"How much do you charge?" Dad asked.

"Mr. Moreno, I've already been helping Jack with his homework. There's no need—"

"Nope, we can't afford you," I said. I finally managed to roll off the sofa. I landed on the floor, true, but a moment later I sprang to my feet. In the process, somehow, I had lost a sock. "You heard him, Dad, he's super expensive."

"In a minute, Jack," he said in the tone that meant he hadn't heard me. "I can pay you in Hamburger Helper, but you'd probably get better food at the dining hall."

"Yes, that's a great idea," I said. "H, you go get some grub at the dining hall, and—"

"I accept," Holmes said over me.

Dad gave the Hamburger Helper an overenthusiastic stir. "Great. Since my son isn't leaving the house again, possibly ever, you can start tonight."

"Excellent."

"I don't think you two have thought this through—" I tried to say while also looking for the sock. "H is so busy, and on top of that, um, what would people think?"

"Give it up, buddy," Dad said.

"It's under the pillow at the far end of the couch," Holmes said in what he clearly considered a helpful tone.

Since Holmes had betrayed me and my father had apparently been indoctrinated by a helicopter-parent cult while my back was turned, I freed my sock from where it was trapped at the end of the couch, yanked it on, and glared at both of them.

"You should have seen him when we made him try the violin," Dad said to Holmes, and for some reason, both of them started to laugh. Even Holmes. Who never laughs at any of my jokes.

"I'm going to my room," I announced. "I don't even want any Hamburger Helper."

"Set the table, please," my dad said.

"I'll help you," Holmes said. "And you've put your sock on backward."

"You can't put a sock on backward," I not-shouted at the back of his head, but I did turn it around so the stitching at the end was above my toes. "It only has one hole."

I don't know what my dad said, but it made both of them burst out laughing again.

"Traitors," I said.

"Why don't you call Ariana?" Dad asked. "See if she wants to come up for dinner."

"We'll be done with dinner by the time she gets here." I took the plates from Holmes and laid them out on the counter. We didn't have a dining table, so setting the table meant making sure there were enough clean plates and flatware and then laying them out on the counter. "And she wouldn't gang up on me like the two of you."

"I don't know about that," Dad said to Holmes. "One of the things I like about her is she doesn't let him get away with anything."

Holmes made a noise that could have meant anything as he laid out the forks.

"Anyway," I said — at a not-shout volume — "I thought I was grounded, so she can't come over."

"Did I say you were grounded?"

It seemed safer not to answer that question.

Dad divided the Hamburger Helper across the three plates — it was called crunchy taco, or something like that, if anything can be crunchy after it's been steaming and simmering on the stove for twenty minutes — and we ate in the living room area.

Holmes, as usual, picked at his food.

"Can I get you something else?" Dad asked.

I snorted. "We don't have anything else. He's fine."

"I really am fine, Mr. Moreno."

"He hasn't taken two bites," Dad said.

"It's because he's a pillhead." I saw the look on Dad's face and hurried to add, "That was a joke. He's on ADHD medicine, and it affects his appetite."

"Oh."

I portioned off some of what Dad had given Holmes, pointed to it so that Holmes couldn't pretend he hadn't seen it, and scraped the rest of his Hamburger Helper onto my plate.

Holmes opened his mouth.

"Yes, all of it," I said.

He shut his mouth and began eating what I'd left him.

I looked up in time to see something strange on Dad's face, but it was gone as soon as I noticed it, and then I wasn't sure — maybe I'd imagined it.

When we'd finished, Dad said, "Maybe Ariana can come over for dinner on Sunday."

Holmes slid to his feet and began collecting plates. "I'll wash up."

"Help your friend."

"You heard him," I said as I kicked my feet up onto Holmes's recently vacated spot. I took out my phone. "He wants to do it. He loves things that are clean." Which wasn't the exact same thing as loving the cleaning process itself, but I didn't want to get into that.

"Jack."

"I'll do them tomorrow. H, don't do those."

"Jack Sixsmith Moreno."

I swore under my breath as I swung my feet down again.

"What was that?"

"I'm just so happy I have a helpful friend."

Dad tried for a hardass look, but he was also trying not to smile, and they canceled each other out.

Holmes and I cleaned up, and before I could do anything smart like jump straight through a window or slam my head in the refrigerator door a few times, he said, "We should probably get to work on that chemistry now."

"About that—" I began.

"Did you text Ariana about Sunday?" Dad asked from where he was watching the BYU game.

I grabbed Holmes by the oxford. "We're going to study now."

"We could eat earlier or later if it works better for her schedule."

"Can't hear you," I said as I towed Holmes down the hall. "Too busy learning about codependent bonds."

"Covalent," Holmes said.

I wasn't sure, but I thought Dad was laughing.

When I closed the bedroom door, I said, "Good call with the tutoring thing. That's going to be great cover."

Holmes was staring at the clothes on the floor, dismay rising in his face. It made me feel kind of bad, the perpetually fresh disappointment and distaste that manifested every time he stepped into my room—as if he hadn't been here dozens of times before.

"I know where all the clean ones are," I said.

"Um, yes." He swallowed. Then, tearing his gaze from the floor, he said, "It's not a cover."

"Hm?" I asked as I dropped onto my bed and took out my phone. There had been something about that New Zealand bird—

A pale, fine-boned hand that was ridiculously stronger than it looked covered my screen and pushed the phone down.

"I'm reading something."

"I told your father I'd help you with chemistry—"

"H, no!"

"—and so I will help you with chemistry."

"But that was, you know, talk. It doesn't mean anything."

"I am not going to lie to your father."

"Why not? I do it all the time!"

Holmes looked at me.

"You have got to be kidding me," I said.

"How do you expect to become a physician if you can't pass high school chemistry?"

"I said that one time, and it was stupid, and I didn't even mean it."

His pupils were chemically hard and contracted, but the rest of his face softened. After a long moment, he said, "Sit at the desk, or I'll ask your father if I can handcuff you there during lessons."

"He'd think it was a sex thing."

Color flamed in Holmes's face. "Nice try, but I won't scare that easily."

"I'll tell him it's a sex thing."

"Good," Holmes said. "He'll be pleased that all your hours of mindless pornography are finally paying dividends."

My jaw legit dropped. "H!"

"Desk, please."

"That was so amazingly bitchy."

"Desk."

"And, like, also kind of evil. Which I loved."

"Do not make me get your father."

He was blushing so hard that I was afraid he'd start being oxygen deprived, so I grinned and rolled off the bed. When he held out his hand, I rolled my eyes, but I slapped my phone into his palm. I sat at the desk, and Holmes brought back a second chair to sit next to me.

"Show me your notes," Holmes said. "And the relevant section in the textbook."

I opened the textbook. I flipped to the page where I'd written—succinctly and, I thought, brilliantly—*Ionic and Covalent Bonds*.

Holmes looked up from the page.

I tried for another grin, but this one slipped away. "Don't, ok? I tried. It...it didn't make any sense."

For a long moment, Holmes was silent. Then he said, "Let's begin with the structure of an atom."

It was a lot. He was a lot. I mean, I'd known he was smart—genius-level brilliant—but it was one thing to know it, and it was another thing to have him recite atomic structure without once having to look at the textbook. And then ionic bonds. And then covalent bonds.

"But they're both about sharing electrons," I said. "There's no difference."

"They're quite different, and to be more precise, they're not both about sharing electrons."

"This one takes an electron, and they get stuck together. This one shares an electron, and they get stuck together. It's the same thing."

Holmes took a slow breath. His pupils had dilated somewhat—maybe only in response to the dark room, but maybe the addies were wearing off. The shadows softened the palette of his face: giving him blues and grays that made him look like a chalk rubbing. We had done those (seventh-grade art, Ms. Prinze). The most important part, she had told us, was to get the paper tight against the surface of the object underneath. Conform—that was the word. It must conform to the surface. The way his cheek would fit into my hand.

"Think of it this way," Holmes said, the words startling me back to myself. "Let's say that an ionic bond is like a theft. One atom steals an electron from another atom."

"But you said it gives its electron—"

"For the sake of the example, please. Let's continue the metaphor. There's an arrest. Both atoms are involved in the criminal proceedings—bound together, we might say, even though they are not sharing the electron. They are attached to each other through this process of transfer. It's an imperfect analogy because it doesn't address the question of ions, but I hope you'll bear with me."

He seemed to expect a response, and his face was so earnest that I hid my smile and said, "Of course."

Nodding, Holmes continued, "Now, think of covalent bonds as something else. Not a theft, but—but an ongoing relationship, if you will. A friendship. Both atoms desire more out of their existence—in this case, to have a full outer shell of electrons. But they can achieve it only in partnership with another atom, by sharing one or more atoms."

"Ok. I guess that makes sense."

If Holmes heard me, though, he gave no sign of it. He struggled with the next words. "Like a friendship, when sharing electrons in this way, both atoms become more stable. Their bond is more stable. It's stronger than an ionic bond. They continue to share electrons, in the same way that people must continue to share experiences, emotions, and intimacy. They require ongoing effort and investment. Covalent bonds are often found in molecules; they allow individual atoms to become more than what they would be on their own."

He stopped, the silence sudden and punctuated, and his throat moved reflexively.

"That was really cool—" I began.

Holmes's expression stilled. It was the only word for it: every sign of animation and life in his face ceasing, arrested mid-motion. He drew out his phone, angled himself away from me, and said, "Yes, Father?" After listening for several moments, Holmes said in an unexpectedly tight voice, "I thought it was understood that my past behavior posed significant public relations challenges and, as a consequence, it would be better if I did not attend." Sometimes, when someone else was on the phone, you could hear the buzz of the other speaker's voice. Not so with Blackfriar—the other end of the call was like a bottomless well. "I believe it would be best—" Holmes tried. It seemed impossible, but his voice ratcheted down further—an icy control that betrayed, more clearly than anything else, how distressed he was. "Father, I would prefer—" I didn't know how much it cost him to say in a tiny voice, "Please."

Whatever Blackfriar said, it made Holmes snap his jaw shut. His teeth clicked. His face was bloodless again, and after a few more of my thudding heartbeats, he disconnected and pocketed the phone.

In that same iron-dead voice, Holmes said without looking at me, "Jack, you'll have to excuse me. I can't continue our tutoring—"

"He treats you like shit," I said. "In case you need an outside observer to tell you that."

"I do not." He stood. "I do not require your commentary on my family or my relationship with my family. Ever. Is that clear?"

"Yeppers."

He was trying to set his jaw, but it was trembling.

"You know what you need?" I asked.

"I need to return to my residence—"

"You need to beat me up."

Holmes stared at me.

"Definitely," I said, stretching as I got to my feet. "You definitely need, like, an hour of nothing but beating me up."

Chapter 12

The Polite Thing to Do

Holmes left via the front door, and he was annoyingly polite as he said goodnight to my dad. They even arranged the next torture—I mean tutoring—session. They both looked so pleased with themselves, I was tempted to fail chemistry just to teach them a lesson.

I said goodnight to my dad too. Then I went out my window. It was the polite thing to do. So my dad wouldn't worry.

My phone said it was a few minutes after nine, and at this hour, the athletic center was closed and dark. Emergency lights puddled shadows everywhere, and on the other side of the windows, workout equipment was reduced to bulky outlines. No music, no voices in the halls. The lights on the tree in the atrium were off.

I still had my spare keys, so I let us in through the service door. After retrieving our gear from the locker room, Holmes led the way to the wrestling room where we'd run into Emma and Rowe and Glo. We were alone except for the mirrors, the weights, the tinsely Christmas tree. Wordlessly, Holmes began to change, and I followed suit: shorts and a t-shirt, mouth guard, headgear, shin guards. It was new, changing like this in front of each other—in the past, Holmes had always arrived ready to go. When it came to the hand wraps, he had to help me. His whole body buzzed with barely capped anger, but his touch was controlled as he wrapped my knuckles.

We'd started doing this in October, when Holmes was still recovering from a gunshot wound—which meant, since he had one functional arm and was moving slowly from head injuries and blood loss, we were almost evenly matched. At first, he'd been tentative, hesitant—pulling his punches, watching me each time like I might shatter, offering corrections in a very un-Holmes, mealy-mouthed mishmash. We'd had a talk about that. We'd had several talks, actually.

Now, he just tried to kill me every time.

I mean, sure, he called it other things. He said words like *aerobic exercise* and *cardio* and *drills*, but it all came down to trying to work me to death. Even the warmup was murder—stretching, plus moves that he didn't call punches or kicks but were clearly designed to get your body ready to throw them. I wasn't exactly gasping for air by the time we'd finished, but I was drenched in sweat, and I couldn't smell the wrestling room's engrained funk anymore—I could only smell myself.

He launched into a series of drills. Punches and kicks and blocks, at first in slow motion, each time with a correction. "Your shoulder is too high," or "Bring your knee up," or "Pivot at the waist." And then (either because I was getting better or, more likely, Holmes gradually got worn down by incompetence), we ran through them faster and faster. When we finished, I was gasping for air. Holmes was breathing faster too, and a sheen of sweat glowed on his forehead and nose and cheeks. He looked alive, awake, alert. His pupils had dilated as his body burned off some of the speed. And there was an edge in his face, a blade that he normally kept hidden, and he whetted it every time we clashed.

The focus mitts next, with Holmes barking instructions as my breathing became more and more ragged. Then the self-defense scenarios. Holmes would charge me from behind, or we'd begin in a grapple, or he'd instruct me to pretend that the Christmas tree, our reflections in the mirror, his shadow—that they were other opponents, and I had to keep them controlled while fending him off. He took me down with a hip throw—harder than he'd done with Rowe, for sure; hard enough to drive the breath from my lungs. He put me flat on my back with a knee strike, and I swear I felt my ribs creak. He knocked me on my ass with an open-handed blow that was barely more than a slap. My whole face felt like fire, and my eyes welled up with tears.

"When I tell you to keep your hands up," he said, standing over me, "keep your hands up."

I nodded, breathing through the pain, at the crumbling precipice of pain and humiliation that would spill me into full-out crying.

"Get to your feet."

I nodded again, measuring my breaths.

"Get up."

Somehow, I got onto one knee, and the whole world went wobbly.

"Get up, Jack."

"Give me a minute."

"No, I will not give you a minute. Get up. Get up! I am not doing this for my entertainment, and I do not enjoy having my time wasted. I've told you time and again to keep your hands up."

Someone had torn the paper rings on the Christmas tree, I noticed through my scrambled vision. Somebody had come in here and been an asshole enough to do that, knocking all the tinsel to the ground, ruining it.

Holmes caught the collar of my shirt and hauled me to my feet. "When I say get up, get up!"

The world—or maybe my vision—went a little more scrambly. I nodded, and when Holmes released me, I stumbled in a circle. I was having a hard time finding him. Maybe this was a trick. Maybe he was secretly a ninja, and he'd thrown a smoke bomb, and—

Something loomed up at me out of the darkness, and I threw a kick.

Well, kind of.

I didn't hit the mat face first only because Holmes caught me, and the next thing I knew, I was propped up against one of the mirrors, the glass cold against my neck and shoulders. Holmes's face swam in my vision. Fresh blood showed at his lip.

In a tight voice, he said, "Close your eyes until the dizziness passes."

So, I closed my eyes.

He was holding my arms, keeping me upright. His hands were warm. He had this one knobby knuckle, and I thought I could feel it, but maybe that was my imagination. His breaths came fast and short, and after a moment, I could tell he was trembling. The smell of our sweat mingled in the air.

"H, I think I'm done for the night."

He let out a bitter, tangled laugh. "I should take you to a hospital. I'm worried I've given you a concussion."

"I'm all right. I'm all lemons purple upside-down cake."

I cracked my eyes. Horror painted Holmes's face.

My smile rolled downhill. "Kidding."

His outrage was better than his horror.

"I'm fine," I said. "Got a little dizzy at the end."

"That blow disrupts the fluid in your inner ear," Holmes said. "I shouldn't have done it."

"Should you have broken all my ribs?"

He touched my chest, his composure reassembling into a familiar frown, and palpated each rib.

"Ow."

"Be silent."

"You don't have to dig in like that."

"I said be silent."

"You're the one who beat me up. Jesus Christ, H! Are you trying to dig out my spleen?"

He pulled his hand back. "That's not where your spleen is located."

For a long moment, he watched me.

"I want to be wheeled out of here on a stretcher," I said.

"Dear Lord."

"I want a hero's parade. I want weeping widows lined up on either side of the sidewalk."

The corner of his mouth trembled; someone had tried to beat it out of him, this last fragment of childhood, and watching over and over what it had done to him was one of the most terrible things about knowing Holmes. He gave up and bit his lip, and then, in a broken voice, he said, "Am I forever going to be apologizing to you? Why can't I do things right for once?"

I struggled to sit up, my skin peeling away from the glass in a way that told me my sweat was cooling and somebody (me or Dad) was going to have to clean the mirror. "First, yes, you're always going to be apologizing to me because I'm perfect and, you know, never mess up."

He shook his head. In the low light, his eyes looked like broken concrete.

"Second, I told you I wanted you to beat me up, and you did exactly what I asked. So, no apology necessary."

"I hurt you. I—I used you as an outlet for my emotions."

"Oh, really? Because I had no idea you were upset when I told you to beat me up. I'm just a simple janitor boy who can't figure out what a complicated superior lifeform like a Holmes might be feeling."

The outrage was back again. Apparently, Holloway Holmes hadn't grown up with enough people giving him shit.

"But if you knew—" He bit his lip again. His teeth came away red. "Jack, I could have hurt you. Seriously, I mean."

"No, you couldn't have. You get a little carried away sometimes. And, yes, I could have done without the yelling at the end. But you're my friend; you're never going to hurt me."

"I hurt everyone," Holmes said in a savage whisper. He stopped for a moment, gathering himself. "I tell myself every day that your life will be better without me and that if I am to do one good thing, it would be to stay away from you. But I can't. What does that say about me?"

"You're as fucked up as the rest of us." I shrugged. "Welcome to the club; we made jackets."

He cocked his head.

"It's a saying," I said. "Do you want to tell me what your dad said?"

He hesitated. Then he shook his head.

"Want to beat me up some more?"

"No," he said quietly. "But I would like to work the heavy bag. Unless you'd like me to accompany you home first."

"See? That's why you're the genius. I should have thought of the heavy bag. Then I'd still have all my ribs."

He glowered at me for a moment before remembering he was supposed to be feeling guilty, and I pushed him away with a laugh.

When Holmes came back from the storage room, he was wheeling the heavy bag on its portable stand. He settled into a relaxed fighting stance, and then he began to move: punches, kicks, elbows. His body flowed, everything becoming starlight and shadow. It was one thing to run through drills with him. It was another thing to know, firsthand, how easily he could hand my ass to me over and over again. But seeing this was something else entirely. We didn't have rain much in this part of Utah, and I didn't go to the Provo River often. But I had gone one day, when clouds were scudding across the sky. I remembered the dapple of light and shadow streaming over the water.

For a while, Holmes kept it up. Then, by degrees, the punches got slower, the kicks got sloppier, the elbows came farther and fewer between. His breathing became ragged. It hissed through his teeth, the sound high and whistling. And then he threw a final punch, the blow arcing and wild and jelly-loose, and it didn't come anywhere near the bag. He bent over, hands on his knees, his whole body shaking. He was still taking those shrill breaths through his teeth. Like if he opened his mouth, he might scream.

By then, my legs had decided to work again. I peeled myself up from the vinyl mats and got over to him. He was still shaking, still hinged at the waist. I carded his sweat-dark hair, and I don't know if he couldn't stand up anymore or if he wanted it, but he leaned into me, head and shoulder making a fork against my thigh. I ran my hand down his back, the bump of vertebrae like stones on a fairy path.

"Want to talk about it now?"

He shook his head against my leg.

I rubbed his shoulder. I tickled the back of his neck, where sweat made my fingers move with stuttering slickness over bare skin. His breathing slowed, changed. Goose bumps climbed his neck to the neatly trimmed hair. I felt it too, like a static charge building in my balls.

With a suddenness that startled me, Holmes stood upright and herky-jerked toward the door.

"H—"

"I need to be alone," he said raggedly. "I—I need to shower, and I would like to be alone."

"Are you ok?" Which, yes, I undermined slightly by adjusting the semi in my shorts.

"I need to be alone!" he called back.

I rubbed my eyes. I walked in an unsteady circle and thought about the BYU basketball game. I needed to call medical science and report this, because apparently you could have your inner ear discombobulated and get skewered by your own ribs and still violently need to jerk off.

But after a few minutes, I had my head on straight (so to speak). I put away the heavy bag, my arms trembling in the aftermath of the workout, and I stripped out of my gear. I carried my stuff and Holmes's to the locker room. The pieces were identical; Holmes had given me the set with the offensively blatant lie that he'd outgrown it, which was interesting since it fit me perfectly and we were the same size. But since I couldn't afford any of my own, I didn't have any other options. I cleaned our gear, and my only company was the sound of the water running in the showers—a steady, hissing spray uninterrupted by splashing or the echoes of movement. If he was showering, he was doing it Holmes-bot style. He might have been crying, and he needed the water to cover the sound. He might have been doing something else, and I chubbed up a little at that thought, but I dismissed it. My guess was that he was sitting there, the water washing over him, motionless and shut away from the world as he locked up all the parts that had threatened to come unchained. How did you tell someone that it was ok to let the feral parts out sometimes? Look at me; maybe that would work. Look at me, I'm basically a hundred percent feral emotions and unmitigated horniness.

I won't lie; I was tempted. It would have been easy to walk past the showers. They were open, and I could have turned my head, looked. He'd be there, the water sluicing over the arrows of his shoulders, hugging the vee of hips, rounding the curve of that jack-in-the-box ass. The little patch of blond hair on his chest would be dark. The hair under his arms would be darker. And lower? The little treasure trail? I'd thought of his vertebrae as a fairy path, but now I was thinking about each dark, wet hair below his navel.

It took me a couple of minutes. But I was determined to be, if not a good person, then at least a semi-decent one. I carried our gear back to our lockers. His was still open, which wasn't like him, but then, he'd been in a hurry, maybe even in a panic. His black leather notebook lay at the bottom of the locker, and I wasn't trying to snoop, but it was hard to miss the piece of paper that had fallen out.

When I saw it, I stopped, and I tried out a few different explanations. Then I kept staring.

It was a sticky note, the kind people keep at their desks to jot something down. And I recognized this particular sticky note because I was the one who had drawn it—a happy janitor blowing a kiss. Nothing but a few lines in ballpoint. Nothing at all, really.

But here it was.

He'd forgotten it was in his notebook.

I let out a breath I hadn't realized I was holding, and I stored our gear.

That was all; he'd forgotten it was in his notebook. He'd picked it up back in September, when he still thought I might be involved in Sarah Watson's death, and then he'd forgotten about it.

Never mind that he was a Holmes. Never mind that he never forgot anything, never did anything without a lacework chain of reasons and logic and evidence.

I took a few deep breaths and told myself: he forgot. That's all.

The sound of the water had changed, splashing mixed in with the steady hiss of the spray. He'd finish quickly; Holmes liked to be clean, and that meant sometimes after we sparred, he wanted to shower immediately. I'd gotten used to his maximum-efficiency showers, even though I'd tried to explain how nice it was to stand under the water and zone out (and yes, monkey around with your dangly bits, but that would have made his head explode), Holmes had never taken to the idea. He'd be done in a few minutes, and he wouldn't be happy to find me lingering here. He'd probably say I was lurking.

I let myself out into the hall, and the door fell shut behind me, closing off the sound of the shower. I walked and stretched and got a drink, and I was telling myself—again, firmly—that he'd simply forgotten about the sticky note when the voices reached me.

Girls' voices. More than one. And then peals of laughter.

For a moment, I froze. Then I turned for the locker room.

I was too late. They came around the corner before I could reach the door, five of them. And then I suppressed an internal groan.

The Bloopies.

The Boy Band's equivalent weren't as actively cruel as their counterparts, but they could be life-endingly cataclysmic in their own way.

I'd sold to each of them, some more frequently than others, so I knew them, and they knew me, and there was no way to get out of their path now.

They all wore athleisure gear—tech-fabric tops and expensive yoga pants. Skye was tall and willowy, and she wanted fashion magazines. Obscure ones, which I had to go to Salt Lake to get. D'Layne had long, dark hair with bangs and a French braid, and she also had a serious booty. She'd only bought from me once: morning-after pills. Remmi had feathery blond hair and, even in the gym, she wore concealer to cover a rash of acne. She collected vinyl, and I'd spent an ungodly number of Saturday afternoons digging through old boxes to find something good for her. Kaylee was that painful kind of white that made her look half dead, and while she was pretty now, in twenty years she'd be pinched, the skin on her face too tight. Like D'Layne, she'd only bought from me once, and she'd wanted brownies with pot in them, even though I'd offered to get her edibles. Marielle was last, olive skin like mine, hair held back with a velvet bow, small and with a painted-on smile like a doll. A chess set, chess books, even, once, a chess video. Hey, there's something for everybody.

"Hi, Jack," D'Layne said.

The other four cooed echoes, and the sound of high-priced sneakers squeaked along the linoleum toward me.

"Hi, ladies. What are you doing here?"

"You mean because it's after hours?" Remmi asked.

"It's none of your business," Kaylee said.

"You're here too," D'Layne said over them with a smooth smile. "What are you doing here?"

I gave her my best smile—assuming Holmes hadn't knocked out any of my teeth without my noticing. "Trouble. Mischief. General bad-boyishness."

Remmi and Kaylee rolled their eyes. Skye laughed. Marielle gave me that painted-on doll smile. And D'Layne's own smile became a little more suggestive.

"Trouble," was all she said.

And then they reached me, and I stepped aside. They passed me, all five of them giving me looks that ran the gamut from frozen fish to cat scratch, and when they'd gone a few yards, they broke out into a flurry of whispers. The laughs came next—they cracked themselves up.

"Bye, Jack," D'Layne called without looking back.

"See you at Wintersmash," Remmi said, just to be a bitch.

They knew I hadn't been invited; they were in charge of the invites. But saying it cracked them all up again, and they were still laughing when they got to the end of the hall and turned the corner. I started moving toward the locker room again, but I stopped when one of the Bloopies backtracked. In the shadows, I didn't recognize D'Layne until she was halfway to me.

"Sorry about them," she said with the same suggestive smile she'd given me before. "They're all PMSing hard."

I shrugged. "What are you doing here? For real?"

"The boys wanted to show off. Have you met the new guy?"

The boys could only mean the Boy Band, and I had an idea who the new guy was. "Paxton?"

"He's your competition, Jack. You need to pay attention. Anyway, it was boring, so we left." She smiled. "And now I'm talking to you."

"What do you mean they were showing off?"

"You could come to Wintersmash, you know." D'Layne knew what she was doing—the way she stood, for one thing—and she hadn't missed me checking out her butt earlier. "Everyone likes you. It'd be fun."

"Yeah," I said.

"So, you'll come?"

"I'm washing my hair."

She rolled her eyes. "You don't have to have an invitation. Just show up."

"And give Axle and Riker an excuse to kick my ass? No thanks."

"You're tough, though." She put her finger on my arm and traced my biceps. "You could handle them."

"No invite," I said, "no Wintersmash."

"What if I promised you that they'd let you in? For real."

I wasn't as smart as Holmes, but I was smart enough to know that asking, *What do you want?* probably wasn't a good idea. So, instead, with my own brand of genius, I said, "Yeah?"

"You have to make sure they're interested. We're all bored. Because we're all so boring."

"And I'm interesting?"

Her laugh was bright and amused. "Oh God, no. Not really. You're cute, Jack, but no. But you know somebody interesting."

Her smile flashed again, and without waiting for an answer, she turned and left.

Well, I thought, that one went straight to the 'nads.

The door to the locker room opened, and a damp-haired Holmes emerged in his coat and oxford and chinos. He glanced in the direction of the voices, which were still fading, and frowned.

"The Bloopies," I said. "Ready?"

Holmes nodded, and we cut through the athletic center, taking a different route than the girls. In the spaced-out glow of the emergency lights, Holmes's face was pale, and the circles under his eyes deeper. The sound of our steps was strangely out of sync, like there was a third person with us. Huh, I thought. And who the fuck could that be?

"My father insists I come to the annual Holmes family holiday party," Holmes said.

We walked a few more feet. "Is that bad?"

"I am welcomed back with open arms, it seems. All is forgiven. Or, at least, forgotten."

We went on for a while. In the atrium, the Christmas tree seemed much larger with its lights off—a cancer that had grown to fill the opening.

Finally, I said, "Do you want to go to your family party?"

"It's a tradition."

"Yeah, but do you want to go?"

"Everyone important will be there. People from both coasts, anyone significant in Utah, Idaho, Colorado, Arizona, Nevada."

"H."

We passed through the vestibule, and the deeper darkness there dropped over us like a cloak, and when we stepped out into the night, his face was as cold and unmarked as fresh snow.

"When," he asked, "has it ever mattered what I wanted?"

Chapter 13

Surprise

We could hear the shouting in Aston's room from the stairwell.

It was Friday afternoon, and Baker House had hit its typical lull. I'd spent the morning in class, pretending to pay attention while groveling via text. Ariana still hadn't forgiven me, but at least she was talking to me. Holmes had barely been able to stay in his seat; Aston wasn't in class, and Holmes couldn't wait to track him down. We needed to talk to Aston about, among other things, a man named Kazen Bates—who was an attempted murderer and possibly Aston's former booty call.

I shot a quick glance at Holmes as we hurried down the hall.

"Maybe we'll be too late," Holmes said, brows drawn together. "Maybe someone will have murdered him."

He'd been like this since I got to his room: an aspen-haired thundercloud. His answer, when I pestered him, was that he was fine. When I pestered him some more, he finally admitted that he had tried again to locate Paxton, with no success. Oh, and that he hadn't slept last night. Oh, and that he hadn't eaten. Oh, and that he was fine, and that I should stop asking. But he hadn't even made me wait while he fixed the length of his shoelaces, so I had my doubts about the last part.

"I like grumpy H," I said. "In case you're interested."

"I am not."

"I bet grumpy H would love to feed crusts of bread to the ducks and shout at children to watch where they're going and stay off his lawn."

"That scenario is inconsistent—" But he caught himself.

I grinned at him as I hammered on Aston's door.

The shouting cut off, and the silence that followed was prickly and dense.

"Open this door right now," Holmes said. "Or I will open it for you."

"Engage Daddy protocols," I whispered.

Fire flared in Holmes's face.

It was fun until he shattered my ankle.

"Holy shit, holy shit, holy shit!" I hopped and swore. "What the hell, H? Are those things steel toed?"

"That's an excellent idea."

"It wasn't a suggestion!"

The door swung open an inch. Aston stared out at us. His hair was mussed, and not in its usual, artful way, and his eyes were bloodshot, the tip of his nose glistening. "I'm busy—"

Holmes poked him in the throat.

Aston fell back, gagging, and I gave Holmes a look.

Elbowing open the door, Holmes lifted his chin. "I've decided I'm not fine."

"No shit."

"Do you have a comment about that?"

"Hold on. I'm considering if I want to spend the rest of my life walking on two canes." His eyebrows knitted together again, and I smirked. "Nope, no comments."

Holmes pushed his way into the room, and I thought I heard him mutter, "Idiot."

Aston's room was pretty much the same—the high-end electronics, the red U of U flag, a wisp of Axe body spray hanging in the air—unless you counted the suitcases that lay open and empty on the floor. Aston leaned against his bed, both hands around his throat, still gagging and looking like he was trying not to puke.

"Don't be a baby," Holmes said. "You're fine."

"What did you do to him?" The question came from a woman. She looked like she'd just come from the office—caramel-brown hair fell in long, feathered layers, and she wore a white button-up and a skirt with a geometric print. The blazer on the back of the chair probably belonged to her; it looked slightly oversized, and doubtless it would achieve that relaxed-in-a-good-way look that white ladies had when they wore blazers in Nordstrom ads. She was checking her hair in the mirror on the back of the closet door, and the only sign she was hella pissed off was the tension around her mouth. "That's assault."

"Who are you?" Holmes asked.

"Hey," Aston croaked. "I told you—"

"You lied to us," Holmes said. "I suggest you think carefully about the next words that come out of your mouth."

Aston looked like he might have poked himself in the throat again: his eyes bugged out, and he snapped his teeth together, and he slid a little farther down the bed like he might end up on the floor.

"Tell them to leave." She took out a phone. "Or should I call campus security?"

They shared eyes and chin, but if she was his mom, she'd kept herself in great shape. Stepmom, maybe? Even that seemed like a stretch, and anyway, Aston had never mentioned anything like that.

"Who are you?" Holmes said. "I won't ask again."

"I'm calling the headmaster," she said. "This is ridiculous; we paid for a private room."

"No," I said at the same time as Aston.

He shot me a weirdly grateful look, and, voice still a little raspy, he said, "No, Cam, don't. It's—it's complicated. Guys, this is my sister, Camdyn."

She studied us again, phone loose in one hand, her finger poised to make the call.

"He's Holloway Holmes. And he's, uh, Jack. They're helping me. You know. With…this."

"You've probably heard of me," I said.

But the woman's eyes were trained on Holmes. She pocketed the phone and rounded on Aston. "How stupid are you?"

"I—"

"Because I knew you were stupid. I knew you had a gift for making the worst choices over and over again. You're practically a savant when it comes to that. But this is a whole new level, Aston. Holloway Holmes and Jack? Do you hear how that sounds?"

"Hey," I said, "first of all—"

"Pack your bags," Camdyn said. "Now. The argument is over; the conversation is finished. This final proof of your total, abject idiocy means we're done talking about it."

Aston set his jaw and stared at the floor. "You don't know what it's like."

"Your issues with Dad—"

"My issues? They're not my issues!"

"Whatever you want to call them—"

"You don't know what it's like. It's not just him. It's everything. I have to watch what I say, how I say it, how I walk, how I stand, how I dress. They notice everything; you have no idea."

"I have no idea," she echoed.

"I'm not going home."

"Did you hear me?" Camdyn asked. Her volume rose. "The conversation is over. Pack your bags—"

"Cut it out," I said. She whirled toward me, and I remembered how scary white ladies could be. Somehow, I managed to say, "Quit talking to him like that. Quit bullying him. We're actually really good at this stuff. Well, H is. And I don't know what's going on, but it's obvious Aston doesn't want to go with you. If he doesn't want to go, he doesn't have to."

She stared at me. She had honey-colored eyes and, apparently, she never blinked.

"H," I whispered. "A little backup."

"It would be a mistake to take him away from Walker," Holmes said.

Camdyn's gaze slid to Holmes, and, when it seemed safe, I breathed out slowly.

"At the moment," Holmes said, "a dangerous man has already attempted murder. He did so in public, in full daylight, and the police have no idea how to find him or stop him. Based on our investigation, we have reason to believe he has taken an unhealthy interest in your brother."

"He wants to kill him?"

Holmes hesitated. "I don't believe so."

"But he's obsessed with him?"

"Yes."

Camdyn shot Aston a look that made him shrink down, but otherwise, she seemed to be handling the news of a psycho stalker fairly well.

"Removing Aston from his routine, though, may startle this man, which would be dangerous for you and your family."

For a moment, Camdyn frowned. "You said he's already tried to kill people. What more can he do?"

"Come after Aston. Right now, Aston does not appear to be his target. If Aston changes his routine, we're not sure what he will do. He may believe that Aston has become a threat to him and act accordingly."

"A threat? How?"

"Yeah, Aston," I said. "Want to explain?"

He made himself even smaller and shook his head, and after a moment, he looked up at the ceiling and wiped his eyes. The tears came faster. In a choked voice, he said, "It's like you said: I'm so fucking stupid."

He cried harder, and Camdyn sighed and moved to sit on the bed next to him, one hand straightening her skirt. She put her arm around him, and he cried into that expensive white button-up, and she rolled her eyes at me and Holmes while she patted his hair and scratched his back.

"Aston was a surprise," she said, and her voice thawed a little. "You're wondering about the difference in our ages. I was seventeen; my parents thought they were done." A tiny smile creased her cheek. "Surprise."

Holmes nodded. I tried to look anywhere but at Aston because he was still sobbing. Then I noticed Holmes was still watching, so I jabbed him in the ribs and shook my head at him.

When Aston's crying slowed, Camdyn produced a packet of tissues from her blazer, and Aston wiped his eyes and blew his nose. He didn't look salon pretty anymore; he looked like an overgrown child—a terrified one. He hiccupped as Camdyn rubbed his back some more.

But her words were clipped steel when she said, "What did you do?"

"It's Kazen, isn't it?" he asked in a tiny voice.

"When we asked you if anyone—" Holmes began.

"I know!" The cry tore its way out of him. "But I swear to God, I thought it was the exact opposite."

"He's closeted," I said. "So, you figured he couldn't be the blackmailer because he'd be too worried about keeping his own secrets."

"Something like that." Aston gave a one-shouldered shrug. "Before things got…serious with Dawson, I was on the apps, you know. I can't leave campus, but there are guys who will drive up here. Some of them like it. The thrill."

Camdyn shook her head, her fist tightening around the tissues.

"Would you like to leave?" Holmes asked. "I understand this may be difficult to hear."

"Because I'm his sister? Or because I'm LDS?"

"Both."

She shook her head. "My parents are—" She stopped. "I'm not like my parents. I don't care that he's gay, but it would be nice if he could use his brain for once."

Aston gave a wet, pathetic squawk.

"Kazen," I prompted.

"I met him on one of those apps. He didn't tell me his real name at first—he said his name was Klip." Aston paused long enough for him and his sister to perform identically dramatic eye rolls. "We saw each other a few times. It got serious for him. Way more serious than I, you know, realized. He let loose one day, telling me about his family, about how he has to hide who he is. And I…I told him about my family."

Camdyn pressed the fist with the wadded-up tissues to her forehead.

"It was a weird moment," Aston protested. "I don't know, he was so vulnerable, and he was crying, and—and so I told him, you know, because I thought it would make him feel better."

"And?" Holmes asked.

Aston shook his head and was silent for a few heartbeats. "It got so much worse. The next time, he told me he loved me. I think he thought it was like a Romeo and Juliet thing—this forbidden love, both of us hiding it from our families, and we only had each other. But that wasn't it, you know? I was still seeing other guys. And things with Daw had gotten, um, more serious. So, I, you know."

"You what?" Holmes asked.

I groaned. "You ghosted him? You ghosted a psycho closeted militiaman?"

"What was I supposed to do?" Aston shouted. "He wouldn't leave me alone!"

"Tell him like an adult how you feel!" I shouted back. "Be a fucking man about it and treat him like a human being!"

The echo of my shout bounced back to me. Holmes was staring at me. Camdyn was staring at me. Aston set his jaw and looked away. In my head, I heard what I'd said, tasted the after-rush of my anger, and my face filled with heat. Huh, a little voice at the back of my head said. I told that little voice to shut the fuck up, and then I copied Aston and looked away.

The silence that came after was like paper towels packed in my throat. I started when Holmes said, "What happened when you stopped responding to Kazen's messages?"

"He went insane." Aston snuffled. "He started messaging me all the time. At first, they were desperate. I love you. Stuff like that. Then they were…scary."

"How so?"

"Demanding I answer him. Calling me names. Saying all these horrible things about me."

"Do you still have these messages?"

Aston shook his head.

Holmes's next breath sounded vexed, but his voice was smooth when he said, "And?"

"He showed up here one day. In that big fucking truck. I saw it, and I knew it was his; I recognized it right away. I sprinted back to my room, and—and he was already in here. He had a gun." Aston's voice broke, and my heart thudded in my ears a few times before he said, "He hit me. Knocked me around. Accused me of tricking him, that he wasn't like me, that I'd given him drugs and made him do things. He said if I ever told anyone, he'd kill me."

"And you believed him?"

"He was in the Army. He told me about it a few times. He killed people, you know, over there. He'll do it again."

"Killing someone as a deployed soldier is different from murder—"

"No, you don't understand. He's crazy. And his whole family is crazy, all his buddies. He really would kill me if he thought I was going to tell someone—because if they found out, they'd probably kill him. They're all part of this weird group—"

"The Danites," I said.

Again, Aston's look was weirdly grateful. "You know about it? He tried to explain it to me a few times. All this stuff about pornography and homosexuality. Do you know he broke into the governor's mansion one time? It was on the news. They didn't catch him, but he told me later it was him. He went there to kill the governor. The only reason he didn't is the governor had a meeting that went late or something. That's what I mean when I tell you he'll kill me—he's out of control."

Camdyn's voice was thick; she sounded sad and tired more than anything when she asked, "What did you do?"

Screwing up his eyes, for a moment Aston looked like he might start crying again. But in a faltering voice, he said, "After you said you'd, you know, find out who was doing this, I panicked. I thought—I thought maybe you'd find out about him, go talk to him, and then he'd think I told you."

"Even though you didn't," I said. "Even though you very specifically didn't bother to mention your lunatic killer hookup."

"You called him?" Camdyn asked, her voice rising with horror.

It was like something heavy pressing down on all of us. A second layer of gravity. Down the hall, a microwave dinged, and a boy shouted, "Booyah! Pizza rolls!"

"I was scared—" Aston began.

"Jesus Christ," I said.

Holmes shook his head.

"You don't understand! I had to tell him. But I made sure he knew it was fine. I made sure he knew you two were cool and that you weren't going to do anything—"

"Have you contacted him again?" Holmes asked.

"No, but—"

"Don't. If he contacts you, you need to let me know immediately. Do you understand?"

"Yeah, but—"

To Camdyn, Holmes said, "Do you agree he should continue his routine?"

Pale, her mouth a thin line, Camdyn nodded.

"I'm right here!" Aston shouted. "You have to talk to me! I'm an adult, and I'm sitting right here, so you have to talk to me!"

Camdyn stood and turned to face him. She eyed him for a moment. And then she slapped him. The blow was quick and precise, and the sound cleared everything else from the room.

Aston let out a broken sound, rubbed his cheek, and started to cry again.

Turning back to face us, she said, "The blackmailer contacted my family last night. That's why I'm here."

A flurry of calculations crossed Holmes's face. "What—"

"We have agreed to pay to have the photographs turned over." The next words were clearly meant for Aston, although she didn't look over her shoulder. "It's the way this situation should have been handled from the beginning."

"You're making a mistake," Holmes said. "Blackmailers don't stop at one payment. If you do this, you will be paying the blackmailer for the rest of your lives."

"No, the agreement is clear: we'll never hear from him again."

Holmes shook his head and opened his mouth, but I spoke over him. "Why would the blackmailer contact you?"

Camdyn looked at me like I might be in the same category of stupid as Aston. "To demand payment."

"Jack's right," Holmes said, his eyes narrowing as he glanced at me. "The blackmailer only recently demanded payment from Aston. Why switch targets so quickly? They didn't even wait to see if Aston would pay."

"They knew he had no money."

"Then why contact him in the first place?"

"I don't know. It doesn't matter. The fact is, they contacted us. That's what's important. It's a family matter now, and the family will handle it."

"Our services are no longer required?" I asked. "Is that it?"

"If Aston promised you something, I'm sorry to disappoint you. I'm sure something can be arranged for your time."

"For our time."

Camdyn turned to Aston. "If you're going to stay here, I'll try to think of something to tell Mom and Dad, but they won't be happy. I'm not going to tell them a—a murderer is after you."

With a glare, Aston said, "I don't want you to tell them that."

"Then, I'm going."

"Ms. Young," Holmes began, "I'd like to accompany whoever your family has designated to meet the blackmailer. An exchange like that can go bad quickly, and I believe I could be of assistance."

"No, thank you. We've got it all under control. Aston, you might want to pack your bags anyway. When Dad cools down, he's going to realize he can't leave you here, and you know what that means."

Aston dry-washed his face and didn't look up at her.

"I'll try to talk to him," she said, lowering her voice.

He nodded, but he still didn't look up.

"It might help your case if you came home instead of going to a party while I'm handling your dirty business. I'm supposed to be at a charity ball for one of the largest employers in the state tonight, and instead, I'm driving crisscross over two valleys, trying to sort this out." She hesitated, but when Aston kept his hands over his face, she sighed and touched his arm.

When she took a step toward the door, Holmes slid into her path. "The blackmailer called you."

"Yes, that's what I said—"

"No, you said he contacted the family. But he called you."

"And I told my father. What's your point?"

"Did he call you on your personal device?"

She touched her pocket without seeming to think about it. "Why?"

"Ms. Young, would you please show me your phone?"

"Dad said it had to be a burner phone; they didn't even try to hide the number they were using."

"Your phone, please."

With an annoyed breath, she handed him her phone. Holmes tapped the screen. Something ruffled his complexion for a moment, and then everything was glass again.

"What?" I asked. "You recognize the number?"

He tapped Camdyn's phone and passed it back to her.

A moment later, the sound of a phone set to vibrate filled the silence.

Holmes drew out his own phone. A number flashed on the screen. He answered it, and Camdyn's phone connected, and the faint static of the overlapping microphones crackled.

"You're shitting me," I said.

My echo came from both phones before Holmes disconnected the call. Pocketing his phone, he said, "Someone is playing games."

"How did they get your phone? When did they get your phone?"

"That's an excellent question. Ms. Young, the timestamp on that call said 9:37pm last night. Does that sound correct?"

"I guess."

Another of those seismic tremors disrupted Holmes's calm before he locked it into place again.

"Your locker," I said. "Last night, while you were showering. The door was open. I thought you were in a hurry and forgot." But he never forgot — anything, and hearing the words out loud made me shake my head at myself. "Jesus Christ, he was in the locker room with us."

"Someone is playing with us," Holmes said. His voice was stripped down. "Someone thinks this is a game."

"What are you talking about?" Camdyn asked. "What do you mean? Are you telling me someone used your phone?"

"The Bloopies were in the athletic center last night," I said. "And the Boy Band. And Paxton. That's ten people right there, not counting Aston. It had to be someone on campus, someone who knew where we were, someone who knew their way around the building."

"Not necessarily," Holmes said. "Someone could have spoofed my number."

"Someone broke into your locker, H. They didn't spoof your number."

"We can't call the police," Camdyn said. "I don't know what you're thinking, but we're leaving the police out of this. They didn't take anything, did they? From your locker, I mean. It's not that serious. It's all going to be wrapped up tonight. We're on schedule to have it all wrapped up tonight."

Holmes's eyes widened with horror, and he looked directly at me and said, "No."

"Yeah, I think we have to."

"Jack, no. There are other ways."

"I don't think there are."

"What are you freaks talking about?" Aston asked, his voice clotted as he finally dropped his hands.

"Please," H whispered.

"I'm sorry," I said with a helpless shrug. "Somebody on campus is involved in this shit. Everybody is going to be at Wintersmash."

Holmes was shaking his head, hands clenched at his sides.

I grimaced. "Looks like we're going to a party."

Chapter 14

Wintersmash

Every year, the location of Wintersmash was a secret that involved either paying off or outsmarting campus security. This year, it meant outsmarting them—the new head of security, Joanna Urban, had a lot of eyes on her, especially in the aftermath of what had happened in September. Which was why we were going down a flight of stairs that had clearly been burned in a fire. Charred paint came loose underfoot, and the smell of old smoke lingered, even though the blaze had been decades ago.

"I thought we were going to a party," Ariana said.

She looked great tonight: a high-necked black top, a plaid skirt in tan and cream, some kind of heels that did amazing things to an already amazing ass. Her hair was down, curls bouncing with each step. She had forgiven me, which was mostly another testament to how cool she was, although I think the promise of a rich kids party did soften her up a little.

"A secret party," I said as I helped her down the next step. I kicked a fallen board out of the way. "And secret means it has to be somewhere that a teacher or security guard or whoever isn't going to stumble onto it."

Ariana frowned at the soot-blackened concrete; overhead, security lights behind wire cages threw an egg wash glow that barely inched back the darkness. "Rich kids are crazy."

Behind us, Holmes plodded along. He'd been dragging his feet—sometimes, literally—about this party since we'd decided to come, and nothing I said could change his attitude. He'd refused to let me pick an outfit for him, so he looked the way he always did: perfection buttoned into an oxford and driving coat. He caught me looking at him, and something like hope kindled in his eyes.

"It's going to be fun," I said.

Hope died. "I changed my mind. I am no longer willing to support you in this plan."

"Too bad."

"Excuse me?"

"You heard me."

"Jack," Ariana said, "if he doesn't want to go, he shouldn't have to go."

"He has to go. He has zero choice."

Ariana frowned. Her natural human decency was clearly overwhelming her desire to ice me out—at least partially—as punishment for the last few days. Finally, she pulled me closer and whispered, "He looks terrified."

"He's fine."

"Why does he have to come with us? I know he's your friend—"

"It's complicated. I promise, it's going to be worth it."

She frowned again, so I kissed her cheek. Ariana rolled her eyes. I went in for a kiss again, and this time, she pushed my face away.

I laughed, and by accident, I caught a glimpse of Holmes's expression: his features narrow and hard, almost unrecognizable. They smoothed out a moment later, but for a moment, what I had seen there had looked a lot like rage.

Fortunately, we reached the tunnel then, and after that I was too busy navigating to have to think about how much shit I was getting myself into.

The Walker School wasn't actually all that old, but at one point, in the sixties or the seventies, one of the headmasters had decided they needed tunnels. You know, in case those Commie bastards decided to bomb us. So, the massive project had been carried out with, apparently, McCarthy-esque zeal. The buildings already had basements, but in the process of connecting the buildings, they'd added bunkers and fallout shelters, as well as a maze of connecting passageways, some of which seemed to go nowhere. It was a mix of cinderblock and concrete slabs, chain-link security fences and cast-iron grates, old pipes and conduit running overhead, and in the distance, the drip of water, the hiss of steam, the clank of tired machinery. Coming down here was a rite of passage for a lot of Walker kids, as evidenced by the roaches of joints and the used condoms and the empty vape pods clumped up at the base of the walls. Sometimes, just to be a hardass, Taylor made Dad and me come down here and clean some of it out.

I'd been down here alone, and it had scared the shit out of me; the silence had gnawed at me, and once, an explosion of movement—a rat, I guess—had left me close to shitting myself. I'd been down here with Holmes another time, and that had been a lot better. I didn't know how guys came down here to get their rocks off; the creep vibes were a major boner killer.

Tonight, though, the tunnels were different. As we followed the instructions that had come with my invitation from D'Layne—after I'd promised to bring Holmes—decorations began to appear: strands of lights, plastic evergreen garlands, gold-foil decorations shaped like snowmen and stars and snowflakes that had been taped to the walls, even gold ornaments hung on fishing wire from the ceiling so that they looked like they were floating in mid-air. The thump of a bass line reached us, and then a sound that registered as the noise of bodies and voices, albeit too many and too muffled to separate out into individual sounds. The smell of a blunt mixed with the frigid air of the tunnel.

"Oh my God," Ariana whispered, forgetting to be mad in her excitement and squeezing my hand. "This is dope!"

Holmes shuffled along behind us, refusing to pick up his feet.

A massive iron door at the end of the corridor stopped us. It was flaked with rust, and it looked like it weighed a ton. When I touched it, though, it moved surprisingly easily. I checked Ariana's face; she was smiling, her eyes bright with anticipation. Holmes was a shadow—nothing more than an elegance of bone and those colorless eyes. I decided my death was going to be historic. I was going to be the first person Holloway Holmes ever murdered.

I swung the door open, and a wall of sound and light met us. It looked like half of the student body had been packed into the room, and if I'd been the fire marshal, I would not have been pleased. A DJ was set up at one end, with colored lights swiveling in time with the music. Kids danced, made out, vaped, drank. At the other end, an impromptu bar had been set up on an ancient I-beam that rested on the floor. The air felt moist and warm from too many sweating bodies, and the smell of weed was much stronger, mixed now with the stink of overheated synthetics and a hundred different perfumes and a chemical fruitiness I decided was the vape juice.

"Holy shit," Ariana breathed, leaning into my chest. She turned her face up for a kiss, and after, she laughed, her eyes wide.

We went inside, and I swear to God, Holmes kicked me in the back of the knee.

Before we'd managed to wriggle more than a few feet through the crowd, Emma and Glo appeared. The differences between the two girls were even more apparent tonight: Emma statuesque, the red tone to her skin even more noticeable when the colored lights splashed over her; Glo petite, her golden complexion accented by sparkly eyeshadow.

"Are you Jack's girlfriend?" Glo asked, grabbing Ariana's arm.

"That skirt is amazing," Emma said.

Then something happened, and I have no idea how to explain it. All three girls started talking at once, and then they were all laughing, and then they were talking again and looking at me and laughing, and Glo even pointed and started laughing harder. I stood there. I realized I had no idea what people were supposed to do with their hands when they were doing nothing but standing there while their girlfriend made friends in that totally impossible-to-understand way girls had. I thought about shoving my hands in my pocket, but that seemed wrong, like maybe normal people didn't do that. I felt like I was covered in hives.

"Ok, bye," Ariana said with a huge grin, and the other two girls towed her out into the ocean of bodies. They disappeared almost immediately, even though—if the world were still sane and the rules of logic applied—I should have been able to track Emma because she was so tall.

"What the hell was that?" I asked Holmes.

But Holmes was gone too. There was no sign of him in the crush of bodies around me.

Well, fuck.

I thought about going after Ariana, but there had been no mistaking the chattering and the laughing and the pointing. Sure, if I wanted to shred the last scraps of my ego and then set them on fire and piss on them, I could go after them and learn what they were saying about me. Or, dear God, what Ariana was telling them. But, because I'm so smart, I decided maybe that wasn't the best use of my time.

And, anyway, I was here to find a blackmailer—or, at the very least, a blackmailer's accomplice.

Someone jostled me, and a guy swore, and that was my sign to get moving. I threaded a path through the bodies toward the bar. I got a rum and Coke—open bar because, well, rich kids—and I found a spot along the wall and watched. I recognized most of the faces. These were kids I had class with, kids I'd seen throughout the school year. Kids whose rooms I'd vacuumed. Kids whose trash I'd picked up. Kids whose shit I'd plunged. Tonight, they looked transformed: faces hot and sweaty, in expensive clothes with brands I'd probably never heard of, most of them high or on their way.

I drank the rum and Coke too quickly and then, because I was a coward, I fished out my vape. It was good stuff. Strong. I hit it, and then, to be safe, I hit it again. Less than a minute later, some of the tightness had gone out of my skin, and I could feel my pulse in my face, and it felt excellent.

Ok, I told myself. Technically, you have two options. You can talk to rich kids and try to find a blackmailer. Or you can track down your girlfriend and pretend you don't have fourteen how-to-break-up articles open on your phone.

I went in search of a blackmailer. Like I said, I'm smart.

At first, it seemed impossible. The best I could do, moving through the throng of bodies, was keep my feet as I got tossed back and forth. Guys and girls screamed along with the music. Or they screamed to talk to each other. Or they screamed just to scream—one girl, a pocket-sized little blonde with glow sticks in each hand, screamed directly into my ear like she was trying to rupture an eardrum. There was no way, in this madness, that I was going to be able to gather any information. Hell, there was no way I was going to get out of it with my ribcage intact, to judge by how many bros wanted to chest bump me.

No homo, of course.

I cut across the room at an angle, shading my eyes against the dazzle of the colored lights, trying to catch a full breath—which is harder than it sounds when someone body-slams you every half second. I scanned the crowd around me as I moved. No Ariana, no Emma, no Glo. I guess I should have been worried since, technically, Emma was on my list of suspects. But the truth was that Emma and Glo had actually been kind of cool, and the weed was taking the edge off everything nicely, and, most importantly, Ariana knew how to take care of herself better than I did. If I'd tried to pull her away, she would have been pissed—and if I'd explained why, she would have been even angrier.

No Holmes either, which was more worrisome, even under the insulation I'd packed inside my head. I'd expected him to be glued to my side tonight. I'd expected that it would be weirdly endearing—him being at the edge of what he could stand, and me being there for him, because I knew him, and I knew how to help him and take care of him and shit like that. I'd expected it to be—well, about us. The two of us, together, the way we were when we were at our best. And instead, the little shit had ditched me.

Someone checked my shoulder, and when I turned, Aston was stumbling through the crowd—his face sagging with a chemical looseness that told me he was already massively stoned. I changed course and went after him. At the far end of the room, additional passageways opened up, and Aston turned down one of them. The suffocating noise and heat faded, leached from the air by cinderblock and steel. Aston's sneakers scuffed the concrete as he shuffled along.

When I caught up to him, I said, "Do you seriously think it's a good idea to get high tonight?"

For a moment, Aston stared at me, eyes empty. And yes, I was aware of the hypocrisy. But then he mumbled, "Hey, man," and tried to shuffle off again.

"No," I said. "Come on, back to the party. Whatever's going on tonight, you shouldn't be wandering around alone."

He said something, the word too mushy to understand.

"What?"

"Fake!"

"Uh huh."

"They're all fucking fake!"

"So, you're not even fun when you're high. Fantastic."

"What's going on down here?" The voice echoed off the bare walls, and I recognized the half-breed of macho playfulness and overdeveloped testosterone. Dawson was in the lead, with Axle, Jaxon, and Riker behind him. The whole Boy Band. No Paxton, though, which was interesting—even though I'd only met him once, I had the feeling he wouldn't be able to stay away from something like this. Who had he glued himself to? "Getting a quickie from Abercrombie?"

"He wishes," I said. "What's he on? He's seriously messed up."

"He was freaking out." Riker was one of those annoying humans who never seemed to suffer any of the ill effects of puberty—no blemishes, no voice cracking in the middle of sentences, not even a single awkward boner on record. "He needed to chill."

"What'd you give him to 'chill'?" I let the contempt in my voice form the air quotes.

"He's fine." Some of Jaxon's family was from the Middle East—Dubai, or maybe Qatar; I forget—and you could see it in some of his features: the silky black hair that fell to his jaw, the olive skin, a strong chin. "Aren't you fine, Aston?"

Aston made a noise. Saliva glistened at the corner of his mouth.

"Somebody needs to take him home," I said.

"Sure," Dawson said with a leer. Caveman hot or not, nobody could pull off a leer. Not since, like, the 80s.

"Not you."

"Abercrombie, what the fuck?" Dawson laughed, and that meant the rest of the hyenas laughed too. "You his nanny or something?" Before I could answer, Dawson said, "I always take care of him; he's helpless. We're going to stay and smoke for a while, and then I'll take him home." The leer was back—barely a tracing of it around his mouth. "I'll make sure he's fine."

Axle snorted a laugh—he had that tousled, hockey-boy hair and a pink cast to his skin, and snorting didn't exactly help his cause.

I opened my mouth, but Dawson produced a joint and said, "Wanna smoke?"

I thought about the joint. I thought about my vape, which was almost empty. I thought about what Holmes would say, but he wasn't here to say it. Besides, this might be considered an interrogation tactic. "Fuck." I shrugged. "Why not?"

Dawson sparked the joint, and we passed it around. I hadn't sold him the weed, which meant either somebody else was dealing or—more likely—this was from Paxton. It was good. It was also some seriously strong shit, and after my first hit, I felt like I was swimming. After a while, somebody pressed a shot into my hand, and I did that too. Whatever it was, it was fire in my throat, and as soon as it hit my belly, I felt like somebody had kicked me between the eyes.

"See?" Dawson said. It was like somebody talking while you were underwater. "Abercrombie can be cool."

"Fuck yeah I can," I said, but the words dribbled out.

This was investigative work, the last rational part of my brain said. I was investigating.

And another part of my brain said, You are seriously fucked.

And a very quiet part said, This'll show him.

The joint went around again. It was like someone blowing the smoke straight into my brain, packing it in until there wasn't room for more. I could feel it leaking out my nose and my ears, and somebody must have said something funny because Riker burst out laughing and said, "He thinks it's coming out his ears."

"Settle a bet," Jaxon said, pausing to take a toke. He tilted his head back, the smoke escaping in a thin stream, and then he shook himself all over. "Are you fucking him, or is he fucking you?"

I burst out laughing. "I'm not fucking Aston."

"Not Aston," Axle said. He started to say something, and then he stopped himself and grinned. "Holmes."

I stared at him. That underwater feeling had changed into a kind of pressure. Someone had packed too much of the smoke inside my head, and my skull was tight like it might burst. I wavered, turned, started off toward the party, but Dawson caught my shoulder.

"Relax—hey, relax! It's a question, that's all. Come on, hit it. There you go."

I barely felt the joint being pressed between my lips. Dawson's other hand found my cheek. His face swam in front of me: the strong brow, the dark stubble. I thought I could feel the texture of his skin just by looking at it. The heat from the toke ran through me, snaking down, down, down. Dawson's eyes studied my face. He ran his thumb at the corner of my mouth.

"You're some kind of lightweight, huh?" he said softly. "Abercrombie is full of surprises."

Maybe I was still smart enough to realize it would be a bad idea to tell him I'd been pregaming, and my own shit was catching up to me, and I was in a state of serious crossfade. Or maybe it was simpler. Maybe I couldn't make words anymore.

"Come on," Dawson said, and he hooked two fingers in my waistband and tugged me down the hall.

Jaxon groaned.

"Seriously, Daw?" Riker asked.

"He's pretty," Dawson said with a laugh and tugged me after him. "What do you want?"

"You're messed up," Axle said.

"Abercrombie's going to be a good boy," Dawson said, and he pulled harder on my jeans this time; it felt like he was pulling me up off the floor. "Aren't you?"

"Hey—is that Jack?"

I thought I recognized the voice, but I couldn't put a name to it.

"Fuck off," Jaxon said.

"Don't worry about it," Dawson said to me in a low voice. "We're having fun, right? We're going to have fun."

"You know Aston's right here," Riker said.

"Aston's so blitzed he doesn't know he's standing up," Dawson said. "Quit being dicks, and I'll have Abercrombie blow you when I'm done."

I shook my head, but Dawson had caught one of the loops on my waistband, and he used it to pull me in his wake. My vision was blurry, and I had an impression of dark spaces, the flutter of fluorescent tubes like wings against my face, the smell of urine and old iron.

"You've got a mouth on you," Dawson said, and then his body pressed against mine. I hit the wall, and my knees buckled, but I didn't fall because there wasn't enough room. "You think you're so fucking tough, but all it takes is a couple of hits, and you're like all the rest of them."

Even through the fog of the weed and the rum, I knew, then, what this was about. It was about him on his knees, taking it while Paxton watched himself in the mirror. It was about the fact that we'd seen it. That we knew.

He parted my flannel and slid his hand under my tee. His fingers were cold. I pushed on his wrist, and he laughed and moved my hand away. He found my nipple and twisted, and I cried out. This time, I grabbed his wrist, but he broke the hold and pushed my hand away again.

"Knock it off," he said, laughing. And then he pressed his knee against my erection. "Just go with it."

My throat was too thick for me to swallow. I tried to say something, but the words were like fishes, down here in the dark water with me, swimming out of reach.

"Good boy," Dawson said huskily as he undid my waistband. "You're going to be my good little cocksucker, aren't you? Bet you wish you'd been nicer to me. I asked for one little favor, and you had to be the big swinging dick. Half up front, you dumb shit."

I shook my head. I made a noise that wasn't a word.

"Yeah, you are," Dawson said. He slid my jeans and boxers down, and my dick bobbed up, hard and hot against my belly, even through my shirt. "Be real good for me, and I'll even take care of this for you. If you play hard to get…" He pinched the head of my dick, and I shouted. Then I caught him with an elbow to the side of his head.

The crack of the blow echoed, and Dawson swore and stumbled back. I ran, but my body wasn't working the way it was supposed to. The message from my brain took forever to reach my legs. And then I remembered that my ass was hanging out, and with my jeans and boxers around my knees, all I could do was shuffle.

"You fucking piece of shit!" Dawson roared.

He caught me by the shoulder and spun me toward the wall. With my legs still caught in my jeans, I fell. Concrete scraped the sensitive skin on my lower back, my ass, my thighs. My head bounced once and turned scrambly.

When it was a little less scrambly, Dawson was saying, "I didn't do anything to him! He wanted to smoke, and then he wanted to fool around."

"He didn't know what he was doing," said that familiar-without-a-name voice. "He's so stoned he has no idea what's going on."

"Look, man, I didn't realize you two—"

"Get out of here."

Dawson's accelerated breathing suggested some final calculation. Then hurried footsteps beat away on the concrete.

I tried to sit up, but a hand on my forehead pressed me back down. "Jeez, you're a mess."

"Rowe?" That was a girl's voice.

"No, don't come in here. God. Find his girlfriend, will you?"

"Emma took her somewhere."

"Just find her."

Steps moved away from us again. Now that someone had said his name, I could match the voice to the memory. Rowe said, "I'm going to cover you up. That ok with you?"

I guess the noise I made must have been agreeable enough. Rowe rolled me onto my side and tried to pull the boxers up, but then he swore. "You're scraped up pretty bad. This isn't going to feel good."

Anywhere in the world, I would have known it: the woodsy heat that came in on my next breath. When Holmes spoke, his voice was like well-machined metal. "What happened?"

Rowe was quiet for what felt like a long time. Then he said, "Dawson."

First, nothing. Then, by degrees, Holmes's breathing became ragged.

"I don't think—" Rowe began. "I think I got here in time. I saw him when Daw was taking him down the hall."

Holmes's breathing continued—those sheared-off, thready breaths. But somehow he managed to say, "Thank you."

"You don't need to thank me. He's still pretty messed up. And, uh— well, you can see."

"Yes." I could hear the gear work engaging, the metal shutters coming down, Holmes's iron fortress sealing itself off again. "I see. I will take care of him."

"I'll help you get him home."

"No." Holmes stopped. And then, in a more even voice, "No, thank you. Jack will be embarrassed by this later. It's better if you leave him to me."

Rowe gave a surprisingly full laugh.

"What?" Holmes asked.

"Uh, I think you're the last person he'd want to see him like this. No, don't get mad." He laughed again. "Never mind. How about this? I'll see if I can help Glo track down his girlfriend, and then we'll get him out of here."

They talked some more, low voices, and then Rowe's footsteps drew away.

It was dark, and my vision was screwy, so I heard more than felt him kneel next to me: the whisper of the driving coat, his knees meeting the concrete. He held himself still and, as far as I could tell, was completely silent for a long moment. Then he caught me under the arms and sat me up. He was always so much stronger than I expected, and even though it was awkward—only in part because of the unstoppable boner I had going—he shifted me around and pulled my boxers and then my jeans up. Rowe had been right; it didn't feel good, but that sensation was packed away.

Holmes did his best to keep me upright, but I ended up on the floor again. I swam deeper as the dark waters rose. When I came up for air, my head was pillowed on his coat. When I came up again, much later, I lay with my head on his stomach, and his fingers were moving slowly through my hair. If the boner of the century had flagged at all, it was back at full force now, pressed against his thigh, which on top of being the single most humiliating thing of my life, also felt fucking awesome.

I rocked my hips to get an inch of saving grace between us, and in an unusually strained voice, Holmes said, "Jack, for the last time, no."

"Hwa?" I managed. Then, somehow, I got my head angled toward him.

His face was red.

Not his usual adorable red circles. Flaming red.

"Hwuh?" That was a little better.

"Are you awake?"

I nodded against his belly. His oxford had rucked up. The little blond hairs below his navel felt like silk against my cheek.

"I'm sorry." Holmes sounded on the brink of tears. "You were—I had to tell you to stop, repeatedly—"

There was probably a better way to find out you had been sleep-humping your best friend's leg, but that ship had now sailed, and all that remained was to figure out how quickly and conveniently I could kill myself. Holmes breathing was fast and shallow, the panic building again. It wasn't hard to tell why; the way we were positioned, and the, uh, phenomenon in his chinos, meant we were in what I would have called, at another time, an ideal sword-swallowing position. I knew he needed me to move, put distance between us. But I couldn't. So, instead, I rubbed his side (because I honestly couldn't move my body any more than that), and even though my throat was so dry it felt like it was cracking, I shushed him.

We were like that for a while as my brain put itself back together again. I had the beginning of what I could sense was going to be a fantastic headache, which didn't make sense—I hadn't had that much to drink, and weed, even green-outs, didn't hit me like that. Music pounded in the distance. Occasionally, someone screamed with excitement. The echoes came twisting down the corridors to us. After some time, Holmes's fingers came back to my hair. He was trembling as he ran them through it.

"Jack," he whispered, "what's going on?"

"I'm an idiot." My throat was raw, and it hurt to talk, but it would have been worse not to say anything.

His fingers continued their slow, uncertain movement.

"I overdid it." I swallowed, but it didn't help. "My therapist calls it—called it—high-risk behavior."

His fingers slowed. He followed the side of my head, brushing the curve of my ear. "I don't want you taking any risks."

I breathed so I wouldn't cry.

"I'm not angry with you," Holmes said.

"What?"

"About the party. I was apprehensive, and perhaps you mistook that as anger—"

"I don't care if you get mad at me. You get mad at me all the time. I like it when you get mad at me. Well, the cute kind of mad."

His fingers stopped. His whole body radiated outrage.

"Like this," I added helpfully.

For another moment, his whole body was tense with indignation. And then he slapped my ass.

I jerked upright. "H!"

The bright circles were back. "Do you like that?"

"No! My ass is scraped to hell! What the fuck?"

"I'm angry at you!"

"You just said you weren't angry!"

"Well, I am! I'm—I'm fucking furious!" The swear was endearingly awkward in his mouth, and he was sounding less and less American by the word. "You took a terrible risk, and you didn't tell me, and then you almost got yourself hurt, and—"

"You took off! You left me! You were sulking because I made you come, and you've been in a shit mood because you haven't slept in twenty or thirty hours and you haven't eaten anything and you're living off those fucking pills, and it's all about some fucking game you're playing with Paxton, which by the way, don't fucking tell me there's nothing there, because the two of you clearly have some un-fucking-resolved shit going on, like, orders of magnitude of shit!"

The fury in Holmes's face was weirdly beautiful—all his defense mechanisms disabled, all the security measures forgotten, a vital passion animating every inch of those perfectly chiseled features. The corner of his mouth trembled like he wanted desperately to bite his lip, and then he gave in, and tears welled in his eyes. He rolled onto his knees, his back to me, every movement suggesting flight.

"H, wait!"

He stopped. For a moment, he knelt like he was about to launch himself to his feet and run. His body rose on each swell of his breath. Then he sat back on his heels, fists pressed to his eyes.

"I shouldn't have said that," I said. "I'm still—uh, full disclosure, I think I'm still high. Like, I'm definitely a little high. Which is probably why your hair looks like a golden swan and I want to touch it so bad." Ok, I hadn't meant that last part to get out, but again, definitely still a little high. "Please?"

His body was an arrow of perfect, hard lines, and he shot toward the door. "I can't be around you right now."

"H!" And then, proof of my utter dumbass-ishness, "Your coat!"

I scrambled after him, clutching the coat in one hand. By the time I got to the passageway, though, he was gone.

I looked left. I looked right. The corridor ran as far as I could see in the weak light. When Dawson had brought me here, I'd been so out of it that I hadn't paid attention to the turns. I tried to listen. In the distance, the party was still alive: a thrashing, growling thing with a pulse. There was a high note that kept going, and it sounded like a fast drill, but maybe that was only inside my head. No sound of retreating footsteps. Nothing to tell me which way Holmes had gone.

Without any better option, I turned toward the sound of the party—or, at least, I hoped it was the right direction. The weed was still messing me up a little. Now that the adrenaline spike had faded, the sense of clarity was going with it, along with the ability to hold my head up. I wanted to sleep, preferably for a week, and my steps dragged as I made my way toward the thudding bass and the occasional scream.

I passed a branching corridor, this one darkened, with the bulky shapes of conduit and pipes running overhead, when the sound of steps behind me made me pause. My thoughts ran in a clear line: he had been embarrassed of his display of emotion; he had needed time to recover; he had chosen a dark spot, somewhere no one would find him; and now he was ready to talk things out.

I turned, but too slow. I caught a glimpse of someone before the bag went over my head—someone who wasn't Holmes. The world went dark, and I smelled high-end cologne and the dank weed that must have still been clinging to me.

"Wotcha, bruv," Paxton said with what sounded like a smirk.

Then he kicked my legs out from under me, and I went down.

Chapter 15

Truth or Dare

He didn't knock me out or inject me with some super fancy drug. There were no terrorizing threats. He didn't need to. He had a bag over my head, and he held my arm and marched me along. A couple of times, I tried to pull away, took a swing. Once, he let me, and I smashed face-first into a scalding hot pipe. The next time, he kicked my legs out from under me. When my head cracked against the floor, the world went woozy, and it was all I could do to let him guide me, blind, through the maze under Walker.

By the time I was functioning again, I was somewhere else. I tried to take stock of my surroundings. I was sitting on something, my hands bound behind my back, and a quick check told me they were zip-tied. We were still in the tunnels; I was fairly sure of that because we hadn't gone up any stairs. But the sounds of Wintersmash had died completely. Even through the bag, through the musk of weed and whatever cologne was giving me a headache, the reek of moldering wool filled my mouth. When I rocked forward, the thin padding under me felt slick, and sagging springs almost gave way completely.

I had an idea of where we were, and panic was scaling the back of my brain. One of the old fallout shelters. They had beds and chemical toilets and old Cold War-era posters on how to survive a nuclear blast—yeah, good luck. Oh, and they had rats the size of Dobermans. Something moved, and a squeal startled me. I jolted upright, banged the top bunk that was above me, and fell back so hard that the springs did give this time, dropping another few inches.

Paxton laughed. "Settle down, bruv. You're all right."

"What the fuck are you doing?"

"Guess it's kidnapping, innit?" He touched my face through the bag, and I yanked away from his touch—only to hit one of the bunk's posts. He laughed again. "Easy, easy. Making sure your brains are still in your skull. Holloway's going to be proper mad as it is."

"Can you take this off?" I asked, and this time when he touched my head, I let him. "I can't breathe."

"You're breathing fine," he said absently. "Don't start thinking you're smart; I'd hate for things to get ugly."

"You kidnapped me!"

"No need to shout. And it's nothing personal, Jack. You're pretty as sin, and I bet you're a hell of a fuck, and I think we'd get along real nice. Proper friends."

"You're insane."

"Come on, it's only a game. Nothing's going to happen. Here, you want the hood off?" He bunched up the fabric and eased it back from my face. The room was dark except for a distant shell of light at the far end. It only hinted at the outlines of more bunks, metal cabinets, concrete that was pitted and stained, but it was still bright enough, after wearing the hood, that I had to blink and try to let my eyes adjust. That's why I didn't realize what he was doing until it was too late.

Paxton made a satisfied noise as the face ID unlocked my phone, and then he tugged the hood back down.

"You piece of shit!"

"Easy, bruv. You'll be fine; you've got my word."

I burst out laughing. The sound had an unraveled quality that bordered on insane. "He's going to kill you. You know that, right? He's pissed at me, but he's still going to kill you."

Paxton didn't say anything. His fingers tapped the screen of my phone. That's all—he didn't do anything else. But I could feel him grinning.

"H!" I screamed. "Holloway!"

"Jesus," Paxton said. "You've got a gorgeous mouth, bruv. I'd hate to stuff something in there you don't want."

"Holloway! H! I'm right here!"

Paxton made an annoyed noise. He cuffed me on the side of the head—not hard, but like he wasn't playing around either. "You're making it too easy for him."

"Don't flatter yourself," Holmes said. His voice came from the far end of the shelter, and he had shifted into full-on posh mode. At the sound of it, I tried to squirm to the edge of the bunk. The sagging springs made it difficult, and after a moment I gave up. He spoke as though I hadn't moved, saying, "You have an effective set of tricks, but once they're used up, you become predictable."

"Hello, luv."

"H, he's fucking insane. He grabbed me in the hall, and he's talking about a game—"

"Jack, be calm," Holmes said in that perfect accent. An emotion I couldn't totally recognize hardened his voice. "It's always a game, isn't it?"

Paxton chuckled. "Come off it. You like them as much as the rest of us. You're only sore because you never win. I did think you had me this time. When I couldn't find the drive, I have to say, I was impressed. But you made the same mistake you always do, Holloway. Heart on your sleeve and all that." Paxton's foot bumped mine. "He is pretty, isn't he? But I did think you liked them smart."

"Let Jack go."

"And you'll give me the drive back? Not good enough, luv."

"No. Let Jack go, and I won't hurt you."

Paxton's laughter was full and round with delight. "God Almighty, Holloway, he's really got his hooks into you, hasn't he?"

"I won't tell you again."

After a moment, Paxton said, "Nah. I think we'll play my game after all."

We had been here before; in September, when we'd confronted Margaret Moriarty. She had wanted to play a game, and the leverage she had used against Holmes had been me. I struggled to get up again, but the disintegrating mattress and the loose springs made it harder than it should have been. At least one of the springs had broken completely and was now poking me in the back. "H," I said as I shifted and squirmed, "don't do what he wants. Just go—if you leave, he's not going to hurt me."

"Maybe," Paxton said. "But maybe not. And Holloway can't stand not knowing. He loves secrets, does our Holloway. Loves them to death. Probably because he thinks he's got so many of his own."

"Jack." Holmes's words were surprisingly gentle. "Be still. You're giving him what he wants."

I wanted to see his face. I wanted to see his eyes, to judge the corner of his mouth, to know how close this was pushing him to that impossible limit the world seemed determined to test. I wanted to tell him I was ok, and what mattered now was for him to be ok too. That I'd be ok if he was ok. That was my whole definition of ok. But the part of me that wasn't bogged down with the leftover weed and exhaustion understood that Holmes was probably right, and so I gave up and lay back, trying to avoid the sharp piece of broken spring.

"Move back, Paxton."

"Luv." He said it with so much tenderness that a feral part of me raised its head to sniff the air. "Don't make this hard. It's a game; when it's over, we'll go back to the way things were, the way we always do."

Holmes's laugh startled me. "Do you believe that? Oh God, I think you do." Even under all that poshness, his voice annealed, hot and cold like the best steel. The next words were almost a shout. "You left me. There's no going back—"

"Hol—"

"You left me!" This time it was a shout. "You knew, and you left anyway." Paxton's silence had a strangely miserable quality that made counterpoint to Holmes's snuffly breathing. After a few moments, Holmes sounded more under control. "Move away from Jack."

"Sorry, luv. I am sorry. And one day, if you let me explain…" He trailed off, the words wistful. "But right now, we're both going to play the game. Because that's how it has to be."

Holmes breathed steadily. "Very well. I will try not to cause permanent damage—"

"If you take another step, I'm going to forward this one to the whole school."

Holmes stopped breathing—at least, that's what it sounded like. And then I remembered: my phone.

"It's a nice one, innit? That gorgeous cock in his hand? How big do you think he is?"

I squeezed my eyes shut, even though it made no difference in the hood. Blood rushed to my face until the skin was hot enough to crackle. Oh my God. Oh my fucking God. How stupid was I? How incredibly fucking stupid had I been?

Sometimes I didn't see Ariana all week.

Sometimes, we messaged.

Her parents wouldn't let her have Snapchat.

I thought I'd deleted them but—

"Or this one," Paxton said, and his voice changed as he read from the phone. "'What were you thinking about the last time you jerked off?' Do you want to know what he told her?"

"Enough," Holmes said, the word gravelly, almost inarticulate.

"H, don't do it," I said, but tears filled my eyes and wet the hood, making the fabric cling to my face. The humiliation. Not just of the pictures and the things I'd said, but that Holmes, of all people, had to know. "It's—it's stupid. It doesn't matter. You don't have to do anything. Let him send that stuff; I don't care."

"He's sweet," Paxton said and nudged my foot again. "Not much of a liar, and doesn't know you at all, but sweet."

"What is the game?" Holmes asked. His voice wasn't much clearer.

"No, H—"

"Shut up!" Holmes snapped.

My face stung. I squeezed my eyes shut and tried to swallow the noise in my throat.

In a more normal voice, although still marked by that unfamiliar huskiness, he asked, "What is the game?"

"Truth or dare," Paxton said quietly.

There was a strange sound I didn't recognize, and then I realized it was Holmes laughing—barely audible, nothing more than a breath.

"Which is it, luv?"

"Truth."

"Is he your friend?"

The hesitation lasted only a beat. "Yes."

"Is he your best friend?"

His silence drew out longer this time, and the word was frayed when he finally said, "Yes."

"Good job. You're doing so well."

Holmes's voice shook as he said, "I will never forgive you for this."

Paxton made a soft, distressed sound, but his voice was as easy as ever when he asked, "Did you miss me?"

The silence was a wound. I knew Holmes. I'd slept with him (only slept). I'd eaten with him. I'd watched him skate on addies, and I'd watched him come down. I knew when he was pissed off, when he was tired, when he was hungry because he always forgot to eat. I knew he liked Double-Doubles from In-N-Out more than any human being should. I knew that he was something more than me, something vast and wonderful that I could only touch the edges of. But for someone like me, the edge was enough—just a glimpse was enough. And, more importantly for right now, I knew what he sounded like when he'd been hurt, the quality of his breathing, because I'd hurt him in a way few people ever had. Which was why, in those rare midnight hours when I could be honest with myself, I knew it was better this way, as friends. Because I didn't deserve him.

All that passed through my mind in a heartbeat. And then, the decision to kill Paxton Adler crystallized in my head.

"Or you can ask for a dare," Paxton said, the words approximating kindness.

Holmes's labored breathing continued.

It was like someone had flipped a switch in my head. The tidal flow of adrenaline surged through me, and my brain lit up. This ancient bunk, the broken springs, the zip ties. Of course Paxton had used zip ties; he was easy breezy, he was chill, he was all gritty savoir-faire with a huge swinging dick (we'd learned savoir-faire in Mr. Scholz's unit on world lit).

But the thing about zip ties? If you work custodial, you use a lot of them—they're amazing for all sorts of fixes; you can use them for pretty much anything. And if you use a lot of them, then you know they're only plastic. And you know that if they're too tight, and if you put pressure on them—especially with something sharp—they'll snap.

"It's too much, Hol," Paxton asked—sympathy with the bottom dropped out. "Say you want a dare."

Clothing swished; I pictured Holmes shaking his head savagely. I knew that sound, that movement, that look.

"Every day," Holmes said, the words thick but clear. "Until I wanted to die."

Paxton breathed out slowly; it was the only sound in the room.

When he started to speak again, I moved—shifting my position on the bed, trying to find the broken spring that had been jabbing me in the back. The rotting mattress slipped under me, and the springs let out a muffled noise. But whatever messed-up game Holmes and Paxton were in, they were too deep now to notice. Fine. Let them mind-fuck the shit out of each other. They could keep on doing it right up to the point where I bashed in the back of Paxton's skull.

"Do you love him?" Paxton asked.

The noise Holmes made wasn't a laugh, but it sounded like one. It was despair tinged with something else—the void of something bottomless. "Dare."

Paxton made a tiny noise—that bullshit compassion, with a hint of understanding, maybe even acknowledgment.

I found the spring. It sliced the heel of my hand, but I barely felt it. Forcing my wrists apart, I made the zip ties tighten until the plastic was stretched as far as it would go. Then I bore down on the broken spring, forcing the rigid plastic against the edge.

"All right," Paxton said. "How about a kiss?"

Holmes's silence had a stuttered shock to it. "What is this? Who put you up to this?"

"Answer the question, then."

"You were always selfish, but never cruel."

"It's a kiss, that's all."

Holmes was silent. "I'm sorry, Paxton. I'm sorry that someone is making you do this. You will regret it for a long time."

For the first time, Paxton's voice took on an edge. "The only one who's going to regret anything is your boyfriend; he won't want his friends knowing he likes his balls sucked."

"I will offer once to help you. Whatever they're using against you, you don't have to do this."

"Fuck off, luv. Go—go fuck yourself." His voice was barely controlled when he barked, "Either answer the question, or take the dare."

"Very well. The dare."

"Come on, then. And no funny business, Holloway. I know your tricks too, and whatever you try, it won't be fast enough to keep me from hitting send."

"No," Holmes said. "No tricks. I am sorry, Paxton. Even after everything."

"Do you know why you lose?" Paxton asked, his voice nasty in a way I hadn't heard before. "Do you know why you lose every time, Holloway? You focus on the wrong thing, let yourself get distracted. Like now."

The plastic split. The zip ties broke. My hands came free.

Another time, I wouldn't have had a chance. It was awkward, getting up from the sagging bunk, and the springs creaked and groaned. But I had a moment of opportunity when Holmes and this psychopath were totally fixated on each other. Paxton must have realized what was happening because he started to turn.

My knee should have caught him in the balls.

Instead, the blow connected mid-thigh. Paxton grunted, more annoyance than pain, and his next move was one that I'd seen plenty of times sparring with Holmes—and that I was never fast enough to block. His elbow snapped toward my head.

Before it could connect, though, Paxton grunted and staggered and spun to bring Holmes into his field of view. The three of us made the points of a triangle: Paxton with his hands up, favoring his side where Holmes had landed a blow; Holmes in that loose, liquid stance I associated with kill mode; and me, focusing on the cans of food storage racked against the wall, wondering if I could brain Paxton with some dehydrated eggs.

Paxton lunged at me, and I saw Holmes's mistake too late. He moved to intercept Paxton, obviously intent on protecting me, but Paxton pivoted at the last moment. Instead of the punch he'd been telegraphing, his leg came around in a tight arc and swept Holmes's feet. Holmes crashed into me, and we both went down on the sagging bunk. Springs made a metallic racket as we tangled with each other.

With an inarticulate cry, Holmes levered himself up. Paxton's footsteps beat a retreat, and a moment later, Holmes sprinted after him.

It took me longer to get free of the broken springs and slimy mattress.

Let's not discuss exactly how much longer.

Paxton had dropped my phone in the fight, so I recovered it and made a solemn vow never to sext again. Or only with one of those apps that automatically deletes the photos. And only if I really, really liked the other person. I'm talking true love. That's me, a bona fide romantic.

I took off after Holmes and Paxton, but after a minute of sprinting through the maze of corridors, I gave up. I'd lost them before the chase had even started, and there was no point pretending otherwise. The party was still going, and I dragged myself toward the sound. The phone said it was past two in the morning, and although I'd slept off some of the weed, the night had drained my reserves: Dawson, then the argument with Holmes, and the fight with Paxton. I wanted to find Ariana and get the fuck out of here.

But I couldn't find her. I stumbled through the party, the multicolored lights making the room spin, the music hammering at me so hard that I felt each pulse like it was pushing me off balance. I recognized faces, some of them; a lot, though, I didn't. I thought I spotted Glo, and a wave of drunk white boys broke over me as I tried to fight my way to her, but by the time I got through the crowd, she was gone. Or hadn't been there before.

Ok. I tried to think through the haze. Where would they go? Emma and Glo and Ariana. The athletic center, so Ariana could brush up on how to beat the shit out of me? Or had she gone home; it'd been hours since I'd seen her. Maybe she'd tried to find me, discovered I was even more worthless than she'd realized, and called it a night. But this was Ariana we were talking about. She loved parties, and she'd been excited to see how the other half did it—even though that meant grudgingly forgiving me for being a shitty boyfriend. She wouldn't have gone home, not until the party burned itself out. But she wasn't at the party. Which meant she was somewhere else.

Elementary, my dear shithead.

The best I could come up with was the possibility that they'd gone back to Emma and Glo's residence. I knew the tunnels connected to Butters Hall, where the girls lived, but I wasn't sure exactly how to get there. I started in what I hoped was the right direction.

The sounds of the party faded behind me—first to a muted roar, and then to a buzz that settled at the base of my skull, the same high-wire tension as the sound of ballast in fluorescent lights. And then it seemed like that sound was enormous, so loud it was blocking everything else out. I tried to focus on finding my route and not having one of my infamous green-out panic attacks. Slow breaths, I told myself. Hand on the wall. Yes, your legs are definitely still attached to your—um, I wanted to say knees? On the walls, people had scribbled cryptic directions and, occasionally, even drawn arrows. My fogged-up brain did its best to decipher the instructions as I shambled toward (I hoped) Butters Hall.

At first, I thought the noise was a variation on that high-pitched static in my head. But then part of me recognized that it was too different, too irregular. High-pitched, yes. But unsteady. Broken. And filled with something that the animal part of me recognized, even stoned, as terror. The sounds were coming from ahead of me; if I'd been going in the right direction, which was a big if, then I was close to Butters Hall. Maybe a girl had snuck down here to get some privacy to cry herself out. Maybe the best thing to do would be to ignore it, to get into the residence hall and—I hadn't thought this part through yet—find Emma or Glo without waking up every other girl and getting myself arrested, expelled, and possibly murdered in the process.

But, my brain said.

I cocked my head, trying to detect where the noises were coming from. Then I turned and started toward them.

When I came around the corner, following those high, terrified sounds, I stopped. It was a small room, with what looked like an out-of-service antique boiler with a soggy plywood barrier crumbling around it. Aston leaned up against the wall; his eyes were half open, and although he was the one making the noises I had followed, he didn't look conscious. Dawson lay on the floor, blood pooling around his head. I went to him first: no breathing, no pulse. I checked Aston next—broken fingernails, marks on his face and neck, one eye a constellation of broken blood vessels. He'd been in a fight, and it had been nasty, but he was breathing.

Digging out my phone, I stumbled to the closest stairs to get service and call the police.

Chapter 16

Stuff

The representatives of the Utah County Sheriff's Department interviewed me at home. As a courtesy, I guess. After all, Detectives Rivera and Yazzie and I were good friends.

At four in the morning, Rivera wore a Dodgers t-shirt under a shearling-lined trucker jacket, which was so unreal that the whole thing felt like a dream. Yazzie wore jeans and a tee too, but she managed to make it look professional. She was one of those white ladies with a sharp chin and a no-nonsense bob, the kind you didn't want to mess around with even if they were wearing jeans and a tee. Her square glasses looked like they needed cleaning.

"Let's try it a different way," Rivera said.

I groaned. My head was killing me, every inch of my body ached, and being seriously stoned was clearly giving way to an epic hangover. Plus, I'd been through this a million times already—first with the deputies who'd responded to the call, and then with Rivera and Yazzie after they'd gotten there. Now we were doing it again, after they'd done whatever it was detectives were supposed to do at a murder. Look at things, I guess. Talk to other people. And then do it all again. They'd been kind enough to assure me that Ariana was ok and had gone home, but my gratitude was wearing thin.

Dad gave me a warning look, but he ruined it by yawning and scratching his buzzed gray hair.

"When did you meet up with Dawson and his friends?" Rivera asked.

"I didn't meet up with them. I was talking to Aston, and Dawson and the other guys showed up."

"What time was that?"

"I don't know. Eleven? Eleven-thirty? We hadn't been there long."

"And how long after that did you and Dawson go off together?"

"We didn't go somewhere together." My face heated, and I tried not to look at Dad. "We just, you know, were walking, and we ended up somewhere."

"Walking," Yazzie said. "And talking."

The silence sharpened to a point.

"Jack," Rivera said, and his tone added, *Come on.*

"We already went over this!" The words came out louder than I intended. "That's the last time I saw Dawson. Then Holmes and I hung out; he didn't want to be around anybody because he doesn't like parties. Or people, actually. Then he left, and I went to find Ariana. Instead, I found Dawson. I called you. That's all."

"But you placed that call at two thirty-seven," Yazzie said. "That's a lot of time between when you met up with Dawson and his buddies.

The prickling in my face intensified. "I told you: I fell asleep."

"You fell asleep," Rivera repeated. "With Holloway Holmes."

"Not with him."

Dad rubbed his eyes.

"We were fucking," I said. I didn't know where the words came from, but they had a kind of gut-punch quality, like someone had knocked the wind out of me and the words came with it. "How about that?"

"Jack," Dad said.

"Were you having sex with him?" Rivera asked.

I met his eyes. "What if I was?"

"Jack!" Dad barked.

"You didn't answer my question," Rivera said.

"I fell asleep." I enunciated each word clearly. "That's all."

"Are you sexually involved with Holloway Holmes?" Yazzie asked.

"Excuse me?" Dad asked. "That's my son you're talking to."

"Mr. Moreno—" Rivera began

"No. If you want to ask him questions, fine. But I don't need you coming in here, trying to scare him or—or whatever you're doing."

"No," I said. "I'm not. We're not."

"Jack," Dad said, "they know that. They're trying to rile you."

Rivera's dark eyes fastened on me. It was like someone closing a hand around my throat. He knew; he'd been with me, those days after Holmes had been shot. He'd driven me to the hospital. He'd waited while I'd sat with Holmes, held his hand. How could he not know?

"If that's all—" Dad began.

"We talked to Rowe," Rivera said. "Do you want to reconsider what you told us?"

In the silence, the wind howled up the canyon.

"I want to talk to them alone," I said without looking at Dad.

It took him a moment. "What?"

I stared at my hands.

"No," Dad said.

I leaned forward, rubbing my knees.

"Absolutely not," Dad said. "This is serious, Jack. In fact, I think we should have a lawyer—"

"Fine." The laugh escaped me like the words had: the sense of something forcing its way free, whether I liked it or not. "Dawson wanted me to—" For a dizzying moment, I almost said *suck his cock*. It would have been like falling, to say something like that out loud. "—to do stuff." I cleared my throat. "Sex stuff." As soon as I heard it, I knew how it made me sound: like a child.

"Did you want to?" Yazzie asked.

"Hold on," Dad said.

I pushed my hair back.

"Jack," Yazzie said.

"Hold on," Dad said again, more loudly this time. "What are you saying? He wanted you to do stuff?" His voice got louder. "What are you talking about?"

"Mr. Moreno," Rivera said.

"No, I didn't want to." I was scrubbing my knees now. "I wasn't thinking clearly. I was—something was wrong with me."

"Did Dawson give you something?"

I remembered the shot that someone had pressed on me while we'd been toking, and my head came up too quickly. I tried to say, "No," but I saw it in Rivera's eyes.

"We're going to need a sample, Jack," Rivera said.

"Rowe and H stopped him," I said, dropping my eyes to the floor between my feet. "Nothing happened."

"We're still going to need a sample." Yazzie's voice was kind as she added, "I'm sorry, Jack."

My vision blurred, and I breathed through my mouth and blinked rapidly.

"I don't understand what's going on." Dad rubbed the stubble on his jaw. "He gave you something? He wanted you to do something? Why would he—" He shut his mouth so hard that his teeth clicked. And then, in a different voice, he said, "We want a lawyer."

"Mr. Moreno—"

"No, this conversation is over. If you think Jack did something to that boy, if you think what happened was—was revenge, or some kind of terrible accident—"

"We don't think Jack did this," Rivera said. "But we're pursuing all lines of inquiry."

"What about that boy, Aston? He was right there, wasn't he? Jack said he looked like he'd been in a fight."

"Mr. Moreno—"

"Or what about that truck?" Dad said. "Somebody shot at them yesterday, right? Did you even think about that guy?"

Yazzie and Rivera shared a look, but before I could process it, Rivera turned his attention to me. His voice was different when he said, "Jack, I need you to do your best to remember: was Holloway Holmes with you the whole time?"

I didn't understand the question at first. "What?"

"Holloway," Yazzie said. "After he and Rowe found you, did he leave you alone? Even if it was only for a short time?"

I remembered waking. I remembered his coat under my head, and then sleeping again. Had he been with me? I thought so, because when I woke the next time, my head had been pillowed on his stomach. But—

My head snapped up. Rivera's dark eyes were waiting for me.

"H didn't do this."

"Answer the question, please," Yazzie said.

"You're crazy if you think he did this. He couldn't do something like this. He wouldn't."

"He's an incredibly dangerous young man," Rivera said. "You know that better than we do, I think. He's attached to you. He's protective."

"What does that mean?" Dad asked. "What do you think you're saying?"

"I was there that night," Rivera said in a low voice. "I saw what he did."

What he did was save my life, I wanted to say. What he did was stop Aston and Burrows from murdering me. All I could get out was "H wouldn't do something like this."

But I remembered the boy named Nick at Hewdenhouse, and Holmes saying, *I did something precipitous.* And I remembered Holmes's anger when he'd caught me in Aston's room, the tundra of expression on his face. *Are you frightened, Jack? Are you scared of me?*

I shook the thoughts off, set my jaw, and met Rivera's gaze. "H didn't do this. And if you think he could, you're out of your mind."

"Do you know where Holloway might be?"

"What do you mean?"

"You understood the question."

"He's missing? You can't find him?"

"Jack," Yazzie said, "why don't you make a list of all the places Holloway might be?"

Round and round we went like that. It was hard, keeping the story straight, making sure I didn't say anything about Paxton, or about the blackmail, or about everything else that led in a scarlet thread back to me and my never-ending stupidity. And it was harder because I kept thinking about Rivera saying, *He's attached to you. He's protective.* And Holmes, his voice detached in the way I had come to recognize as the sound of him hurting the most, *I did something precipitous.*

The sun was coming up by the time Rivera and Yazzie left—and yes, with a sample. Bundled in their coats, their faces unreadable, they both looked tired, beaten down by the long, frustrating night. Rivera's last glance at me was considering and, to my surprise, on the verge of compassionate. Then Dad shut the door, and I couldn't decide if I'd imagined it.

The three-quarters fridge chugged, filling the air with that faint, burnt smell. Light came in low and oblique, dusting everything with silver. There hadn't been much black left in Dad's stubble, but it looked totally gray now. He had lines I'd never seen before.

"I'm sorry," I said.

He rubbed his eyes again.

"Are you getting a migraine?" I asked.

"What they said about you, about that party—" He stopped himself. "I am so disappointed in you. I don't even want to look at you." But he dropped his hands anyway. "Go. Get out of here."

"Dad, it was a party. You said you wanted me to go—" I stopped at the look on his face. It was the way he looked at strangers. "I mean, something terrible happened. It's not like I knew—"

"Stop talking. Did you even think about what this might do to us? Drugs, Jack. What the hell were you thinking? Going down into the tunnels, getting drunk, passing out, that's bad enough. But what if Headmaster Cluff orders a drug test? If they search the cottage, are they going to find something?"

I didn't say anything.

"I cannot believe you. We'd be out on our asses, Jack. I cannot fucking believe you." Dad shook his head and took a deep breath. His voice was buckled down when he added, "Go to your room."

I opened my mouth. The look on his face made me close it again, and I turned for the hall.

"You're grounded. You don't leave this house until I say you can."

It was everything. The way my body felt after the shit Dawson had given me—not to mention the shit I'd loaded up on myself. The long, disorienting hours in the tunnels. The feel of Dawson's hands on my waistband. My head in Holmes's lap. Paxton saying, *How about a kiss?* Not knowing where Holmes had gone, or where Ariana was, or if they were ok. Finding Dawson. The way Dad had said, *What are you saying? What are you talking about?* Like the closest I'd ever come to the truth was incomprehensible to him.

"Sure," I said as I started down the hall. "Until you need me to run an errand, or pick up your meds, or help you dig a trench, or clean the west-side bathrooms because you can't get there today, or buy groceries, or do one of those task-app jobs so we can pick up an extra forty bucks. I guess I'll be in my room until the next time I have to carry your fucking water."

"Hey," Dad said.

A ringing noise filled my ears; I wondered if I'd blown an eardrum at Wintersmash.

"Get back here," Dad said.

I kept walking.

"Get your ass back here and say that to my face."

Outside, the rhythmic steps of joggers came on the asphalt, and someone laughed—the sound startling and clear in the morning stillness.

Dad started after me.

I didn't run; I was proud of that. But I did slam the door, and I was less proud of that. I pushed my chair under the handle and threw myself on the bed.

A moment later, the door rocked open and caught on the chair.

"Open this door!"

I rolled onto my side, back to the door.

He slapped the door. "Jack!"

I pulled the pillow over my head.

He slapped it three more times—three hard, staccato beats, and in between, his breaths sounded like explosions. Then his steps hammered toward the front of the cottage, and a moment later, the door crashed shut.

Drawing the pillow tighter around my head, I held on as long as I could. Then I started to cry.

Chapter 17

Migas

When I woke up, the light was different, and someone was knocking at the front door.

I rolled out of bed. I was still in my flannel and jeans and, yes, somehow, one Cortez—the other had been kicked off mid-sleep, and a quick scan didn't locate it. My mouth tasted like dick, and not in the good way, and my head was pounding. For about twenty seconds, I stood there and thought about collapsing onto the bed again.

But the knocking continued.

When I got to the front door, Ariana was there. She had showered and changed and, presumably, slept, and in a hoodie and yoga pants, she looked the way she did most Saturday mornings. If it still was Saturday morning.

"Is it Saturday morning?" I croaked.

"Barely," she said. She gave me a once over, and then she smiled, and I had no idea what to make of that smile. "Rough night?"

"You have no idea. Ariana, about last night, I'm really sorry—hey, come in—" And I shifted to make room. "I'm really sorry—"

She stepped inside, eased the door shut behind her, and said over me, "Jack, your dad called me because he was worried. Actually, he sounded pretty upset."

"My dad called you?"

"So, you officially have permission to take me to get migas. Only I'm driving, so I'll be taking you."

"How did he get your number?"

"Go get ready." She smiled that totally incomprehensible smile as she sat and folded her legs under her. "And for once in your life, don't take forever."

I brushed my teeth. I did a quick underarm scrub and applied fresh deodorant. I looked in the mirror and despaired.

"Don't start with your hair, or we won't get there in time for migas," Ariana called from the living room.

I gave it a quick try. And then just a little more. And then I thought maybe, if I was quick, there was time for a shower, and I could start on my hair from scratch.

"Time's up," Ariana called.

One more quick fix. Ok. Two.

Then, before I left the bathroom, I texted Holmes. Ok, a series of texts:

Are you ok?

Call me.

Please.

I'm lowkey freaking out.

Then I paused, telling myself I might stop there and then trying to figure out who I was kidding. The last message said: *I'm worried about you.*

"Is this how men feel when they pick up their dates?" Ariana asked as I reached the living room.

I gave up on the remaining Cortez and pulled on my Stan Smiths. "Is there a right way to answer that?"

"No," she said with that bright smile.

We went down the canyon in her little green Geo, and the fact that it was still in operation long after the Human Rights Commission had banned all people everywhere from driving Geos was a sign of: a) Ariana's determination to be independent; and b) her dad's skill as a mechanic when he wasn't drunk or fired for being drunk. It sounded like we had a lawnmower sitting between us, and every bump shot me up from my seat and cracked my head against the roof. Normally, when Ariana drove because I couldn't cadge or steal the truck, I bitched solidly the whole ride. Today, I kind of enjoyed it. There's nothing like smashing your face against the window while you've got a hangover hammering against the inside of your skull.

El Mexsal was a strip-mall establishment, wedged between a transmission shop with a Spanish-language sign and an off-brand, Spanish-language Western Union. It was hard to see any of it, though, because of the skyscraper-sized, rotating, illuminated sign for Freedom Car Wash, which featured an abundance of stripes and stars and red, white, and blue. Inside, the tables were chipped, and the chairs were cheap and stackable—the kind with splitting vinyl seats and trapezoidal backs. Gumball machines. Toy machines, the kind that dispensed junk in little plastic balls. Pepsi coolers with bottles of Modelo on the bottom shelf. It smelled like cilantro and onion and hot pork, and '80s Latin pop was playing in the background—not my usual, which mostly consisted of Dad's grunge CDs, but Selena was still dope.

Ariana sat, and I got us each a Pepsi, and a waitress came. We both ordered migas. The lady had mile-high hair and looked sorry for me, which, you know, was nice. When she left, it was Selena again, interrupted only by the hiss of the bottle as I unscrewed the cap.

"You wish it was Nirvana," Ariana said. "Don't you?"

"It's ok." Then I shrugged. "Who knows? Maybe 'Lithium' is up next."

That made her laugh. I liked making her laugh. It was one of those things I was unexpectedly good at, like making waitresses feel bad for me, and stumbling onto dead bodies, and fucking up everything real and good in my life. My dad. Holmes. Exhibit A was currently opening her Pepsi.

She stopped, her knuckles white against the cap. "Jack, I'm sorry about last night. That must have been horrible."

The music switched to someone I didn't recognize.

I said, "Are you kidding me?"

"I never should have gone with Emma and Glo. If I hadn't, I'd have been with you when—" She sounded like she was going to cry. "I hate that you were alone."

Staring at her didn't help me make sense of what was happening, so I said, "If anyone is going to apologize, it's me. I can't believe I left you alone for that whole party. That was—that was stupid, I guess. I should have been with you. I asked you to go." Too late, I realized what I should have said first: "I wanted to be with you."

"Yeah," she said slowly. "And I wanted to go with Emma and Glo." She waited, as though I might say something, and then, like someone explaining something, said, "To make you mad."

The best I could come up with was, "Uh…"

"Well, I was still mad at you. Am still mad at you. But, like, suspended mad because this is so awful, and I can't be mad at you while you're going through this."

I drank some Pepsi. It was cold and sweet, and the caffeine helped, a little, with that hammering inside my skull. "But you went to the party with me."

"Well, yeah. Because how was I going to show you I was mad if I didn't go? Plus, it was the rich kids, and you know I've always wanted to go to a party like that." She laughed. "It was fire, actually. Even though it got weird with Emma later."

I knew the Emma comment was the important part, but I couldn't let go of another bit. "You went to the party because you were mad at me?"

GREGORY ASHE

"Yeah."

I rubbed my face.

She laughed again. "Have you seriously never dated anyone before?"

I kept rubbing my face. Saying, *Not anyone as complicated as this*, but I thought I might get a Pepsi bottle in the eye if I did. "No. I mean, hooking up and stuff."

"Ok, well, I'm mad."

"Suspended mad."

I got a tiny smile for that. "Suspended mad," she said. "And I'd already done the thing where I didn't answer your calls and texts, and that wasn't fun anymore, so I decided to make my point in person. And I couldn't do that if I was avoiding you, right?"

"No," I finally said. "I guess not."

"So, I had to go to the party. Plus, I wanted to go. Like I said."

"Uh huh."

In the kitchen, a cook shouted something in Spanish, and somebody shouted something back, but it all sounded good natured and relaxed and ordinary, and everything at Walker felt like something happening in another world.

"And you're mad at me because I screwed up on Thursday."

"Well, you screw up a lot. But yes, Thursday was the breaking point."

I drank some more Pepsi. "Did my dad make you take me to migas so you could break up with me?"

She burst out laughing. She was still laughing when the waitress came with our food, and the laughter made the waitress smile and look at me, and for some reason, I started fumbling with my silverware and trying to tear the little paper band that kept it sealed. When I finally got it open, the waitress was laughing too, and she patted Ariana's shoulder as she walked away.

I forked some migas. Savagely.

"No," Ariana said when she'd finally finished. "I'm not breaking up with you. But I am—I don't know. Worried, I guess. About you, specifically, right now. Your dad told me someone shot at you, Jack, and you—you freaked out. And then, last night, finding that boy. And I know you—you have some stuff in your past. And I'm worried, you know, that you aren't ok, but because you are a boy, you aren't going to talk to anyone."

"And because I'm dumb."

She smiled with the corner of her mouth and took my hand. "I already said you were a boy."

I poked the migas some more. I thought about what Rivera had said, the horror in Dad's voice, the questions that he refused to accept the answers to. My voice was lower when I asked, "What else did he tell you?"

"Nothing, really. You know, that you found that boy. About the shooting. He's worried it's going to be like September, but it's not, is it?"

I shook my head. "He didn't say anything else?"

"No. Why? What happened?"

I hesitated. Then I told her a little: Dawson drugging me, passing out, Holmes's disappearance and the police's suspicion that he might have killed Dawson.

She didn't ask why Holmes would have done that, and I didn't know what to make of it. All she said was, "Are you all right?"

"I'm fine. Just, you know, a worse hangover than usual. What about you? I tried to find you."

Ariana frowned. "It was...weird. I mean, most of the night was fun. Emma and Glo are nice, and we had a good time dancing." A tiny giggle escaped her. "They wanted to know all about you."

I knew better than to ask. That's why I said, "What did they want to know?"

She giggled again. "Oh, you know. Girl stuff."

Since I had zero idea what that meant, my brain supplied all sorts of horrifying possibilities.

"Of course, I made them talk too. They're both totally in love with the same boy, even though neither of them will say it. You can tell from how they look at him. To be fair, he's super cute."

"Rowe?"

"You know him?"

"He's not that cute."

Ariana's laugh sounded shocked, and then a huge grin exploded on her face.

"He's not," I said. "It's the beard, that's all." If anything, her grin got bigger, so I decided to take advantage of the opportunity to say, "Did they say anything about a guy named Aston Young?"

"Emma's ex?"

"So, they did talk about him."

"He sounds like a piece of shit. He's been spreading all these stories about her, about stuff they did together, but it's bullshit. Emma said they never had sex together. She got super upset about it, actually. She said he's making the whole thing up."

Which was what I'd say, of course, if Paxton decided to repeat certain choice phrasings from the texts I'd sent Ariana. What I said aloud was, "Because he's gay."

Ariana made a noncommittal noise. "Maybe, but she didn't say that."

"Trust me, he's definitely gay."

"Oh, I know. He's very pretty."

"He's not that pretty," I said before I could help myself.

This time, Ariana's laugh sounded much more knowing. "Anyway, that was most of the night. Dancing. Drinking. Trying to talk over the music. These stupid boys kept coming up to us, and we kept having to get rid of them. We definitely had too much to drink. So, you know, migas."

I did know. Migas were a miracle cure for hangovers—for me, anyway, and apparently for Ariana as well. Scrambled eggs, tortilla chips, salsa, avocado, beans, carnitas. You could have it without all that extra stuff, just the eggs and chips and salsa, but then, you could also choose to drive a Geo. I forced myself to take a bite instead of pushing the food around on my plate.

"But it was weird?" I asked.

"Yeah. Glo and I were, you know, drinking. But Emma was getting stupid drunk. I don't know how she was still on her feet after a couple of hours. Then, they got in a big fight. I couldn't hear what they were saying because the music was so loud, but they were mad. Emma pushed Glo." She stopped and shook her head as though she still couldn't believe it. "And then she grabbed my arm and said, 'Ariana will go with me, then.' And she pulled me after her."

"Where'd she take you?"

"I don't know. That place—you know how it is. But we walked for a while, and after the first few minutes, we didn't see anyone else. I started to get a little freaked out. I mean, not as freaked out as I should have been, because of the shots, but still a little freaked. It's cold down there, and it's quiet, but there are all these noises." She stopped again, and I looked down and realized my migas were gone and my stomach was gurgling contentedly. "Finally," Ariana said, "we got to this hallway, and she told me to wait."

"For what?"

"For her. She said she'd be right back."

The clatter of flatware, of plates skidding on laminate tabletops, of voices mixing Spanish and English—it all swelled to fill the void.

I shifted forward in my seat. "And?"

Ariana shook her head. "I feel crazy saying this. I mean, Emma is so sweet, and last night, she and Glo went out of their way to make sure I had a good time."

The silence lasted longer this time.

"Ariana, what happened?"

"She was arguing with someone. And then—and then someone shouted. It sounded like they got hurt."

"Who?"

"I don't know. A guy. I don't know." She shook her head. "I think it was a guy."

"Ok."

"And Emma came back, and—and she was freaking out. Not like a panic attack, but—I don't know how else to describe it. She was talking nonstop to herself, and none of it made any sense, and she couldn't stop moving. It was like watching someone have a breakdown. And—" Ariana stopped and ducked her head. "And she didn't have her gloves."

"Huh?"

"Those gloves, the cute gloves she was wearing? She didn't have them, and her hands were all messed up—knuckles split and bloody, cuts and scratches." Ariana laid her fork down and touched her eyes.

"Hey," I said. I shifted around to the seat next to her and put my arm around her. "Hey, hey, it's ok."

"It's not ok. She was so messed up, Jack. And I didn't know what to do, so we went back to the party to find Glo, only Glo was gone, and then everything went insane because people found out that boy had been killed—I mean, I still don't know how we got out of there. Followed the crowd, that's all. I kept thinking if I fell, if I got lost—" She cut off with a choked noise and touched her eyes again.

I crushed her against me. She didn't fall apart crying (unlike me, exhibit: earlier that morning), but she sniffled for a few minutes and then wiped her eyes with the napkin. When she'd finished, she patted my leg, and I eased up.

"Here," she said with a wet laugh and pushed her plate of (seriously inferior) migas toward me. "I can't."

"Do you think Emma killed Dawson?" I asked.

"If you don't eat them, they're going to go to waste. I can't eat anything."

"Ariana."

She held the napkin under one eye and stayed like that for half a minute, shaking her head. Then she said, "Maybe. I don't know."

"Did she say anything about Dawson?"

Ariana shook her head. But she said, "I don't know. They talked about how his parents were poor now. They lost all their money, I guess? Nobody seemed to know how."

That explained some of it, I thought. Nobody had been blackmailing Dawson; he'd been broke because his parents were broke, which was why he'd tried to buy from me on credit, why he'd hit everyone up for money, why he'd sold his clothes and his shoes and his PS5.

"Did you see this?" She unlocked her phone and tapped it a few times, and then a video began to play. It was of Aston bottoming, his face red, only inches from the camera, his eyes unfocused as he moaned and rocked under each thrust. She stopped the video and shook her head. "The links showed up this morning. They're all over; if you know anyone at Walker, you've seen those videos. Emma said—she said how would he like it. How would he like it if someone had videos of him?"

I tried to think. Someone had released the videos, which didn't make any sense. Why not continue the blackmail? Unless you hated Aston so much that it wasn't about the money.

"Did she say anything about where she was going, or why she wanted you to go with her, or—"

"She didn't want to go alone. She was scared; she wouldn't have gone if she'd been by herself. And I don't want to talk about this anymore."

"The voice, the one you heard shouting, like maybe they got hurt—"

"Jack, I said I don't want to talk about it."

She didn't shout, but her voice was louder. Across the room, the waitress gave me a death look from under that mile-high hair. So much for feeling sorry for me.

"Ok," I said quietly. "I understand. But the police need to know—"

"Know what? Nothing happened."

"They need to know something happened, even if we don't know what it was."

"Fine. You can tell them."

"No—"

"Nothing happened, Jack. It was weird, that's all. I shouldn't have said anything."

I thought about asking again. I figured the waitress might decide to intervene personally at that point, so I didn't. I was still thinking about what to do when I caught myself plowing through the rest of her migas and, distantly, realizing I felt much, much better. Almost human, in fact.

"Do you want to come to my family Christmas party?"

I was so caught up in my thoughts about why Emma might have murdered Dawson, or, if she hadn't killed him, what she might have been doing, that it took me a beat too long to answer. "Uh, yeah. I mean, maybe? Do you want me to?"

Ariana let out a noise that was part annoyance and part amusement. "It's only my family. It's not a big party, you know. I mean, it's a lot of people because my family is big, but it's not like we invite everyone from church or our neighbors or anything."

My phone buzzed. The message from Dad said, *I'm sorry I lost my temper. When you get home, I'd like to talk.*

When I looked up, Ariana was watching me. I put my phone away.

"Well?" she asked.

"Yeah, sure."

She smiled.

"If you want me to," I said.

"Jack."

"What?"

"Never mind." And then, as though she couldn't help herself, she added, "Joslyn told me I was rushing things."

I sat a little smaller in my seat. I unscrewed the Pepsi's cap and screwed it back on. "What do you want to do?"

"I said never mind."

"I think your mom and dad might not be super impressed if you bring home a guy who's a part-time custodian and, like, drives his dad's truck and stuff."

"I'm in high school. They don't expect me to bring home a dentist."

"What if Joslyn says something about the party? What if she starts talking about how I, you know, get stuff for the kids at Walker?"

"You're worried my parents—who, by the way, are worthless, and you know that, and that's why I'm moving out as soon as I turn eighteen—are going to be upset that my boyfriend deals weed?"

I didn't particularly like the weed-dealer label, since it made me sound like I had scraggly facial hair (which, let's be fair, it was still coming in) and like I was a useless stoner (which, let's be fair, last night had pretty solidly proved). What did I want to be called? Reverse blackmailer? Although reverse wasn't quite right—

"Are you serious right now? I'm trying to have a conversation with you, and you're not even paying attention."

"Sorry," I said automatically, "whatever Dawson gave me—"

But I stopped because a zigzag path lit up in my brain. Last night, Paxton had said two things I didn't understand. At the time, still coming out of whatever I'd been drugged with (not to mention the rum and the weed), I hadn't been able to focus on them. Now, though, I heard them again, and I still didn't understand. Paxton had said something about a game. About Holmes having found the external hard drive, and now it was time for the next part of the game. That suggested we'd been right in part—Paxton's appearance, and the subsequent blackmail against Aston, weren't a coincidence. But it also didn't make sense. Holmes hadn't found anything; I would have known if he had. In fact, one reason he'd been so pissy last night was because he hadn't found Paxton—or anything else that might help us wrap up Aston's blackmail.

The other thing Paxton had said, the thing that felt like a puzzle piece falling into place, was that Holmes (and, by extension, I) had been focusing on the wrong thing. I didn't know what that meant, but together, I thought I had a few ideas.

First, someone else now had the blackmail videos—the external hard drive Paxton had mentioned. Paxton didn't have them. Holmes didn't have them. Therefore, somebody else did. (Jack Moreno, everyone. Boy genius.)

Second, someone had killed Dawson, and I was pretty sure it had happened while Paxton and Holmes and I had been playing patty-cakes. The most likely possibility was that Dawson had been part of the blackmail operation. He'd needed money, if what Ariana had told me was right, and he knew Aston would pay—had paid, already, when he'd been blackmailed earlier that year. He'd had access to Aston. With a little help from Paxton, it wouldn't have been hard to hide a few cameras, record a few fucks, and go from there. It wasn't a stretch to believe that Dawson had decided to branch out on his own, stolen the hard drive from Paxton, and tried to collect from someone. Aston, most likely. In the process, he'd gotten his head bashed in.

But if someone had killed Dawson because of the blackmail, why release the videos? Maybe Dawson had some sort of backup plan—a contingency. If he didn't call a friend, the videos got posted. Something like that. The problem with that was, well, it was way too smart for someone like Dawson—who had been the kind of criminal genius to blackmail his own sexual partner and then meet someone in person for payment. Hell, the only reason he'd thought of telling us that he was being blackmailed too was because we'd given him the idea by asking. For a moment, it all seemed so...repetitive. Unbelievably so. We'd done this all before—the blackmail, incompetence, the stupid meet-ups—and now it was happening again.

But what really troubled me was the third thing. The third thing was that something else was going on. This game, maybe, the one Paxton had mentioned. Or maybe something else. Something we hadn't been paying attention to. Because we'd been distracted. No, that wasn't quite right. Because, I was starting to suspect, we'd allowed ourselves to be distracted.

And, worst of all, Holmes was missing.

"I'm really, really sorry," I said to Ariana. "I've got to get back to campus."

Chapter 18

St. Holmes

Instead of the cottage, I asked Ariana to drop me off in front of Walker Hall.

She said goodbye and smiled. I said goodbye and smiled. When I leaned in for a kiss, she bent to check her phone, and, like a good boyfriend, I pretended not to notice. I got out of the car, and she drove off so fast the Geo sounded like a string-trimmer. Like a good boyfriend, I pretended not to notice that too.

Or maybe like a not-so-good boyfriend.

I headed to Baker House, and the first thing I noticed was that campus was empty. Saturdays were a free day, and although it was winter, you'd usually see at least a few Walker kids out and about—going to the athletic center, or the dining hall, or the library, or a study session, or to chill in someone else's residence hall for a few hours.

Not today. Today, the campus looked abandoned. The redbrick, pseudo-Victorian buildings huddled under shawls of ice, and the walks were gritty and water-dark where Dad had salted them this morning. The only signs of life were the plumes of vapor rising into a cut-glass sky.

Lockdown, I thought. Which would make my job more difficult.

At Baker House, I went in through the basement. I grabbed a mop and bucket from the utility room and carried them up the central flight of stairs. Life hack: people don't actually see custodians. It's the next best thing to being invisible. Not that it mattered; the building was unnaturally quiet, and I didn't see anyone on my way. Apparently, Headmaster Cluff had been serious about this lockdown.

My first stop was 221. I used my spare key to open the door, let myself in, and stared.

Holmes's room had been destroyed. I'd seen something like this before—the mattress pulled off the bed and slashed, the side of the desk staved in, the closet emptied and the contents mounded on the floor. The last time someone had done this to Holmes's room, it had been his father's work—Blackfriar had been looking for Sarah Watson's laptop. But it couldn't be Blackfriar again. He'd found the laptop, and he'd done something—corrupted the data, maybe? (Jack Moreno, everyone, hacker wunderkind)—to ensure Holmes couldn't access it. As far as I knew, there was nothing else Blackfriar wanted, aside from his lifelong efforts to break his son down and mold him into a high-functioning sociopath. Traditional family values, and all that.

So, who had done this? And what were they looking for?

It was obvious that Holmes wasn't here, so I turned to open the door, but then something caught my eye. A piece of paper on the top of the desk. At first, it looked like one more of the papers that had been scattered around the room, but when I looked more closely, it was clear that someone had left the paper on purpose—there was enough of a suggestion of space around it, as though someone had cleared a spot, to make sure this wouldn't be overlooked.

A single line of words crossed the page in small, blocky handwriting. *Where is it?*

It meant nothing to me, but goose bumps spread across my chest anyway. Whoever had written it, their rage came through in the handwriting—at the question mark, the pen had left a jagged tear in the paper.

Where was what?

And the more important question was: if Holmes had something important, something valuable, why hadn't he told me?

There were a million answers—it was something I didn't need to know about, or it was something from before he had met me, or it was something he wanted to protect me from (which would have been an annoyingly Holmes thing to do). At a rational level, I knew that Holmes was entitled to his privacy, and that it meant more to him than perhaps anything else—probably because most of it had been stripped from him as a child. Paxton had been right, even if he'd been cruel, when he'd said Holmes loved secrets. Holmes had told me once, when we were first getting to know each other, that every Holmes had their obsession.

But none of that made me feel better. I was sick to my stomach as I stared at the page. Paxton had said we'd been focused on the wrong thing, and I got the feeling that this—whatever it was—was why we'd been distracted.

I didn't let myself think through it. I found Holmes's overturned trash can. It had a clean liner, and based on a quick look, I judged Holmes hadn't had anything but a few pieces of paper in there when the room had been tossed. I shook out the liner, and then I used it to pick up the scrap of paper on the desk. After wrapping it as tightly as I could in the plastic, I tucked it into a pocket of my coat.

Then I left.

Mop and bucket in hand, I went up to the third floor. My spare opened Aston's door just as easily, and it looked how I remembered it. The U of U flag, the massive TV, the PS5, the rumpled blue bedspread. It still smelled faintly like his body spray, and a little like weed. No Aston. He'd already been high when I'd seen him at Wintersmash, so he must have pre-gamed here. Nerves, maybe. Fear. It was easy to let myself follow that path, to imagine Aston's mixture of terror and fury when he realized Dawson was behind the blackmail. If I was right, and if Dawson and Paxton had been working together until Dawson branched out on his own, then Dawson was stupider—or more desperate—than I'd realized. The same kind of stupidity or desperation that might make him meet someone face to face to get his payout. And, instead, get himself murdered.

But that was a lot of abduction, to borrow Holmes's word, for a little skunky, day-old weed fug.

I did a quick search, checking the dresser and the desk and the closet, but I didn't find anything. I took out my phone and called Aston. It went to voicemail, so I left a message, and then I texted him: *Call me.*

It was possible the police still had him in custody. It was more than possible; it was probable. They might be questioning him about the night before. They might be waiting while he was treated for his injuries—for all I knew, they hadn't even had a chance to talk to him yet. Or they might have arrested him, and he was being processed. I didn't have a number for Camdyn or his parents, and while I could probably find one, I decided that could wait. If Aston was charged, I'd hear about it. And if he wasn't, he'd call me. Or not. Whatever happened, it would tell me something.

I was starting to let myself out of the room when I stopped. I hadn't found anything interesting. So, I did another quick search, and I still didn't find anything interesting. And that made me wonder: where was the blackmail note? Where were the photos? I didn't think Aston would throw them out without asking me or Holmes.

My phone buzzed with another message from Dad: *Are you home? We need to talk.*

I left Baker, but I kept the mop and bucket. The invisible janitor act— you have to see it to believe it.

First, I tried Woody Hall; I wanted to see Dawson's room. But two Utah County Sheriff's Department cruisers were parked outside, and the building's door was propped open like they were tired of unlocking it every time they went in and out. Invisible janitor or not, there was no way I'd be able to get close to his room, not while they were still processing it. As I watched, a deputy came out of the building. I recognized Deputy Fitzgerald—he'd kind of arrested me when I'd found Sarah Watson's body—and he was still a sixty-year-old string bean who hitched up his trousers every few paces. He was carrying a cardboard box, and I would have given my left ball to know what was inside it.

He glanced around, so I lowered my head and shouldered the mop and kept moving. Dawson's room would have to wait.

Butters Hall, where Emma and Glo lived, was as deathly quiet as Baker House had been. I did my disappearing act, walking through the basement, up the stairs, and onto their floor. I tried Emma first; I wanted to know about Wintersmash. I wanted to know all of it, including—a vicious part of me thought—why she'd gotten Ariana involved.

When I knocked, though, no one answered. Down the hall, a distant thumping rhythm suggested Cardi B. I knocked again, and still nothing. I thought about the depths of shit I could get into for using a key I wasn't supposed to have to go into a girl's room. But Holmes was missing.

I unlocked the door, opened it a crack, and called, "Emma?"

No answer.

Inching the door open the rest of the way, I braced myself. But the room was empty. I hadn't been here before, and I took a moment to examine it: the bedspread printed with an androgynous Asian boy's face, the black-and-white photos on the walls (lakes, mostly—apparently, she had a thing for lakes); a black velvet Elvis, only he was wearing a clown costume. She had a pile of athletic shoes near the door. A lot of guys seem to think girls are incapable of smelling bad; I've got a pile of shoes if you ever need to prove them wrong.

I moved through the room carefully and—more importantly—quickly. I checked the most common hiding places. I tried not to think about the fact that I was touching her underwear. I found an unopened Juul in the desk and four tubs of a creatine mix in the closet. So much for contraband. The velvet Elvis was the closest thing in the room to a crime. There was no sign of where she might be—or why she might have ventured out when the school was on lockdown, so I left myself out into the hall. Sweat was prickling at my hairline.

When I went down the hall, I could make out the music more clearly. Not Cardi B. Megan Thee Stallion. The explicit version (of course).

This time, I lucked out. Glo cracked the door and looked out at me.

"Hey, can I talk to you?"

She looked like she'd been crying: her skin was sallow, her eyes red and hollowed out, her nose puffy. "About what?"

"Last night."

"What about last night?"

"Well, lots of stuff. Emma—"

"Emma and I aren't talking."

"Ok. Um, why?"

"She blocked me. On everything." Glo said it like a challenge.

"Ok," I said again. "What happened?"

"She lied to me, and I called her out on it. She was such a—" She had to work herself up to it. "Such a bitch!"

"Glo, what did she lie about?"

"I don't want to talk about it."

"This is important."

"I said I don't want to talk about it. I don't know where she is. I don't know where she went. I don't know why she went psycho. We're not friends anymore, get it?" And then, through a sob, "I was trying to help her!"

"I know you were. I know—"

But Glo shut the door. Something thunked the door, like maybe she'd hit it with her hand.

"Glo?" The Meg Thee Stallion song ended, and in the silence, my voice sounded too loud. I tried again in a whisper. "Glo, you've got to tell me what happened last night."

Nothing.

The radiator down the hall began to knock and clank.

"Glo. Glo!"

Still nothing.

I said, Fuck it. I tried my key.

It worked, of course. But the door didn't open more than a quarter inch.

"Glo," I said through the opening. I tried the door again, and it caught on whatever was wedged under it. "Glo, please, H is missing, and somebody killed Dawson—"

"I'm going to call the police! If you don't go away, I'm going to call them right now!"

I stopped pressing on the door. "Don't call the police."

"Go away, Jack!"

"Don't call the police, please?"

She didn't say anything, but a moment later, the door slammed shut again.

"Hello?" someone asked from the next room. "Is someone out there? I thought we were supposed to stay in our rooms?"

That seemed like my cue, so I jogged toward the stairs, the mop sliding along my shoulder.

It took me a few tries to find Rowe; I hadn't been to his room before either, so I had to check the lobby of the boys' residences until I saw his picture on the wall in Hunt. When I knocked on his door, he answered it. His eyes were red like Glo's, his face blotchy, and he sniffled as he looked at me and, without seeming to realize it, pulled up his shirt to wipe his face.

"Hey, man—" I started.

"You can't be here," he blurted. "Jack, you've got to get out of here."

I took a beat to center myself. I looked at him more closely. Then I said, "What happened?"

He was gripping the door like he might shut it, but then he shook his head. His face twisted, and in a broken voice, he said, "I really screwed up."

I let him have that moment. Down the hall, a boy shouted something that sounded like "That is so unfair!" Then nothing. No radiators knocking. Silence settling down like snow.

When I started into the room, Rowe fell back. His movements were stiff. I'd seen him move before, and he had the kind of easy comfort in his own body that most natural athletes show. But now he hobbled, every movement drawn up and shortened. He ended up on his bed, head down, hands between his knees.

His room was what I would have called comfortable and Holmes would have considered panic inducing: clothes on the floor, clothes on the back of the chair, clothes on the bed. There was even a shirt hanging off the windowsill. He had a Vikings poster on one wall (football, not the TV show), and his dresser was cluttered with photos of a family that looked equally hale and hearty and Scandinavian. A quick glance made me think they all might actually like each other, and I wondered how Rowe had gotten himself here.

He looked so miserable on the bed, his shoulders hunched, his breathing pained, that it was hard to remember in the moment how much bigger than me he was. But it didn't matter how big a puppy was; they were still a puppy.

"What'd you do?" I asked.

He gave another miserable shake of his head and pressed his fingertips to his eyes. Definitely a puppy, although most puppies didn't have beards that some grown-ass men would have envied.

"Who hurt you?" I asked.

His head came up, and the shock in his face almost made me grin in spite of everything. I wondered if this was how Holmes felt all the time. It was probably how he felt when he was dealing with me.

"How did you—" Rowe stopped himself. "I was serious, man. You've got to get out of here. You should—" He had to gear himself up to say it. "You should call the police."

The silence sounded like white noise in my ears.

"Did he break anything?"

After a moment, Rowe shook his head, but he touched his side. "I don't think so."

"You probably need to see the nurse. You might need X-rays."

He shrugged.

"Let me guess," I said. "Anywhere your shirt covers."

After a moment, I got another of those hesitant nods. Rowe dropped his eyes again, and tears filled his voice as he said, "He used his belt." He flinched as he shifted his weight. "Like I was a little kid."

I wanted to say something about how different the world was. How one day, you were sure you knew how it worked, and then something happened—someone ran your car off the road, or someone caught up with you in a dark alley, or someone took off their belt—and you realized that everything you'd taken for granted was only the face of the world, and when you peeled it back, you found out you didn't know anything. I thought about telling him that you could get your balance back, kind of, but that it wasn't ever the same. But I didn't say any of that.

I sat on the bed, offered a mental prayer to St. Holmes, patron saint of awkward boys everywhere, and put an arm around Rowe.

He started to cry. Not huge sobs, but he was shaking a little. And then, through the tears, he said, "Man, you can't," and then he cried harder.

Fortunately, handkerchief-alternatives were abundant. I passed him a Rowe-sized shirt that featured, for some reason, a banana having a party on the beach and the words BANANARAMA ST. CROIX, and he held it against his face. After a while, he wasn't crying anymore.

His voice was thick when he said, "Are you ok?"

I laughed. "Am I ok?"

He twisted the poor Bananarama banana. "I mean, you know. Last night."

"Oh. Yeah. Uh, thanks for that, I guess. I mean, yes, definitely, thanks. It was just, uh—"

For the first time, I got a smile. "The kind of thing we should never talk about again?" Rowe asked. "Like this thing right now. Like, never talk about them again ever?"

"Yes, Jesus Christ, thank you."

The expression widened to a grin, and Rowe wiped his face again. He was still smiling when he pulled the shirt away.

"That shirt is dope, by the way," I said.

"It was for my grandma's eightieth." Rowe flattened the shirt on his knee. "Emma hates it. Well, Glo does too, but Emma really hates it."

He'd left that conversational door wide open, so I nudged it a little more. "So, the three of you."

"Man, don't ask." He dug his thumbs into the corners of his eyes and laughed. He sounded ninety percent genuine and ten percent out of his mind. "I mean, we were just friends. There aren't a lot of people, normal people, up here. You know?"

That felt like the understatement of the century.

"And now, it's, like, horrible because they're best friends, and—" He stopped himself.

"And you're in love with both of them?"

He looked up at the ceiling. "It's not just me, though. If it were just me, they'd both tell me to get lost. Or they'd get in a fight, and one of them would hate the two of us. But we, like, love each other." So fast he almost bit off his tongue, he added, "Not sex, man."

"I got you."

He rolled one massive shoulder. He scratched his beard. "So, like, what do I do?"

"Excuse me?"

"You're smart. I've got these two amazing people, and, I don't know, I'm not poly, so I can't say, 'Hey, let's all three of us be together,' but I don't want to hurt either of them, and some days it's so freaking hard, man, that I swear my brain is going to explode."

Not to be unkind, but I didn't think Rowe suffered tremendously from a risk of an overfull brain. But the question was genuine, and he was clearly distressed.

"That's hard," I said, and then the words were coming, and it was like I'd been waiting for someone to let me say them. I couldn't have held them back if I'd tried. "There are a lot of reasons people get together. Some of them are good. Some of them are bad. Sometimes people change. Sometimes what seems right at one point isn't right later on. And yeah, obviously it would be ideal if you could go up to one of them, and you could say, 'I like you. You're super cool, and you're so smart, and you've made so much of your life already, and I know you're going to keep being amazing. You've been there when I needed someone. But also, there's this other person, and I don't even know how to describe what I'm feeling, but it's—it's something else, and I can't pretend it's not happening, even if the other person doesn't feel the same way.'" I was hot, and my skin felt too small for my body. I flapped the hem of my shirt.

"I guess," Rowe said dubiously. "I mean, that's not exactly my situation, but I kind of see what you mean."

I barely heard him. I had a hand up under my shirt, holding it away from my body to get air, and my belly felt sweat slick and feverish.

"So, like, H is fire, right?"

The question startled me out of my—what? Low-grade panic attack? I tried to focus on Rowe.

"He threw me like it was nothing," Rowe said.

"Yeah, I was there, remember?"

"Yeah, but did you see it?"

"Yes, Rowe. I saw it."

"He's super cool."

"No, he's not cool at all. He is seriously the biggest dork you will ever meet in your entire life. He uses a ruler on his shoelaces sometimes."

Rowe's face changed.

"No," I said.

He smiled. "It's cool, man."

"No, it's not like that at all."

"My little bro is gay. I love gay guys. I'm the best with gay guys."

"Ok, well, one, that actually makes a weird kind of sense, and two, H and I are just friends."

Rowe waited a moment. He gave a doubtful nod, but he was still smiling.

"We're friends," I said.

His smile brightened. "Ok, man."

I considered slamming my head in the door a few times.

"But, like—" Rowe said.

I groaned.

"—if you're ever not just friends, you know, it would be freaking fire. Emma and Glo and I talked about how cute you two were for, like, two hours."

"Rowe," I said, and then I stopped because I honestly didn't know how to respond to that comment.

He nodded. "It's ok, man. Life's complicated. I just wanted you to know we're team Hack. That's your celebrity couple name."

Slamming my head in the door a few times wouldn't be enough, I realized. I needed one of those anvils the coyote was always dropping. I needed to stand directly under one and let it happen. The peace that only Acme brings.

"Rowe," I said, making my voice more serious, "what happened?"

He frowned.

"Yeah," I said. "You're cute, and you're sweet, and the puppy-dog eyes probably get you out of a lot of trouble. But I didn't forget. Tell me who hurt you."

"He was a guy," Rowe said. His shoulders were already hunching again, and he twisted the Bananarama shirt in his hands. "I don't know."

"White? Latin? Black?"

"White."

"Your size?"

Rowe hesitated. "Maybe not as tall, but close."

"Long hair or short?"

"Short."

"Brown hair or blond?"

"I don't know. Brown. No, maybe blond. I don't know."

"That's ok." It sounded like Kazen Bates. "What was his voice like?"

"Mad. Like he was really mad."

"Ok. Now you've got to tell me what happened."

Rowe twisted the shirt until his knuckles were white. His breathing shortened.

"Hey, I saw H put you on your ass," I said. "And you saw me with my shorts around my knees while Dawson tried to get me to swing on his dick. We're officially friends, unless you hate the Dodgers, and then I'll have to kill you." He didn't smile, but some of the blankness in his eyes went away. "A lot of people don't know what to do when shit happens. Even if they've had training. Even if they're strong and smart and kickass. It's ok."

"He walked into my room. Just walked in. And I lay on the fucking bed and stared at him. I—I froze." A single, disbelieving bark of laughter escaped Rowe. "By the time I sat up, he had already crossed the room. He flipped me, and he had something—tape, I guess—and he wrapped my wrists. And my brain was telling me to scream or shout, but I couldn't do anything, and then he put tape over my mouth." Rowe was crying again, but he didn't seem to realize it. "He hit me like you said, where my shirt would cover it. My stomach. My chest. My sides. With his fucking belt. I thought he was going to kill me, and I didn't know why, and I couldn't breathe cause of the tape, just through my nose, and I was crying so then my nose was all snotty, and I thought that's how I was going to die, because I couldn't get any air while he beat the shit out of me. When he finally stopped, he told me he was going to take the tape off, but if I tried to scream, he'd put it back on and we'd keep going. So, he took it off, and I didn't scream. I just wanted to breathe. I just wanted him to stop."

"Rowe, it's ok. You didn't do anything wrong."

"I did." The words were caught in a sob. "I really, really fucking did, Jack. And then you came here, and you were so fucking dope, and I'm sorry. I'm really sorry."

"What do you mean?" I asked. "What are you talking about?"

He stared down as he wrung the t-shirt between his hands again.

"Rowe! What did you do?"

"He wanted to know where a boy named Jack Moreno lived." He gulped, and I could hear the snot in his throat. "Jack, I am so sorry."

Chapter 19

Overthinking It

I ran across campus. No mop. No bucket. No disappearing janitor. Just me, and the razor wind off of Timp, and my Stan Smiths carrying me toward the cottage. My mind was playing a million nightmares, like cutting-room snippets from a horror fest: Dad shot; Dad stabbed; Dad with tape over his mouth, struggling to breathe, as Kazen Bates circled him, Kazen with a belt, hurting him in all the places we'd worked so hard to make better after the accident.

When I crossed the Toqueah, though I stopped. My breathing was tattered, exploding in huge white clouds, and my hands were shaking. I had to think. I couldn't run straight back there. I had to do this smart, the way Holmes would.

As the first surge of terror ebbed, the world began to come back into focus, and my thoughts with it. The creek babbled as it passed through the culvert beneath me. A bird—a falcon of some kind—was an ink stamp in the sky. The next breath of frozen air stung my throat and lungs. Ok, I thought. First things first.

I texted Holmes: *I need you.*

I didn't wait for a reply; either Holmes would come, or he wouldn't. Instead, I considered my options. Option one was to run straight back to the cottage. If Kazen were torturing Dad, or if he'd hurt Dad and then left, then time was the most important factor.

But, the other part of my brain said, if it's a trap, if he's waiting for you, then running straight home is exactly what he wants you to do.

And since both options were fucking terrible, I had no idea what to do.

I tried for a compromise. I scrambled down the slope to the bank of the Toqueah, and then I went north, up the canyon, slipping on wet stone and scraping my hands on the bark of cottonwoods. The Toqueah ran straight up through campus, which meant it was a way to move around without being seen. I'd used it before—once, memorably, the night Sarah Watson had been killed.

When I got close to the staff housing, I worked my way up the bank and stopped at the tree line. The staff housing was screened off from the rest of campus by a line of scrub oak and aspen and pine—when the trees were bare, you could make out the cottages, but most of the year, they were safely invisible. You know, so the students wouldn't be troubled by the existence of lesser folk.

By coming up the Toqueah, I gave myself a view of the staff housing without coming down the side street and making myself visible to anyone who'd been waiting. So, I took advantage of the opportunity to study the street. No black truck, like the one Kazen had brought up to Walker last time. No red sports car, like the one Holmes and I had seen at his house. My breathing eased, and mixed with the smell of the water came the scent of broken pine duff. I pressed my hands against my thighs, aware now that I couldn't feel my fingertips because of the cold.

After a few more minutes, I left the trees and jogged toward our cottage. The windows were dark. The doors were shut. That didn't mean anything; we never locked the doors, a policy I was starting to seriously reconsider. Dad might still be working. But he might be home, waiting for me. To talk.

For the first time since he'd texted me at breakfast, I wanted to know: talk about what?

The porch boards creaked when I crossed them, and the front door opened easily. The familiar warmth and sounds of home greeted me, and then a sour-body smell that made me stop in the doorway.

In the living room, with only the afternoon light slanting through the windows, he was an outline with a few highlights: the pink flush of his cheeks, a glint of cropped brown hair, the black bulk of the pistol in his hand.

I opened my mouth.

"Dad's sleeping," he said, and his voice wasn't what I expected—so soft that it approached a lisp. But mean, too. That's what Rowe had said, and I could hear the coiled-snake meanness in those two words.

I stood with my hand on the door. Sweat needled me under the arms, across my chest, down my belly.

Kazen stood. "We're going for a ride."

I still hadn't moved. The edges of the doorknob cut into my palm.

"You're overthinking it," Kazen said. "We walk down the street. We get in my truck. If you run, I'm not going to chase you. I'm going to walk down the hall, and I'm going to wake up Dad. If you shout, you're going to wake him up, and that's the same thing." His index finger slid from the barrel of the gun to the trigger guard. "You still overthinking it?"

My throat was too dry, so I shook my head.

"Ok," he said. "Here we go."

Chapter 20

The Thing about Duct Tape

He'd parked at the entrance to campus, so we walked together. I saw one person I knew, Mr. Thompson, who waved, and I nodded and hoped he wouldn't notice how jerky the motion was. Kazen held the gun low at his thigh. He'd shot at five teenagers in public, in the middle of the day. I didn't think he'd slow down for Mr. Thompson.

When we got in the truck, he taped my hands together.

"Behind your back, bitch," he said with a kind of weary disinterest.

Then he made me get down in the footwell. It would have been cramped under any condition, but with my arms bound behind me, I was wedged in. There was no way I could get myself out—let alone do it quickly—and I figured that was the point: I was trapped (and seriously uncomfortable) until he decided to get me out. As he started the truck and we rolled down the canyon, I tried to think about options. Even at a stoplight, I wouldn't have a chance of jumping out of the truck and getting away. Zero possibility of surprising him with an attack. And nobody would see me. He'd look like a regular guy driving by himself, so if—at some future point, after somebody discovered my corpse—the police tried to figure out how I'd disappeared from campus, everyone who saw the truck, anyone who might remember it, would remember Kazen driving alone. Maybe Mr. Thompson would remember, but by the time he realized he needed to tell somebody, it would be too late.

That left option number whatever-the-hell.

"You don't have to do this."

The engine rumbled.

More loudly, I said it again: "You don't have to do this."

We hit a rough patch in the pavement. The truck didn't bounce as badly as the Geo did, but it still clicked my teeth together, and a jolt ran from my bound arms to my shoulders.

"I know you think you're in a bad spot," I said. I tried to make the words sound calm, compassionate. I wanted to make a connection. Currently, though, the only thing I was making a connection with was the glove box. "I know you think you have to do this. You're trying to protect yourself. You think this is the only way."

His voice was almost as low as the sound of the engine; he still sounded tired. "You don't know anything about me."

"I know you're in an awful situation." I twisted, trying to get him in my line of sight, but all I did was jank up my shoulder. "I know what it's like. A little. I mean, my dad—I didn't think he cared, but now that I think about it, we never really talked about it. He never said that, you know? That he didn't care. I guess I was wrong." My head bounced as we went over a pothole. I closed my eyes. "It's not like he'll disown me. I mean, I don't think he will—"

"Shut up."

"If I tell him I'm bi, he'll probably just—I don't know. Hug me or something. But now I know it's going to be weird. Now I know it's going to be…bad. If I come home with a guy."

"Shut the fuck up."

"I'm saying I understand it's hard when what you feel and what your family wants—"

Over the sounds of the truck, I didn't hear him move, so I wasn't prepared when he grabbed my hair. He yanked, and I had to arch my back, my head moving with his hand, so that he didn't scalp me. A startled cry escaped me, and then, when he kept pulling, a second one, full of pain.

"I'm not like that."

"Ok!"

"What you're talking about, that's not me."

"Ok, ok, ok!"

"I told you to shut your fucking mouth!"

"Oh my God, I'll stop, I'll stop! Please, I'll stop!"

He pulled harder, and I felt some of the hair pull out, and this time I screamed. For one terrible moment, I couldn't move any farther, and he kept pulling, and I was sure he was going to rip more hair out of my head. Then he released me, turning the movement into a shove. My head bounced off the dash hard enough to make my eyes water, but the relief in my scalp was so great that I barely noticed. I slipped down into the footwell again, trying not to break out into tears as my brain started to catch up with my body and all the different agonies pressed to the front of my awareness.

The walls of the canyon were peeling back, more light filtering into the cab of the truck, when Kazen said, "You're going to help me get that Holmes boy. Do what I tell you, and nothing bad's going to happen to you."

We drove the rest of the way in silence.

When we got to Kazen's house, the garage door rolled up to the soft hum of the motor, and we pulled inside. The garage door went down, and as my eyes adjusted to the dim yellow light from the single bulb, Kazen got out of the truck and went around. He opened my door. My shoulders and back, arms and legs—they were all cramping, and the pain took all my attention. I barely noticed when he grabbed my arm and, with his other hand, my hair. He looked at me until I nodded that I understood. Then he applied pressure to my arm, helping me up from the footwell.

The freedom to move sent blood rushing to every inch of my aching body, along with a fresh wave of hurt. Kazen didn't give me a chance to slow down, though. He pulled me out of the truck, and it was either stumble along or get my hair ripped out. My legs felt soft, and as he marched me toward the door, my knees kept folding when I didn't want them to. I caught a whiff of his sweat and the smell of last year's grass clippings, a hint of gasoline, and then we were inside.

We crossed his kitchen to the basement stairs.

"You can go down yourself," Kazen said. "Or, if you try something funny, I'll throw you down."

I tried to nod, which was hard with him holding my head like that.

He released me, and because my arms were still bound, I crabbed sideways down the steps to keep my balance. He came with me, always one step behind, obviously still thinking I was going to try something. A hysterical giggle lodged in my throat. He and Rivera should be buddies. They could share conspiracy theories about what kind of shit Jack Moreno was capable of.

I only had a moment at the bottom of the stairs to take in shadowed outlines of the steel shelves. The now-familiar smell of lubricant and solvent and metal—gun smells, my brain said—met me, and then Kazen caught my hair and my arm again and marched me forward. At one of the doors that Holmes had inspected, he stopped and fished out his keys. He unlocked the door and gave me a two-step bum rush. When he released me, I pitched forward, landed on my knees, and rolled. The room was dark, and I had only an impression of space as I tumbled across the floor. My brain showed me another pressure plate, like the one I'd stepped on before. Only this time, there was no Holmes to disarm it, and I was moving too quickly to stop myself—

But then I smashed into the wall. I lay there for a moment. Dazed, I was dimly aware of the fact that I'd stopped moving and, somehow, hadn't exploded. Something moved above me, and Kazen's outline materialized in the dark. He crouched, patted me down, and took my phone and keys. He rolled me over, found my wallet, and looked through it. After tossing it aside, he got to his feet. He put one foot on my belly and pressed down hard.

"Don't give me a reason," he said.

The pressure eased, and the outline above me dissolved. Then the door shut, and the lock clicked, and after a while, Kazen's steps moved away.

Maybe it was minutes. Maybe it was a lot of minutes. I lay there, staring up at the dark, breathing. The pain in my scalp had faded to discomfort, and now that I wasn't human origami, the cramps had eased in my legs and back. But my arms and shoulders were killing me. I flopped onto my side and lay there for a while longer. Breathing. In the dark.

In the past, Holmes had always come for me—a few months before, when Shivers had hunted me down; then again with Dawson; and, of course, with Paxton. He had an uncanny ability to know when I needed him and, against all odds, to show up and kick ass. But hoping that Holmes would miraculously appear and save me wasn't what our guidance counselor would have called a self-actuating goal, which meant it was the equivalent of sitting on my ass. So, I sat up, wincing as fresh aches hit me.

First thing, I kicked off the Stan Smiths. Then, although it took some contortionist-level wriggling around, I brought my arms down and under my feet. With my arms in front of me, my shoulders could relax a little. I leaned against the wall to let the burn in my muscles die down. Then I went back to work.

The thing about duct tape is that everyone thinks it's amazing for everything—and to be fair, actually, it kind of is. But it's not perfect for absolutely everything, and if you do enough maintenance work, you start to figure out when duct tape is good and when you'd be better off with something else. Sometimes painter's tape. Sometimes electrical tape. Sometimes (shocking) no tape at all—my least favorite option.

And the other thing about spending all that time doing maintenance jobs? You find yourself doing a lot of jobs that require you to hold something in place with one hand while you try to get a strip of tape with your other. And that means using your teeth to tear the tape.

Saying I chewed through the tape is undignified and inaccurate. I nibbled. I did some light biting. I savaged the tape with my teeth sounds appropriately butch. And once I got a tear going, I could twist my hands

GREGORY ASHE

back and forth to spread the tear, and after enough of that, my hands were free.

Downsides: you lose some skin off your lips, and your mouth tastes like adhesive-slash-ass.

Other downsides? Ripping the tape off my arms meant losing some more skin and accompanying arm-hairs.

The important part was that I was free. My pulse was pounding, body felt warm and charged, and I was ready to kick some ass. Or at least get out of here and successfully run away.

I took a moment to examine the room. Like the one where Holmes and I had entered, the window was a horizontal slider that led to a window well. It was still afternoon, but the angle of the house meant that little sunlight reached the basement window, leaving the room only dimly lit. No pressure plate marked the floor, but I inched over to the window anyway, testing each step.

When I got to the window, I let out a breath. A wire ran across the bottom of the window. Another wire was connected to the latch. They both ran to a small gray block of what looked like (but most definitely was not) plastic.

Great. Another booby trap. Why couldn't he have used a pressure plate? Why did he have to change it up? But maybe this was like home decorating for prepper extremists. Showcase your arts and crafts for visitors by including a variety of deadly explosives.

The window was out—for now—so I collected my wallet and moved to the door. This was more in my wheelhouse. I'd had to fix my share of doors at Walker—when a kid busted the hinges, or when time had made them stick in the jamb, or when some asshole put his foot through a hollow-core. They weren't all that complicated.

Someone—most likely Kazen—had switched the door; normally, interior doors, especially in a home, opened inward. That meant the hinges were on the inside. Pop the hinges, and you could remove the whole door. This door, however, was hung to open out, with the hinges on the other side. I guessed that was an after-market change. It told me that, in addition to the fact that Kazen was crazy, he had planned on the possibility, at least, of holding someone captive. On the other hand, he hadn't planned enough to install a deadbolt, so I decided he was crazy with a dash of stupid.

I flipped through my wallet, waffled between my Albertson's card and my CVS card, and went with Albertson's. Back in September, Holmes had used a Café Rio card, which just went to show that he had absolutely zero priorities. The plastic was stiff with a little give to it, and after two tries, I got it between the door and the jamb. It was tight, and I had to slide the card up with short, hard jerks. As soon as it slipped between the latch and the strike plate, though, the door popped open. Fresh air wafted in with the smell of gunmetal. I rested my head against the jamb and took a few deep breaths.

For a minute, I stayed where I was, listening. Nobody shouted. No alarms went off. Nothing went boom. I nudged the door, and it swung open a few more inches. The basement's main room was dark, bulky with the outline of shelves. Nobody was aiming a laser sight at me.

I stepped out of the room and started toward a door across the basement. That was where Holmes and I had come in, and odds were good Kazen hadn't noticed yet that someone had sawn through the latch and disarmed his landmine.

When I was halfway across the basement, though, a high-pitched whine began. I stopped. A cold sweat broke out over me, and in that first moment of reaction, I stayed exactly where I was—I'd obviously triggered something. Then, after another second, realization caught up with me: it was the sound of a printer. The office must be right overhead, and the sound had carried through the ductwork.

I had to press my hands over my mouth to stifle another of those hysterical laughs.

Kazen's voice shattered the moment. "Yes, I got it." He was silent. His steps rang out in the kitchen, measured but hard. "Don't give me ultimatums; I'm not a child." More silence. "I don't know. I should tell you no. I should tell you it's too late." Another of those pauses. "I said I don't know. I'll see what I can do."

The silence that followed felt charged, a buildup of some kind of emotion that I could feel even in the basement. Then those heavy steps hammered across the floor, fast. I shrank back, turning toward the room I'd escaped. But before I could reach it, a door crashed shut, and a moment later came the unmistakable sound of the garage door rolling up.

He was gone.

He'd left.

I could walk out the front door.

Why?

That seemed to be an important question. Kazen had told me he wanted me so he could get to Holmes. (Stand in line, buddy.) I thought I could see the chain of reasoning there: Aston had told Kazen that Holmes and I were investigating the blackmail, and now Dawson was dead and Aston had probably been arrested and Paxton was in the wind, all of which Kazen would know if he'd been watching Aston as obsessively as those recordings on his computer suggested. Securing me and Holmes until he knew what was going on was understandable, even if it didn't seem particularly bright or, in this case, well executed.

But something had happened. Someone had called and sent him something. *Yes, I got it,* he'd said. And they'd demanded something. An ultimatum, Kazen had called it.

I looked at the door to my escape. I looked at the stairs that led up to the kitchen.

Jesus Christ, I thought as I started up the steps. Maybe everyone's right. Maybe there is something wrong with me.

The lights were off upstairs. The kitchen smelled like trash that needed to be taken out, and a scum of protein shake lay across the bottom of the sink. He'd taken apart my phone, and it lay in pieces on the counter. I replaced the battery and snapped the case shut and said a silent prayer until the screen lit up and it began powering on.

The dead eyes of the photographs on the walls followed me as I moved toward the office.

Several pieces of paper lay on top of the desk. Photographs of a house taken from different angles, focusing on a second-story window. In one picture, you could see the name on the mailbox: Young. I wondered for a moment why Kazen had printed the pictures out instead of looking at them on his phone. Old, maybe. Old people loved to print stuff out. Dad printed everything out on the printer in the maintenance office.

But when I got to the final page, I understood. It was a rough floor plan drawn by hand and showing two stories. Windows and doors had been marked in the printout, and in red marker, Kazen had added arrows outlining different possible paths through the home. In one of the second-floor bedrooms—the one the pictures focused on—he'd drawn a large, red A.

Shit.

I tried calling Aston. I got nothing again, but I left him a message: "Kazen just left his house, and I think he's going after you. He's got a map, notes. It's a plan. You've got to call the cops and tell your family to get out of there."

I hung up and tried again. Then I texted him.

Still nothing.

Maybe he was in jail, I thought. Maybe he was safe, getting processed.

But he wasn't. Someone had called Kazen. Someone had set this up for tonight because they knew Aston's family had money and influence, because they knew Aston would be home.

I tried Holmes. Nothing there either.

I wanted to scream. Something bad was going to happen. Was going to happen soon, since Kazen had left in a hurry, no matter what he'd said on the phone. And Aston wasn't answering, and Holmes wasn't answering, and if I called the police, I had no idea how to explain this mess.

Wait a second.

I found my best bud Rivera in my phone and placed the call.

"Jack—"

"Kazen Bates is going to kill Aston Young tonight if you don't stop him."

The silence only lasted a beat, and Rivera said, "Who's Kazen Bates?"

"The guy with the truck. The one who tried to shoot us. He's got it all planned out. He's going to break into Aston's house—his family's house, I mean—and kill him. Tonight. He just left. I think he's in his truck, but—" And then it hit me. "Oh my God."

"Hold on, hold on. This man, the one who shot at you—you know his name? And you're in his house? Where are you right now?"

"Send somebody to the Youngs'."

"Jack—"

I disconnected. I took a few pictures of the photos and the floor plan, making sure to capture the address inked in the corner, and then I ran to the bedroom. If Kazen were like most guys, his keys would be either somewhere in the kitchen or—

On his dresser, in one of those little organizer trays.

I snagged the keys and ran to the garage. The smell of gasoline and frozen concrete met me. The little red sportscar was still there—a Mazda MX-5. Fun to drive until it snowed; then it would be like sitting in a block of greased ice.

Since I had so many great options, I got in the car and started driving.

Chapter 21

That's Kind of Insulting

By the time I got to the Youngs' home in Heber and then buttonhooked back up into the mountains (per the GPS instructions), the sun had set. The sky was a cinder gray that hadn't quite turned black, and the pines were pencil sketches until the headlights touched them and they sprang into 3D. At least the roads were clear. The MX-5 had handled fine—a lot smoother than the truck.

My phone buzzed again in the cupholder. I checked the screen, expecting another call or text from Rivera. Instead, Dad was calling.

I slowed the car, and then I nosed over to the shoulder, close enough that I scraped the snow packed along the side of the road. The phone continued to buzz. If Rivera called him, he'd be worried. Afraid.

Of course, if I picked up, what was I going to say? Sorry you're scared, but I've got important shit to do?

I compromised with a text message: *Can't pick up now, but I'm ok. Call you soon.*

A text came through from him almost immediately: *Where are you?*

And then another: *Detective Rivera sent someone with a warrant to search your room. Call me right now!*

I wanted to close my eyes. I wanted to smack my head against the steering wheel. Off the top of my head, I could make a list: some fairly good weed, a lot of addies, condoms (not that those were illegal), unopened vapes (those were), this rare tentacle porn manga that Ty Bryce had paid me for but asked me to hold on to. After I got out of prison in thirty years, I already knew, Dad was going to make me have a super awkward sex talk.

Another text came through: *Jack, call me!*

I locked the phone and shoved it in my pocket.

It had been stupid to hide stuff in my room again; I should have learned my lesson. But I'd assumed getting caught up in a murder investigation would be one of those once-in-a-lifetime experiences. Plus sometimes it was really cold outside, and I didn't want to walk to the maintenance building if I had to get something from my stash. Of course, being homeless and jobless and unable to pay for Dad's meds was going to be a lot more inconvenient.

Pushing it all away, I tried to get my head in the game. Stop Kazen first; everything else later. I needed to get into the Youngs' home. And then I needed to—what?

I guess I could tell Aston. Or, maybe better, his father. But what would I say? I got kidnapped by your son's crazy hookup, and I think he's coming here to do something serious, although I don't know exactly what or when, but probably tonight.

Very convincing. Jack Moreno, Toastmaster.

First things first: get inside.

Farther up the road, cars were parked on the shoulder, which suggested the Youngs' guests had been forced to walk. I left the Mazda where it was and hurried up the hill. The cold stung my ears and the tip of my nose, and when I breathed, I tasted snow and pine sap. After a hundred feet, music reached me, and light showed through the trees.

When the house came into view, I shook my head. It was massive, even by Utah standards: gray siding with white trim, fieldstone accents, windows lit up like a gingerbread house. Something glittered in the air, and I realized it was starting to snow. I huffed a laugh, my breath clouding up in front of me. Of course it was starting to snow.

I stayed where I was for a moment, trying to gauge the best approach. A middle-aged white couple was making their way up the driveway ahead of me. When they reached the front door, they knocked, and it opened immediately. A white guy with no neck and, I guessed from his face, no sense of humor said something, and the woman handed him a piece of paper. He stepped aside.

Invitation only. Great. One of the perks of having Dad and Grandpa be big, important muckety-mucks at church, I guess, was you got to throw parties that were invite only. And I had a theory that No-Neck had dealt with his share of raving lunatics before—people who had to see Dad or Grandpa right now because it was an emergency. If I went up there, demanding to see them, telling them they were all in danger, I'd be lucky if all they did was slam the door in my face.

I cut up to the right, climbing over the bank of snow that had been plowed to the side of the road. It was slick underneath me, where it had melted and refrozen, but once I got past it, fresh snow crunched underfoot. I kept to the tree line. The glow from the house gave enough light to see by:

the blue-green of spruce, the reddish-brown of cedar bark, a shadow moving at the corner of my vision. I stopped and waited for it to move again, but after a minute, when nothing had happened, I started walking again. An animal. A rabbit. Or a—I don't know. A badger. Did badgers live up here? But it had definitely been bigger than a badger. And coyotes lived up here. And mountain lions.

Ok, so, I was going to get eaten by a mountain lion while trying to save Aston Young's life. That was probably karma.

I stopped at the side of the house and consulted the photos on the phone. Whoever had sent them to Kazen, they had focused on a second-story window on this side of the house. In theory, it would be a fairly easy climb to get on the roof of the porch and, from there, get to that window. The only problem was that tonight, the porch was crowded with people. Kerosene heaters hissed, a hint of their smell drifting to me, and someone in catering apparel was manning what appeared to be a hot cocoa station.

With one last glance for the mountain lion—nope, nothing—I reversed course. This time, I moved toward the opposite side of the house. The three-car garage looked invitingly dark, and although the downspout was ice cold, it was solidly attached. I took a few deep breaths, exploding each one out into the night—oxygenating the blood and, more importantly, psyching myself up. Then I grabbed the downspout and hauled myself up.

I made it on the first try—when I reached the garage roof, I hauled myself up, the shingles scraping my chest and belly as I dragged myself over the edge. Then I lay on my back, the snow melting in my hair, my breath glowing as it dissolved against the stars. My face was numb with a hint of heat behind it that made me think of sunburn, and even through the coat and shirt, my chest and belly felt raw. What are you doing, part of my brain asked. What in the world are you doing?

Instead of answering it, I flopped over and got to my feet. At least two inches of snow made the shingles slippery, so I moved at a diagonal until I reached the ridge of the roof. Ahead of me, several darkened windows on the second floor suggested access points. I scrambled toward the house proper, careful to keep myself centered over the ridge—a good idea, as it turned out, since my feet threatened to slide out from under me every few feet.

The rattle and creak of a storm door made me stop moving. Steps clipped against pavement, and the familiar sound of a vape reached me. Then the storm door rattled again. I recognized Camdyn's voice when she said, "You're going to freeze to death out here."

"I can't do this. I can't…pretend." That was Aston. "All those fucking faces smiling at me, like they don't know I'm all over the internet taking it up the ass." He let out a sharp cry and then, in outrage, "You made me drop my vape!"

"Watch your mouth."

"Fuck off."

"I'm telling you to watch what you say. Not everybody knows, but they will if you stand out here shouting about it."

In the silence that followed, the frozen air seemed to crackle. Finally, in a low voice, he said, "I'm so fucking sick of pretending."

"I know. A couple more years, though. You can do it."

The silence lasted longer this time. "I'm going to my room."

"Mom and Dad want us on parade tonight."

"Fuck Mom and Dad."

"At least say hi to the Smiths—"

But the storm door crashed shut, and Camdyn bit off the rest of the sentence. A few moments later, the door creaked once more. I counted to thirty before I started moving again.

The closest window was a vertical slider, double hung, and I wiggled it a few times and got absolutely nowhere. I had no tools. No plan. I was probably going to die of exposure if that mountain lion didn't get me first. The next window was farther down the roof, which meant abandoning the safety of the ridge. I sat and scooted slowly down the shingles, one hand braced on the second-story wall to control my speed. When I got to the window, I used the sill to steady myself as I stood. Another vertical slider, double hung. Even if I'd had a screwdriver, I probably couldn't have gotten it open. I gave it a shove, more out of annoyance than anything else, and the bottom sash slid up.

I stared. And then I decided not to overthink it. The window was open; that was what mattered. Maybe it was good karma, although I had no idea how I'd generated that. Maybe it was God; maybe he wanted to keep Dad and Grandpa Young safe, so he'd paved the way, or whatever you were supposed to say from the Bible. Whatever it was, I had a chance, so I hoisted myself up, wiggled through the opening, and landed hard on the other side.

I scrambled to my feet and shut the window. The thump from when I'd landed had been loud. Loud enough to be noticed? I wasn't sure, but I didn't want to find out the hard way. I had a moment to take in the room: even in the dark, I could tell it was an office, complete with a desk and club chairs and the smell of leather and wood polish. A door near me suggested a closet, and another door probably led to the hallway.

Maybe ten seconds had passed, and I was starting to tell myself nobody had heard me. That's when footsteps moved in the hallway.

I ducked toward the closet. The door was locked. I turned back to the window, and I made it two steps before the office door opened, and lights blazed to life. I put my back to the wall, my eyes still adjusting to the sudden brightness, my brain rapid-firing suggestions. Maybe I could dive out onto the roof. Maybe I could brain him with that bust of Jesus.

"Jack? What are you doing here?"

I took a moment to process that. And then to process the rest of it: Holloway Holmes standing in front of me, dressed in a knit blazer and a white button-up and dark slacks and polished wingtips, every stitch tailored to show off the perfectly worked lines of his body. Then I frowned.

"You realize that's kind of insulting," I said. "Right?"

Chapter 22

A Game Afoot

Holmes still hadn't recovered. He stared at me. The corner of his mouth trembled. And then he said, "Jack, you can't be here."

"You'd better shut the door."

He shut the door and leaned against it. It had been less than a day since I'd seen him; it felt like it had been months. He'd shaved. His hair was back to its Ivy League perfection, the color softer and burnished in the mellow office light. His jaw. His throat. Had I seen him in a tie before? It was distracting, but not so distracting that I didn't get an eyeful of the rest of him. When I got back to his face, I noticed the shadows under his eyes.

"You have to go," he said. "Now."

"It's nice to see you too."

He came across the room and took my arm. There was a slight tremor that might have been nerves—he was never comfortable with touching—but was more likely a compound of taking too much speed and not sleeping or eating or being human. "I can help you get back down," he was saying, trying to turn me toward the window, "but then you must run, Jack." Some of the English was slipping out again. That was even more distracting than the tie. He reached for the window, and the woodsy heat of him filled my lungs.

I squeezed his hand and, as gently as I could, detached it. When he slid the window up, I pushed it back down.

"Jack—"

"When was the last time you slept? Without a million addies running through your system?"

"You don't understand. Certain events have been set in motion—"

"You didn't sleep last night; I already know that. And I don't think you slept the night before. You must have slept a little, but I bet you were so wired that it was more like a crash and reboot." I turned his head. "Let me see—"

He knocked my hand away. His breathing quickened. "You aren't listening to me."

"I heard you; I don't care. Dawson drugged me. Paxton used me as bait. Kazen Bates kidnapped me today and pulled out some of my hair, and you know my hair is one of my top five best features. Everywhere is dangerous, H. Big fucking deal. I asked you a question, and I expect you to answer me."

"You expect me?" Yes, we were definitely getting the full English now. "You expect me?"

"Let me see—"

He knocked my hand away again. His voice was brittle when he said, "Don't touch me."

So, I touched him. Poked him, technically. In the chest.

He swiped at my hand, but I'd already pulled back.

"Jack—"

I poked him again.

He was slower than usual, but that's what happened when you never gave yourself a moment's rest.

I poked him again, and this time, he made a feral noise and grabbed my arms. He shoved me, and my back connected with the wall. The corner of his mouth was twitching harder. His eyes were bloodshot, the pupils like tiny lead dots.

"Enough," he said with that posh whip-crack of a voice. "If I have to, I will incapacitate you. Those are your options, Jack. Leave, or I will ensure that you remain safe, albeit slightly uncomfortable. For your own good."

"Interesting," I said. "When I want to do something for your own good, like make you eat three whole chicken tenders, you have a million excuses and protests and complaints about human rights and privacy and how it's your body and you know what's best. But when you—"

He made a choked noise, hauled me away from the wall, and slammed me against it. My head connected with the drywall this time, right where Kazen had torn out some of the hair. It was as much shock as pain, but I cried out anyway.

Holmes's face transformed. The color bled out of it, and his mouth opened, and his eyes widened. He dropped his hands from my arms, and then he reached out, and then dropped them again. "Jack, I'm so sorry!"

"That hurt, dumbass!"

"I'm very sorry. Jack, I'm so very sorry. I don't know—I don't know what I'm doing. I didn't mean to do that."

I glowered at him. I rubbed my head. I rubbed it a lot, but it wasn't that much fun because he looked so miserable. Finally I said, "Do I have a bald spot?"

"This medicine makes me reactive—"

"It's not medicine; it's speed, and you don't need it, and you definitely need to stop using it the way you have been. Check me for bald spots."

Holmes's mouth worked soundlessly several times. Then he inched around me. His fingers parted the hair on the back of my head, and his touch was light. He was trembling harder than before. "There is scabbing in several places, and the hair here is thinner than on the rest of your head, but to a casual glance, it does not look significantly different."

"So, no bald spot?"

"Not as such."

I blew out a breath. "Thank God."

"Jack—"

"No, go away." When he didn't move, I looked over my shoulder. "I'm mad at you."

He gave me his guilty look and fiddled with his cuffs. "I am sorry I laid hands on you—"

"Not about that. Well, yes, about that. But mostly because you disappeared." I turned to face him. "Where have you been? I needed you. The police think you killed Dawson—you didn't kill Dawson did you?"

"Of course not. He was already dead by the time I found him."

"Uh...but you were planning on killing him?"

"I was planning on breaking his knees and elbows."

I chewed on that. "When the police ask, don't tell them that, ok?"

"Jack, I apologize that I worried you—"

"Someone tore apart your room."

He nodded like he'd been expecting that.

"They left you a weird note," I said. "Where is it?"

That one went home. His mouth quirked, and then he went totally still.

"H, what the hell is going on?"

It must have cost him. He was silent for a long time, but when he finally lifted his eyes, they were the color of starlight. "There is a game afoot, Jack." The words were delivered simply, evenly. Like facts. "I must make my move."

For a moment, I had no idea what to say. Then I cuffed him on the side of the head and said, "What game, dummy? What the fuck is going on?"

"I understand you're angry—"

"You're goddamn right I'm angry. To repeat: in the last twenty-four hours, I got drugged and almost date-raped by Dawson. Paxton used me like bait. Kazen kidnapped me—"

"What do you mean—" Holmes began, and then his jaw snapped shut, and calculations began in his face.

"—and my best friend, the guy who's supposed to be helping me with all this, he's not anywhere. I can't find him. He doesn't answer his phone. I don't know if he's alive or dead. Do you know how freaked out I've been?"

Absently, Holmes said, "Jack, please, lower your voice."

"I'll talk as loud as I want to talk," which was actually more like shouting. "Everything has been terrible. I'm exhausted. I feel like shit. I got in a huge fight with my dad—" But my throat closed around that because I couldn't tell him, of all people, about that. My voice was too tight for shouting when I finally managed, "Do you know how scared I've been?"

The array of thoughts and plans and scenarios playing out in Holmes's face died, and then he was just Holmes again, his gaze intent as it settled on me. He reached out like he was about to pet a viper and touched my shoulder. I wiped my face and focused on the enormous bust of Jesus, but he wasn't any help, so I had to wipe both cheeks this time.

"Jack," Holmes whispered.

He sounded so out of his depths, so lost, that I laughed, and then I had to pull my shirt up to dry my eyes. He was still petting my shoulder, and he was such a creeper, and I wanted to tell him he was the biggest dork I'd ever met. Instead, I started legit crying, and all I could do was shake and mop at my face with my shirt and try not to fall apart into sobs.

Holmes's hug was tight and, of course, stiff, but his shoulder felt nice under my chin. He smelled like Holmes, that green heat, and underneath the fancy clothes, his body was the same maze of hard lines that I remembered. The sounds of the party—Christmas music and excited voices and the accumulation of lots of bodies moving in a relatively small space—filtered up to us through the floor. It was snowing harder, the flakes seeming to spring out of nowhere when they passed from the dark to the light of the windows, sudden and spinning and glittering.

"I'm ok," I said and gave him a nudge, but he didn't release me. "Get off me, you big dork. I'm ok."

He released me slowly.

"I'm still mad at you."

He nodded. Warily. "Will you be less angry if I tell you I disposed of my phone so I couldn't be tracked?"

"No, H. No, I will not be less angry. Because you could have told me. You could have found a way to tell me."

The dilemma in his face surprised me; it was rare to see Holmes indecisive about anything, much less torn. Finally, he said, "I couldn't be sure your phone hadn't been compromised as well. I'm sorry; it was important that no one know I was no longer carrying my phone. But I wanted to tell you. I did not like…"

The words crumbled into silence. He didn't like what? Not talking to me? That was bullshit because he never wanted to talk, not even about fun stuff like *Dead by Daylight* or which Stream Queen was the bitchiest or why he had a crush on Niall, of all the options in One Direction. He didn't like being away from me? A part of me kindled at the thought, but that wasn't true either—most nights, after I forced him to hang out, he couldn't wait to be alone again. He didn't like not being in control of the situation? Well, yes, that shoe fit.

"H, what's going on? Paxton said something about a game. You said it too. What game?"

Indecision showed in his face again. "It's complicated."

"Bullshit."

"If you can trust me, for now, I swear I will tell you later."

I grunted. My eyes had that stinging warmth that came as the last tears dried and began to crust, and I rubbed at the irritation. "Is it about Aston?"

"Aston is simply the battlefield."

"What does that mean?"

"It means whoever is behind this, they don't care about Aston."

"I don't understand. Paxton was blackmailing him. Then the blackmail disappeared—and my guess is that Dawson stole it—only Dawson got killed. It'd be easy to say that Aston's family had Dawson eliminated, but the killer released the blackmail, and now Aston's the lead suspect in the murder investigation. Well, you might be tied with him."

Holmes huffed a little breath. "It's insulting, really. If I were to kill someone, I'd at least do it well."

I raised my eyebrows.

Holmes shot his cuffs and looked anywhere but at me as he mumbled, "It's the principle of the thing."

I'd been thinking about this for almost three months; before I could stop myself, I said, "Is this about Watson?"

Holmes's head came up, and his eyes were flat and unreadable. "What do you mean?"

"The stuff on her computer. The stuff about Zodiac."

A tension I hadn't realized was there went out of Holmes's body, and he shook his head. "No, Jack. Someone has arranged events to keep my attention occupied. The question is who; that's why we're here tonight."

"What do you mean, to keep your attention occupied? What don't they want you paying attention to? Does it have something to do with someone searching your room? Because we already know Paxton—"

"Paxton is a tool, and, more importantly, he is not to be trusted, even when he is telling the truth. Especially when he is telling the truth."

That was so bizarre that for a moment, I didn't know what to say.

"I plan on learning who sent Paxton to Walker," Holmes said into the silence. "But Paxton may not know why he is here. He may not even know who sent him. And he is, ultimately, always his own agent. That is an important thing to remember about the Adlers. It would be foolish to believe that these events were only about Paxton and Aston."

"So, what? You think somebody, this mastermind, was behind Dawson's death too? Why would they kill Dawson?"

"I don't know what to think, Jack. I have hypotheses. I am testing one hypothesis tonight, which is why you must leave—"

"Holy shit. You called Kazen."

He was remarkably good at stilling his body, but in that moment, I was better at reading him. The slight curl of one finger against his thigh. The tension at the corner of his mouth.

"H, are you out of your mind?"

"Don't be ridiculous," he said. "I didn't call him."

I crossed my arms.

The music downstairs switched. Mariah Carey now, the one everybody plays every year. I wondered what marble-bust Jesus thought about it. And in a religious home, too.

Holmes ducked his head and muttered, "I did not call him." And then, as though it had been ripped out of him: "I forced Aston to do it."

"Oh my God."

"This is why I wanted you to leave."

"H, oh my God. He's insane. You realize that, right? He's going to come up here, guns blazing, and try to kill Aston and anybody else who might out him for being queer."

Holmes let out a dry little laugh, and then he checked my face, and his eyes brightened with atypical amusement.

"What?" I asked.

"Jack, he's not coming to kill Aston."

It took me a moment. And then I couldn't keep the horror out of my voice: "Your genius plan was a booty call?"

"Don't be crass; obviously the ideal lure for Kazen was a sexual rendezvous—"

The horror turned my whisper shrill. "Don't call it that!"

"Jack, you're being very immature about all this. You saw that video on Kazen's laptop. There's a strong possibility that Kazen saw whoever met Paxton that night outside Aston's residence. Thus, Kazen is the next thread to follow."

I opened my mouth to respond to that, but I had no words. Zero words.

The sound of voices in the hall startled both of us. Holmes grabbed my arm and propelled me toward the closet. I was about to say something about the door being locked, but he had a card in his hand, and he ran it between the jamb and the latch so fast that I could barely track the movement. The door popped open, and Holmes pushed me into a wall of coats. For a moment, the world was wool and hangers, and then Holmes crowded in next to me. I heard him test the handle to make sure the lock hadn't reset, and then he pulled the door shut. A moment later, the hall door opened, and steps moved into the room.

"You're being a child about this." It was a man's voice, older, with the kind of engrained confidence that came from bossing people around. "I told you we weren't having this conversation."

"Why are these lights on?" That was a woman's voice.

There was the slightest hint of metal on metal as hangers shifted, and then Holmes's mouth was at my ear. "Bruce and DeeDee Young. Aston's parents."

I nodded, but I was having a hard time focusing. Holmes's breathing tickled my ear, and it was having…an effect. His thigh was between my legs. The closet was packed with clothes, full of the smell of musty fabric and a hint of rubber soles and cedar. We'd been in such a hurry, and the space was so tight, that I was leaning against the wall at an angle, and as the snow on my Stan Smiths melted, I felt like I was slipping. No, scratch that, I was slipping. And that meant more of my weight was coming to rest on, uh, a certain area and, in the process, pressing that area against Holmes.

Holmes shifted. I could feel the definition of his quadriceps, which, let's be fair, the boy was jacked as hell. But worse, the movement increased the friction and pressure. I let out a little breath, and the sound was distressed, maybe even a little panicked, as blood rushed to my face.

I grabbed Holmes's wrist, my nails biting into the skin. I shook my head.

He didn't say anything. He didn't do anything. Then he moved again. Only a fraction of a turn, but there was no chance he didn't feel a death-defying boner grinding on him, and a part of me wondered if this last movement hadn't been done exactly for that purpose. My sneakers slipped again, and I dropped a few more inches. His hand slipped behind my back, and his breath on my ear made me fight back a whimper when he said, "I've got you."

It was either fall on my ass and, in the process, announce to the Youngs that we were hitting second base in their closet, or let him help me. So, I gave up and embraced death by sheer humiliation. I let my weight come to rest fully on Holmes's thigh. His arm flexed behind me, securing me. If anything, it made me harder, and it felt so good to be against him like this that I was breathing too fast. His face was next to mine. He was so warm, and the closet was so small, and sweat was slowly dampening my shirt. If I turned my head, we'd be kissing. I was starting to realize it would take a team of shrinks to unpack how fucked up I was.

The angle of our bodies made it impossible to know if he was having a—um, a reaction—as well. I wanted to know. Part of my brain had accepted back in September that he didn't feel the same way. But I had felt him against me, that first time we'd slept together on the sofa, and I wanted to believe that meant something—even if he wasn't ready for it, maybe never would be ready for it. Maybe something had changed in the last couple of months. He hadn't started screaming and trying to get away from the hard-on that was literally about to kill me, which was how things had gone last time.

His arm tightened against me, and his lips brushed my ear. "Stop thinking about it," he whispered. "You're hyperventilating."

Easy for him to say. His traitorous dick wasn't currently trying to drill through a semi-new pair of jeans. But I took deep breaths, and I dragged my attention away from our bodies. I wasn't sure how much time had passed—it had felt like an eternity, but it couldn't have been more than a minute, maybe two. On the other side of the door, Camdyn was yelling.

"—Aston needs to stay and face the consequences of his own actions. How's he ever going to learn?"

"DeeDee," Bruce said, "will you talk to your daughter, please?"

"Don't do that," Camdyn said. It was like she'd never been shouting at all; her voice was ice, smooth and clear. The change made the hairs on my arms stand up. "I'm not hysterical, and you can't let Mom run interference for you on this one."

"Sweetheart," DeeDee said, "I don't understand what you're getting so upset about."

"You can't pack him away. You can't make it all disappear and act like nothing happened."

"Look who's talking," Bruce said. The tone matched the words—elementary-school snideness, like a spoiled kid.

In the silence that followed, the music downstairs changed. An organ played in the background. A choir sang. Probably the Tabernacle Choir, or whatever they called themselves these days. It might have been a Christmas song, but it had as much cheer as a funeral march.

"Your grandfather's changed the music," DeeDee said, as though that were somehow Camdyn's fault.

"He's gay," Camdyn said with that same cold detachment. "You tried bullying him into being straight. You tried scaring him into being straight." She laughed, and the sound was empty and shell-shocked. "You and Grandfather have certainly tried praying him straight."

"In my house, you will speak respectfully about the apostles of the Lord—" Bruce tried.

Camdyn spoke over him without raising her voice. "He's not going to change. He's not going to be different. You're going to ruin his life, or you're going to make him kill himself, or maybe first one and then the other. And I'm not going to let you do it."

"Sweetheart," DeeDee said, "don't you think you're making a big deal out of all this?"

Whatever had been happening to my body, it was over now. I felt sick to my stomach every time I pulled in that stale, musty air. Wool scratched the back of my neck, and sweat made my clothes itch. Holmes's body was steady as he supported me, but he had changed too. I could feel the tamped-down rage in him.

"I will not let you—" Camdyn began.

"Who are you to tell me what you're going to let me do?" Bruce slapped the desk, and the sound made me jump. Holmes tightened the circle of his arm. "This is my house. You are my daughter. After everything your mother and I have done for you—"

"Dear," DeeDee said, "Grandfather will hear you."

Bruce's silence had a choked quality before he continued in a lower voice, "He's going to the camp. Six months. Then we'll reevaluate."

The pause yawned.

Steps moved toward the door.

"Sweetheart," DeeDee said, "you're a little blotchy."

The door slammed shut.

For ten seconds, there was nothing.

Bruce said, "You'd think we were throwing him to the wolves."

DeeDee's answering noise was sympathetic.

"I want what's best for him."

"I know, dear." Their voices were moving toward the hall now. "And she knows too. She's upset; that's all."

The lights went out, and the door closed again—more softly this time. I could feel Holmes's heartbeat like a metronome. Half a minute had passed before he settled both hands on my hips and helped me stand, and hangers screeched along the rod as I got my feet under me. The closet still felt stuffy and hot, and I couldn't stop sweating.

"I'm only going to say this once," I whispered, "and if we ever talk about it again, I'll literally die and go wherever pervert ghosts go, but I'm—" I had to rush through it. "I'm sorry."

Holmes cocked his head. His face was nothing more than lines limned in the darkness. His voice was tentative as he said, "I'm sorry too."

I laughed and let my head thunk against the closet wall. "No, dummy. This is not one of the times when you say you're sorry too."

He let out a bothered breath. "It's very confusing when you continue to change the rules—"

Too late, we heard the sound of the window, rapid patter of steps, and then the click of the closet door's latch being set. Holmes tried the handle, but it didn't turn.

A familiar laugh came from the other side of the door, low and darkly amused, and Paxton said, "Your move, luv. Give it to me, and we can end the game right now. No hurt feelings."

"Give him what?" I asked. "What's he talking about?"

Holmes jostled me as he squared up with the door. There was barely enough room for him to stand like that, which meant I had my back flat to the wall and had to make myself as small as possible. With a savage noise somewhere between a grunt and a growl, Holmes brought his heel up and drove it into the door. He connected with the wood next to the handle, and something splintered and gave.

Paxton laughed again. "As you like." His steps moved toward the hall. A door opened and shut. And then, unmistakable even against the dull, background roar of the party, came the sound of a gunshot.

Holmes's expression tightened, and he kicked the door again. This time, wood cracked. He kicked again, and the door's paneling gave. His heel caught; if it had been me, I would have wobbled and fallen ass-backward, but Holmes just gave a legit growl this time and yanked his foot free. The next kick separated the handle and latch from the door itself, and the door tried to swing open under the force of the blow. Something caught it and held it. Holmes kicked again, and the door stuck again on whatever Paxton had wedged under it. Holmes's breathing was wild, his pupils still contracted into tiny dots, in spite of the darkness. He steadied himself for another kick.

"H." Nothing. I grabbed his ankle. "H!"

He jerked free of my touch, and for a moment, he stared at me like he didn't know me.

"He jammed something under the door." Still nothing registered in his face, so I said, "Ease up for a minute, ok?"

It was like watching the real H step back into the room. His eyes slid away from mine, and he gave a tiny nod. I squeezed past him, pulled one of the hangers from the rod, and shook the coat to the floor. The musty smell mixed now with the unmistakable scent of Holmes's body, worked up and overheated in the tiny space. I dropped to my knees and peeked under the door. Chair legs canted toward us; Paxton had propped a chair against the door.

I slipped the hanger under the door. It took some squinting and wiggling around, but then I got the hanger lined up with the chair leg. I pushed. At first, nothing happened. Then the hanger started to bend. I let out an annoyed breath, hooked the door with my free hand, and pulled it toward us. The movement created a slight gap between the chair and the door. It only lasted a moment, as the chair rocked toward us and tried to settle into place again, but it was enough. I thrust with the hanger, forcing the chair's leg back. It was enough to change the angle at which the chair stood, and it fell.

Holmes shouldered open the door and stepped over me. "Stay," he said as he sprinted toward the hall.

I scrambled after him. I had a glimpse of dove-colored walls and dark floors. Holmes turned right, but I glanced left and saw someone going down the stairs—nothing more than a silhouette. I opened my mouth to tell Holmes, but he shouted, "Put your hands where I can see them!"

When I turned, he was facing Emma. She wore a green dress, and she'd spilled something on herself. Punch. Then I saw more of it: on her hands, running down her arms. Not punch; blood. Her face had been emptied out, and she was looking at both of us without any sign of recognition.

"Keep your hands in the air," Holmes said. "Get on the floor."

"Emma," I said, "what happened?"

"Get on the floor," Holmes said.

"Are you ok? Hey, it's Jack. Emma, do you hear me? Nod if you can hear me."

The nod came a half-second later. A lag. Like somewhere in her brain, there was a bad connection.

"Get on the floor," Holmes said, "where you will remain until the police—"

She stumbled toward us. Holmes reached for her, and I reached for him, saying, "H, she's scared—"

He listened to me because he trusted me, and my mistake caught both of us. While Holmes was distracted, Emma drove her fist into Holmes's solar plexus. He grunted and staggered, and I caught him under the arms. Emma shoved past us. I tried to grab her, but I was too busy not falling on my ass while keeping a hold of Holmes. She shot toward the stairs.

Holmes twisted in my grip, muscles and bones like silk, and raced after her—all while I was still getting my feet under me. I moved to follow, but through the open doorway, something caught my eye.

The room that Emma had been leaving—the one where Holmes had heard the gunshot, where we had intercepted her as she fled—must have been Aston's: another U of U flag, a *Point Break* movie poster (the original) that should have raised questions about his sexuality for anyone who was paying attention, a desk, a bed. The window was open, arctic air making me shiver.

It was the bed that held my attention. The bedding had been pushed to a heap at the foot of the bed, as though someone had been in a hurry, and a naked man—too big to be Aston, and covered in blood—lay on the mattress. His clothes lay on the floor next to him: pockets turned out, tossed in random directions. Because someone had gone through them, I realized. Because they'd been looking for something.

The room was silent the way empty rooms are. Downstairs, the music changed, and Mariah was back.

I knew. But I had to check.

Kazen Bates was dead. He'd been shot in the chest.

Chapter 23

He's Not Your Friend

Sixteen hours later, they still hadn't found Emma, and I hadn't slept—not unless you counted dozing upright in a holding cell, or chained to a bench, or handcuffed to a table in an interview room.

The Heber police had come—before we even had to call them, actually. Rivera had notified them, but everything had gotten mired in the typical bureaucratic morass. Holmes and I had been taken into custody and questioned, and then we'd been carted back to the station and separated. Holmes had been put in an interview room, and I'd gone to a bench in the jail—not a cell, but near the processing desk, where a duty officer could keep an eye on me. After a few hours, detectives had come and started hammering on us. I'd asked them to call Rivera, and after a while, he and Yazzie showed up, and they did some hammering too.

It all came out, everything. Why I'd rushed to the Youngs' party. Kazen kidnapping me. Paxton. Mine and Holmes's first—and disastrous—attempt at being consulting detectives. I spared myself the embarrassment of using that phrase; Yazzie, however, had read her Holmes.

The only thing I managed to hold back was that I was still dealing on campus. Rivera asked. Yazzie asked. The Heber detectives asked. And Rivera asked a few more times—calm, relentless, because he knew I'd done it before. The hours took on a nightmarish quality where nothing seemed real, but a part of me could think clearly enough to recognize that if they were asking, they didn't have proof. So, I admitted to selling Beanie Babies and condoms and energy drinks and some sort of crushed spider egg powder that one girl insisted was good for acne, but that's all.

At some point, a lawyer came for Holmes.

My dad came for me.

It was Sunday afternoon by the time they let us go, and we drove into Provo Canyon in silence. The mountains looked like folded cardboard—

brown corners peering out where the snow had melted. A winter-thin doe poked her head up near the reservoir and then froze, watching us. The truck rattled and thudded, and the vents hissed, and it had a faint smell like machine grease, the way the maintenance building's garage smelled sometimes. Dad had some of it worked into the skin around his nails. He'd been doing something last night when Rivera had sent someone to search my room. He'd been interrupted. He'd been scared. All night, he'd been scared something had happened to me.

I drew in a breath.

"Not right now," he said.

My eyes filled with tears, and I let my head fall against the window, and I nodded.

When we got home, he slammed the truck door, and he slammed the carport door, and by the time I got inside, he was slamming the fridge door. Bottles clinked against each other. I had no idea what he'd been looking for. He stood with his hands on his hips, staring at the fridge.

"Go to your room."

I toed off my Stan Smiths and went.

When I checked my phone, I had messages from Ariana: *Jack, is everything ok?* And, *Your dad is super worried.* And, *Call one of us, please.* On and on like that. I started to reply, but I didn't know what to say. I locked my phone and put it on my chest.

Later, I woke up. The light washed in, the angle different, textured and deep like honeycomb. I hadn't meant to sleep, hadn't realized I'd fallen asleep. I was at an eleven on a scale of one to ten for needing to pee, so I slunk to the door and tested the handle. Dad hadn't done anything drastic like nail the door shut, which said something about his faith in humanity, so after a moment, I eased it open.

His voice came down the hall. "You can come out."

I hesitated. The words sounded dry and crumbly when I called, "I'm going to pee."

Dad didn't answer, which I guessed was permission. So, I peed, and I washed my hands, and I stared in the mirror and saw Kazen, the blood soaking the bedding, the clothes tossed everywhere. *Give it to me*, Paxton had said. And Holmes: *I must make my move.* And Emma, the scrabbling terror behind the blankness in her face. So much blood.

I was shaking, so I got in the shower and cleaned up, and I brushed my teeth, and I tried to make my hair look the way it was supposed to look, which was a constant defeat. Eventually I gave up and realized you could only put off your execution for so long. When I left the bathroom, pans clattered in the kitchen, and I could smell eggs and sausage and hot tortillas.

Now that I wasn't one of the walking dead, I could see that my room had been searched: the desk torn apart, clothes everywhere, mattress askew on the bed. I decided the adult, responsible thing would be to ignore it for now. I found joggers and a big LA Rams sweatshirt that had been Dad's before I stole it. I tried to stand up straight, but when I got to the kitchen, I sank onto a stool and put my head on my arms. Dad was cooking at the stove. Tacos. It was quarter of five and, unless I'd slept a whole day, still Sunday.

"You need to eat something," Dad said. He'd washed up since the ride home; his hands were clean. He had strong hands—fingers thick and powerful, the way they get when you work with your hands every day. He filled a tortilla with cheese and ground beef and rolled it up. He could do that, gentle stuff like that, without tearing the tortilla. I screwed it up every time. He slid the plate to me. "Get yourself some water."

I did. My throat felt slightly more human, but the words were croaky when I said, "Dad, I'm sorry."

He nodded. His eyes met mine. "I'm sorry about our argument yesterday. I didn't say things the way I wanted to."

I looked down at the taco and picked at the tortilla, tearing off tiny pieces and ruining the great job Dad had done. I tried to say something and couldn't, so I shook my head.

After what felt like a long time, I ducked my head, my face stinging as tears rushed into my eyes. Dad let out a long breath. He leaned over the counter, one of the strong hands cupping the back of my head, and pressed our foreheads together. I really started to cry then. We stayed like that for a while. Then he came around the counter and sat next to me, and I cried into his shoulder for a long time.

He rubbed my back. He shushed me. But he didn't say, *It's alright* or *Everything's going to be ok.*

When I'd cried myself out, I pulled away from him. His shirt was wet where my face had been pressed, but if it bothered him, he didn't show it.

"Did Headmaster Cluff—" I couldn't say it. "Do we have to—I mean, did she call you or anything?"

"She came by," Dad said. "She wanted to talk face to face."

Fresh heat rolled through me, and I pressed a hand over my eyes.

"She's a decent person," Dad said. "She wanted to talk to you, but I didn't want to wake you. There are some serious consequences for your behavior, buddy. But, as she put it, she didn't believe in punishing one person for another person's mistakes. So, we're staying. For now."

"Oh my God."

He nudged me with his knee. "Eat your taco."

"Dad, oh my God! That's amazing!"

But he didn't answer my smile, and his face hadn't softened. "Your friend Detective Rivera didn't tell her about what they took from your room. Maybe that's because they're still deciding if they want to charge you. I don't know."

That struck a false note—like the interviews at the Heber station, it was a piece of the puzzle that didn't fit. But I didn't know what to make of it, and Dad nudged me with his knee again, so I forked up some taco and had a bite of literally the most delicious thing in my entire life.

"Jack," Dad said as I melted into the perfection of cheese and ground beef. "We need to talk."

I hesitated, fork hovering above the plate. The hot electric smell of the refrigerator hit me, and I lost my appetite.

"I need you to understand that these last couple of days have been the worst of my life, except when I lost your mom. I didn't know where you were. I didn't know if you were safe. I didn't know if you were alive. You are the single most important thing in the universe." He stopped and ran a hand over his buzzed gray hair. "I can't tell you what it feels like. You won't understand until you have a child of your own."

My first thought was of Holmes. How he had disappeared. The agony of not knowing if he was alive, if he was safe, if he had gotten hurt and needed help, if he was alone and afraid. Maybe, I thought. Maybe I don't understand. But I know some of it. I know something.

"I want you to understand that what I say next is for your own good." The words had a practiced quality—a rhythm, a cadence, everything controlled and reasonable. "Do you believe me when I say that?"

I nodded.

"Since we moved here, you have...changed." Dad's eyes slid away from me. "I understand that some of what you did, you did because you felt like you had to. And, Jack—" He stopped; frustration locked his voice. "I wish things were different. I wish I were different. I wish you hadn't had to do those things. And I'd be a liar and a hypocrite if I didn't tell you the truth: yes, what you did helped our family, and I am grateful for it. I understand that you had to be an adult way too early, and that you had to make tough choices. I hope you know—I want you to know—that I am so proud of you. Every day, I'm proud of you."

He waited like I had to do something, so I nodded again and looked down at the mangled remains of the taco.

"But," Dad said and stopped and ran his hand over his hair again. "But, Jack, you've also started acting in ways that make me worried about you. That scare me, frankly. You disappear."

"The last two days—"

"I'm not talking about the last two days." The words were louder, harder, slapping me down. He took a deep breath, and in a more level voice, continued, "You disappear. You're late to class. You skip class. You're failing chemistry. You take the truck without asking—"

"Only when I need to!"

"—even though you don't have your license. You lie to me—"

"When have I lied?"

"—about where you are and who you're with—"

"Tell me one time I've lied."

"—and what you're doing—"

"You can't! You can't tell me one time!"

His hand cracked so hard against the countertop that my fork rattled against the plate. Water sloshed in the glass. "I'm talking right now!" Under the brown of his skin, a flush rose in his cheeks. His words tumbled out. "Every time you're with that boy. Do you realize that? Every time you're with him, this is how you act."

I stared at him. Something popped, the sound of the house settling. Then I said, "H?"

"You weren't like this before you started—started hanging out with him. Do you realize that?"

"What has H ever done to you? You've hated him since the first time you met him, and you don't even have a reason."

"You never got into trouble before you met him."

"He's smart, and he's nice to me when all the other kids here treat me like shit."

"People shooting at you. People kidnapping you. Kids turning up dead, Jack."

"It's not his fault! It was my idea to help Aston—"

"What do you think is going on, Jack? What do you think this is about? You don't understand kids like him. You don't know how this is going to work out. For a couple of years, while you're both here, you're convenient for him. You're useful. You get him what he wants, and he lets you hang out with him and his friends because you're a novelty. But you're not from that world. They've got money, they've got power, they're in a totally different league."

I shook my head. "He's my friend."

"Buddy, he's not your friend. If he were your friend, he wouldn't be asking you to deal drugs."

"That's not how it is."

"Give me a little credit."

"You don't know what you're talking about."

"Jack, the deputy found them. He showed me."

"H helps me with my homework." The tears were just below the surface again. "He doesn't have anybody else. He needs that stuff because it's his medicine."

Dad let out a soft noise that was somewhere between disgust and pity, and he rubbed his face. "You're dealing drugs—"

"Stop saying that."

"You have been dealing drugs—"

I stood before I'd realized it. My elbow caught the plate, and it skittered across the counter, the fork chiming against the ceramic. "You don't know what you're talking about!"

Dad stood too. He jabbed a finger at the stool. "Sit down."

I glared at him.

"Sit your ass down!"

"No! He's my best friend! I'm not going to listen to you talk shit about him."

"Jack, what is going on with you? Do you hear yourself? What happens if Detective Rivera decides to charge you with possession? What if he charges you with intent to distribute? You've got a shot at a good life here. A good school. A great girlfriend. What's going to happen with Ariana if you get thrown in jail?"

The fridge's compressor shut off with a long, loud knocking. I stared at Dad. My head felt like it was full of all the blood in my body, the pressure building and building. I started to laugh and stepped around him.

Dad put out his hand. The muscles in his neck stood out against the skin. "We're having a conversation."

"What is it with you and Ariana?"

The flicker on his face was there and then gone. "She's a good girl. You two are good together."

I laughed again.

"Is something funny?"

"We're good together," I said. "You don't know anything about her."

Dad dropped his arm. He turned on the stool to face me.

"You definitely don't know anything about me," I said.

"Sit down," Dad said in a low voice.

"Where do I want to go to college?"

He tried not to take the bait; it showed in his face. But he said, "UCLA."

"I haven't wanted to go to UCLA since I was nine. What's my major going to be?"

"I don't know what's happening right now, but I want to make something clear to you. You're not going to hang out with him anymore. Not here. Not at his residence. I'll ask the counselor to make sure you aren't in the same classes."

"You don't know. How many nights a week do I have nightmares?"

The hurt in his face surprised me, the way it stayed open like a wound. His voice was different when he said, "Jack."

"How many nights do I have to get high to sleep?" I couldn't catch my breath. "You don't know me. What the fuck do you know about who I'd be good with?"

For a moment it was us and the silence. The keys on his belt loop jingled when he shifted forward. He had his hands turned up the way people did in stained glass sometimes.

"You can be angry at me; I can handle that. And you're right: I didn't know you were still—what was going on. But I want you to be safe, and I want you to be healthy, and I want you to be happy—"

"I don't want to be happy! Mom's dead because of me! Why the fuck should I be happy?"

I thought I could see myself in the darkness of his eyes. "What do you— Jack—"

"But you know what's worse?" I turned, fumbling my coat off the hook by the door, grabbing the second set of truck keys.

"Hold on," Dad said.

"What's worse is the real thing, what this is really all about, is you're so fucking scared of it, you can't even say it."

"I said hold on!"

I got halfway to the carport door before he caught me, fingers biting into my shoulder, and spun me around. He must have been off balance, and I caught him by surprise, because he still had more mass than me, and he was definitely stronger. It didn't matter, though, because when I shoved him, he clipped the end table and fell into his recliner. Something fell. Glass broke. He stared up at me. His mouth hung open, and he looked old.

It had been the picture. The one of us, where he'd folded Mom out of it. It lay face up, surrounded by shards of glass.

"Get back here," Dad said, levering himself up.

I headed for the door.

"Jack! Where do you think you're going?"

"Ariana's," I shouted as I slammed the door behind me. "Since we're so fucking perfect together."

Chapter 24

Did I Fuck Up?

But I didn't go to Ariana's. I went to Joslyn's. Her sister had an apartment on the south side of Provo, and on the weekend—yes, even on Sunday—she had parties.

On the drive, I blasted Pearl Jam. "Animal." I kept seeing his face at the end, and I put the song on repeat and turned up the volume. The sun had dropped behind the horizon as I tore down the canyon. There wasn't enough light to give the stone texture, so draws and curves and sheer granite faces were nothing more than shadows hemming me in. Provo was a collection of broken amber and the eggshell halo of streetlights, and then her street was a dark tunnel leading to her stairs, and then I was at the door, the darkness tight around me, like silk drawn close around my throat.

I didn't recognize the guy who answered—some humper on his way to middle age, hair receding, in a t-shirt and blazer that made him look like the dumpster-kid version of a tech bro. He shouted, "Joslyn," over his shoulder, and gave way to her a moment later.

"No," she said. She looked like Ariana—a few years older, her hair straightened, press-on nails. "Get lost."

But when I pushed past her, all she did was make an annoyed noise.

The wall of sensory input swallowed the sound. The tiny one-bedroom was crammed with bodies, the air close and hot and hazy from joints being passed back and forth, and the reek of cheap tequila hit me. Someone had swept a broken bottle into the corner of the kitchen, and nobody seemed interested in getting rid of the glass. Electro house music thudded loud enough that I didn't have to hear my own heartbeat anymore. A girl with an armory's worth of piercings in her ears turned around and blew vapor in my face—sweet, damp, sticking to my skin. They had a keg tonight, and somebody had brought one of those enormous party subs—probably the guy in half a Subway uniform who had his hand up Roukaia's skirt.

Ariana appeared in the hallway. She looked great tonight: her curls loose, a black jumpsuit, white sneakers that had to be new. Her face went flat when she saw me, and she charged through the party at me.

"I don't want you here," she shouted over the music. She waved at the door. "I want you to go!"

"Can we talk?" I shouted back.

She waved her hand again, her face twisting, and shook her head. Then she turned and slipped between a pair of dudes trying to figure out how to work a beer bong, moving toward Joslyn on the opposite side of the party.

I made myself a rum and Coke, and I stood in a corner. The pretty boy was there, the one who'd tried to make a move a time or two. His eyeliner must not have been sweat proof because it was streaking badly, but he caught my gaze a couple of times, and he made a big show out of rucking up his tank top to show a pale, flat belly. I shook my head at him and pounded the rest of my drink. Then I got another. There wasn't much Coke in the third.

I'd killed my vape at Wintersmash, but after a few drinks, I was loose enough to go up to a girl I didn't know and get a toke off her joint. She was still in her chef whites, minus the hat, and her septum piercing had little red stones in it. I got a second toke, but when she wanted to dance, I went back to the corner. Maybe if she'd had the hat, I would have considered it. Maybe, a part of my brain suggested, I was fucking myself up a little too fast. The green-out came in like a storm.

"I just want to talk." I had the echoing sense that I'd repeated myself a few times already, and I was surprised to find myself on the opposite side of the room. Ariana and Joslyn were standing together—Ariana half-turned into Joslyn, refusing to look at me, and Joslyn staring daggers at me. "Things would be totally fine if we could just talk."

"She doesn't want to talk to you," Joslyn shouted over the music. "She doesn't need a piece of shit part-time fuck-up who deals baggie weed when he's not jerking off into his socks. Get the fuck out of here before I make you leave."

"Jos," Ariana said.

"I just want to talk," I said. I steadied myself with a hand on the wall, but it turned out the wall was glass or smoke or a force field, because my hand met it and went through it—or slid along it. I was trying too hard to stay upright to tell. "Why can't we just talk?"

"Get out!" Joslyn screamed.

"This guy bothering you?" He was the sandwich artist, still in his Subway visor, and he had three inches of party sub—ham and turkey and

American on white, shredded lettuce, tomato. I thought maybe that was a metaphor. Or an analogy. Or a simile. They don't teach you to make metaphors while you're high. He looked at me, and his chest puffed up, and he said, "I think they want you to leave."

"That's a fucking cliché," I said. It would have sounded better if somebody didn't keep turning off all the force fields.

"Jack," Ariana said, "we can talk tomorrow. Can you please go?"

"You heard her," the sandwich jockey said. "Let's go."

"Is that three inches of sandwich," I asked, "or are you just happy to see me?"

What might have been a smile—albeit an exasperated one—glimmered on Ariana's expression.

The sandwich specialist glowered at me. He ripped off a bite of the three inches, and I guess maybe in some other universe, it was threatening.

"Two and a half," I said and giggled.

"Jack," Ariana said, but she was smiling and trying to hide it. "Knock it off."

"You think you're funny?" the sandwich supervisor asked through a mouthful of turkey and shredded lettuce.

"I'm a joke," I said. "I'm a fucking punchline."

Ariana put a hand on my shoulder. "Jack—"

Enough time spent having Holmes knock me on my ass meant it was easy to see when the guy started winding up for the punch. The smart thing to do—the thing Holmes had trained me to do—was to hit first and hit hard. End the fight before it even got started. But this guy had some space-time manipulation bullshit going on; I swung, and the punch whistled through the air. The sandwich surfer swung at me, and my brain told me exactly how to block it, which I did. Successfully. With my face.

A lot of white. And then I was lying on the floor.

Hands dragged me up, propelled me. My feet might have touched the floor, but I thought maybe I'd learned how to fly. A moment later, they pitched me out the airlock. Dark. Cold. Silent. Apparently I didn't know how to fly because I hit the concrete hard and rolled until I came up against the rail.

This is a good place to sleep, my brain said as it started shutting down. She wants to talk in the morning.

I woke up when someone started stabbing a needle of ice through my eye. I jerked away from the attack, hands coming up to defend myself.

"Cut it out," Ariana said as she settled the icepack against my eye again. Her other hand stroked my hair.

She was a werewolf, it turned out. She had grown fur. But now that I was awake, the ice felt kind of good against the puffy heat of my eye, and I decided to let this werewolf have her way with me.

"I'm not a werewolf," she said, laughing softly as she repositioned the pack. "It's Joslyn's coat. It's so ugly, but I can't find mine."

"That's what a werewolf would say."

She laughed again, but the sound was different now.

I don't know if I actually sobered up or not, but consciousness reassembled. I was aware that I was cold in a way that seemed dangerously comfortable, and the icepack against my eye narrowed my field of vision, and everything else was Ariana: a hint of her perfume that clung to her with the musk of weed, the bristly magic of her werewolf coat, the hint of copper in her curls under the porch light, her nose.

"I'm sorry," I croaked.

She pulled the icepack away and set it in her lap and chafed her hands.

"Did I fuck up the party?"

"It's not a Joslyn party if at least one annoying boy doesn't get laid out."

"Joslyn hates me."

"Joslyn already hated you."

I wet my lips, and it was like spreading cold fire across them. "You hate me."

The crinkle of plastic came as she rewrapped the towel around the icepack. "I'm pretty mad at you, yeah."

That seemed fair. I lay there. I wondered if medical science had ever seen a guy with one eye that was twice as big as the other.

"I was scared," she said, her voice taut and humming with an energy I didn't recognize. "You disappeared. Your dad said the police were looking for you. You weren't answering your phone."

"Yesterday was a bad day."

"Fine. But you didn't call me today? You didn't even text? Nothing?"

"I'm sorry," I whispered.

"We talked about this."

"I'm sorry."

"And you show up tonight and get tanked, Jack, just—just fucking tanked as fast as you can, and you're an asshole, and you get yourself in trouble, and now I have to spend my night sitting out here in the cold with you."

I squeezed my eyes—well, my eye—shut. "I'm really sorry."

The fake fur of Joslyn's coat made a whispering sound when Ariana leaned forward, and then the icepack came to rest against my eye again.

"We talked about this," she said. "Before we started dating. We had a whole conversation about this."

"I know."

"Is this how it's going to be? You—you do crazy things, get yourself involved in, God, I don't even know, Jack. You disappear? You won't answer calls or texts? And it doesn't matter what I feel, or how scared I am, if it's not convenient for you, too bad?"

I swallowed.

"I asked you a question," Ariana said.

"I'm a piece of shit."

"Don't do that."

"Like Joslyn said. I'm a piece of shit."

"I don't want to hear you tell me you're a piece of shit. I want to know if this is how it's going to be."

I opened my good eye, but it didn't focus right, and she was a blur, an outline, a shape in the water. I thought about lying. I thought about my dad's face, and if I could keep doing this to everyone I cared about. And then I thought about him.

So, I said, "I don't know."

"That's not good enough."

My voice was small when I said, "I know."

She was crying. I could hear it in her voice, even though she wasn't making any other noise. "I don't want to live like this. My dad gets drunk and disappears. Or he gets drunk and comes home and picks fights with anyone he can find. I look at my parents, at how they live, and I don't understand it. Why they settled for so much unhappiness. Why they keep settling for it. And Joslyn is just as bad. Everything in Joslyn's life is drama—guys in prison, guys getting out of prison, guys dealing, guys fighting. But she takes it because she looks at our parents, and she thinks somehow she's doing better, even though it's the same thing. You're sweet, Jack. And you're smart. And I care about you. But I don't want to live like this. I don't want this." She stopped as though hearing herself, but she said it again. "I don't want this. Not anymore."

I don't want this, I thought. I don't want to keep doing this. I could. If I said the right thing tonight, we could. It would be easier—for me, anyway. In the short term. But it wouldn't be fair. He would always be there. And she had asked me, months ago, if there was someone else.

I wanted to close my eye, but I made myself sit up. I found her hand, and I squeezed it, and I made myself meet her gaze. She knew; we both knew, and she started crying harder, and it took a long time for me to find my voice.

"You deserve that." I rubbed my thumb over her knuckles. "You deserve the life you want. I'm sorry—I'm sorry I'm such a fuckup. I wish I could promise I'd be different."

She shook her head and cried harder.

"I think we should break up," I said.

Music thudded inside the apartment. A girl screamed with excitement. Shapes moved behind the blinds like shadow puppets. Ariana wiped her eyes once, snuffling into the fur of Joslyn's coat, and shook her head. Then she let go of my hand and went inside.

Chapter 25

Let Me Show You

It was stupid to drive, but I drove. High-risk behavior. A typical response in males after serious trauma. They threw money at people who came up with stuff like that.

The moon was up by then. The canyon looked like someone had carved it out of ice, the black marks of the cottonwoods gouged out against the brightness of the walls. The Provo was running low and scaly with ice. The old serpent. In the rearview mirror, headlights grew in a blinding rush, and, for a moment, I saw myself: the hollowness of cheek and eyes, puffy flesh starting to bruise, dirt and grit on the side of my face where I'd lain on the concrete. And then the lights passed me, and a horn blared, and I realized I was driving twenty. I inched the speedometer up to thirty. I was somewhere between giggling and crying.

I couldn't go home, maybe ever, so I left the truck on the main campus road where Dad would find it. I sat there for a long time. Or maybe it was sleeping. A knock at the glass made me jerk upright, my hand tightening around the keys.

Holmes peered in at me. For a moment, I thought I was dreaming. He was wearing that ridiculous driving coat over a Rudolph t-shirt and boxers printed with candy canes. The December wind raked lines into his golden hair.

"What the fuck?" I said.

"Jack?"

I opened the door. "What the actual fuck?"

He shivered and hugged himself and continued to look at me. "Are you all right? Jack, your face."

"Are those candy canes?"

His face transformed into a scowl, which meant this wasn't a dream. Then he shivered and shifted his weight.

"What are you doing? You've got to be freezing."

"I was on my way to hot-wire Mrs. Shaughnessy's minivan. To look for you." Hugging himself, he studied me, his eyes roving my face. "Your father came to my room."

The wind rattled pinecones in the bed of the truck. The weed and the rum were making me even smarter than usual, so I said, "Aren't you freezing?"

"Yes. I'm going to get in the truck now."

He came around, and I started the truck. We sat there with only the grumble of the engine for company, and as the heater warmed up, Holmes pulled his coat tighter and hugged himself. I forgot sometimes how white he was, and his pale legs were pebbled with goose bumps. Some of the clarity from earlier that night—the rush of adrenaline when I had realized what was happening between Ariana and me, the surge of startled awareness when Holmes had woken me—was fading. Fog crowded my thoughts.

"It's genetic," he said, his voice stiff. "I can't help that I have a fair complexion. And you shouldn't mix alcohol with cannabis."

I hadn't realized I'd been talking out loud. I tried to shut my mouth, but it felt like somebody had cut the strings to my jaw.

"Jack, your father is upset. And worried. We both are."

"My dad is mad. Dad. Mad dad."

"I understand that you argued. Your father said he's sorry, and I believe him."

It was getting sleepy inside the truck again, so I leaned against the window. The cold of the glass bit into my cheek. "He hates me," I murmured.

"He doesn't hate you."

"He hates who I am. Do you ever feel like there are a million of you, and it's like a vending machine, and somebody's pushing E7 because that's the only one of you they want?"

Over the Dodge's rumble, Holmes's answer was barely audible. "Yes."

"He wants a Snickers, but I'm like—I'm like the one with the pretzel. What's the one with the pretzel?"

"I'm not sure."

"He wants a Snickers." Tears filled my eyes, and my voice caught. "Why does he want a fucking Snickers? Snickers are the fucking worst."

"It's ok," Holmes said hurriedly. "Jack, it's ok. Don't cry. He doesn't want a Snickers."

"He does."

"No, he doesn't."

I ran my arm across my eyes. "He wants a fucking Snickers."

"Maybe he doesn't know what he wants. Maybe he doesn't even know about the one with the pretzel. Maybe if he knew, that's the one he'd want."

For a while, I was still, my breath fogging the glass. "It's got caramel too."

Holmes nodded, opened his mouth, and paused. Then he said, "What are you on?"

I smiled. "Cloud nine."

The noise he made sounded annoyed. "That makes this conversation more difficult."

"Your hair looks like aspen leaves. Can I touch it?"

For some reason, color rushed into his face, and a touch of English slipped out. "Later, perhaps. Jack, you're intoxicated, which means you're in no condition to be driving. You certainly shouldn't be alone."

I shook my head. "I'm not going—I'm not going—I'm not—" I giggled and thunked my head against the window. "I forgot what it's called."

Holmes sighed. "I'm going to turn off the truck now."

"Home! I'm not going home!"

His sigh was even louder. He reached across and took the keys from the ignition.

"Hey—"

"Come along."

When he got my door open, I knocked his hands away. "I'm not going home. I'm not going back home. I'm not going back ever again."

Holmes had a lot of hands, like eighty million of them, which explained why he could get me out of the truck even though I was doing a great job of pushing him away. The cold slapped my cheeks, and my eyes watered, and for a moment, I felt more awake.

"H—"

"Jack, I understand that you're not going home." A little more English now. "Please stop talking before I become vexed."

He took my arm and marched me down the dark road, but someone had been messing with the asphalt, and it all slanted to one side, so I kept going into the drainage ditch.

"Dad's going to be so mad when he finds whoever did this," I mumbled, picking leaves off me.

"Good God above," Holmes said. "Why couldn't meth be your recreational drug of choice?"

After that, he kept two fingers hooked through my belt loop, and he towed and tugged and manhandled me all the way back to Baker Hall. I leaned on him as we went up the stairs, and someone had been messing with these floors too because as Holmes got out his keys to unlock his room, I kept falling over—well, falling into him, anyway—and he kept shouldering me upright until he finally got his keys in the door.

When we got into the room, I said, "You fixed it."

The furniture had been replaced, everything had been straightened, all signs of the destructive search had disappeared.

My eyes welled up again. "It was broken, and—and—and—"

"Dear Lord," Holmes muttered as he maneuvered me toward the bed.

Through a sob, I managed to say, "You fixed it."

"Yes, Jack. It's fixed. Everything is fine. Please don't be upset."

"Not upset."

He let out a long breath.

"Happy," I said and started sobbing harder.

"It would be another thing," he said as he sat me on the mattress, "if you weren't so cute."

He didn't seem to understand how big a deal it was that his room was fixed, so I tried to explain as he shucked my shoes and then my socks and helped me stand. He undid the button on my waistband, and where his knuckles pressed into my belly, they struck sparks. Weed did that to me, I tried to tell him as he yanked my jeans down over my growing hard-on. My boxers didn't have reindeer; they had hot dogs. I started to cry again.

"I cannot," Holmes said in that crisp, taut accent as he rolled me out of my shirt. "Jack, you must stop."

I lay on the bed, wiping my eyes. I could feel every thread in his comforter. My skin was alive.

"Stop talking about the bedding," Holmes ordered.

"I like your voice." I fumbled with the elastic of my boxers, got my thumbs under it. "I like when you talk like that."

"I've noticed," he said.

"I want to—I want to—I want to—hey!"

Every time I made progress, he dragged my boxers back up. The cotton rubbing against my boner sent something through me, something I felt in every joint. Something like thunder.

"No," Holmes said. "Stop it, or I'll leave."

I stared at him. Then I stopped.

"Get under the covers."

"You're mean."

"Good. You're too pretty for your own good, and consequently, you get your own way far too often."

"Everyone's mean to me."

"Get in bed, Jack."

I slid under the covers. They felt like water running over me, like electricity, like light. Almost instantly, it got sleepy in Holmes's room — well, everywhere except my boner. He looked at me, made a noise that could have meant anything, and turned off the light.

"H?"

Silence. In the dark, I couldn't even make out his form.

"H?"

The darkness was a void pulling me into it.

"H?"

"Yes," he snapped, "what is it?"

The pull of all that darkness made me dizzy. My blood pounded in my head, and something was sitting on my chest, making it impossible to breathe.

The bed shifted under new weight, and a hand stroked my forehead. Holmes shushed me. "You're all right. You can breathe. You're breathing right now. Listen. We're both breathing." He put his hand on my chest, and then he brought my hand to his. His hand was a feather on my chest, but under my fingers, he was warm and solid, the ridges of his ribs, the familiar density of muscle. His chest rose and fell rapidly; mine seemed so much slower.

Through the haze of sleep, I managed to say, "Did you take your medicine?"

His voice was different when it came back to me. "Go to sleep, Jack."

I did sleep, and my dreams were fragments: Kazen pulling my hair; the cramped, dark heat of the closet at the Youngs' home; Holmes's leg bearing my weight, the friction of my dick against his thigh; the fight with Dad; the look on his face; the look on Ariana's face; the compression of the green-out, squeezing the air from my lungs; the car crash, the night of broken glass and twisted steel, and the man who was a shadow.

When I woke, I didn't know where I was, and my head was killing me. Someone was in bed next to me, and I held myself very still. A hookup? Had I finally been drunk and high and stupid enough to go home with somebody I didn't know? And then pieces tumbled into place.

His breathing changed when he woke, but he didn't say anything for what felt like a long time. Then he rolled away from me, and the air was cold where his body had been. When he shifted back, he found my hand and pressed two tablets into it. "And drink all the water," he said as he passed me a bottle.

I swallowed the pills and drank and lay back again. There was no clock. It could have been any time. It could have been anywhere. He lay next to me again, his body a composition of straight lines that refused to bend into me, and I was lying with my knees tucked toward him, my head angled to his shoulder, and I knew I needed to move. I just couldn't.

After a while, my head felt better, and I said, "I broke up with Ariana."

His breathing was still fast, and I wondered if that was the addies. "Tonight?"

I nodded into his shoulder.

"I'm sorry, Jack. How do you feel?"

"Horrible. But hydrated."

"You sound…better."

I croaked a laugh. "I'm not stoned out of my gourd, if that's what you mean. How long was I asleep?"

"A few hours."

"Did you sleep?"

Those accelerated breaths were my answer.

"So," I finally said, "is this our thing? I get messed up, and you watch over me while I sleep it off?"

"Other people have worse patterns."

I moved my head on the pillow, and then it hit me: he only had one. I scooted over. "Here."

"I'm fine."

"H."

He shifted, his head flattening the pillow, and I was surprised at how close he settled next to me. My head was against his shoulder again. He had run, the last time we had been like this.

"It was fucking awful," I said between our mixed breathing.

When he spoke, his voice was so detached that it reminded me of the Holmes bot I'd met a few months before. "I'm sure Ariana will be willing to talk once you've both had a chance to calm down."

"I don't want to talk to her. Not like that, I mean. It was awful. And the fight with my dad was awful. But—but they needed to happen, I guess."

Holmes shivered. Seconds turned into minutes, and I didn't have anything left. My eyes were drifting shut when he said, "Why?"

I thought about that. "Because I don't love her. Not like that. Because I rushed into things. I was scared and alone, and I cared about her, and that felt like enough."

"And it wasn't?"

I thought about that too. "No. Not when there's so much more."

His breathing changed, becoming raspier. He pushed at the sheet like he might climb out of bed, but he didn't go anywhere.

"I love you," I said. "I'm sorry if that makes things weird. But I had to tell you. I think about you when I'm trying to go to sleep. I think about you when I'm in class. I think about you when I'm brushing my teeth because you're a psycho and use a million yards of dental floss every day. You're this—this miracle that I get to be close to, and I don't know how to tell you what that's like. It's everything. You're everything. And I know you don't feel the same way, so I'm not expecting you to say anything. We can go to sleep, or I can leave. Whatever you want."

His voice was thick when he said, "I don't want you to leave."

I tried to sound lighter when I said, "It's actually easier, you know? With Paxton. I understand. It's somebody else, and that means I don't have to spend all this time wondering what's wrong with me."

"Paxton?"

"Knowing you're in love with him." His silence stretched out, and I propped myself on one elbow. "You are, aren't you?"

Another long, shattered emptiness came, and his voice was broken when he said, "I used to think so."

I was aware again of my body, every bruised and battered and aching inch of it, aware of every micro-movement, the faint give and chime of the mattress springs.

"Jack." Holmes's voice trembled in the darkness. "It's not Paxton."

"Oh."

"And it's not you, either. You are—you are perfect, I think."

I cleared my throat. "I'm not perfect. You've seen my room."

"Do you remember when I told you that you terrified me?"

I did. It had been the first night like this, when we had lain together in the dark.

"A Holmes is always in control," he said, his voice shaking harder. "It is how we survive. We control ourselves. We control our thoughts, our reactions, our emotions. Discipline and focus are our weapons."

I sat up. The air was cold against my chest. "Let me guess: Blackfriar taught you that."

"My father taught me that. Yes."

"Jesus Christ."

"Whatever you might think of him, he has worked tirelessly to help me—"

"To help you? He's fucking brainwashed you!"

"He has helped me in spite of my own failings—"

"What failings? You bite your lip? So the fuck what? He hurt you. He— H, I don't even know what he did to you, but I know it wasn't right, and I know it wasn't good."

"My training—"

"Your brainwashing."

"I owe my father everything—"

"For what? For him fucking with your head? For making you think you have to pump your body full of that shit so you can have an edge? For what, exactly, should you be so fucking grateful to that abusive fuckwit asshole?"

Holmes sat up. "Stop shouting!"

In the dark, he was nothing more than an outline. We stared at each other. I could feel him trembling. When he spoke, the words were so shaky that they were barely intelligible. "I cannot be in control of myself around you. I become distracted. I make mistakes. I have no perspective. I spend so much time and energy thinking about you and worrying about you that I become useless for anything else."

"For these stupid fucking games that you and your mindfucked family play."

"For keeping you safe, you idiot! How do you not understand that you are the most important person in my life, and if I am not in control, I cannot keep you safe? If something happened to you, I would die!"

The fury in his voice sucked the air from the room. I rubbed my chest. His trembling had become violent now; I thought I heard his teeth click together.

"I don't need you to keep me safe," I said. "And that's all bullshit. The stuff about your dad. The stuff about being in control. It's bullshit. It is fucking bullshit."

His breaths were labored and pained. The springs rattled as he continued to shake. He sounded on the verge of tears.

"I'm sorry," I muttered. In a louder voice, I said, "H, I'm sorry."

He was still taking those panicked, struggling breaths.

"I shouldn't have—I didn't mean it. It's like you said. I don't understand, that's all. If you say he helped you—"

"Stop," he said as he started to cry.

I watched him, his shoulders heaving as he came apart. Then I reached for him. He stiffened in my arms, and then he twisted. He probably could have broken my jaw and my elbows and all my ribs if he'd wanted to—hell, he probably could have done it while he was still crying himself to pieces.

But when I tightened my hold, he let me, and he let me pull him against me. I leaned against the wall, and he lay against me, sobbing. I stroked his hair and rubbed his back. It didn't last long; a Holmes must always be in control.

When he'd calmed himself enough to take a deep breath, he sat up and wiped his face with the sheets. He sat there in silhouette, head down. I knew the curve of his spine. I knew the span of his shoulders. Anywhere, I thought. I could be anywhere and know you.

"Do you want me to leave?" I asked.

He shook his head. His voice was rough but surprisingly steady when he said, "I will never want you to leave."

"Do you want to lie down, then? We can lie down. How about that? Let's get some sleep."

He let me pull him down, and this time, his body bent into mine. We fit together perfectly, my arm around his waist.

"If I have a, um, reaction," I said, "please don't freak out."

He gave me one of those dry little huffs of breath.

I wanted to kiss the back of his neck. Instead, I tucked him against me more closely and closed my eyes and thought pure, chaste thoughts about traffic accidents.

When he moved, I knew. He couldn't stand it. It was too much, being vulnerable like that, and (full disclosure) I was already chubbing up. So, he'd ask me—politely—to leave, and—

His mouth was hot against mine, uncertain, hard.

When he pulled back, I got up on one elbow. I could feel my pulse in my throat, in my face, in my lips.

"What are you doing?" I asked.

"I don't know," he said. His voice was sandy, dissolving. "I've never kissed anyone before."

I found his hip with one hand, his jaw with my other, pulled him closer, cupped his face, fingers curling along his nape. He was close enough that his breath felt hot and made my skin tighten. I wanted to say again, *I love you*, but instead I whispered, "Let me show you."

Chapter 26

Even a Holmes

We didn't do anything—not that it's any of your business. I was a perfect gentleman. Basically. He didn't even take off his Rudolph shirt, in spite of my best efforts.

But I will say this about Holloway Holmes: he's a fast learner.

At some point, we slept again, and I mean slept. I woke twice during the night to the sound of Holmes's deep, even breathing. I wondered how long it had been since he had slept—days probably—and how long since he had slept this deeply, without the night terrors that came for him. Since September, when we'd shared the couch in my living room? I kept one arm around him, and he stayed close to me all night.

The next time I woke, though, there was the distinct aroma of onions and hot carbs and a slight, vinegary kick. A herd of horses had been running through my head, taking horse dumps wherever they pleased, and where I'd gotten punched, my eye was swollen and throbbing. I groaned.

"We're skipping class," Holmes said. "It's only a matter of time before they begin looking for truants."

"How are you up so early?"

"I slept six hours." Like he'd said sixteen.

"I'm dead."

"You're not dead."

"You can't be truant if you're dead."

His touch was hesitant as he brushed the hair from my forehead. I opened my eyes. He had showered and dressed, of course, and his hair was dark where it was still damp. The oxford and chinos were back, but I was having a hard time not thinking about what was underneath them. I smiled at him, and after a moment, he smiled back at me. You could see it then—how unsure he was about what was happening, about what would happen next, and how dangerously happy he was and, at the same time, aware of the danger of that happiness. I held out one hand (flopped it onto an empty expanse of mattress, if we're being technical), and after a moment he took it.

"A-minus," I said and squeezed his fingers. "You're still a dork."

Relief softened the lines around his mouth and in his shoulders. "Since you're dead," he said, "and I am such a dork, I suppose I should throw away these breakfast burritos."

"No!"

"Then you'll have to get up and eat—quickly—before the truant officer finds us."

I tapped my mouth.

Holmes rolled his eyes.

"You're my dork," I said.

"Jack."

I puckered up.

He didn't roll his eyes, but he did give me that amused little breath. He bent, and it was clear he was going to try to get away with one quick little brush of lips. So, instead, I twisted his collar and dragged him closer and gave him the business.

A while later, while I had my hand up his shirt, Holmes wriggled away. His hair was mussed, his cheeks were flushed, the waistband of his chinos hung open. "No," he said, more like he was trying to convince himself. He started stuffing his shirt back into his chinos, and that's when he noticed the waistband. His head came up. Shock painted his face. "Jack!"

"Just in case," I said.

"In case of what?"

"In case of a medical emergency."

He fastened the button on his waistband, face flaming. His hard-on was more visible when he finished, and I watched him hesitate, trying to decide if this was worse.

"H?"

He threw me a wary glance.

I pointed to my own below-the-equator situation, which my boxers were doing nothing to hide. "It's ok. It's good. We're good."

He nodded, but his gaze slid away from mine.

"It's supposed to happen," I said. "It's supposed to feel good, and it's, you know, a way for us to show each other how we feel."

He nodded again, but he still wouldn't look at me.

"H—"

"Jack, please."

I stopped. After a couple minutes, Holmes's face cleared into its usual cold reserve. He moved over to the desk, where he'd improvised takeout containers by doubling up foam plates. He brought them over to me and sat on the bed. When I touched his back, he flinched and tried to hide the movement by removing the top plate from one of the makeshift containers. It held a breakfast burrito the size of a small bus, along with several salsa packets of varying heat, and plastic flatware. I propped myself up, tried to resign myself to blue balls for my foreseeable future, and went to work on the burrito. Fire-level salsa, by the way. There's no point if it doesn't burn going down.

"It's not that it doesn't feel good," Holmes said. He released a jangled laugh. "Quite the opposite."

Bacon, eggs, crispy potatoes, cheese. I took another bite.

"I didn't want you to think I didn't enjoy it."

"Trust me, I know you enjoyed it."

He turned enough to glare at me, and in spite of my best efforts, I grinned. After a moment, his face softened, and he said, "It is frightening to me. And more frightening that—that I can be so distracted that I don't even notice…"

"Me trying to free the weasel?"

"Jack!"

I laughed, almost choked on some burrito, and saved myself by coughing and hacking and eating more burrito. Holmes didn't do anything to save my life, of course. He also didn't often look quite so satisfied, but I figured he deserved this one.

When my airway was clear of breakfast deliciousness, I said, "It was when I bit your nipple through your shirt."

Holmes's jaw dropped. He raised a hand halfway to his chest, where the wet mark was drying on the oxford.

"You were distracted," I said through another mouthful of bacon and potato and eggs. "It happens to the best of us."

Something changed in his face.

"No," I said and put the burrito down. "You're human. You're allowed to be human. I only make out with human boys, and I only let human boys grind on me like it's going out of style."

He let out a frustrated breath and shook his head.

"Yes," I said.

"Jack."

"Yes."

He was quiet for a long time. "You do not understand." And then, before I could say anything, he added in a small voice, "I do not want to fight with you this morning."

I thought about that. Then I flipped the plate off of his burrito and pushed it toward him.

He shook his head.

"You want to try that again?" I asked. "Seeing how you don't want a fight and all."

In the end, he ate half the burrito, and I did garbage disposal duty by finishing it off for him.

"So," I said, "not trying to be weird, but could I borrow some clothes? I'm not moving in, I promise, but I've got to figure out what I'm going to do next. I should be able to get some of my stuff while my dad is out of the house today."

"Jack, you have to talk to your father eventually."

"No, I don't."

Holmes looked at me.

"I'm not going back there," I said.

Holmes reached out, hesitated, and touched my eye. How long, I wondered, would he hesitate before he felt safe touching me? How long before it wasn't always the ultimate risk? He asked, "Did your father do this to you?"

"God, no. Some Subway douche. It's a long story."

Holmes let his hand fall. A familiar rattle came from the window — the blinds were closed, but I recognized the sound of snow spitting against the glass.

"Your father loves you," Holmes said. "He's worried about you. I understand that you had a fight—"

"He doesn't love me, actually. He loves the me—whoever he thought I was. And I'm too old to care what he thinks about me."

Holmes's mouth slanted with amusement. "You're sixteen."

"I've been taking care of myself for over a year. I'm not going to let him make me feel like shit about—" But I stopped. In part, because Holmes was some of it. And in part because I didn't want to hear it out loud.

Holmes waited for the rest of it, but when I stayed silent, he didn't press. Over the sound of the snow spinning against the window, he said, "The situation is more complicated than that."

"I'll figure it out."

"Jack, please. He was desperate when he came here last night."

"I said no. I'm done talking about it."

He opened his mouth.

"Are you going to lend me some clothes or what?"

Whatever he'd been about to say, he changed it to, "Of course."

So, I showered, and naturally, Holmes had an extra toothbrush. His clothes fit me alright; we were the same height, but I was broader across the shoulders, and built—well, *thicker* didn't sound super flattering, but maybe *more substantially*. I mean, I wasn't a speedhead with a jack-in-the-box ass. I settled on a Lake Powell t-shirt I'd never seen him wear and, surprise of all surprises, a hoodie and joggers he kept folded in one of the drawers. I tried to figure out my hair in his mirror, and after a while, Holmes came over and did it for me.

"How did you do that? I can spend an hour and it doesn't look like that."

He frowned. "It's hair, Jack. What do you mean?"

Instead of engaging with that, I gave him a look and said, "What now?"

"Class—"

"Unh-uh. Nice try. The minute I walk into class, they'll call my dad."

"Jack, consider your long-term options."

"No. I refuse to consider anything long-term, options or otherwise. Besides, you're trying to distract me. What are you going to do next? Scheming? Plotting? Skulking?"

"Even if we omit, for the moment, the question of food and housing and other necessities, your education—"

"Holloway Holmes."

One corner of his mouth fish-hooked. "I don't know what you mean."

"Yes, you do. The game. This stupid game with Paxton."

He thought about this for a while. "It's not with Paxton. Or rather, he is a piece being moved in the game. He is not one of the players."

"Are you sure about that? Because it looks like he's been playing us pretty well."

"I'm sure." He bit his lip, the movement unguarded, and seemed to be thinking. Then he said, "I was given something valuable. Someone is trying to steal it."

"Who?"

"I don't know."

"Maggie?"

"Possibly."

"Aren't the Moriartys your family nemesis? Nemesises? Nemises?"

"It may be Maggie. I don't have enough information yet."

There was another option, of course. Holmes's father, Blackfriar, might have been the one behind these events. It could have been one of his bizarre trainings, another way to test his son. Or it could have something to do with whatever secrets he was hiding—he'd killed Sarah Watson to keep them, so I didn't think he'd be bothered by a little blackmail and theft.

"I still believe our best course of action," Holmes said, "is to discover the truth behind Dawson's murder. That is the moment when everything went awry; up to that point, my opponent's—"

"Our," I said.

Holmes's eyes flicked to mine. His throat moved, and after a moment, he said, "Up to that point, our opponent's gambit had been successful. They deployed Paxton to distract me, which Paxton did quite effectively by embroiling us in this blackmail investigation. But something changed. Someone stole the blackmail material and killed Dawson. Now someone has killed Kazen. This suggests a possible opening; any disruption to the initial plan offers a chance to see who has orchestrated these events."

"It's hard to believe we're dealing with two killers, so I guess we can assume that whoever we're looking for, they were at the party at the Youngs' house. Do you think it was Emma?"

After a pause, Holmes shook his head.

"Neither do I, but it looks bad for her." I told him what Ariana had told me, about the night of Wintersmash, and Emma's bizarre behavior in the tunnels. "She got into a fight with somebody. I guess it could have been Dawson, but honestly, I just can't believe it. I've talked to her. Rowe and Glo love her. She's not a killer."

Holmes studied me.

"What?"

"Do you believe you can tell when someone is lying to you?"

"That's not what I said."

"But you believe you can sense deception?"

"No, not all the time. But I think I would have gotten a vibe if she was the crazy killer type."

In the silence that followed, a door opened and shut somewhere else in the building.

"The evidence suggests that Emma is not the killer," Holmes finally said. "She was not in possession of the weapon used to kill Kazen, and more to the point, if she were the killer, there would be no reason for her to be covered in blood the way she was. Kazen was killed with a single shot from close range. Emma would have been covered in blood spatter. Instead, she had blood on her hands, as though she had tried to turn the body or check him to see if he was still alive."

"Or search him," I said. "Someone went through his clothes. They were looking for something."

Holmes grimaced and nodded.

"You're sure it's not Paxton?" I asked. "He was there that night. Hell, H, he locked us in that closet."

"Aston was there. His father and mother and sister were there."

"This is what I'm talking about. I don't know what this thing is between the two of you, but I think it's affecting your judgment."

"There is no thing between me and Paxton," Holmes said. "There is nothing between us."

"H, come on."

He drew in a breath. Then he flattened his hands on his knees and let it out slowly. I watched him, and when he still didn't say anything, I picked up one of the takeout plates and folded it. The foam squeaked as I creased it.

"When I was younger," Holmes said, the words brittle and cut like crystal, "Paxton was a guest of my family's. For quite some time, actually. The Holmeses and the Adlers go back; they are one of the three families: Holmes, Adler, Moriarty."

"Four, right? Watson?"

He gave me a strange look, but all he said was "You've met Paxton. He is brash. Charming. Intelligent. In many ways—perhaps in every way—he was the son my father wanted. He was also, believe it or not, kind, which is not a trait my father cultivates." Holmes swallowed. "I found my father's training to be…difficult. There was always another lesson. Always another game. Always another difficult truth or unyielding reality against which I was expected to test myself. I understand, now, that it was for my benefit. But at the time, I wished it were otherwise."

"H."

"Paxton is four and a half years older. At that age, it seemed like a lifetime. He was everything to me: brother, friend, confidante. When I thought I couldn't stand it any longer, he did what he could to help."

"Were you—" I didn't know how to finish that, so I stopped, and my face grew hot.

Holmes laughed. "No. But I'd be lying if I said I hadn't wished it were so. You asked me if I loved him. I thought I did. I was infatuated; I would do anything he asked. He was my lifeline to sanity. He promised me that as soon as I was old enough, we would leave together, travel the world. He has always had grand plans."

The pain in his face was so bright I wanted to shade my eyes. I swallowed and asked, "What happened?"

"He turned eighteen and left for college, and my father sent me to Hewdenhouse." What Holmes didn't say was, *He abandoned me.* But I could hear it in the timbre of his voice. "My father is influential. At Paxton's request, he helped him gain admission to a prestigious university on the East Coast. With a full scholarship, of course."

I reached for Holmes's hand, and he let me take it. "Jesus."

"It was a game, you see? One of many. A long game." He touched his lip and examined his finger, as though surprised by the scarlet stain there. Then he looked at me, and the gray in his eyes was cold and flat like old snow. "It was a valuable lesson."

We sat in silence, and I tried to think of how to say it. The world isn't like that. People aren't like that. There are billions of people who want to be kind and generous and patient and good, and I'm sorry you were born into a family of psychos who taught you that the world was barren and hard and cold. But none of that would be right; he'd shake his head or laugh or stare through me. And in the end, I said nothing.

"Paxton is many things," Holmes said, "but he is not a murderer. If he knew about the—the valuable object I acquired, he would attempt to steal it, of course. He might even have chosen something like this to distract me. He knows me too well."

"But?"

"But, among other things, Paxton is vain. He would never have engineered a plan in which he appeared to be outsmarted."

I laughed in spite of myself.

Holmes looked at me, searching my face. "Jack, there is nothing between me and Paxton. When he left my family home, what I felt—what I thought I felt—ended. I want you to know that."

I nodded. But I remembered the look on Holmes's face when we had stumbled onto Paxton in Dawson's room. I remembered how he had held himself when Paxton had kissed his cheek. We all lie to ourselves, I thought with a kind of bemused detachment. Even a Holmes.

But I said, "If not Paxton, then who?"

"That's the question, isn't it?"

"We should talk to the Youngs. We haven't talked to them yet."

"Definitely," Holmes said. "But we should talk to Emma first."

"How? She ran away, and the police have no idea where she is. She's obviously not dumb enough to keep her phone with her."

"Simple: we ask Rowe and Glo where they've been hiding her."

Chapter 27

B-Plus

Because Holmes was a bit of a showboat, he actually didn't walk right up to Rowe and ask him where he kept his fugitive quasi-girlfriend. Instead, we skulked and snooped and scouted, just like I'd predicted, until we spotted Rowe coming out of class at the lunch break. We trailed after him to the dining hall and waited outside behind a tamarack.

My breath plumed, and I shivered and kicked the dirty hump of snow left by the plow.

When Rowe emerged, he was carrying a plastic bag. He did a quick glance around, managed to miss us entirely behind the tree, and hurried off with his head low and shoulders hunched.

"They didn't offer me a bag," Holmes said.

"Could he try to look a little more suspicious, please?" I said. "He's practically wearing a striped jumpsuit with PRISON on the back."

"They were well aware that I was taking food to go, and they didn't offer me a bag."

"Don't feel bad; Rowe's basically a human-sized puppy, and not in the kinky way. He's lovable."

"It should be an equal policy," Holmes said. He was going a bit English at the edges. "Everyone should receive a bag if they require one."

Sighing, I hooked his sleeve and tugged him forward. "You're lovable too."

Bright red circles glowed in his cheeks, and he didn't say anything after that.

It might have been hard, following someone else across campus during the lunch break without being spotted, when most of the paths were empty and the snow made a white backdrop. But Rowe kept his head down and powered on, not even looking side to side.

"Five bucks he goes to the athletic center," I said.

Holmes huffed that tiny breath.

"You don't think he will?" I asked.

"Of course that's where he's going. I'm not interested in giving you my money, that's all."

True to my—our—prediction, he walked straight to the athletic center. He passed one of the PE teachers—Mr. Patrick—in the vestibule, nodded, mumbled something, shrank away when the Mr. Patrick laid a hand on his shoulder, and then put his head down and powered into the building.

"Jesus Christ," I muttered. "You're going to have to give him lessons."

"Hello, Mr. Patrick," Holmes said as we passed him.

"Hello. Jack, I heard you were sick."

He was one of those big guys, still young, who shaved their heads, and his no-bullshit attitude wasn't as effective once you'd seen him play with his kids. I tried for a sickly smile and said, "Feeling better. I left some of my books in my locker—gotta grab them before class this afternoon."

Mr. Patrick watched us for a moment. "Well, hurry up. Break's almost over."

We jogged deeper into the building—as much to get away from Mr. Patrick as to catch up with Rowe. The warm air was pleasant; the smell of rubber and feet and Fabuloso, less so.

"Like that?" Holmes asked.

I poked my head down a hallway and didn't see Rowe, so I jugged down the hall. "Huh?"

"I assume you mean Rowe should be performing at that kind of level."

No Rowe in the next hall. I spared Holmes a glance. "What?"

"What book would you have left in your locker? The logistics of it are, frankly, ridiculous. The personal storage lockers aren't big enough for more than a few effects, and a textbook of any size would have made them impossible to use."

I stopped for a moment. "Are you talking smack?"

He pointed. "Rowe went down that hallway."

"Rowe didn't—" I poked my head around the corner. Rowe was halfway down the hall. "I was going to check that one next."

Holmes didn't say anything, but his eyes were silver bright.

"It worked, didn't it?" I asked as we hurried after Rowe. "I mean, Mr. Patrick didn't say anything?"

"I pulled a muscle and need to see the trainer. Someone sent me to get ice. I've got to grab a book from a friend. And you've always got your trump card: my dad asked me to do something."

I scowled. I waited until Rowe rounded the next corner. Then I shoved Holmes hard enough to send him stumbling. He burst out laughing—the sound short, almost immediately controlled, but one I hadn't heard from him before. I smiled in spite of myself.

When we came around the corner, we found ourselves at the end of the hall. Three doorways stood in front of us. Two were unmarked, and the third said simply STAFF ONLY.

"Got anything smart to say?" I asked Holmes. When he opened his mouth, though, I said, "Don't you dare."

He shut his mouth, but he looked like he was trying not to smile. How many people had ever seen him like this? How many had known he could be a goof? I mean, everybody knew he was a major dork, but how many knew he could be this weird, sweet goofball who was still trying everything out for the first time, who sounded so much younger when he laughed?

I studied the doors again. I decided to try the staff one first, and Holmes took a breath. I stopped, set my jaw, folded my arms. He looked like he wanted to help, so I shook my head.

Snowmelt shone on the floor, leading toward the door on our right.

I pointed.

"Very well done."

"Stop."

"No, Jack." He was poshing it up again. "That was quite well done."

"You're doing that on purpose, aren't you? Because I told you I like the accent."

He cracked that big, doofus grin. "Of course."

I tried to dead-arm him, but he slipped away, his grin spreading across his face.

When he rapped on the door, silence greeted us. Holmes raised his hand to knock again, but I shook my head.

"Rowe, we know you're in there. Open the door."

Still nothing.

"I've got keys," I said. "I can open it myself. Or I can call my dad. Or I can call security." I gave him a few seconds, and then, in a softer voice, I said, "Come on, man. It doesn't have to be like this."

The latch made a noise, and the door swung open a few inches. Rowe stared out at us from under disheveled blond bangs. The usual open friendliness was gone, and in its place was a strange hardness. Warlike. Thousands of years ago, puppy dog boys like Rowe had been called Vikings.

"Number one," I said, "we already know you have Emma in there. Number two, you know there's no way you can keep this going forever, so you're looking for a solution. We're it. Number three, you owe me, man. You sent that son of a bitch to my house." I tried it again, blunting the sharpness in my voice, letting it drop down. "And number four, I thought we were friends."

It was a low blow, but it was the truth. That's why shit like that works.

Rowe's face crumpled. Tears leaked out, and he wiped them away. "Promise you're not going to call the cops."

"We can't make any promises," Holmes said.

I squeezed his arm, and I said, "Rowe, let us talk to her. That's why we're here. If we wanted to call the cops, we'd have done it already."

After a moment, he gave a slow nod. He wiped his cheeks again, leaving the glisten of a salt smear, and he snuffled and inched the door open until it was barely wide enough for us to slip through. He shut it again and set the lock.

We stood in the front room of a small, three-office suite. Now that I was inside, I vaguely remembered this space—I'd wiped it down maybe a grand total of once when I'd been helping Dad. The football offices, I was pretty sure. Until a donor came up with a lot of money to give them better facilities. Doors connected with each private office, set with frosted glass. Two were dark, but the third had a light on.

"Stand where I can see you," Holmes told Rowe, indicating a spot across from us.

Rowe glanced at me.

"This is a weird situation," was the best I could come up with.

Rowe shook his head, but he moved across the room. He folded his arms. Some of the fight was rising in his face again, as though he were starting to think he'd made a mistake. He was bigger than I was. Built a lot heavier. Holmes had disabled him pretty easily, but personally, I was having some doubts about myself.

When Holmes cocked an inquisitive look at the lit door, Rowe nodded. Holmes reached for the handle, but it turned before he could grab it. The door swung open, and Glo stepped into view. She had a box cutter in one hand, and she gave an experimental slash at Holmes—not trying to get him, but testing out her range and, at the same time, warning him.

Holmes drew back and looked at me, of all people.

"Hey," I said. "You picked that door. You get to deal with her."

"You can't have her," Glo said. She was vibrating, all five feet of her, and her makeup was smeared. The hand with the box cutter bobbed and wove unsteadily. "You need to go, right now!"

"Rowe—" I tried.

"Rowe wasn't supposed to let anyone in! Get out of here!"

"Glo," I said. "Come on. This is crazy. What are you going to do? Kill me?"

A sob hitched Glo's tiny frame. She sliced an X in the air.

"I can take the knife," Holmes whispered.

Rowe was staring at us, his fists balled at his sides. If Holmes moved, Rowe would start swinging, and if that happened, this whole thing would fall apart. Likely, Emma would run again in the confusion.

"Why don't you ask Emma?" I said to Glo. "Ask her what she wants. Ask her if she wants to do this forever, hiding and running and being afraid, and making the two of you accomplices."

Another sob tore through Glo. She turned her face into her shoulder, the box cutter dipping. Holmes tensed, but I shook my head.

Emma stepped into view. The cat-eye glasses were crooked, and her pixie cut stood up in places, probably from sleeping on it. She had changed into joggers and a sweatshirt, but she still wore the fingerless gloves I recognized from every other time I'd seen her. Her skin was ashy, and her eyes were hollow and smudged, but her face was strangely composed. "It's all right," she said quietly and put a hand on Glo's arm. Glo turned into her, and for a moment, they embraced.

Then Glo pushed herself away from Emma. "No. Run, Em; we'll keep them here—"

"Glo, it's ok." Emma set her hand on the smaller girl's arm again and gently forced it down. "He's right. I didn't know what to do. I don't know, I guess. But it's not fair, putting you and Rowe in danger like this."

"You're not putting us in danger," Rowe said huskily. "We're doing it because we love you, Em."

She nodded. When she looked at us, her face had that stripped-down quality of emotional exhaustion, all the layers and masks and veils fallen away. "What do you want?"

"To talk," I said. "We need to know what happened last night at the Youngs' house."

"She didn't kill him," Rowe said. It was almost a shout.

"I'd like her to answer the question," Holmes said.

"If you think she could have killed him—" Rowe began, still at full volume.

"Rowe," Emma said in a small voice.

He stopped and rubbed his cheeks.

"I was going to look for something in Aston's room. That's why I went upstairs. And instead, I saw—" She stopped and drew a deep breath. "That man was already dead when I found him. I shouldn't have touched him, but I thought he was hurt. He was hurt, I mean, but I thought I could help him. And then I realized he was dead, and I was covered in blood, and—" When she spoke again, she sounded burned out. "I didn't kill him."

"Of course you didn't kill him," Holmes said. "I want to know why you were there, and I want to know why you ran."

Emma drew a deep breath and shook her head.

"What do you mean?" Holmes asked.

"That's all I'm going to say," Emma said. "If you want to call the police, go ahead. Please don't—if you could please not tell them about Glo and Rowe, I would appreciate it. They didn't do anything wrong."

She turned and moved back inside the office.

Holmes made a frustrated noise, but when he took a step, Glo brought the box cutter up again. She was still sniffling.

"You've got to be kidding me," I said. "Glo, give me that thing. Right now. Rowe, stop looking at me like you're going to tear my head off. You two are nut-cases—you realize that, right? I like you, but God, you are legit psycho about each other. Glo, I'm still waiting. Box cutter. Now."

Her eyes were wide and startled. After a moment, she wiped her nose and handed me the box cutter. I retracted the blade and stuffed it in my back pocket. Rowe was opening and closing his hands—not in a threat, but like he was trying to get the blood moving again. His face was ruddier than usual, and when he met my eye, he gave me an embarrassed half-smile.

"All of you wait here," I said.

I stepped past Glo and shut the door, forcing her into the outer room. They'd made up a pallet for Emma out of their own bedding. A little nest, kind of. She had a hot plate, God only knows where they got it, and a steel mug like the kind you find in camping gear. About ten Cup of Noodles. Lots of hot chocolate packets from the dining hall. Her uneaten meal—fish tacos, it looked like—waited in a genuine takeout container. Holmes would be devastated to know his two-plate system was completely unnecessary.

Emma sat on the pallet, her knees drawn up to her chest, arms wrapped around her knees. When I sat, she twitched, but she didn't look at me.

"Something's going on," I said. "And you don't want to tell us because you're embarrassed or you're frightened. But whatever it is, it's not worse than going to prison, or having your life turned inside out."

She turned her face into her knees. Her breathing sounded thick, clotted.

I tried to think. I didn't know her that well. I knew the rumors Dawson had told us—that she was crazy, that she'd almost killed her last boyfriend when he tried to break up with her and that's why she'd been sent to Walker. I knew she and Rowe and Glo were caught up on each other, desperately in love but none of them poly. I knew she and Glo had been kind to Ariana. And I knew what Ariana had told me about Wintersmash: how Emma had gotten wasted, her fight with Glo, taking Ariana into the maze of tunnels and abandoning her, and when she came back, the sounds and signs of a fight. She had been upset. She had told Ariana she'd never had sex with Aston, and then she'd clammed up, but it wasn't like that was a secret because—

"Oh," I said.

Emma looked up at me through bloodshot eyes.

"Hey," I said. "Listen. They're not going to care. I promise."

She started to sob. "They. Are." She struggled for breath between each word. "They're. Going. To. Hate. Me."

I let her cry. After a while, she pressed the heels of her hands to her eyes, and her body fell into a slower rhythm, and she dried her face on her sweatshirt. She breathed through her mouth and traced the seam of her joggers with her thumb.

"They love you," I said. "They're not going to care. I promise. If anything, you might actually—don't take this the wrong way—but you might actually make things easier for everyone."

Her breathing stuttered.

"Really," I said to the unanswered question. "You don't have to tell them if you don't want to. I know it's—it's a lot, trying to put something like that into words. You expect the people around you to know. You expect them to see, to understand, because it's obvious to you—or it's obvious once you actually let yourself start thinking about it. And it's scary, realizing that who they think you are, who they care about, that doesn't match up with who you think you are." My mouth tasted bitter, but I forced myself to keep my voice even as I said, "But that doesn't mean you shouldn't give them a chance. They deserve a chance, right? To show you they love you no matter what?"

She sniffed and dried her face and pressed her fingertips against her eyes.

"I bet you've got a hell of a headache," I said.

That made her laugh weakly, and she opened her eyes. "But what if they don't?"

"I don't know. Life goes on, I guess. It sucks ass. Isn't it better than lying, though?"

"No. I don't know. I don't think so." She stood, and halfway up, she stopped, hands on knees. It was the way people stood when they were hurt. When they'd taken a body blow. And the way you knew if someone had guts was if they forced themselves up the rest of the way, even if it hurt, and kept going.

Emma had guts. "Will you ask them—will you stay?"

I gave her a crooked smile. "Sure. You've still got to tell me about all these murders."

They filed into the room like they'd gotten in trouble: Glo with her finger marking a place in a book—*PAWsitive ID: A Friendly Feline Mystery*—and Rowe, because he was Rowe, clutching a football, and Holmes with that particular kind of fluid grace that marked his annoyance. We took up position around the room, with Emma still on her pallet. And then we waited.

Emma looked up. Struggle played out in her face. She opened her mouth, and a little whimper escaped her, and then she started to cry.

Glo dropped *PAWsitive ID* and knelt on the pallet to wrap her arms around Emma. She gave me a furious look. "What did he say to you? Did he threaten you? You don't have to do anything he says—"

Slowly, Emma fought free of the embrace. Squeezing Glo's hand in one of her own, she shook her head. And then, tears still streaking her face, she said, "I'm—I'm ace."

Holmes's expression didn't change. Glo's flickered indeterminately. Rowe shrugged and said, "Yeah?"

"Rowe!" Glo slapped his leg.

"Ow! What—oh. I mean, ok." Rowe looked at me of all people, rubbing the back of his neck, and then back at Emma. "Thanks for, um, telling us?"

"You knew?" Emma asked.

"No," Glo said.

At the same time, Rowe said, "Well, yeah."

Glo tried to smack his thigh again, but Rowe leaned out of the way. Then he grinned and pushed back the blond fringe above his eyes. "I mean, you never wanted to make out, and I'm super good at making out."

"That doesn't mean she's ace, you—you pig!" Glo turned back to Emma. She looked her friend in the face for a long moment. And then she wrapped her in a hug—different from the one before, just as tight but with a new kind of energy. "We love you whoever you are," she said, her voice choked. "It doesn't change anything."

"Well, it does, kind of," Emma said with a wet laugh, but she hugged Glo back. When the girls separated, Emma wiped her eyes. "It means you two can finally be together, and we can stop dancing around all this. I should have said something a long time ago, but—but I was scared. My parents are going to lose their minds when I tell them, and I didn't want—" She stopped herself, but the rest of the sentence hung in the air.

"We love you," Glo said. She was beaming as she took Emma's hands in her own. "Whatever that looks like. However you want it to be." She glanced over her shoulder at Rowe. "Say something, you big dope!"

"Well, yeah, we love you," he said. When Glo gave him another look, he asked, "What? You already told her."

"I can't," Glo said as she hugged Emma again.

"You have to," Emma said with another laugh—a stronger one, this time.

"Don't make me."

Emma laughed harder, mixed with tears now, but full of relief. Rowe moved over to crouch next to her, and he pulled her into a hug too, and she cried into his chest for a couple of minutes while he stroked her hair. Then the three of them sat there, faces glowing, holding hands.

"I was serious," Emma said. "I meant what I said. I was afraid for a long time that if I told you, you wouldn't want this anymore. But now I realize what we had, it wasn't a true thing anyway. So, I want you two to be together. I know we'll still be friends, but I want you two to—I want you to be happy."

"Em," Glo began.

Rowe spoke over her. "The three of us," he said firmly. "This is a true thing. Right here."

"But I know you don't want—" Emma began.

"Em," Glo said. "Stop. You're right on the verge of making Rowe sound smarter than us."

Rowe gave them his puppy-dog grin, and the girls shared a look, and it was obvious that they'd forgotten me and Holmes—forgotten the rest of the world, in fact. Holmes was watching them, his face closed off, and when I touched the small of his back, he started. He looked over at me, but I kept my fingers there. Contact. A link from my body to his. Something changed in his countenance, and for a moment, I could see him behind all the armor.

"Oh my God," Glo squealed.

I looked over. The three of them were staring at us.

"You hooked up!" Emma shouted.

"Oh, they totally hooked up," Rowe said. "You could see it as soon as they got here."

Holmes flinched, and he would have moved, but I gave his back a reassuring rub. "We didn't hook up," I said. "We—"

"Dope hickey, man," Rowe said.

"Nobody has a hickey!" I snapped.

It was too much for Holmes; he shifted his weight, breaking that point of contact between us, and his face was as smooth as ice again. His voice was ice too when he said, "If the three of you have finished, Jack and I need to ask some questions."

"I bet Jack took his shirt off," Rowe said.

I couldn't help it: "Rowe!"

"He totally took his shirt off," Glo said. "The real question is, did he flex?"

"Stop talking," I said. "This is a murder investigation."

Laughing, Emma pulled the collar of her sweatshirt up to hide her mouth. But I could hear her perfectly fucking well when she said, "Look how red he is. He definitely flexed."

"You—" I stopped. "The three of you—"

And then I saw Holmes's face. Some of the rigidity had melted, and a kind of wary amusement showed now. This was all new to him. He was still trying to figure it out.

"For your information—" I began.

"Oh my God," Glo squealed again. "He's going to say he was a perfect gentleman."

"You know what? I'm not going to dignify any of this with a response. Holmes, arrest all three of them, and throw them in the brig or whatever we have on campus."

"Respect, man," Rowe said, holding out his fist for me to bump. "He's super hot, and if I were into dudes, I'd go for him too. Same goes for you too, so don't feel bad."

"This is what the two of you want?" I asked Glo and Emma.

"He's sweet," Emma said, stroking Rowe's bangs.

"And he really is good at making out," Glo said and then giggled into Emma's shoulder.

"One day," Emma said to Holmes, "you can tell us if Jack is any good."

Holmes hesitated, and his gaze slid to me. I rolled my eyes. Holmes said, "I don't know if that would be appropriate." Then, he added, "Jack likes to give letter grades. B. B-plus."

"B-fucking-plus?" I demanded.

"I was simply demonstrating the scale."

"You're out of your goddamn mind."

Emma and Glo had collapsed against Rowe, and all three of the psychos were laughing.

For a moment, Holmes looked…young. His face was still that cold-chiseled perfection, but radiant now as one of his dorky smiles slipped out. I wanted a snapshot of that moment, of him, like this, forever. I never wanted the night terrors to come back, or the training, or the games. I wanted to kiss him right there, and I probably would have except for the *Looney Tunes* brigade. He must have noticed something in how I was looking at him, because those fine blond eyebrows arched. I smiled and shook my head. And then I pursed my lips in a tiny kiss, and his face caught fire.

"Emma," Holmes said when their laughter had died, "I understand that the last few days have been hard, but we need to talk to you."

She nodded and sat up. "You two can go—"

Rowe shook his head. Glo clung to Emma's arm.

With a sigh and a reluctant smile, Emma nodded again. She looked at Holmes and said, "I told the truth: I didn't kill anybody." When Holmes didn't say anything, Emma squirmed, and her eyes dropped. "I—I made a mistake, though. I did some dumb stuff."

"Start at the beginning," I said.

She let out a dry noise that might have been a laugh. "The beginning is my parents being so obsessed with this whole 'get married and have babies' life plan—it's a Mormon thing. It's also why being ace is such a big problem for them. No sex means no babies." She shook her head. "If they hadn't been so excited for me to start dating, I never would have been in that car with Darvey, and I wouldn't have beaten the crap out of him for trying to pull my skirt off."

"This is the ex-boyfriend?" Holmes asked. "The one you attacked?"

"She didn't attack him," Glo said.

"She was defending herself," Rowe said at the same time.

"Peanut gallery." I snapped my fingers. "No comments, or I'll kick you out. Understand?"

Rowe gave me a hurt look. Glo glowered.

"He wasn't even my boyfriend," Emma said. "He was a creep. But yes, I—I overreacted. I'd been doing kickboxing classes, and I just started swinging. He had to go to the hospital. And my parents sent me here. And, like I told you, at the beginning, I dated Aston. It was a way to placate my parents, who were terrified I might be a lesbian." Glo giggled into Emma's arm again, and Emma smiled reluctantly. "And it was a way to fit in. You know how it is here. It's hard to make friends—hard to find anyone who's actually decent."

"When you told Ariana that you'd never had sex with Aston," I said, "I thought you meant because he was gay. But that wasn't it, was it?"

She shook her head. "He wanted to. Or he wanted to do it once so he could say he'd done it, I think. But for the most part, like I told you, he wasn't interested in any of that stuff. It made him the perfect boyfriend."

"When did he begin telling people that you'd slept together?" Holmes asked.

"It started when we were dating; that was one of the reasons I broke it off, actually. Then, for a while, he left me alone. I kind of knew about Dawson and the other guys—I suspected, a part of me, and I figured he was happier with us broken up. And then, a couple of weeks ago, he started messaging me again. At first, he was sweet, telling me how much he missed me. Then he was annoying. He wanted to get back together. He wouldn't take no for an answer. He'd show up during passing period and walk with me between classes. He'd come to my residence after hours."

"He's super annoying," Rowe said.

Emma smiled and squeezed his hand. "When I still wouldn't agree to start dating him, he threatened me. He'd tell Rowe and Emma, he said. He asked me if I thought they'd still want to be with me if they knew I had— his words were 'a block of ice for a pussy.' I didn't know—I was afraid—" She stopped and swallowed. Rowe made a grumbling warning noise, and Glo scooted closer to her. "It shouldn't have been such a big deal. But it felt like such a big deal. It felt like if anyone knew, if I said anything, it would ruin everything."

"Did you help Paxton blackmail Aston?" Holmes asked.

"No!"

"Did you know he was planning to blackmail Aston?"

"No, of course not."

"What happened at Wintersmash?" I asked.

"I got drunk," Emma said. "I was so angry, and I thought it would calm me down, loosen me up. But I just got angrier. Glo tried to stop me—"

"I shouldn't have fought with you," Glo said. "I shouldn't have abandoned you."

"You said Emma lied to you," I said.

"She said she changed her mind. She said she wasn't going to let him get under her skin."

Emma let out a slow breath and shrugged. "I decided to confront Aston. I was tired of being scared of him. I was going to scare him. I was going to tell him I knew about Dawson. If he said anything, then I'd start talking. Let him see how it felt to be afraid your secret was going to come out. You'd told me someone was blackmailing him, and I figured if I said something, he'd back down." It was hard to tell under the umber cast of her skin, but she looked like she was blushing. "I followed him, trying to catch him alone for a minute. That's when I heard him talking to Dawson about where they were going to meet. So, I decided I should catch them, you know, in the act. Maybe even get a picture." She was silent for a long moment, and when she spoke again, her voice held guilt and embarrassment and a hint of challenge. "I just wanted him to stop."

"You took Ariana with you?"

"I shouldn't have done that, but I was drunk. And, to be honest, scared. I left her alone—I know I shouldn't have done that either—and I went to confront Aston. Only, before I got to where they were supposed to meet, I saw him."

"Aston?" Holmes asked. "Where?"

"I don't know."

"Where was he supposed to meet Dawson?"

"The old boiler room for Walker."

Holmes looked at me, and I sounded a little unsteady when I said, "That's where I found Dawson."

Emma nodded. "You know that passage that runs toward Butters? That's where we were." She took a deep breath. "He wasn't alone."

"What do you mean?" Holmes asked.

"There was someone with him. I don't know. It was dark, and I was drunk, and I was—I was so worked up, I wasn't really paying attention. They were all in black, and they had something over their face. I don't know; I'm sorry."

"What were they doing? Fighting with Aston?"

"No. No—actually, that's the weird thing. They were…leading him away. I guess that's what they were doing. They had a hand on his shoulder. He was out of it, you know? Even worse than me. Stumbling. Bumping into the wall. When that person saw me, they stopped. There was this moment when I thought they were going to do something. I don't know what. Come at me, I guess. And then they turned and ran. I—I didn't really think about it because I was so focused on Aston. I walked right up to him, and I told him." Her voice tightened again. "I thought it was a good idea. I thought he'd leave me alone. But when I said I was going to tell everyone his secret, he went crazy. He tried to hit me. And I was so mad, I hit him back." She stopped to dry her cheek on her shoulder. "We were both so—so messed up that it didn't last very long. Then I went back, and Ariana was waiting, and I didn't know what to say. And later, when they told me about Dawson, I knew if I said anything, they'd ask me about Aston, and I couldn't. I just couldn't. Not again." She sniffled and peeled off the gloves. Her knuckles were split and scabbed. "It's not from hitting Aston, not really. I...hit things when I'm mad. But I knew the police wouldn't care; they'd see my hands and Aston's face, and they said somebody hit Dawson in the head, and I knew that'd be it."

"And?" Holmes asked. "What then?"

"Nothing. I blacked out. Glo and Rowe got me home."

"And the following night? At the Youngs'?"

Emma shrank down. "I knew they'd let me in. They wanted Aston to date me as much as he did—maybe more. I told them Aston and I were patching things up, and he stood there, staring at me, and went along with it."

"What were you looking for in Aston's room?"

She shook her head. "Aston. I was looking for Aston. I heard him say he was going to ditch the party and go to his room, so I went to talk to him. I wanted to see if he remembered anything from that night. And I wanted to—to make sure he wasn't going to say anything to the police. The rest of it was the truth. I went in there. I thought I could help that man. When I came out into the hall, you two were standing right there, and I knew what you'd think. I panicked."

I frowned, but it was Holmes who asked the question: "You didn't pass anyone in the hall?"

Emma shook her head. "When I was going up the stairs, I heard a door close, and I figured someone was in the bathroom—there's one in that hallway." She swallowed. "I swear to you, I didn't hurt anyone. Well, Aston, a little, but he deserved it. I didn't kill anyone. You've got to help me."

Holmes set his jaw, but then all he did was look at me.

"We'll see what we can do," I said. "The smart thing right now would be to find a good lawyer and have him negotiate a way for you to come in. You need to tell the police what you told us; it can only help you. The longer you stay on the run, the worse things are going to get."

"We'll find someone," Rowe said.

"My parents can help," Glo said.

We left them, the three of them huddled together in that abandoned office, looking miserable and happy at the same time, charged with that feeling you get when you love someone and begin to feel what it's like to be loved back.

"The killer heard her coming," I said when Holmes and I got to the hall. "They were leaving Aston's room, probably with the gun still in hand, and ducked into the bathroom. Then, as soon as Emma was in Aston's room, they hurried back to the party. That's who I saw on the stairs. Lot of fucking help that was."

Holmes gave a distracted nod.

"I'm going to try Aston," I said, following as he retraced our route through the building.

He gave me another of those nods, but I wasn't sure he'd heard me. The phone rang until it went to voicemail—Aston hadn't bothered with a personalized one, so all I got was a recording reading me the number. I left a message for him to call me, and I tried again. Then a third time. I still had the phone pressed to my ear when we emerged from the athletic center.

Clouds had hunkered down, and the snow came thicker now, swirling and drifting and spinning back in huge gusts. What remained of the day had taken on the color of steel. A few lingering students trudged across campus, barely more than fingerprint smudges in the distance. Closer, an older guy, heavyset, his complexion like a peach going bad, smoked near the service road. When he saw us, he pitched the cigarette down into the snow and hurried off. Some kind of contract maintenance, I guessed, not Walker staff. The kind of guy who didn't care that it was a smoke-free campus.

"I don't get it," I said. "You tell me it can't be Paxton. Fine; I believe you. But I don't see who else it could be. Aston's family wouldn't be behind this. His parents don't want this kind of information getting out, and there's no point to blackmailing him if they're providing the money, much less framing him for murder."

Holmes was biting his lip. The tip of his nose was already getting pink, and the cold stoked color in his cheeks. I thought about what it would feel like to rub my knuckles against the blade of his jaw. I remembered what his hair had been like between my fingers. I thought maybe I should find a snowbank and shove my head in it.

"H," I said.

He looked at me, but his eyes were only half with me.

"It doesn't even make sense for it to be Camdyn," I said. "Yeah, she's a little mean to him, and she obviously finds him annoying, but she doesn't hate him. You'd have to really hate Aston to try to ruin his life like this—blackmailing him, framing him for murder. But you heard her at the Youngs'—she was begging them not to send him away. And what Emma told us, about the killer walking Aston through the tunnels. What was that about? Do you think they were trying to kidnap him?" Still nothing from Holmes. "I don't get it. We've gone through everybody in his life, and nobody has reason to hate him enough for something like this."

Holmes's eyes were almost the same color as the sky.

I opened my mouth to ask him if he was done rebooting, but my phone buzzed. I checked it, hoping to see Aston's name. Dad flashed on the screen. I dismissed the call. It started again, and I dismissed it again. Then I silenced it.

When I looked up, Holmes was frowning. "He's worried about you."

"Great. He can spend the rest of his life worrying about me."

"Jack—" He stopped, and a surprisingly helpless look crossed his face. "I don't know what to do."

"We'll keep looking for clues—"

"Not that. This—this isn't like you, this anger, this—" If anything he looked even more lost. "This recalcitrance. You're such a kind person. So gentle. So quick to forgive. It is why you're the only person in the world, perhaps, who can tolerate me. I don't understand what's happening. I know you love your father. He loves you. He's desperately sorry for what happened, and he's frightened, and he'd do anything to make sure you're safe—" It was like watching lightning run through his face—a streak of something that was there and then gone. That, combined with how suddenly he cut off, made me worry something was wrong.

"H?"

"Dear God," he said, a bit of the posh slipping out again, voice tight with excitement. "We've got it all wrong."

Chapter 28

You Love Him

The truck wasn't where I'd left it, and it wasn't parked at the cottage, which made me think Dad had purposefully hidden it so that I couldn't take off again.

So, we stole Headmaster Cluff's car.

I mean, it's not like we targeted her. But there it was, a boxy brown Volvo idling in front of Walker Hall. The quad had emptied. Everybody was inside, either on lockdown or avoiding the storm. It was too convenient. Besides, we didn't even know who it belonged to until we were halfway to Lehi.

Holmes found the registration in the glove box.

"She should have known better," I said. "She's the head of school for a bunch of delinquents."

Holmes grimaced. He was probably wondering how much his dad would have to pay to keep him from getting expelled.

"This will be a valuable life lesson," I said as I pushed the Volvo to eighty.

In a storm like this, the canyon went dark. The snow veiled everything, riding currents of air, billowing and rippling like curtains in a breeze. In theory, the whole world was still out there, the parks and the pull-offs and the reservoir. But the storm became a tunnel for me and Holmes, the two of us. There were still people out, of course, and occasionally, the dark bulk of a car or truck became a staticky outline that either passed us or dropped back again. For a while, one seemed to follow, staying just within sight. Then it, too, dropped away. Most of the traffic was headed in the opposite direction, south, as people tried to get home from work before the roads closed or an accident stopped their commute. We didn't even have music because all Dad's CDs were in the truck and, of course, the Volvo didn't have a CD player. Holmes refused to man the radio, and I had this weird thing about not spinning off the highway and killing both of us, so we drove in silence. It was like being packed in wool.

Holmes was biting his lip savagely, his pupils big enough to tint the gray of his irises so that they looked like graphite.

"Ease up," I said.

Holmes hammered the door. When he moved his teeth, I could see where he had chewed his lip to the quick.

"H, stop beating yourself up. Or I'll pull the car over, and we'll have a fight, and we'll probably get stuck in the snow."

"It should have been obvious," he snapped.

"Well, since you refuse to tell me what it is, it's kind of hard for me to be an objective third party. But I don't like when Big-brain Holmes starts beating up on Cute-butt Holmes."

He made a disgruntled noise and turned to look out the window. The snow tapped steadily against the glass, and the tires hissed as they threw up the slush that was thickening on the road. I still heard the familiar rattle, even though he kept the bottle between his legs.

"One," I said.

"It is not your decision—"

"One. Or I'll stick my fingers down your throat."

He whirled to face me. "How dare you—"

"One, H!" I didn't mean for it to be a shout, but it was, and Holmes reared back like I'd slapped him. "Don't make me say it again."

He breathed hard. The fingers of his free hand clutched the driving coat. His nail beds were white. In the corner of my field of view, he nodded.

"Show me," I said, my voice still rocky.

He held out his hand, where he cupped a single pill.

"Give me the rest of them."

"May I take this first?" he asked. The words had been unplugged from anything like emotion. "I need both hands to close the bottle."

I grunted.

A moment later, the pills rattled against plastic again, and he slid the bottle into my coat pocket.

"Did you lie to me?" I asked.

His answer took a long time: the ticking of the snow against the windshield, the hiss of the heater, the engine's purr. "No."

"Did you think about it?"

He took even longer. "Yes."

I nodded. "Could you have gotten away with it?"

"Of course." Then he shifted in his seat. Some of the Ivy League part had come loose and tumbled across his forehead. His voice held a faint note of chagrin as he added, "Until you asked me. I find it difficult to...prevaricate. With you."

"What every boy dreams of hearing."

The storm was verging on a blizzard, snow whipping back and forth in front of us, the mid-afternoon gone dark. On either side, the canyon had become nothing more than impressions, what the storm hinted at when an eddy of air spun in a new direction: the granite draws, the rock walls, the glass needle of the Provo.

He sounded more like himself a few miles later when he said, "Jack, I appreciate that you are worried about my well-being. But in cases like this, I need you to accept that I know best."

I nodded. I didn't look at the bloody wreckage of his lip. I didn't let myself think about the night terrors. Or about the need I'd felt when I'd touched him, because he'd been touched so little in his life, and never with love. I didn't say anything because if I did, I thought I'd burst out crying.

"Please don't be upset," Holmes said.

"I'm not." But the words were thick with snot, so I tried again. "It's fine, H. I guess it's fine. I guess everything's fine."

He clasped his hands. He gave up on that and grabbed his coat. Then he switched again and squeezed the seat so hard I thought the springs were going to pop through the upholstery. He got a little smaller and stared straight ahead as he said, "Perhaps you could keep the medicine. If that would make you happy."

"Who the fuck cares what makes me happy, H? Is that really what you think this is about? Jesus Christ."

He got even smaller.

Heber came on in snapshots: a Sinclair huddled under an amber light; a strip mall with half its storefronts dark, a window in one of them saying, THE SECRET IS HERE; the unreality of a self-storage facility—the corrugated steel walls and white paint and security lights like a dystopian leftover after the apocalypse of snow.

"I'm sorry," I said. "Yes. Let's start there."

He nodded.

"I'm sorry, H."

We had to stop at the next light, the tires lurching as the brakes sent us into a tiny slide. We stopped well before the white line, and there weren't any other cars, and the intensity of the red glare, after so long with nothing, made me squint. I shifted into park, unbuckled myself, and stretched over the center console.

Holmes's head came up.

I touched his cheek, guided him, found his mouth. At first, he hesitated, and then, when I applied a little more effort, he let my tongue slip past his lips. He tasted like Holmes, which was a new taste for me, and I was determined to familiarize myself. He tasted like copper—the fading vibrato of his blood. He made a noise that no Holmes bot had ever been programmed to make, and some of the wires in his neck and jaw softened.

"I'm sorry," I whispered and rubbed his nose with mine.

His words were flatteringly raspy when he said, "The light has changed."

"Forgive me?"

"Always," he said, voice still raw. "Anything." His Adam's apple moved. "This is a misdemeanor traffic violation."

I kissed him again, just to show him how brave I was, misdemeanors be damned. When I was buckled, we started off through Heber. A car rolled up behind us—a Charger, black, with tinted windows—and I thought of the car that had ridden our butts for part of the way up the canyon. But then, with a throaty roar, the Charger swerved past us and shot into the next spindrift of snow.

"Will that work every time?" Holmes asked with what sounded like—and, because he was Holmes, probably was—genuine curiosity. He touched his mouth and seemed to realize what he was doing and dropped his hand.

"It depends on how big I screw up," I said. "And how sorry I am. And how many dirty things you let me do to your body."

He huffed that tiny noise, but his face was scarlet. Later, when he must have thought I wouldn't notice, he ran a finger along his collar. All things considered, it's nice to be appreciated.

When we got to the Youngs' home, the storm crouched and blew in our faces. It flipped my hair back from my forehead, and it turned Holmes's into a haystack. Snow stung my cheeks, and I had to squint and shield myself with a hand. The cold ripped through my coat and shirt, and I was shivering before we'd gone two steps. The house itself was nothing more than a bulwark against the wind—a darkened outline, with no light in its windows, no music, no warm bodies or happy voices. I had the strange thought that it was a dead thing, a corpse, and that the party the night before had been a grotesquerie—a cadaver made to dance on strings. I thought maybe this was what happened to your brain when you used up all the oxygen kissing your not-quite-boyfriend.

Holmes pounded on the door with a fist. The echo came back to us, the sound torn apart by the wind, muffled by the snow. Holmes hammered on the door again. I decided to give the doorbell a jingle. Still nothing. Holmes shook his head and said something, but the storm tore the words away. He pointed, and I figured he was saying something about the garage, or going around the house, so I started to turn.

The door opened, and Aston stood there. I knew it was him. Even in the storm light, which was barely anything at all, I recognized him. But for a moment, it was like the house: like I was seeing something dead and made to dance. He said something, but the wind shrieked, and he shivered and wrapped his arms around himself. Then he shook his head and waved and started to close the door.

Holmes caught it on his shoulder, and I followed him inside. When I hip-checked the door shut, the silence that followed made my ears ring.

"You guys shouldn't be here," Aston was saying. "You need to go home."

Holmes ran a hand along the wall, searching for the switch.

"I'm going to get in so much trouble," Aston said. "You need to go."

A chandelier blazed to life overhead. I blinked to clear my vision. In that first moment, the light had the unfamiliarity of sudden, artificial brilliance after too much time in the dark—the light too yellow, almost waxen, laid over everything with a kind of gratuitous opulence.

Aston looked even more like shit today—the combination, I guessed, of the natural course of bruises and scrapes looking nastier after a full day, when they really started to get some color, when the swelling and inflammation were at their worst. His face was mottled, his nose puffy, his lower lip almost comically fat where it had split. Emma had worked him over. His eyes were dull. His hair was lank and hadn't been washed. He'd chewed the salon nails—clear coat only—to ragged ends. In mesh shorts and a Bear Lake tee, he must have been freezing, and he was hugging himself. But I got the feeling that was more about us than about the cold.

"Who is home?" Holmes asked.

"Nobody."

"Jack," Holmes said and started off.

He took the main floor, so I jogged upstairs. Aston hesitated at the bottom, his protests turning into squawks of "Hey!" and "Get back here!" In the end, he followed me as I went from room to room: the study, Aston's bedroom—now sans bed—an impersonally decorated room with a bed that had its sheets balled up at the foot (I guessed this was the guest room, now temporarily Aston's), and then a room that had to be Camdyn's—pink wallpaper, a canopy bed with gauzy white curtains, posters on the wall suggesting the simpler times of the early 2000s. An enormous Avril Lavigne, in full-on Sk8er Boi mode, stared down at us. I wouldn't have known who she was except Mom had made a dig about a kid with a skateboard one time, and I'd had to look it up to understand.

By the time I got downstairs, Holmes was in the kitchen. He'd dumped the trash out on the floor and was poking through it.

"What the hell?" Aston shouted.

When Holmes looked up, I said, "All clear."

"This floor is as well." He spared Aston a glance. "Where are your parents and sister, and when will they get home?"

"They're not coming home," Aston said, and his tone said the answer should have been obvious. "Because of the storm."

"Where are they?"

"Mom had to run to Salt Lake for some errands. Dad had to go to a meeting. Camdyn had an event to help set up." He must have been feeling his inner fourteen-year-old because he added, "They all had better things to do than sit around with me."

"Ok," I said to Holmes, "we're here. Are you going to explain?"

"Not yet. Aston, this isn't the garbage from the party. Was it already collected?"

Aston goggled at him.

"The garbage," Holmes prompted.

"What?"

"Wake the fuck up." I slapped the granite countertop. "We're trying to save your ass; get with the program."

The dishwasher hummed, and silverware clinked.

"There's no trash service up here," Aston mumbled. "We have to drop it off. Dad took it this morning. What do you mean you're trying to save me?"

"At Wintersmash," Holmes asked, "the night in the tunnels, who was there with you?"

"I don't know. A lot of people—Dawson, Riker—"

"Later," Holmes said. "Someone was with you when you met Dawson. Who?"

Aston shook his head.

"That's not going to help you," I said.

"I don't know, I swear."

"Aston, who was in the fucking tunnels with you?"

"I don't know!"

Holmes's words were measured and clipped. "Who was Dawson meeting?"

"I don't know."

"Who met him there?"

"I don't know."

"Who was walking through the tunnels with you?"

"A lot of people!"

Holmes stood and dusted his knees. "He's worthless."

"I was blitzed, man." Aston rubbed red eyes. "It's all a blur."

"You're blitzed now," I said.

He hugged himself and wouldn't look at me. "It's my fault," he finally said. "He's dead. Daw's dead, and Kazen's dead, and it's my fault. I asked him to come here."

"What about the night of the party? I heard you say you were going to your room; you knew Kazen was coming, but when we went upstairs, you weren't there."

"You heard me say that?"

"Focus. Where were you?"

"Downstairs. Some of my dad's friends wanted to talk to me. They all wanted to talk to me because of the videos, not that they'd say it to my face."

"Did you see anybody go upstairs?"

Helplessness bled across his face, and he shrugged.

I threw Holmes a look, but Holmes only said, "Watch him," and started for the stairs.

"H, the master bedroom is down here."

"I know," floated back to me from the stairs.

Aston shivered and stared at the floor. The dishwasher swished and rattled.

"Come on," I said, grabbing his arm.

"What—"

"He said to watch you, so come on."

I propelled Aston up the stairs in front of me. When we got to the hall, the light in Camdyn's room was on, the sound of hangers sliding on a rod reached me. I steered Aston through the doorway. Holmes had dumped out Camdyn's hamper, and clothes were scattered across the floor. As I watched, he gave a disgusted shake of his head and shut the closet's double doors. He turned to the dresser and opened a jewelry box.

"Uh, H?" I said.

Aston tried to take a step forward. "Stay out of my sister's stuff, you pervert."

I hauled him back, and he gave me a wounded look. "H?"

"I'm quite busy, Jack."

"Want to explain what you're doing? You know, while you're being busy."

"I made a mistake."

"Let me go out on a limb: I made a mistake too."

He raised his head long enough to offer me the glint of dry amusement in his eyes. Going back to his search, he said, "We made a mistake. We knew, as soon as Dawson was killed, that two parties were involved. I was angry at myself for letting Paxton distract me; I was overeager to believe that by unraveling the events behind Dawson's death, I might find out who had arranged things."

"Ok, maybe I didn't make a mistake. That wasn't my theory."

"No, that's not the mistake I was referring to. The mistake that we both made was in believing that similar motivations drove both of our perpetrators. You asked the question, who could hate Aston enough to do this to him? But it should have been obvious we had it wrong. Paxton and Dawson didn't hate him; they wanted money. Yet when Dawson was killed and the blackmail leaked, we continued to ask the same question." He opened a drawer and began dumping out Camdyn's underwear. "Who hated Aston enough to do such a thing—to frame him for the murder of his best friend and lover, and then, to add insult to injury, to expose the motive by releasing videos of their sexual encounters?" Holmes inspected the drawer's underside and set it aside with a noise of disgust. "We had it wrong the whole time."

The wind shrieked around the house. I had this momentary mental image of something huge, something vast, a beast of snow and ice with the house gripped in its jaws. The wolf of winter.

"Ok, well," I said, "I'm using my amazing powers of deduction to guess that the person behind all this is Camdyn, since we're searching her room. But she wouldn't release those videos, H. And she definitely wouldn't frame him for murder. She did everything she could to protect him—including going up against his psycho parents. No offense."

"No, man," Aston said, "they're legit psycho."

"In the first place," Holmes began, "deduction does not yield guesses—"

"Forget I said deduction," I cut in quickly.

"—and in the second place—"

I shook my head and rolled my eyes for Aston's benefit.

"—deduction relies on premises that, if true, always yield a true conclusion."

"It's my fault," I said. "Never say deduction. Never ever say deduction."

This time, Aston rolled his eyes, and I was pretty sure it wasn't for my benefit, but he said, "He's right, H. I mean, um, Holloway. Cam wouldn't do this. She's the only one who's nice to me. I mean, she's a total bitch sometimes about stuff like, well, everything, but she's actually a decent human being, and she cares about me."

Holmes let out that dry little huff that passed for his laugh most of the time. "That's what puzzled me and Jack, of course. Who would do such a thing? Who could hate you enough to do it? And, of course, that was our mistake."

A voice behind me, cool and feminine and slightly shaking, said, "But not your only one."

I started to turn. Steel snubbed up against my neck. The muzzle of a gun.

"Cam?" Aston said, facing the door. "I thought you had an event."

"Don't move," Camdyn said. "Mr. Holmes, show me your hands. I'd hate for something bad to happen to your friend."

Holmes stared at her. Then, slowly, he lifted his hands and displayed them.

Most of the power to my brain was off, big sections of it going dark. Sweat broke out everywhere—cold flop sweat on my forehead and chest and back and underarms.

"Would you like me to tell him?" Holmes asked. "It might be easier, hearing it from someone else."

Camdyn trembled. The gun dug into my nape hard enough to hurt. When she spoke, her voice was almost unrecognizable. "No more talking."

"Cam, what's going on?"

She took a few deep breaths. Her free hand closed around my collar, and her nails felt cold and smooth between my shoulder blades. "I'm taking care of things."

"What do you mean? They're—they're helping me."

"Get in the closet."

Aston's silence lasted a beat too long. "Is that a gay joke?"

"Aston, get in the goddamn closet!" she screamed.

Aston flinched and took a couple of nervous steps toward the louvered doors.

"Now! Right now! What don't you understand?"

"Cam—"

Her next scream was wordless and full of helpless fury. Aston blanched and yanked open one of the closet doors. He fumbled it, trying to pull it shut, and then, finally, it clicked.

"Tie the handles," Cam said. Her voice was still thick, the words heavy and distorted. "We don't want him to get out and call the police, do we?"

Holmes nodded. He found a scarf in the mixture of clothes on the floor, and he looped it around the handles of the closet doors. Every movement was steady, assured. A Holmes must always be in control. A Jack, on the other hand, was allowed to piss himself, I figured, if he had a lunatic jamming a gun against his neck.

When Holmes had finished, he displayed empty hands again. "Camdyn, the police are already investigating your family. Your time has run out. The best thing you can do now—for everyone, including Aston—is put the gun down and let us contact the authorities."

In the seconds that followed, her breaths came rapid and shallow, like she was on the verge of crying. Then her hand tightened on my collar, and she yanked me back a step. "I said no more talking. Come on."

I moved backward with her, all my focus on keeping my footing so that I didn't fall. I had the sense that if I was no longer useful as a hostage, she might blow my head off, and lately, I'd been pretty attached to my head. It's what I used to kiss H with. A wild giggle started in my chest at that thought, and I had to fight to clamp it down. It took everything I had to concentrate on walking, on breathing, on not tipping over into a total batshit meltdown.

The stairs were the worst part. She moved the gun to the base of my spine and her other hand to my waistband, and she said, "It might not kill you down here, but it'll be enough."

So, I stumbled down the steps backward, blindly, my heart pounding behind my eyes. If she slipped. If she came down wrong, and her finger tightened automatically. If the dishwasher sang its happy song when she wasn't expecting it.

Holmes came with us, keeping a ten-foot gap. His face was unreadable, but his eyes were intent and fixed on me. I focused on him. Holloway Holmes. The water-silk of his movements. The hollow fires of his rage. The tremendous power of mind and spirit that worked through him. In another time, they would have called him god-touched, and he had let me hold his hand.

We made it down the stairs, and she walked us through the kitchen, the silverware still clinking, and out into the garage. The cold met my fevered cheeks like the edge of a knife. A black Infiniti sedan was parked in the middle of the garage, and Camdyn moved us around it until we stood at the back of the car. She released my collar long enough to do something, and the car beeped, and the trunk popped open.

"Get in," she said.

I took a step, but she caught my collar and pulled me back. "You."

Something flickered in Holmes's expression.

Seeing it, whatever it was, woke something in me. I'd let her haul me around like a sack of potatoes, and yeah, that had been shock and whatever else. Now, though, the first wave of terror had broken, and I found my voice. "You don't have to do this. Please, Camdyn, we're trying to help Aston."

"Get in the trunk," she said again.

Holmes hesitated. Then he lifted one unscuffed chukka. It had salt and water stains from the snow; he'd have to get rid of the pair because he couldn't wear them like that. It was probably driving him crazy. It was the kind of thing we'd have to work on, something maybe I could help him with. I realized my brain was slipping again, trying to find a mouse hole to slip through so it wouldn't have to deal with the gun at my neck.

"Camdyn, you don't hate Aston. You love him. Why are you doing this? You're his sister."

She let out a bizarre little laugh, and the muzzle dug into my flesh.

"No, Jack," Holmes said, but his gaze had moved past me to Camdyn. "She's not his sister. She's his mother. Aren't you?"

Camdyn's fingers flexed, nails scratching my back. Then she said, "The trunk. Now."

Holmes nodded. He climbed into the trunk, folding himself up to fit. If anyone could look neat and packed away and perfectly comfortable in the trunk of a mid-sized sedan, it was Holloway Holmes. Apparently. When Camdyn told me to, I shut it. The last thing I saw was Holmes, his gaze meeting mine, the look calm and confident. His eyes were the silver of the moon.

"Get in front," Camdyn said, and she shoved me toward the driver's door. "You're driving."

Chapter 29

Darkness and Snow

We drove across Heber—at least, that's what I think we did. I was behind the wheel, but I was on autopilot: turning when Camdyn told me to turn, stopping when she told me to stop. She sat behind me, and for the first few miles, she kept the gun pressed against my neck. Then she sagged back, and the gun dropped away. I got my first glimpse of her in the rearview mirror: makeup ruined, face sallow, hair flat and wet from snowmelt. I hadn't realized she'd been crying.

And then we were through Heber, hurtling down the darkness of a canyon: the bones of the mountain, the black brushes of cottonwood and willow, slashes of silver—water, but not the Provo. The storm had intensified. When the winds were strongest, snow billowed against the windshield in a total whiteout, and all I could do was grip the wheel and maintain course until the wipers let me see again.

"Are you his mom?" I asked. I wet my lips and tried to work moisture into my throat. "Really?"

"No talking," she said dully. Then she gave that weird laugh again. "What am I doing? What in the world am I doing?"

"It's not too late. We can stop. Pull over. We can wait here for the police."

She said nothing. We drove, and the wipers scraped the windshield. She needed to replace them—they squeaked every time, both directions. The kind of thing that, another day, would have driven me crazy. One thing about guns? They're great for perspective.

"You hear on TV—" Her voice was small, almost lost in the sound of the tires churning slush. "—all those stories about moms who lift a car off their child, or who throw themselves into a river, or who fight off a dog. It sounds made up. People are people. Some of them are good. Some of them are not so good. Having another person come out of you, it doesn't change any of that."

We drove another mile. I blinked; one of the vents was pointed at my face, and my eyes were dry. "Maybe it's not having a person come out of you. Maybe it's loving someone."

She was quiet for so long, I thought she wouldn't answer. But then she said, "How did you know?"

"I didn't. Holmes did. But now that he said it, I can see it too. The age gap, sure. I think about it now, and yeah, I should have wondered. A sister that much older, I think she wouldn't have been in his life much. She wouldn't have shown up on campus, swooping in like a surrogate mother. The way you treated him when you came to his dorm room. My mom sounded the same way when she got after me about my room. And we heard that argument you had with your parents. You were so worried about him."

She let out a long breath. "You're sweet. I can see why Aston likes you. Not that he'd ever admit it; he's so scared about fitting in, about being liked. We did that to him, of course. But when he was a child, he was so—so open. So loving. Sometimes, I'd hold him, and I thought it was too much. That my body couldn't hold all of what I was feeling. I'd give him to my mom, and I'd go to my room, or I'd go to the store. Anything so I didn't have to feel so much." In the rearview mirror, I saw her slump against the door, her cheek fogging the window. "I was fifteen, and I thought I was in love, and he was persuasive. He was desperate, which was its own kind of persuasiveness. That anyone could want me so much. When my parents found out, they were furious. My dad was a stake president at the time. His father was on the shortlist to become an apostle. After they calmed down, when they explained everything, I understood. It seemed so simple. Necessary, even. I spent a year studying abroad." She gave the two words a bitter edge. "I came home to meet my baby brother. Everyone was so happy. So excited. It was a miracle, wasn't it?"

"Aston doesn't know? Seriously?"

"How could he? I'm his older sister. He was my parents' mid-life surprise. It's an easy explanation. We look alike, but then, of course we do. We thought it would be better this way."

Asphalt and snow and black ice sped past us. The wind buffeted the car, and I had to fight the Infiniti to keep it on the road—and, I hoped, in the right lane.

"Is that why you killed Dawson?" I asked. "Because he was threatening Aston?"

When I looked in the mirror, she was checking her hair, and for a moment, our eyes met. Her gaze slid away. "I didn't mean to. I told you the truth: someone contacted the family. They wanted money. We were willing to pay. I met him in the tunnels, and—and I couldn't believe it. I knew Dawson. He'd come home with Aston. He'd been polite to my parents. He wasn't the kind of guy I wanted Aston to be with, not forever, but I could tell he was fun, and he was into Aston, and it was…good, I thought. Good for Aston to be with someone who wanted him. Good for Aston to have a chance to be himself, his real self. And then there he was, with that smug smile, like—like it hadn't meant anything. I tried to talk to him; all he cared about was the money. I gave it to him." Her voice changed, opening into something between disbelief and amazement. "And he wouldn't give me the videos. He said he'd keep them safe. He said nobody would ever see them. But I knew. Right then, I knew he was going to keep doing it." She swallowed, the sound audible even over the Infiniti's engine. "I don't remember it. I was so mad."

I tried to keep my eyes on the road, but they slid to the rearview mirror. She was waiting for me, watching me, death in her face. I yanked my attention back to the road. My brain started talking, trying to cover up that moment, and I heard myself saying, "And then Aston showed up."

"He was supposed to meet Dawson, he told me, but he was confused." She laughed. "He was stoned. I need to stop doing that. I need to stop…editing. I think he was early. I don't know; that's the only thing I can think. Or he'd followed Dawson. It might have been that. Aston is insecure about a lot of things. He can get jealous."

"You tried to help him. We thought you were trying to get him away from there, maybe kidnap him. But you were trying to take care of him."

"He needs it," Camdyn said with dry amusement. "He can't take care of himself. I tried telling him that if he'd wait, if he'd play their game, they wouldn't be able to touch him once he turned eighteen. But he wouldn't listen. He wants so much, and he wants it so badly—to be seen, to be known, to be loved. I tried to give it to him, but it wasn't enough. There was the boy at Scout camp. And then, when he didn't learn his lesson, there was Dawson. And then that awful security guard was extorting money from him, and I thought maybe that would be the thing that made him stop, think, be smart." A click came from the back seat. The sound of metal—something on the gun. My chest tightened until I wasn't sure I could draw another breath. "He's a child still," she said as though speaking to herself now. "It's not his fault."

"It's not anybody's fault," I said. I had to force myself to suck in air, and I felt dizzy. "Nothing is anybody's fault. We can pull over."

"They were going to send him away to one of those camps. They were going to cover it up. Again. Just like last time. Make it all go away." She let out a weird laugh. "I was going to do it too. I took the pictures from his room, the blackmail note, all of it. And then I realized the truth had to come out. They won't be able to cover this up. The videos are out there; everyone knows. And me…" She trailed off, the words dissolving in the dark.

"Camdyn, please." I tried to think. I tried to make my brain work. I was distantly aware that I wasn't getting enough oxygen, and if I blacked out, we'd probably both die. All those fucking Wikipedia articles. All those fucking Great Courses videos on YouTube. I needed the one on hostage negotiation, or crisis de-escalation, but all I could think of was the page on Holmes (Sherlock, that is), which I'd read about a million times in the last two months, or the one that was entirely dedicated to hills that were shaped like boobs, or the Dry Valley in Antarctica. They hadn't had rain in over two million years. Instead of reading about what to do when a lunatic holds a gun on you, I'd read about BackpackersXpress. Which was great if Camdyn was open to the idea of changing the purpose of our trip. We could pick up a bunch of off-key, drunken backpackers and adopt a fucking terrible business model. And then I couldn't think about any of that. All I could think about was Holmes, who had been silent in the trunk, and if he was getting enough air, or if he was suffocating from carbon monoxide, and how it had felt to kiss him while snow flurried against the car, while the whole world was cold but we were warm.

"Slow down," Camdyn said. "There's a turn ahead."

The words yanked me back to this moment. I scrambled for something to say. "What about Kazen?"

"Slow down."

"Did he threaten you? If it was self-defense, that makes a big difference."

"Yes. He threatened me." But she sounded confused, like she was reading the words off cue cards. "He was…he was lying there. Naked. In Aston's bed." The next silence writhed with something like horror. "He was touching himself. The first thing he said was, 'Hey, baby.' Then he realized." I caught a glimpse of her in the mirror: eyes wide and frenzied, cheeks flushed, lips parted. "He threatened me. He was going to hurt me. He was going to hurt Aston. I was so scared."

Headlights appeared behind us. Part of my brain dissected the lie she was telling both of us—Kazen naked, unarmed, shot in the chest; the way his clothes had been rifled—but the rest of me focused on the headlights. Another car meant people. Witnesses.

Camdyn cleared her throat. "Do you know the thing about secrets? We're all convinced there's this part of us we have to hide. That we'd be better off if nobody knew about it—and maybe the world would be too. But the thing about secrets is that they always come out. Who you are? It comes out. Sooner or later. Whether you want it to or not. And you know what? I think that's a good thing. To be seen as who you are, finally. Not how someone wants you to be. I think maybe it's for the best."

"This isn't a secret," I said. "This isn't who you are. We can fix things. We can make things better."

She laughed, and it was gentle and a little sad and sounded way too sane for my liking. "You really are sweet, Jack. I'm sorry."

The car rushed up behind us, the headlights flaring in the rearview mirror.

"Pull over," Camdyn said.

"Fuck off, buddy," I said to the mirror.

"He's trying to pass," Camdyn said. "Slow down and get over so this moron doesn't kill us."

I burst out laughing. It was way too much, and it hit me way too hard, and it wasn't even funny—just a release valve for everything that had been building since she jabbed a gun in my neck. I was still laughing when the car started to pass, coming up alongside us. And then it slowed to match our pace.

The police, my brain suggested. Or then, grasping at straws, Aston. Hell, I'd take anybody. I risked looking away from the road. If I could catch the driver's eye—

In the first moment, it seemed unreal. I recognized him. The overweight guy with the peachy complexion, the one who had been smoking outside the athletic center. He was looking back at me, his gaze intent as he inspected me and Camdyn. And then my brain connected the dots: the car following us up the canyon, the car that had passed us in Heber.

He tapped his brakes and started to fall back. Some of my tension unknotted itself. A weird coincidence, that was all.

Then he swerved into the Infiniti.

I lost control immediately. Our car slewed across snowy asphalt, and the movement turned into a spin. I grappled with the wheel, trying to correct course, straighten us out, stop the movement. It didn't help. We spun.

Part of my brain strobed, and I was back there, back then. A year and a half ago. Mom driving. The car hurtling toward the guardrail.

Gravel hissed under our tires, and then we were airborne, flying into the vortex of darkness and snow.

Chapter 30

Silver

Impact was a series of blows that threw my body: against the roof of the car, against the door, against the seat, against the seat belt. We must have rolled once, maybe twice. Camdyn was screaming. I was screaming. And then it was over.

Darkness speckled my vision. A rushing noise filled my ears.

My first thought was: H.

Do not black out, I told myself. Don't you dare black out. He needs you.

I clawed away from that abyss. Bits and pieces of the world came together around me. I was hanging from the seat belt—sideways, I realized after a moment. The car lay with the passenger side against the ground. The engine was still idling, and another sound accompanied it now: the rush of water. It took me a moment, staring out the windshield, to understand what I was seeing. We were halfway into the creek; the headlights showed me the ruffled surface of the water, where snowflakes melted as soon as they settled. Then the car made a weird whining noise, and the electronics— including the lights—went out.

I yanked on the seat belt, but it wouldn't give. A panicked sob built in my chest. Part of me was back there, back then, alone and afraid in the car after it had stopped moving. And Mom and Dad weren't moving either. I gave another yank. Then another. I tore at the belt with my nails. Something crowded the edges of my vision. My breaths were high and ragged. I had to get out. I had to get out. I had to—

"Jack!" Holmes's voice was muffled but recognizable. "Jack, you have to talk to me."

Another sob escaped me—a different kind, this time. My fingers stung where I'd torn some of my nails, but whatever had been crowding me, stuffing me down that black tunnel, it eased.

"Jack, I understand this is difficult, but please, you must talk to me."

A little posh. I shouldn't have told; he'd do it all the time now, not that I had any complaints.

"H," I said. That was all I could manage before another sob constricted my throat.

"Good. That's very good. Are you hurt?"

I tried to take stock, but too much of my brain was still screaming at me, so finally I said, "No. I don't think so. No."

"Wonderful. I need you to find the trunk release; the one in the trunk doesn't seem to be working. Can you do that?"

It rushed over me again: the darkness, the fall, how still they were. I squeezed my eyes shut, but tears leaked out. I managed to say, "Yeah." I coughed, cleared my throat, and did a little better. "Yeah, yes."

"Good. You're doing perfectly. Find the trunk release."

Now that my brain was marginally less swamped by terror, I realized the seat belt was still buckled. I undid it, fell awkwardly against the center console, and steadied myself against the head rest of the passenger seat. I risked a glance back. Camdyn had ended up against the passenger window, and she was pale and unmoving. No sign of the gun. Something glistened, and when I bent to look closer, I realized it was water. The car was flooding.

Well, we were half-submerged in the creek, after all. Jack Moreno, Boy Genius.

"H, are you getting water?" I asked as I lowered myself to stand on the passenger window. The water came halfway up my Stan Smith's, soaking my feet and freezing them instantly.

"Find the trunk release, Jack."

I opened the glove box, located the release for the trunk, and pressed it. "Got it."

Silence. Something thumped. And then another, harder thump came. Holmes swore.

"H?"

"Jack, I need you to listen carefully. I assume Camdyn is incapacitated because she hasn't been screaming or shooting. You need to find her gun, and then you need to run. Cross the creek, continue in our direction of travel, and find the turn that she mentioned. Follow it until you're sure that you're not being pursued. Then you must find shelter."

"What are you talking about?"

"Do you hear me? Find her gun and run. Now."

"H—"

"Jack, you must go!"

I risked another glance into the back seat. Camdyn's gun wasn't anywhere I could see it, and while part of me knew Holmes was right, that the gun was a good idea, I couldn't bring myself to climb back there and look for it. I couldn't be in the back seat. Not now. Not again. I used the center console as a stepstool and reached for the door. It took me two tries before I remembered the door was locked. Then it opened, and I snaked my way out—albeit a bit more clumsily than usual, since it kept trying to fall shut and, you know, crush me.

I'd just finished getting my legs free of the Infiniti when I heard a man's voice—Peachy, I guessed, since I hadn't seen anyone else in the car.

"It was my call," he shouted over the howling wind. "It's the first time all day he hasn't been glued to the Holmes kid." His steps crunched on the gravel at the shoulder of the road, and I knew I should move, but I was frozen, listening. "Don't tell me how to do my job. And don't ever fucking call me again when I'm working. You don't like it, next time, do it the fuck yourself."

The sound of his steps changed to hard thumps against earth, moving closer toward us through the storm.

I had to move.

I slid off the car. Snow pelted me, and the wind sweeping down the canyon cut at my exposed skin, ripped at my hair, shrieked in my ears. I staggered around to the trunk, and I saw immediately the problem: the back of the Infiniti was lower in the creek than the front, and water pressed against the trunk lid, keeping it closed. I splashed into the water. My already frozen feet turned into frozen feet, ankles, and calves. It was the kind of cold that closed around you and compressed—so painful that my eyes watered and I forgot about my torn nails and the bruises from the seat belt.

By the time I reached the trunk, it was up to my waist, and part of my brain reminded me about hypothermia. Bugger off, I told it. Maybe it was the shock. Maybe I'd been reading too much British porn.

"H," I shouted over the wind, "you've got to help me. I'm going to pull. You push."

He said something back—probably something bossy and sensible—but I couldn't hear him over the wind. And, for that matter, over my chattering teeth. "N-now!" I shouted.

At first, the lid of the trunk refused to move; the water pressed it closed. Then, slowly, it began to rise. For a moment, I thought we had it. Then my numb fingers slipped, and the water forced the trunk shut again.

Holmes shouted something else, but I couldn't hear him. I tried to grab the trunk again, wedging my fingers in the gap between the lid and the bumper, but I couldn't feel my hands by that point, and whatever strength I had left went into holding myself up.

In the distance, a dark figure moved toward us, hand low at his side.

Run, the voice in my head said.

I had been here before. I had done this once. I had lived to have nightmares about it. And for a treacherous moment, my body responded: I angled myself toward the bank, already looking for escape.

But Holmes was here, trapped, the water rising. If I ran, he'd die. The first time, I hadn't known what I was doing. But I couldn't do it again.

The snow blew a curtain between me and that dark figure, obliterating him for a moment, revealing him again. When the snow changed direction again, he was gone.

I had to distract him. I had to get him away from here so Holmes had time to get free. Jack Moreno, I thought. Wonder Boy. Armed with nothing but a trusty river rock—

No, I thought. Not quite.

I checked my back pocket and, somehow, Glo's box cutter was still there. I worked it free and extended the blade. It was more difficult than it should have been. I was shaking pretty bad now, and the cold made my fingers stiff and unresponsive. I'd get one chance; the first bad move, and I'd lose my grip, and the box cutter would be gone. Then Wonder Boy would get his ass capped.

He'd be expecting me to run. And he'd come after me, nice and slow— because he was warm and dry and had a gun, because he hadn't had his brain scrambled in an accident.

Well, fuck that.

"H, find the seat release." I hammered on the trunk and screamed over the storm. "Put the seat down and crawl out the front."

Then I splashed down into the creek and crouched as low as I could. The cold wasn't as bad this time, and that worried a small corner of my brain. Keeping low, I scuttled along the side of the Infiniti that was in the water, using it to hide myself from anyone who might be on the bank. When I got halfway down the car's length, I stopped. The creek pulled at me; I thought I could feel it sucking the heat from me, my body's temperature dropping like the mercury in a cartoon thermometer. I wasn't shivering anymore. That seemed bad.

Something crunched—the sound of brown stubs of winterkill crushed under a heavy tread. It had come from the other side of the car. Then another step came. And another. Steady. Calm. A measured gait. He was moving after me—in the direction I'd started running.

When the sounds began to fade, I slipped around the front of the car and dragged myself up on to the frozen bank. The wind knifed into me again. I couldn't tell if I was still holding the box cutter, so I had to look. It was still there, but my fingers barely moved when I tried to tighten them. Now I needed to—

A shadow loomed, barely different from the darkness, and much closer than I'd expected. I tried to rush him, but I overestimated myself and underestimated my body's response to the paralyzing cold. I stumbled.

He materialized out of the storm, the gun coming up. I was so close that the heat from the flame and gas touched my face. Something tugged at my arm. I twisted toward him and lunged, slashing at his face. The blade was a tiny, inch-long triangle of steel, and it sliced open his cheek. He roared, twisted, and clubbed me with the gun on the side of my head. The world went helter-skelter, and I dropped.

It was like a dream. The edge of a dream. The Christian mystics, Wikipedia told me, had believed they could brush up against a consciousness vaster than their own. A mind that filled the universe, a limitless well of compassion and peace and grace.

Holloway Holmes came out of the spindrift of night and ice and snow, came toward me, came for me. He shone like silver in the stormlight: his face, his eyes, his hair. They used silver, I knew, to kill monsters.

And then I couldn't hold on anymore.

Chapter 31

Nibble, Nibble, Little Mouse

My head hurt, and my arm, and I was hot and sweaty, and my blankets had gotten tangled. Bad dreams waited at the rim of consciousness—the darkness, the cold, the car rolling, the man with the gun. I tried to throw back the blankets to get some air, but I only got myself more tangled. I cracked one eye open, and the lights were too bright.

"Jack," my dad said, "you're ok. Hey, buddy, calm down."

Bits and pieces of it came back: the ambulance ride, the warmth, doctors looking at me and moving my head and forcing me to open my eyes. And then, finally, they'd let me sleep.

Even with my eyes closed, I recognized his hands as he tucked me in. His breathing was different, though. I felt like I could sleep, but in spite of the headache, everything was taking on that total clarity that comes from waking during midnight hours.

I opened an eye again.

The light wasn't as bad this time, although for a moment, it was a spike that went straight to the back of my skull. Then my vision adjusted: the bedside lamp, the dark room. Dad was a wreck. His skin was gray, and he had bags under his eyes. He wore a Walker polo over a white undershirt, and the collar stood up in back. He smelled rough too, but I was guessing I didn't have any room to talk on that one. Across from us, an old woman slept with her mouth open in the other bed. A white board on the wall said REBECCA and then a bunch of stuff I didn't understand.

Dad rubbed my shoulder. "You need to go back to sleep."

I smacked my lips and tried to say, *Thirsty*, but what came out was, "Hot."

Dad waffled. Then he untucked one of the blankets. That must have been the load-bearing one, because once it was free, I could wriggle around a little more and get my arms out. I had a bandage around one forearm. I wanted to take a closer look, but just getting myself settled had wiped me out again.

"You're ok," Dad said. "Your body temperature was really low. When you fell in the creek, they say you went into shock."

"H?"

"He's fine. He was sleeping here, but we agreed to take shifts." Something I couldn't read crossed Dad's face. "That boy's a tough nut to crack."

"Did he do that thing where he stares at you until you agree with him?"

That startled a laugh out of Dad. "He does that to you too?"

"He's the fucking worst sometimes."

"Do you want some water?"

I nodded. Dad had to hold the cup, and I made do with the little bendy straw, and Dad said I'd had enough while I was still trying to get more. He touched my hair lightly, but when I looked at him, he pulled his hand back.

It was hard, meeting his eyes, so I pressed my cheek to the pillow and mumbled, "I'm sorry."

"I'm sorry too," Dad said. His voice got all choked, and for a while he didn't say anything else. And then, something I didn't ever remember him doing, he took my hand in both of his. "When they told me there'd been another accident, Jack. My God. If I lost you."

He didn't start crying all at once, but it got stronger and stronger. And then he sat there, weeping silently, face down. He held my hand in his, crushed against his forehead, as he shook. Maybe it was the drugs. Maybe I was all cried out. I'd spent a lot of time over the last few days crying. I scruffed one hand through his buzzed silver hair. My eyes kept closing. The little yellow light from the lamp dilated, and I was able to think, I'm falling asleep. And then I was gone again.

When I woke, it was mid-morning, to judge by the light. My head was better; my arm was throbbing. I didn't recognize the view from the window. I didn't know if I was in Salt Lake or Provo. Or maybe Heber had a hospital, or Park City. I was hot and sweaty and tangled in the blankets again. Detective Yazzie was sitting in the chair by my bed doing a word jumble. I lifted my head, and she made a noise and went out into the hall. The old woman wasn't in the other bed. Maybe they let you out sometimes for good behavior.

A minute later, Yazzie was back with Rivera. He put his hands on his hips. "Are you as stupid as I think you are? Or can you convince me the treehouse detectives had a genius plan all along?"

"My mouth tastes like a tortoise's asshole. Do tortoises have assholes?"

"You're lucky you don't have frostbite," Yazzie said. "Nothing serious, your dad told us."

"I have to pee."

Rivera made a disgusted sound. "You need somebody to squeeze your weasel for you?"

That seemed like permission, so I fumbled around until I got free of the bed and hobbled to the little bathroom. I peed. I gave myself a check in the mirror. I looked like shit on a stick, and I gave up absolutely, immediately, totally on my hair. Then I got my hand wet and at least tried to make it stick up evenly.

When I stepped out of the tiny bathroom, Rivera said, "Did you remember how?"

I gave him a look.

"And next time, take five seconds and fix your hair."

Yazzie must have seen something on my face because she laughed and tried to cover it with a cough.

"Isn't my dad supposed to be here?"

"Your dad hasn't slept in the better part of thirty hours," Rivera said. "Thanks to you, Jack. How about we don't bother your dad?"

"Do you want me to get him?" Yazzie asked.

After a moment, I shook my head. "Unless you're going to arrest me."

"Arrest you." Rivera rubbed his cauliflower ear. "Sit. Talk. Then I'll decide if I'm going to arrest you or just kill you myself."

"Does he have kids?" I asked Yazzie.

A surprised grin creased her face, and she shook her head.

"He's got this weird dad energy, though, right?"

"I don't have any dad energy," Rivera snapped.

Yazzie's grin got bigger. "Huh."

"I think he imprinted on me," I told her as I climbed back into bed.

"Is that what you think?" Rivera said. "You want to see dad energy? How about you spend a couple of weeks in the county jail? You can be a trustee. Mop the drunk tank after the guys piss themselves. See where you're headed."

"He's already coming up with chores," I said. "And life lessons."

Rivera had dark brown skin, but even so, he was turning red. He was making this noise, too—a whistling sound like he had something caught in his throat.

"Jack," Yazzie said, her smile fading. "We've got some serious stuff to talk about."

"It was my idea," I said. "H didn't know what we were doing."

"That's convenient." Rivera had gone back to his power pose. "He said the same thing. Only it took a lot more words, and he brought in a lawyer."

I shook my head.

"Why don't we start at the beginning—" Yazzie adjusted her glasses. "—and you tell us how it happened?"

After a moment, I said, "Do I get immunity?"

"You little shit—" Rivera began.

"Right now," Yazzie said over him, "this is kidnapping and attempted murder. You're the victim. How about you keep that in mind as you tell us about it?"

"Technically, I've been kidnapped three times in the last week. Which time are you talking about?"

Rivera was breathing hard through his nose.

Yazzie caught my eye, and I made a face and nodded. "What...happened? The other night, I mean."

The detectives traded a look. Yazzie said, "Heber police found you and Holloway. He was trying to carry you up the highway. By himself. In the middle of a blizzard."

"He was out of his skull," Rivera said. "He put two of the officers on their asses when they tried to stop him."

I smiled in spite of myself. "And—the man?"

"The responding officers found the treehouse detectives," Rivera said, his tone softening. "They found Camdyn Young still in the vehicle—she was concussed and suffering from hypothermia. That's all."

"No, there was a man. He forced us off the road. He had a gun." And I wanted to say, *Just like it happened with Mom.* Only that hadn't been the same.

Had it?

The memories overlapped now—too many similarities. The collision that forced us off the road. The way the cars had rolled. The desolate stretch of highway, where no one would find us. The peach-faced man with the gun. That had been last night; I tried to hold on to that memory. But the night of Mom's accident, there had been a man. A man with...something. An emergency tool, they had told me. Later.

My heart was beating so fast, I thought I was going to be sick.

Yazzie was studying me, but it was Rivera who spoke. "You have a graze on your arm. Nothing serious, although it'll hurt like hell. The tattooing—that's the black stuff on your skin, where particles of gunpowder got embedded—and the flame burn, those say you were right up next to the shooter when he fired."

"But Camdyn Young tested negative for gunshot residue," Yazzie said. "And when we recovered her gun, it was fully loaded. Unless she stopped to reload, somebody else took that shot."

"We've got people out there looking. The casing is gone, but if we find that bullet, my guess is that it's not going to match the ballistics we take from Camdyn Young's weapon."

I swallowed. I breathed to slow my heart, not that it helped much. "If I'd died."

"Holloway told us," Yazzie said, "that when the man saw him, he ran. Do you know why he'd do that?"

Shaking my head, I started to say no. And then I remembered the man's voice, his annoyance at the phone call that had interrupted him: *It's the first time all day he hasn't been glued to the Holmes kid.* He had been watching me. He had been waiting. Waiting for the moment I'd be separated from Holmes. And when Camdyn had put Holmes in the trunk while we were still in the garage, the man must have thought Holmes had stayed at the house with Aston. He saw his opportunity.

Part of me knew I needed to focus on the fact that someone had been hired to kill me. But my brain was busy with other things. It had to be a coincidence. Mom's accident was exactly that: an accident. They'd said he'd had a tool, the kind people use to break glass. They'd been too polite to say it, but the implication had been clear: there'd never been a man with a gun. I'd imagined it.

I heard myself breathing faster, my heart ramping up.

"Jack?" Rivera said. His hand settled, heavy and solid on my shoulder.

Pressing my fingertips against my eyes, I shook my head. In the distance, someone paged Dr. Hastings over the intercom. When I trusted my voice, I said, "It's just been a lot."

Rivera squeezed my shoulder until I looked him in the eyes. His face was stern. Cop face. But his voice was the same guy who had bought me McDonald's. "We're going to get this asshole, Jack. That's why we need you to tell us everything you can."

I counted to ten and thought nothing, because if I thought nothing, he couldn't see it on my face. Then I nodded.

I was about to start at the beginning, but instead, I heard myself ask, "What about Camdyn?"

"She's all right."

"No, I mean—did H tell you? What she did, I mean?"

They shared another look, and I thought maybe this time, they wouldn't tell me. But Rivera cleared his throat and said, "Camdyn confessed to both murders. We're still working on the ballistics from her gun, but we may not need them. Confessions are tricky, but right now—right now, she seems like she'll go through with it."

"She doesn't want them to cover it up," I said.

Yazzie's eyebrows made a question.

I told them as much as I could.

Dad came back partway through, and he made some noise about a lawyer, but Rivera and Yazzie did their song and dance again about how I was the victim. Dad seemed ok with that, but he kept a pretty sharp eye on me, and a couple of times, he looked like he was going to tell me to stop talking—so I made sure that when I got to those parts, I hurried to get to the next bit. They all must have known I was leaving things out, but they were kind enough not to say anything. Rivera was even cool about whatever his deputy had found in my room—no threats about busting me for possession or intent to distribute. I figured he'd be happy to hang those over my head as soon as he got bored catching killers.

The detectives did want to know one thing that I didn't understand.

"Do you know what happened to Kazen Bates's cellphone?" Yazzie asked.

I shook my head, and they moved on.

By the time I finished, the doctors wanted to check me out one more time, and that meant more poking and prodding and all the vaguely humiliating things that you have to do because a doctor says so. Then there was paperwork. Dad went to take care of that, and I cleaned up a little more in the bathroom and changed into clean clothes Dad had brought from the cottage.

When I came out, the air was cloying with the scent of lilies, and Blackfriar Holmes was there. He wasn't blocking the door to the hall, not exactly, but to get out of the room, I'd have to pass him. He was arranging flowers in a cut-glass vase, his expression focused. Without looking over at me, he said, "Hello, Jack. Glad to see you up and about."

I watched him. He was so much like Holloway, and so much not like him, it was frightening. The way nightmares could be ordinary, everyday things flipped on their heads. It wasn't their coloring; Blackfriar's hair was jet black and combed straight back. And it wasn't their faces; where Holloway had that cold-chiseled, classical perfection, Blackfriar's face was sharp, a prominent triangle of cheekbones and chin. But the eyes. Holloway's were silver or moondust or starlight. Blackfriar's were tin. And the way they moved, the inhuman grace of it, the same but different: Holloway like a spindrift of snow, where Blackfriar was oiled steel.

"I'm leaving," I said.

I took a step, and Blackfriar straightened up from the vase. He didn't do anything else. He didn't move toward me. He didn't block my path. He didn't frown. He didn't so much as raise an eyebrow.

But I stopped. My pulse pounded in my head.

His voice was quiet. Almost gentle. "Where is it, Jack?"

I shook my head, but he kept looking at me, and the force of that gaze ripped the words from me: "Where's what?"

A hint of a smile. Inhuman. The baring of teeth. "It was clever, allowing him to hide it, and then making off with it yourself. I will admit that you fooled me. Not many people have succeeded at that; you should be proud. I did not expect cleverness from you."

A machine was beeping in the next room, and TV voices buzzed at the threshold of being intelligible, but I was suddenly aware of how quiet the hospital floor seemed. Where were all the nurses? Where were the orthopedic shoes, the squeaky casters, the general bustle? Even the old woman I'd shared my room with was gone. Someone had erased REBECCA from the whiteboard.

"I have been, I think—" Blackfriar said, the words so low I caught myself leaning in, moving to hear him better. "—admirably patient. I have not objected, even though you have distracted my son, even though you have caused him to lose focus. I have not interfered." He bared his teeth again. "I can be patient, Jack. You are nothing compared to my son; why should I worry, when I know that you are a speck of dust next to what I have created? He will open his eyes eventually, and when he does, he won't remember so much as your name." The rictus on his face widened. "I have even let you play with him." The way he said the word made the hair on my neck stand up, and heat rushed into my face. "Even though I do not like other people touching my things." He took a step, and I backed up and hit the wall. "Would you agree, then, that I have been patient?"

I couldn't answer. I couldn't swallow. I couldn't shake my head or nod or whatever I was supposed to do.

When he spoke, the words were a whip crack. "Where is it?"

"I don't know." I wanted to hold the words back. I wanted to tell him to fuck himself. But those chips of tarnished tin held me, and I heard myself saying, "I don't know what you're talking about. I don't have anything. I didn't take anything."

Movement at the door drew my eye. Holmes stood there, dressed as always: a white oxford, navy chinos, unmarked chukkas—these ones a buttery, oxblood leather that probably cost more than a used car. His hair was back in its perfect Ivy League part, and his face was bloodless and empty as he stared at his father.

"Hello, Holloway," Blackfriar said. "A bit late, aren't you?"

Holmes's voice was a sheet of ice. "I was disabling your vehicle."

A pleased laugh rolled out of Blackfriar. The rictus was back, pulling his cheeks wide. "Were you? Delightful."

"A tow truck is on its way. If you'd like to keep the Bentley, I suggest you make your way to the parking garage."

"Tremendous," Blackfriar said to himself. "Do you know, Holloway, I think there's hope for you. I really do." He turned to me, and he said, "Jack, what do you think?"

His eyes were dull, flat coins, and I had to force myself to look away. I tried again to tell him to fuck off, but I still couldn't get my throat to work, and what came out instead was barely more than a whisper: "My dad's coming."

"Your dad is coming." Blackfriar laughed again. "You two are quite the pair."

"Father," Holmes said.

"What if I told you your father isn't coming?" Something about him was magnetic—his voice, his attention. It pulled my gaze back to him. "What if I told you that he'd gotten lost? Or gotten busy? There's so much paperwork after something like this, you know. Why, you might sit there, with them putting paper after paper in front of you until you think, 'This can't be possible; someone's taking the piss.' And they'd keep bringing you papers and bringing you papers. And if the papers get lost, you might have to start all over again. It could take hours."

"Father," Holmes said more sharply.

"Do you know what a father's responsibility is, Jack?"

The smell of the lilies made my head spin. I wanted to look away, but the tarnished grip of his eyes held me.

"A father's responsibility," Blackfriar said, "is to watch over his family. Master of hearth and home. To instruct them. To direct them. To mold them." The dead man's rictus was back. His teeth looked like broken glass. "To protect them."

"Jack has done nothing wrong," Holmes said—his voice a little higher now, a little tighter.

"Just the other day," Blackfriar said, and he took a step toward me. I told my legs to move, but then I remembered the wall. Convenient, actually. It was the only thing holding me up. "Just the other day, Jack, I found mice in our garage. Now, they hadn't gotten into the home proper. They hadn't breached the sacred walls of the Holmes family. But they were there. And they are pests, you know. They ruin everything. They spread—" He drew a breath, and when he exhaled, he was close enough for me to feel it on my face: warm, a hint of something that made me think of fish oil. "—disease. And the only thing to do, when you have something trying to infest your family, is to exterminate it."

"He's my friend." Holmes's voice broke. "He's done nothing."

"People go on and on about humane methods." Blackfriar took another step. We were close enough that I could feel him—was aware of him, another body in my space. Not heat, not the warmth of another body; he might as well have been room temperature. Like a corpse, my brain added. But I could feel that magnetic field around him, like the hum of a high-voltage line, a kind of energy that made my skin crawl. "Glue traps. Live traps. Bait. But do you know what works best with mice, Jack?"

I tried to turn my head; his breath clouding against my face was worse than the lilies. But I couldn't. I couldn't do anything. Some snakes hypnotized their prey. Or was that only in cartoons?

"Old-fashioned traps work best. The spring-loaded bars. The jaws. They operate on the same principle: snap."

I flinched.

"It breaks their back," Blackfriar said. "The little things die, of course. They're not like people, you see. Break a man's back, and he could live forever, relatively speaking, with the proper care."

His breathing was slow and measured. His pupils were normal size. His heart, if I could have heard it, would have been calm and steady, I was sure. The hint of red in his cheeks, though. I had seen it on another Holmes. When he had figured out a piece of a puzzle. When he had made me laugh. When I had kissed him. When he was excited.

I could hear my own breathing in contrast: the shrill, barely contained whistle in my throat.

"Nibble, nibble, little mouse," Blackfriar said, so quietly I could barely hear him. The worn tin of his eyes raked me. "Who's that nibbling at my house?"

The dead-man's grin came back, and he reached up, his hand moving to my neck.

"Don't touch him!" Holmes shouted. His voice had slipped into full public-school boy, and it shook on every word. The shout echoed in the small room, fading slowly.

Laughter burst from Blackfriar. He thumbed something from my cheek and displayed it: an eyelash. "My son understands the importance of family,

Jack. I am a reasonable man, but my patience is not endless." Then the rictus peeled back his lips again. "Make a wish."

He stayed like that until I blew the eyelash from his thumb, then he headed for the door. At the last possible moment, Holloway slid out of his path, his body still loose, still charged with potential violence. Blackfriar stopped and considered him, the broken-glass glitter of his teeth flashing again. "Do you know, Holloway, I think we've finally found something to inspire you?"

Chapter 32

Straight, Gay, or Bi

The next day, Dad called me in sick to classes, and he called off work, and we spent the time together in a weird limbo. He didn't talk. Neither did I. There was nothing good on TV, but finally Dad found *Judge Dredd*, and that was better than sitting in silence. I wanted to go to my room, but if I did, he'd think I was mad. I wanted to sleep, but dreams of rolling cars and faceless men with guns waited for me. I wanted to see Holmes, but he'd be in classes.

Solving the murder of a student, as well as that of another man, apparently generated enough good karma that Holmes and I hadn't been expelled for stealing Headmaster Cluff's car. In fact, from what I could tell—although Dad didn't want me reading the news—she was leaning into it, making good-natured jokes about it, like we were plucky teen wonder boys from a book. The Hardy Boys, maybe. I'd never read the Hardy Boys, but I was pretty sure one of them wasn't spending ninety percent of his time thinking about sucking face. I was pretty sure they didn't wake up from nightmares, sweating so bad they thought, at first, they'd peed themselves.

Dad couldn't stay in his chair. He got up. He got a Diet Coke. He sat down. He fiddled with the tab on the can until it broke, and then he got up again to throw it away. He got chips. He put the chips back. He got up "to stretch his back." He had this weird look on his face, and he kept glancing over at me. It took me a while to realize what he was working up to.

When someone knocked, I actually said out loud, "Thank God."

Dad threw me a surprisingly dirty look, but he went to the door—probably because it gave him another reason to get out of his chair. In a voice I barely recognized, he said, "Get off my porch, and don't come back."

"Mr. Moreno—" Aston said.

Dad slammed the door.

When I stood, Dad pointed to the sofa and said, "No."

I stepped into my Cortez and grabbed my coat.

Dad caught my arm.

I looked at him until his face colored, and he released me.

"Ten minutes," Dad said. "And you stay on the porch."

I nodded. "Thanks."

He squeezed my shoulder. Then he sat at the counter, where he could look out the front door and watch us, and I tried not to sigh.

The air was so cold I felt my hair stand up, and my eyes stung, but it was also fresh and clean with the mineral smell of new snow, and in a weird way, it made me think of those people who do polar plunges and stuff like that. I felt awake, maybe. Or just glad to be out of the house.

Aston still looked like shit. The bruises and scratches on his face were healing, but the bags under his eyes were dark and heavy, and he'd obviously given up on the perfectly mussed look for his hair. Now it looked regular mussed, the unsexy version of bedhead. His eyes were red, and he huddled in his coat, his breath steaming. He stared at me, opened his mouth, and shut it again.

I gave him a few more seconds. Then I moved over to the rail, knocked the snow from the wood, and hopped up to sit there. He stood around looking dumb for a while, and then he came over and sat on the rail too. He smelled like too much body spray. It was nice to know that some things in the world didn't change.

"I could really use a smoke," I said.

"Jesus, yes, please."

"Are you ok?" I asked.

He shook his head. His gaze was far off, somewhere on the flank of Timp, where the scrub oak looked like stubble in the distance.

"Police told me you saved us," I said. "If you hadn't gotten out of the closet and called for help, we'd have died out there."

A weird laugh corkscrewed out of him. When I looked over, he laughed again and shook his head. "I didn't get out of the closet. She didn't take my phone. I just—I just yelled for a while. And then I figured I ought to call somebody." His voice clotted, and it looked like he had to make an effort to say, "I'm so fucking stupid."

"You're not stupid. Well, yeah, you are, but only because you're such a douche."

His head snapped up, and he stared at me. Then another laugh got loose, more of a giggle this time.

"Look," I said, "I don't know what to say. Dawson was a shitty person. Kazen too. And they're gone. And you're never going to be able to fight with them or fuck them or scream at them or apologize, not anything, ever again. I'm sorry; I know what that's like, kind of."

He nodded and wiped his eyes.

"Did somebody tell you?" I asked.

The noise he made was like wet paper tearing. "It's in every fucking news story."

"Oh. Shit."

"My dad—I mean, my grandpa. You know what I mean. He told me before I saw it on the news."

In the distance, something moved. A fox, maybe. Fresh powder tumbled down the slope, and then everything was still again, everything white, everything unmarked.

"I'm sorry," I said.

He shook his head again. It was a long time before he said, "Everything is so fucked up."

I was the one who waited this time. The whole thing would have been so much easier if we could have sparked a joint, got lit. Nobody cares about awkward pauses when they're lit. And hell, at least a joint gives you something to do with your hands.

The best I finally came up with was, "Yeah."

He stirred, sitting up straighter, and reached into his coat. Displaced air carried more of the body spray, and when he brought his hand out, he was holding an envelope. It was fat, and where it didn't close completely, a flash of green told me it was stuffed with cash.

"Aston, I can't—"

"I pawned her jewelry." He dropped the envelope in my lap. "That lying, fucking bitch, that's the least she deserves."

"Man, I can't take this."

"Then throw it in the trash. Or burn it. Do whatever you want."

I swallowed. My hand curled around the envelope, and a weary smile pulled at the corner of Aston's mouth.

He slid from the rail, dusted himself off, and looked somewhere over my shoulder as he said, "I'm not coming back. So, you know. This is it."

I nodded.

He watched me, body tight with a tension I didn't understand. Finally he said, "Aren't you gonna do it?"

"Do what?"

"Break my nose."

It seemed years ago. I shook my head.

After a dozen heartbeats, he rolled his shoulders and started for the steps.

"It wasn't your fault," I said. "None of it. You didn't do anything wrong. The detectives told me they got the test results; Dawson drugged me at Wintersmash. He probably drugged you too some of the times, you know..." I paused. "If you need to talk about it—"

"Jack, I hope I never have to talk to you again."

For ten seconds, maybe twenty, he waited there, poised on the first step, like there was more to say. Then he jogged down the steps and disappeared around the side of the cottage.

I went inside. Dad watched me as I stripped off my coat, heeled off my shoes. He was still watching when I walked down the hall.

I cried. Not about Aston, necessarily. About all of it. And then I was done, and I fell asleep.

A tap at the door woke me, and it took me a moment to realize Dad was waiting for me. "Uh, come in."

He came in carrying a tray: a can of Coke, a grilled cheese, tomato soup. Campbell's. You can tell right away. It's the only tomato soup that's good for grilled cheese, which means it's the only kind of tomato soup that's good at all. He laid the tray on the desk, and then he said, "I thought you might be hungry."

"Thanks."

He put his hands in his pockets. He took them out again. He put them in his back pockets. He rocked on the balls of his feet. He looked like an extra in those stupid John Wayne movies. Or like a guy who needed to pee.

"Maybe you want to eat in bed? That's why I brought the tray."

"Dad!"

Something in my voice made him smile. He settled back onto his heels. He stopped doing weird things with his hands. He said, in a voice that was surprisingly firm, "Jack, I want to talk to you about something."

"Then yes, I want to eat in bed."

The smile turned into a grin. He got me settled with the tray. I dunked a corner of sandwich. He'd cut it into triangles, which is the only good way to eat grilled cheese with tomato soup.

Dad sat, put his hands on his knees, took a big breath. Then he said, "I love you. I know I don't always do a good job of letting you know that."

"You do a good job," I said and bit some of the dangly cheese before another dunk. "I know you love me."

"Well, good. But I'm not happy about—about some of the interactions we've had lately. About how I behaved. And—and how I reacted."

I was mid-dunk. "Dad—"

"When Detective Rivera—

"Dad, I can't do this. I need to be high. Or I need to be drunk. Or I need a lot of Xanax." The look on his face made me add, "Kidding. Kind of."

An emotion I couldn't decipher rippled his face, and then it smoothed into a smile. My dad's smile. "You don't have to do anything, Jack. I'm not asking you to do anything. Or say anything. Not now. Not ever. But I want you to know that I love you, whoever you are, and who you choose to love does not matter to me. Not even the tiniest bit. I am so proud of you. And I respect you, even if that's hard for you to believe. I understand that this is a weird time in your life, for a lot of reasons. It's not realistic for me to assume that you can go back to being a kid, not after you spent a year of your life, and more, taking care of me. I'm not happy with a lot of choices you've made recently, and yes, I want to talk to you about those. Later. But right now, I want you to know that—that if I gave you the impression that something else mattered to me, that was wrong. I will never, ever stop loving you."

I pushed some soup around with the soggy-getting grilled cheese. I wanted my words to be a challenge, but they came out a little-kid mumble: "It seemed like it mattered."

He nodded. "I know. And I'm sorry about that. I'm—I'm ashamed of it, actually. But that's not how I feel. I hope you believe me when I say that."

I stirred the soup some more. It was that Elmer's-glue consistency and beautifully orange. My face was pins and needles when I finally looked up and said, "I think I'm bi. Or whatever."

Dad nodded.

"I am bi," I said a little more forcefully.

"Thank you for telling me."

"And it's not a phase or—or because of Mom or because we moved or because I'm acting out. I like guys. I like girls, but I like guys too."

"Ok."

"If that's a problem—"

"Jack." He smiled, but he stopped and had to wipe his cheeks, and his eyes were wet again before he'd even finished. "Yes, I was surprised. This was new to me. And hearing about it that way—hearing what almost happened to you. That was horrible for me because you could have been hurt so badly. If I'm being honest, Jack, I didn't expect this. You never expressed an interest in guys when we were in Salt Lake. You're—I mean, you like sports—"

"Oh my God," I said.

For some reason, that cracked him up, and the longer he laughed, the more I had to fight a grin. Somebody finished my grilled cheese, and I found myself spooning the soup over and over and grinning and being an idiot, more or less.

"Ok," Dad finally said when he had himself under control. He was wiping his cheeks again. "I hear how bad that sounded. I'm going to work on it. I've got a lot to learn. But I'm going to do my best, and I'm sure you'll help me."

That seemed like a question, so I shrugged and moved soup around and finally said, "Well, yeah."

"Thank you." He hesitated. "It's scary, Jack. For me. As your father. Not because I care who you love. But because the world is...unkind to people who are different. I want your life to be perfect. I want you to be happy. But most of all, I want you to be safe."

"I'll be fine. Things are different."

He made a noise that might have meant anything, but he said, "I love you."

I shrugged, but I did manage to drag my eyes up from the soup long enough to meet his eyes. "I love you too."

"Are we good?"

I nodded.

"Anything else you want to talk about?"

The car, I thought. The way it rolled. The man with the gun. The fact that it had to be a coincidence, but that didn't help me when the nightmares came.

I shook out a no.

He came over and kissed me on the top of my head, and he rubbed my back, and after a while, he said, "You know things are going to be different now when Holloway comes over."

"Oh my God."

"Rules are rules, Jack."

"We're not even—we're friends."

"Uh huh."

"That's all."

"Uh huh," Dad said again, but this time he sounded amused. He pulled my hair just hard enough to be annoying, and he said, "Buddy, I might not know how all of this works yet, but straight, gay, or bi, I know what it means when my son stares at a boy and tries to put his shoe on the wrong foot."

"No, that was—on TV, there was—"

Dad gave me a little push, patted my cheek, and laughed.

"I saw boobs! I was staring at boobs. On TV!"

"A little tip, son," he said as he started toward the door. "If you're going to stare in public, at least wipe up your drool."

"Why do you have to be like this?"

He was already down the hall when he called back, "And don't think I missed the time he bent over to pick up his bag and you walked into the stool."

"We were having a nice father-son chat! We were bonding!"

Chapter 33

Something Damaging

When I found Holmes the next day, he was stealing a car.

The noonday skies were blue and clear like glass catching the light, and we were enough days past the snowstorm that the charm had gone, and everything was gray and crusty and half slush. He left Baker House in his driving coat, one hand in a loose fist at his side, his bag slung over one shoulder, and walked around the building toward where Mr. Fischer, the resident head, had a solitary parking spot.

I followed him. When I came around the building, he had one door of Mr. Fischer's red minivan open.

He must have heard me because his head whipped around. When he recognized me, his face only softened slightly.

"Going somewhere?" I asked.

He wanted to lie; the desire, and the conflicting knowledge that he'd probably be found out, muddled his expression for a moment. It was a little flattering.

Finally, he settled on, "Jack."

"Where are you going?"

"You're supposed to be resting. I'm going to bring your coursework this evening."

"From my classes."

Holmes waited. His hand tightened around Mr. Fischer's keys.

"Which is where you're supposed to be," I said. "In about five minutes. When lunch is over."

Somewhere farther off, a chorus of voices swelled—more boys from Baker House, hurrying to make the most of the lunch break. Holmes glanced automatically in their direction. When I took a step forward, his attention snapped back to me.

"Jack—"

"Let's see. It's important enough that you'll skip classes, even though you never want to skip, not even for good reasons."

He looked more comfortable scowling, which kind of made sense. "Afternoon cartoons are not a good reason."

"Well, they're called anime, so the joke's on you. Second, you don't want me to know about it, or you'd have asked me to drive you in the truck."

"You're injured. You're unlicensed. Your father does not want us consorting—"

I put my fists on my hips, and he stopped.

"It's about this stupid game, isn't it?" I said. "With Paxton and—" I almost said *your father*, but I managed to ask instead, "The mastermind?"

He couldn't meet my eyes. "Please, Jack. It may be dangerous, and if anything happened to you—"

"Either we go together, and you tell me everything on the way, or I pull out my phone and call the police, the FBI, the National Guard, maybe even the President of the United States. And yes, I know you could take away my phone and tie me up, which is weirdly cute and kinky at the same time, but you're not going to do that, are you?"

Pink circles lit up his cheeks. He shook his head.

"Then I'm driving," I said.

He tossed the keys to me, but when he tried to circle around to the passenger side, I caught his coat and pulled him closer and kissed him. He made an annoyed noise. He still wasn't meeting my eyes. After a moment, though, they came to rest on mine.

"Even if you're worried," I whispered. "Even if you're scared. It's good practice."

It took a moment. Then he offered me one of those tremulous, uncertain smiles.

We bonked foreheads gently, and I said, "Still a dork," and then I kissed him and sent him on his way with a pat on the ass.

Who says I'm not a gentleman?

We were merging onto I-15, where traffic was steady with minivans and crossovers and SUVs—anything big enough to hold a baseball team's worth of children—when Holmes said, "It's Paxton."

"I thought you said he couldn't be the mastermind."

"Yes. I mean, he isn't." Holmes let out a frustrated breath.

"Would it help if we kissed some more?"

"No."

"I can pull over."

"You are—" He set his jaw.

"Adorable."

"Yes." Then, as though he regretted saying anything, "But not as much as you think."

"Delightful."

"In your own peculiar way."

"Sexy."

Those circles of color darkened, and the muscles in his jaw tightened, and I thought for sure he wouldn't say anything. But then he said flatly, his gaze straight forward, "You have an appeal."

I burst out laughing. Holmes didn't, of course, but his face relaxed, and when I squeezed the back of his neck and left my hand there, I could feel the coiled anxiety in his muscles loosen in response.

"Mischievous," Holmes said. "And insatiable. And...and single-minded."

I smirked.

"It's not a good thing," Holmes said as he leaned into my touch. His eyes half-closed. I wondered if he'd slept, really slept, since the accident in the canyon. More likely, his nights had been full of his stimulants of choice, pushing himself until he collapsed and then, in his dream, pursued by terrors. The shadow of it lay across his face. We had learned a word for it. Eighth-grade Language Arts, Mr. Scholz. A caul. "Stop worrying, Jack," he murmured, his eyes still half shut. "We can't spend all day worrying about each other."

Clearing my throat, I squeezed his neck again. "That's kind of what this is all about. Sorry to break it to you, but I'm going to be doing lots of worrying."

He made a noise that could have meant anything. For a moment, his face was almost childlike as he let himself relax. Then the locks clicked shut, the bolts drove home, and he sat up, opening his eyes as all his defenses fell into place again.

"Paxton turned on Kazen's phone."

"What?"

"Kazen Bates. His phone. Paxton has it, and he turned it on."

"So many questions. How do you know Paxton has it?"

"Because Kazen's clothes had been rifled, and the phone was missing, and the window of Kazen's room was open. Someone took the phone and exited the house. Precipitously."

"But how do you know Paxton has it? He didn't kill Kazen."

"Because Emma doesn't, and Aston doesn't, and Camdyn didn't."

"Ok, but—"

"Abduction. The most likely possibility."

"Fine. Let's say you're right. How could you possibly know that he turned it on? And why does it matter?"

"Because," Holmes said, and he opened the bag between his feet to take out a matte-black laptop. "I have Kazen's laptop, and I'm using it to track his phone."

"Jesus Christ."

"It was the simplest way."

"H, he had bombs all over that place!"

"Landmines and other traps, not bombs."

"Excuse me?" I asked. Loudly.

Holmes's eyes got wide, and he shrank down in his seat, hands tight around the laptop.

"Not to mention—" Like I said: loudly. "—the fact that the police are looking for that, and it's a key piece of evidence."

"It's not a key piece of evidence for anything that concerns them," Holmes said. "And they don't need to build a case against Camdyn because she's already confessed."

"It doesn't matter. They should still have it. Why would Paxton want Kazen's phone anyway?"

"I'm not sure, but I imagine he wants that video—the one we saw synced to his laptop."

The tires thrummed beneath us, and I listened to that until I felt capable of speech. "You know what really pisses me off? You did it without telling me."

"You were in the hospital—"

"Like you don't trust me."

"Don't be ridiculous. Of course I trust you."

"That's why I caught you sneaking off to do this by yourself. That's why I had to threaten to fuck up your plan before you'd let me come along."

"I'm not letting you do anything," H said, and he was getting a little shouty too. "You forced me into this, as I knew you would. I cannot be trusted to make decisions in your best interest, not when I'm in your company, not when I—I can't say no to you. And so, the logical thing to do—"

"Finish that sentence."

He did not.

My pulse beat in my throat.

"I'm sorry," he whispered.

I nodded.

"You're supposed to say it now," he prompted.

Rolling my eyes, I managed not to choke on the words. "I'm sorry too."

We were passing Point of the Mountain now, and as we came around it, the suburban sprawl of the Salt Lake Valley spread out ahead of us. A boner in a Tesla zipped past on the left, horn blaring. I gave him the finger, but too late.

"I'm tired of being kept in the dark," I said. "For my own good or not. I want to know what's going on."

"We will follow the phone to Paxton—"

"No, dummy. I understood that part, thanks. I mean what's this all about? What's this game?"

Holmes was silent for a long time. He slid his fingers on the laptop's aluminum casing, pressing so hard that the tips turned white. When he spoke, his voice had regained the buckled-down, affectless quality I remembered from when we'd first met.

"My family enjoys games. Of all kinds. Not games like other families play. Games with secrets. Games that involve taking away. Or hiding. What can you get away with."

For a moment, the memory of Blackfriar's breath on my face, the fish oil weight of it, overcame me. "So, you think it's someone in your family?"

He shook his head. "The Moriartys play these games too. The Adlers play them. The three families." Something twisted in the next words like a knife. "And their fucking games."

I let us both have a moment. "Ok, so it's someone playing a game. We don't know who, but Paxton might help us figure it out. Do we know what kind of game it is?"

He hesitated.

"No," I said.

"Jack, please."

"No. I want to know."

The corner of his mouth trembled, and then he broke down and bit his lip. Teeth broke skin. Fresh blood welled.

"Someone gave me something," he said. His voice was unsteady with an emotion I couldn't scan. "Something important. Tremendously important."

"What?"

He bit his lip again. He was silent for longer. "On this one thing, will you please trust me? I will tell you anything else you want to know."

"Why won't you tell me?"

"It is something…damaging. Knowing it will place you in danger, and I will be unable to protect you."

I screamed in my head about that for a while, using up all my swear words. Then I said, "You don't have to protect me."

His laugh sounded strangled. "Jack, please. You have no idea—if it were that easy, if I could simply turn it off." He stopped. He released the laptop and pressed his face to his hands and drew long, deep breaths. When he lowered them again, his eyes were liquid and silver, but his voice was calmer. "Whatever else you want, I will give to you. Please don't make me do this."

A dozen different answers sprang to mind. I settled on, "And someone's trying to take it away from you?"

"Yes."

"But you don't know who."

"There are several possibilities."

"It seems like a pretty small pool of suspects, actually. Your family. The Moriartys. The Adlers."

"Perhaps. But unknown descendants appear from time to time. The bloodlines are far flung and tangled now. It's impossible to know them all."

I shook my head at that, and we kept driving.

The Intermodal Hub in Salt Lake City was, well, what it sounded like: a hub for the light rail system, Amtrak, city buses, and Greyhound. It was a long, low building with plate-glass windows and a corrugated steel awning. We had to park a block south, and as we walked to the station, Holmes carried the laptop, studying the signal from Kazen's phone as he tracked it via his own phone's internet hotspot. There were a fair number of people sitting outside the station: a man in a trench coat and sweats that had gone out at the knees; a woman with stringy gray hair and a dozen strands of Mardi Gras beads over a *Leave It to Beaver* t-shirt; a man in crisp new Wranglers and a white tee still creased from the packaging, no coat, whizzing into a trash can. I caught a whiff of urine and body odor, and after that I breathed through my mouth.

"Want to put that away?" I asked as Holmes continued to walk with the laptop open. "People are looking at you."

"Alert me if I need to protect us."

"Alert you?" I grabbed his elbow to steer him around what I was pretty sure was a Burger King bag full of human shit. "And hey, dumbass, I can protect us."

Holmes let out that little huff.

"Excuse me?" I asked.

"I was simply remembering something."

"The worst thing I ever did was let you stick your tongue down my throat. Now you've got all sorts of confidence."

"It's an unusual technique, tripping over a log while flailing with a box cutter, while your opponent has both a firearm and enough distance to operate it effectively."

"He wasn't supposed to turn around!"

"Very inconsiderate of him."

"I was half-frozen, you know. My legs weren't working right."

"Of course."

The guy whizzing was doing some fancy side-to-side action now, like some sort of nightmare human sprinkler, and I had to tug Holmes clear.

"I hate you," I said.

"The gum," Holmes said right before I stepped in chewing gum.

After that, he was on his own. It didn't seem to bother him as much as it should have. When we got to the steps leading up to the hub, he stepped over a lady who was sleeping on a rolled-up Kroger's bag, still studying the laptop's screen, while I paused to scrape gum off my Cortez.

I caught up to him inside. We were in a long, open room. Exposed girders and ductwork had been spray-painted black overhead. Retractable-belt barriers created queuing lines that everyone ignored. Families waited on benches that had been subdivided with metal armrests to keep people from sleeping on them. An overweight man in a North Face coat was screaming into a pay phone (which I hadn't known, until that moment, still existed). On the far side of the room, automatic doors led out to a platform where the salt-and-mud spattered chassis of Greyhounds rumbled.

"If you see—" Holmes began.

A familiar dark faux hawk was moving toward the automatic doors, carrying something—a small box with a handle—at his side. Paxton glanced over his shoulder, the movement unconcerned, probably automatic, and we locked eyes.

He ran.

I sprinted after him.

"Jack!" Holmes shouted.

But I kept running. As I ran, I tried to think—while, at the same time, dodging a double stroller stuffed with toddlers, a woman in a cotton-candy cloud of a coat, an emotional support dog that tried to bite me. Paxton was bigger than me, older, and as he had proven in the tunnels, clearly capable of handing me my ass. If I gave him an opening, he'd do it again. And then he'd be gone, and he'd be smart enough to ditch Kazen's phone. We might not ever find him. So, the solution was simple. Tackle him and make sure he didn't get up again. I wasn't sure how I was going to manage it, but sometimes it paid to be sparing on the details.

At first, I was sure I was going to lose him. I put on the gas, but he was still faster, and the distance between us grew. Then he jinked left as he passed through the automatic doors, and I cut at an angle after him. Holmes was shouting something behind me, but I couldn't focus on that. I lasered in on Paxton, on that stupid faux hawk, on broad shoulders under a waxed leather jacket.

When I passed through the automatic doors, the cold hit me like a slap, and my eyes watered. Paxton was maybe twenty feet ahead of me, and for some reason, he had slowed. He was turning in a circle, looking. People were staring at us. A few—an older man with a cane, a young woman with two roller bags, someone in an enormous hat—were still moving, but everyone else had stopped to watch.

I charged at Paxton. He turned, settling himself, the pose familiar: he was about to flip me or throw me or do the ultimate punch on me—something that would send me ass over teakettle and put me out of the race. And then I saw his focus change. He angled his body away from me, toward something behind me, and started running. It meant he was running toward me now—kind of.

I saw the elbow coming, and I took it on the crown of my head instead of in the face. He still rang my fucking bell, but instead of collapsing, the way I would have done if he'd hit me square, I did a tactical dive. It looked a lot like collapsing, only I wrapped my arms around his legs and took him with me. His momentum carried him another pace before he hit the platform hard, his breath whooshing out of him. I swear I heard his chin crack against the concrete, and the box he'd been carrying hit the ground and skidded away. I scrambled up Paxton's body, clawing at his fancy coat, until I was sitting astride him. Then I locked his wrists between his shoulder blades. A pain compliance hold. One of Holmes's favorites.

"Jack, hold him!" Holmes shouted as he blew past me.

I turned to watch and saw that he was chasing the person in the big hat. He—she?—looked shorter than either Holmes or I, but that could have been an affectation; it was hard to tell because they wore a long, baggy coat that came almost to their ankles. They were carrying a leather pilot's bag in one hand and, in the other, the box Paxton had been carrying. It swung at their side as they raced toward the end of the platform with Holmes in pursuit.

Beneath me, Paxton wriggled, tried to raise his head, and then groaned and dropped back down again.

"Got you, fucker."

"You split my chin, you cunt. And my teeth—I swear to God, if I lose a tooth, I'm going to take it out of your ass."

"Sounds great. I still owe you for that shit in the tunnels."

He laughed, and it sounded surprisingly genuine. Then he winced again. "Come on, bruv. Get off me now."

"Nice try."

His accent was thicker than I remembered. "I fink you should. I really fink you should."

"Lighten up on the act, would you? We're going to sit here and wait until H gets back. Or the police show up. Whichever happens first, I guess."

"I can give it to you. The half I've still got, I mean."

My mouth opened for me to say something snarky about that—and then my brain caught up with me.

"Yeah," Paxton said with rough satisfaction. "But you've got to decide right now. Before the blond bombshell gets back."

I worked on that for a minute. The best I could come up with was "Nice try." Again.

"Spoze you wait. Spoze you let Holloway take it. Do you think he'll let you see what it is?"

"Stop talking."

"You didn't ever wonder, did you? Holloway Holmes and all his secrets. Why's he keeping this a secret from you?"

"I said stop talking."

"What've you got to do with any of it, huh? Did you ever fink about that?"

A voice blatted on the speaker system, the words indistinguishable. The rattle of metal on metal suggested the approach of a train. On my next breath, I felt like all I got was the sickening sweetness of diesel exhaust. An older woman—trim and nicely dressed and with a handbag the size of a bowling ball—pranced a few steps towards us and took a swing with her bag. She missed me by inches, but she shouted, "What are you doing to him? Get off him!"

"Come on, bruv," Paxton said in a low voice meant for me. "You're not that thick. Front pocket. Help yourself."

"Didn't you hear me?" the woman asked with another menacing swing of her bag. A red-faced man in the crowd behind her cheered, and then someone else shouted something. This was my luck: I tracked down a blackmailing fuck boy, and somehow I was the one about to face mob justice. The woman lunged a few steps closer. That time, the bag almost got me. "Get off of him!"

I patted his coat as best I could. Paper rustled under the waxed leather.

"Don't move," I said, shifting so that my knee was between Paxton's shoulder blades. But it was a stupid thing to say because he had to move— rolling slightly so that I could reach into his front pocket. My fingers closed around paper.

I realized my mistake too late. Paxton was still rolling, as though trying to be helpful. But the movement gave him freedom to bring his arm up, and he threw another elbow at my head.

Twisting to avoid the blow, I put myself off balance. Paxton bucked, and I rocked sideways. I kept my grip on the papers in his front pocket, and they slid free of his coat as he snaked away from me. Scrambling after him, I got one hand around his ankle. He drew his other foot back, about to give me a hundred and fifty dollars' worth of sneakers to the teeth, but he never had a chance. That bowling-ball-sized handbag caught me on the side of the head, and the shock of it made me pull back and release Paxton.

He got to his feet and sprinted toward the buses. I started to follow, but another blow from the handbag caught me in the nose this time, and the next one barely missed taking out an eye. Shielding myself with my free hand, I scooted backward and shouted, "Cut it out!"

The older lady was breathing hard. The red-faced man let out a cheer. Two guys with Mexican cross tattoos on their necks were trading looks, and one of them broke away from the line of the crowd to step toward me.

"It's over," I said as I stood. "It's over!" I had to ward off one more blow from the handbag. The guy with the neck tattoo glared at me, and I met his look, and he stopped. Finally, he took the elbow of the lady with the handbag and said something to her, and she let him lead her back toward the crowd. Voices broke out everywhere. The red-faced man cheered again. I wondered how much cheering he'd be doing if he'd caught that bag with his face.

I jogged a few paces down the platform, then back, peering between the buses. No sign of Paxton. I'd lost him.

A woman with two small children was saying in a shrill voice, "Someone call the police! Someone needs to call the police!" And then one of the kids started to cry, and two Karens with matching haircuts took out their phones and started recording me.

Ducking my head, I hurried down the length of the platform in the direction Holmes had gone. The hub of outrage faded behind me, replaced by the rumble of idling buses. A fat man in a gray suit was smoking against the side of the Hub, and he eyed me as I passed him.

"Way to go, champ," he said and flicked what was left of his cigarette at me. The cherry hissed when it landed in the slush.

"For fuck's sake," I said, "I'm the good guy!"

I ducked around the corner of the hub. The tracks ran along this side, with another platform for people taking the light rail or Amtrak. This platform was empty—either nobody wanted a train today, or they'd all gotten pulled away by the disturbance Paxton and I had created. There was no sign of Holmes or whoever he'd been chasing.

Blowing out a breath that steamed in the freezing air, I dropped onto a bench. The jitters came as adrenaline washed out of me. My hands hurt; I wondered if maybe I'd thrown a punch. My head hurt from taking that first elbow on the crown. My knees and hip hurt from hitting the platform when I tackled Paxton.

Maybe that's why it took me so long to remember the paper I'd taken from Paxton's coat. I brought it up and smoothed it across my lap. Not a paper. An envelope. The big manila kind like you might use if you wanted to mail something without folding it. The postmark was from Salt Lake, from October. The address was to Holloway Holmes at the Walker School. I didn't recognize the handwriting, but it was controlled and small and detailed, which made me think it was girly, even though that's sexist. That was borne out by the name in the corner, though. Sarah Elizabeth Watson. Which didn't make any sense at all because she had died in September. Been murdered. By Blackfriar Holmes, although he'd arranged for someone else to do it. Because she had known something about the Holmes family.

It is something…damaging. That's what Holmes had said in the minivan on the drive up.

He'd had this since October.

He hadn't told me about it.

Something that everyone wanted. Something important. Something Blackfriar Holmes would kill to cover up.

The seal had already been broken, so the only thing holding the envelope closed was a metal clasp. My fingers were numb. The cold, probably. It took me a couple tries to get it open, and when I shook the envelope, a single sheet of paper slid out.

A family tree. Names. Lines. It had been printed off a computer. At the top, where the tree started, was John Watson.

I was breathing faster. A whistling sound filled my head. A train, maybe. The sound of something coming, something fast, something dangerous. *It is something…damaging.*

Scanning down the sheet, I tried to make sense of what I was seeing, tried to think. But they were names. Names I didn't recognize. Names that meant nothing to me. Until one.

It was all the way to the right, a distant branch far removed from the trunk of the tree. A woman's name. Camilla Catherine Sixsmith.

My mother.

And below it, circled in red, my own. Jack Sixsmith Moreno.

The paper trembled like a breeze was pulling at it, like maybe it was caught in the draft of something massive rushing past. A train, maybe. The gust of air displaced by its passage. But there was no train. No breeze. My breath floated up in ragged strips of white. My hand was shaking.

"I lost her." Holmes's voice was full of bitter, contained fury. "Or him. Whoever it was, they got away, God damn it."

He sounded far away. I wanted to slide the page back in the envelope. It was important. *It is something…damaging.* I needed to keep it safe.

"I suspect they were meeting Paxton to make an exchange. They didn't drop the bag, which suggests it held something valuable—probably cash."

It is something…damaging. That's what he had said. My eyes were dry. My face was a fever.

When I looked up, Holmes glanced over, and he froze at whatever he saw. His gaze moved to the envelope. Then to the page I held. I'd seen him angry. I'd seen him upset. I'd seen him frightened. He had been so scared that night when he had finally kissed me. It seemed like years ago now. But I'd never seen him like this—a kind of gaping horror in his face, like a wound.

"Ok," I said. My hands moved on their own, trying to stuff the paper back into the envelope. "That's what I needed to know."

"Jack—"

"Something damaging." I laughed. "Yeah, you'd better believe it."

"Jack, you don't understand. Whatever you think—"

"What do I think? Tell me. You're a genius, so tell me, what am I thinking?"

Holmes did that trick of his where he shut everything down, his face becoming glass, his body stone. His voice was emptied out, a purity of control, when he said, "I understand you're upset, and I will explain, but I need you to tell me where you got that."

"It must be really fucking damaging, figuring out a nothing piece of shit like me is related to your precious fucking John Watson."

"Where did you get it, Jack? Where did you find it?"

"Jesus, that's a black eye. The Holmeses and the Moriartys and the Adlers and the Watsons, all so fucking full of themselves—"

"Answer my question, Jack."

"—playing their games in their mansions. And then you've got a nobody like me."

"Did Paxton have it? Or did you find it yourself?"

"What's the worst part? What's most embarrassing?"

"I'm asking you a question—"

"That I'm too stupid for your games? Is that it? That I'm poor? That I'm brown?"

Holmes lunged, caught my coat, hauled me up from the bench. It shook the breath out of me. He was always stronger than I expected. "Answer me!"

Words percolated through the fog in my brain. *Did you find it yourself?* And I remembered Blackfriar in my bedroom, disassembling my desk to reveal where Holmes had hidden Sarah Watson's laptop. I remembered catching Holmes in there a few weeks ago, the expression on his face—a mixture of fear and chagrin. Because I'd caught him going through my desk. Only, I hadn't realized what I'd caught him doing, not really. I wanted to laugh; I thought he'd been trying to pick up a little, clean my room in secret. I thought about how strange it had been that Rivera had sent a deputy to search my room after I told him I'd been kidnapped. And stranger, still, that in the aftermath of Camdyn's arrest, nobody had said a single word about the drugs I'd stashed in the cottage. Almost like they'd never found them. Or, I was realizing now, because the deputy hadn't been a deputy.

"Oh my God," I said. A grin sliced open one side of my mouth. "You fucked up, didn't you?"

Holmes released me. He pressed his hands to his eyes. His breathing came in labored, desperate bursts.

"You tried the same trick again, and it didn't work. Paxton found it. He got to your little hidey-hole in my room, and he took it. He took this. This damaging information."

He was trying so hard to get himself under control again, but he couldn't quite do it. He dropped his hands. His eyes were wet. They looked like the asphalt where the snowmelt was nothing but a skin of water. "Jack, please listen to me. Elements are in play that you do not understand—"

"You told me you'd looked up my mom. You told me you'd checked her maiden name. To make sure I wasn't a Watson. Was that a lie?"

"Jack—"

"Was it a lie?" My shout bounced back from the platform and echoed out across the tracks. The speakers overhead buzzed. We were still alone. How were we still alone in a city of millions of people?

"No," he said in a crushed voice.

"You didn't think to check her mom's maiden name."

A tear spilled and ran down the chiseled coldness of his cheek. "I did not."

"Did you feel stupid when you got this in the mail? Did you feel like an idiot?"

Some force I didn't recognize tore at him, clawing at his face. I could barely hear him when he said, "I felt terrified. Please let me explain—"

"What does this mean? My mom's a Watson. I'm a Watson. What does that mean?" I couldn't help my voice twisting as I asked, "Is that really so fucking awful?"

"Don't be ridiculous. It means nothing. It doesn't have to mean anything."

"It means nothing." I tasted blood and realized, distantly, I had bitten my cheek. "You've known for two months. You've known for two fucking months! A dead girl sent this to you, and you lied about it, and you kept lying! And you're going to tell me to my face that it doesn't mean anything."

"I was trying to keep you safe!"

I swung before I realized what I was doing—my other hand, because I was still clutching the envelope. Holmes dodged; he barely moved, turning in place to let my swing go wide, the force of it making me stumble. Holmes stepped back, giving me space. It was the way he moved when we sparred. Always giving me another opportunity to embarrass myself.

Drawing myself up, I scrubbed an arm across my face. My cheeks were dry. My eyes. Sweat prickled at my hairline. The discord of our breathing was the only sound.

When I'd put enough of the pieces back in place, I said in a low voice, my eyes on the platform, "I told you: I don't need you to keep me safe. I don't need you at all." I threw the envelope at his feet. "Don't worry. Nobody's going to learn your dirty secret."

He grabbed the envelope and held it against himself. When I turned, he reached for my arm. I spun, my fist coming up, and he flinched. But he didn't move, and he didn't let go.

"Strike me," he said, the posh bleeding into the ragged ends of his words. "Beat me. Do whatever you like, Jack. Please. Do whatever you must do, but let me explain."

I tried to shake him off.

"Please!" That look was back—his façade broken, and what was left was a black hole of fear. The next words were torn from him. "Jack, I love you." He stopped. Swallowed. Seemed to hear himself. He was so pale. Bloodless except where he bit his lip and berry-bright drops appeared. His voice made me think of the car when we went into the creek, water coursing over steel. "I love you." He stopped again, and even in that moment, I knew how much this was costing him, how hard he was fighting to say all the things he'd been trained never to say, to feel all the things he'd never been allowed to feel. "I love you," he whispered. "I don't care about anything else. Can't you believe that?"

Three deep breaths. Then I trusted myself to say, "Let go."

He must have heard it in my voice: the end, the finality of it. His hand opened, and he fell back a step.

"I don't ever want to see you again," I said. And then I left.

Chapter 34

Goodbye

Dramatic exits are all well and good, but they're kind of undermined when you have to call your dad, sobbing so hard you can barely get the words out, and then wait on a bench on North Temple while various well-intentioned Mormons assume you're homeless and try to help. By the time Dad finally picked me up, I'd been offered two places to stay, six rides to a shelter, and — if my math was good—four hundred and eighty dollars. Not that I took any of it. It's hard to hold on to cash while you're weeping uncontrollably and covering yourself in snot.

By the time we got back to Walker, I'd told Dad enough: it was over between Holmes and me; under no circumstances was he to allow Holmes into our home; and I didn't want to talk about it, not ever again.

When we pulled into the carport, though, Dad shifted into park and sat for a moment with his hands on the wheel. Then he said, the words calm and quiet, "Jack, if he did something to you that you didn't want him to do, we need to call the police."

So, of course, then I had to deal with that.

The rest of that day was a blur—one long moment that seemed like it would never end, me lying on my bed in the dark. Dad came to check on me. He didn't know what to do, so he made me chicken noodle soup, poor guy. That night, he did something he hadn't done in a long time: he stretched out next to me and scratched my scalp while I cried, and at some point, I fell asleep.

I wasn't any better the next day. But the day after that, I got up. Dad had talked to Headmaster Cluff, and she'd excused me from my classes for the rest of the semester, which was only a few days now. I heard him in the other room when he called. Trauma was a magic word. The truth was, it didn't matter. I could have gone to class. I could have sat in my room. You could have dragged me behind a truck.

Instead of any of those options, Dad made me go to work. I had to plunge toilets again. I had to cable drains. We got more snow dumped on us, and he put me on the plow at two in the morning. When I wasn't sleeping, I was working. If it wasn't jobs for Walker, I was in the maintenance building's garage, where Dad supervised as I tuned up our old mountain bike.

I was falling asleep a week later, sore everywhere, the blackness coming in like a flood, when I realized he had probably saved my life.

And then it was winter break, and everyone at Walker went home. Campus was empty except for a few faculty who chose to spend their holidays here, and, of course, the essential staff who kept Walker alive. If anything, there was more work to do—waxing floors, cleaning carpets, replacing bathroom fixtures. All the big jobs we couldn't do during the school year. And the snow, of course. Even with only half a dozen people on campus, Dad made me plow and shovel and salt.

When the next semester came, I was going to have to tell him I couldn't go back.

I didn't realize how much time had passed until one morning I was stepping into my Vans, and Dad came out from his bedroom in his sleep tee and old gym shorts and said, "Go back to bed; it's Christmas Eve."

He followed his own advice, so I kicked free of my shoes and shucked my jeans and crawled back into bed, too lazy to get rid of the Walker hoodie I'd been wearing. I lay there. A little ambient light came from my clock. The ceiling had the irregularities of old plaster, which was another way of saying it was a pain in the ass when you had to fix it. Compared to drywall, anyway. Outside, the world was still dark. I could go back to sleep. I could sleep all day if I wanted. Dad would let me; it was a holiday.

But I didn't fall back asleep. I lay there, and I stared, and I could feel my thoughts marshaling at the horizon. All the things I didn't want to think about.

After Mom died, I had been devastated. I'd lost my mom. I'd blamed myself. And on top of that, I'd been dealing with the trauma of the accident itself. Devastated wasn't the right word. I'd hurt so badly that for a long time, the only reason I could get out of bed was because if I didn't, we'd be out of food, or the house would look like shit, or Dad would lie on a urine-soaked mattress all day, and if I let that happen, some state-mandated reporter would eventually tell the next person up the chain of command, and they'd take me away. Fear had been the only thing to keep me moving, fear of losing the last piece of my life.

What had happened with Holmes was different. Dad thought it was a breakup. And my friends—if I had any—would have thought I was better off without Supercreep. But it was more than that.

Meeting Holloway Holmes had changed my life. Made it wonderful in so many ways. And, in a few ways, made it harder. I'd brushed up against something amazing, something singular in the universe, and for a few months, I'd been allowed access to another world. It had made me better. I'd done things, impossible things. And I think he was better too. He had pushed me, challenged me—and in that dark bedroom, under that ceiling pocked with shadow, I had nobody to lie to, nobody who needed false modesty. I had risen to that challenge. Maybe not perfectly. Maybe not every time. But I had been more than Jack Moreno, or the Jack Moreno I used to be. And Holmes had been more too. More everything. In World History this semester, when I'd been catching up on the stuff I'd missed at the beginning of the semester, Mrs. Albrecht's slides about Aristotle said that he believed virtue was the quality of being a human as excellently as possible. We had done that, I thought. We had made each other better humans.

It was hard not to hear, in the shadow of my thoughts, bits and pieces of my conversations with Holmes over the last few months. Little things he'd said before he'd learned who I was, what I was. Holmeses and Watsons find each other, he'd told me. In the most impossible places. Under the most improbable circumstances. Some sort of genetic trait passed down through generations. Or quantum entanglement. Or magic. He did, after all, come from the land of Harry Potter. He had told me that the Holmeses were always at their best with the Watsons. And I had heard, in what he didn't say, the pain that those days were past and gone. But they hadn't been, of course. That had been us. Just like he'd said.

And then Holmes had stolen it from me. Because it had been my secret, mine to know. Who I was. Who my mother was. And he had lied about it. What could have been wonderful, what could have explained everything about who we were to each other, he had corrupted. He'd taken a big old stinking shit on it, as a matter of fact. Because it was one thing to be friends with Jack Moreno, to slum with Janitor Boy while you were in high school. And it was another thing to be saddled for the rest of your life with a poor brown kid who had a dad with disabilities, no prospects for the future, and a hell of a lot of emotional baggage—all because of a bloodline that made him the cosmic equivalent of a study buddy.

He had said, *I love you.*

Had he ever said it before? To anyone?

I knew him better than just about anybody, and I thought the answer was no. Maybe to his mom, although it was difficult to imagine Holmes having a mom. But he had said it to me. And in the darkness, his face floated in front of me in those last moments, the pain that was so tremendous that even Holloway Holmes, who had only ever known a lifetime of pain, buckled under it.

But he had lied. He had taken what should have been the best thing in my life, and he had turned it into a knife to slip under my ribs.

I put my arm over my eyes. I was tired of staring at the ceiling. The wind soughed. It was the aspens' long song, it was stone and ice, it was the sound of a great, rushing emptiness.

Sleep didn't come.

I had read about sadness. After Mom died, when I needed help, when I couldn't go to the counselor or the therapist or anybody, because they'd take me away from Dad, I'd gone to my trusty friend Wikipedia, and I'd read. It wasn't the same as grief, and I read about that too. But I remembered learning about sadness, about some bozo who said it was a natural process of growing up—rooted in the experience of separation from the mother, as the child detaches itself from a symbiotic relationship to become an independent organism. I'd had to look up symbiotic. And I'd had to think about it. And I thought if this was what they paid scientists for, to tell you that you were sad when the universe took away your mom, then sign me up because even I could come up with that shit.

The more I'd thought about it, though, the more I'd realized it was more than that. And I thought about it now, with the smell of the store-brand detergent on my hoodie, and the fabric rough against hot cheeks. That sadness wasn't just about your mom. Sadness was about being alone. That wasn't the only reason people were sad, but it was a big one. Sadness, when it was part of growing up, was the experience of learning that you were alone in the universe. No matter who loved you. No matter how many friends you had at school, or followers on TikTok, or anything. We were all alone. We touched each other briefly, and then the world spun us apart again. So, it was all right to be sad. And maybe it was ironic, a little bit, that Wikipedia told me that sadness could be a way to learn through solitude. That being alone with our sadness could teach us something—about ourselves, about life, about the world. I figured I was in the PhD program for that kind of stuff. And Wikipedia said that loss, grief, sadness, when we approached it as a learning opportunity, could lead to a new sense of being alive, a return to the outside world.

I didn't know about that. That hadn't been my experience; my experience was that I'd dragged myself out of the burning wreckage of my life, and I'd been alone for over a year—well, I had Dad, but I'd been alone in the ways that counted—and then I'd met Holloway Holmes, and everything had changed. I didn't even know what it meant, a new sense of being alive, a return to the outside world. Was there a world for me without Holloway Holmes? The question should have sounded silly and dramatic, but in that moment, I didn't know the answer.

I guess I was going to find out.

I sat up. I found a pair of joggers that were probably, likely, clean. I found Dad's Discman, and I clipped it to my waistband and pulled on the headphones and pressed play. The Smashing Pumpkins. "Today." Today, I thought as I pulled the Stan Smith's over my heels. Today. Today.

Letting myself out of the cottage as quietly as I could, I winced at the first crushing wave of cold. Snot froze in my nostrils. My nose and the tips of my ears prickled. I started toward the maintenance building.

The sun was clearing the mountains, the world folding up its shadows, packing them away for the day. Wind rushed against me, stirring up the powder, snow stinging my face. The air smelled like pine and cedar. My breath wreathed up around me, and where the light caught it, it was the color of his eyes. When the wind quieted again, the only sound were my sneakers crunching the crust of snow.

We kept some of our stuff in storage at the maintenance building; there was plenty of space, and as long as Mr. Taylor didn't find out, nobody cared. Stuff that we didn't have room for in the cottage, like Dad's mountain bike. Or seasonal stuff that took up too much room. Like the Christmas tree.

I found it in the lofted storage space you could only get to with a ladder, and I had to shimmy it to the edge of the platform and then let it fall. It survived, albeit with a few bent branches that would have to be straightened out. I found the boxes of ornaments, and those I had to carry down by hand. Then I found the lights. Last Christmas, we hadn't done anything. Dad had still been really bad, even months after the accident. He kept promising we'd put up the tree. He kept promising we'd go out for a nice meal. He kept promising presents. But Christmas Eve and Christmas Day he'd spent laid up with a migraine, and when I'd tried to order pizza, I'd learned all his cards were maxed out. That felt like another boy, someone I barely knew.

Lugging the tree back to the cottage wasn't exactly easy, especially with the snow, but I did it. On my next trip, the sky was a blue so faint it was almost white, and a thin layer of cirrus clouds showed to the west like someone had straightened them out with a comb.

I carried the ornaments home.

Then the lights.

I was kicking snow off the Stan Smith's, shrugging out of my coat, when Dad appeared again at the end of the hall. He looked at me for what felt like a long time. Then he said, "Want some help?"

I shook my head, and he went back into his room.

The tree first, setting it up, forgetting how it was supposed to sit in its base—or maybe I'd never known, since Dad had always done it—and then figuring it out. The branches, which straightened out pretty well except for one, so I put that side against the wall. Then all the needles. I stopped to watch two YouTube videos about fluffing your tree. If Holmes had been there, I would have told him that was a sex thing, and he would have gotten those perfect red circles in his cheeks. Then, because I shouldn't have thought about that, I made myself think about it for a little longer. Because it hurt.

Dad got ready in the background—he showered, he shaved, he emerged from his room dressed in thick woolly socks and dad jeans and a Christmas sweater that showed a drunk reindeer—you could tell it was drunk because it was hiccupping and staggering. Mom had told him to throw it away. I hadn't known he still had it.

I stood back to judge my fluffing, and he came over and put an arm around me and kissed the side of my head. He was warm the way you were after a shower, and he smelled like the little bar of Dial that we needed to replace.

"I'm working," I growled and elbowed him off me, and he laughed and messed up my hair and went into the kitchen. He banged around in there for a while—pans going on the stove, eggshells cracking, the whisk chiming against a mixing bowl. I kept fluffing. He was watching me. Like a Dad. Which meant zero chill, and it was impossible not to know he was watching me.

I did the lights next.

"If you start there, you're not going to be able to plug them in," Dad said.

"Who's doing this?" I asked. "You or me?"

"Do you want your pancakes shaped like Christmas trees or reindeers?"

"You can't do reindeers. They look exactly the same as your alligators. And your dolphins. And your ducks."

"Christmas trees it is."

"Your Christmas trees look like your Valentine's hearts."

"You can tell by the color. The trees are green; the hearts are pink."

I hid a smile and redid the lights.

He was still watching (like I said, zero chill), so when it was time for the ornaments, I didn't let myself hesitate. I opened the box, pulled them out, and started hanging them. He'd kept all of them, probably because it had been too much trouble to go through them when we had to leave our house in Salt Lake. It was kind of a miracle they'd made it here—the tree too. Maybe he'd loaded the stuff without knowing what it was. Or maybe he'd known and had thought, for some reason, it was important enough to keep.

Some of the ornaments were from trips we'd taken: one shaped like Mickey Mouse ears, and one like the Hollywood sign, and one from Yellowstone that was supposed to be a grizzly bear, only whoever had done it had apparently never seen a grizzly. And some of the ornaments were older—they'd been my mom's mom's, and they were small and fragile and were from an entire set that was themed around a tea party. A table set for tea. A little tiered stand with cakes and sandwiches. A teapot. Teacups. Stuff like that. I hung these ones on the back. I thought, if someone bumped the tree on accident and they fell and shattered and no, we couldn't glue them back together, that would be a real tragedy.

A few of the ornaments, the ugliest ones, I'd made. A star out of popsicle sticks. A snowman out of cotton balls. The felt Santa who was totally crooked and, because I'd glued the googly eyes wrong, was slightly terrifying.

I knelt there in front of the tree, staring at it. People around the world had used evergreen trees as a symbol that life went on, even in the coldest, darkest winter. That the sun would come again. That new growth would push its way free from the slowly warming soil. For hope, in other words. You could read all about it on Wikipedia.

I didn't know if sadness would awaken me to a new sense of aliveness. But I knew something in me wanted to live, wanted to be awake, wanted the snow to spark on my tongue, wanted to see dawn coming over the mountain and the light picking out the hares and the voles and the oaks and the pines. Even though it hurt. Maybe even because it hurt.

Before I could stop myself, I went to my room, and I found the small, wrapped package in the bottom drawer of my desk, and I ripped off the paper and opened it and carried the little ornament out to the tree. I had bought it for him because I hadn't known what else to get him, because I didn't know what to get the boy who had everything. You could get any kind of ornament you wanted on Etsy. The same thing, by the way, goes for dicks. Gummy dicks. Decorative dicks. Dicks on mugs. Big bouncy dicks on hats. Dicks on dicks on dicks. In case you're wondering.

It was a Double-Double with animal-style fries, and you could tell it was In-N-Out because the artist had gotten the cup right. On the back, there was a little frame where you could put a picture, but I hadn't done that. It would have been creepy as hell. Even if I'd wanted to, I'd never stolen that picture off the bulletin board in Baker House, and I didn't have any good pictures. Not of us. Not together.

When it hit me, I blinked and pulled up my hoodie and wiped my eyes, and my shoulders shook. In the kitchen, the bowl clunked against the counter, and Dad's steps came toward me.

"I'm ok," I said. But I started crying harder. "I'm ok. I'm really ok."

Dad hugged me, and we stayed like that for a long time. It was different this time. The crying. I mean, it was the same: ruining Dad's reindeer sweater, getting both of us snotty. But it felt different. The emptying out of something—infection, poison, whatever you wanted to call it. And, in its place, a kind of relief.

Eventually, Dad got me settled at the counter, and he plated Christmas tree pancakes that looked (if I'm generous) like arrows. If I were being honest, they looked kind of like dongs, but that's not the kind of thing you can say to your dad. Or I couldn't say to my dad, anyway. He didn't even pretend to eat. He just stood there, watching me.

"Creep much?" I asked around a mouthful of pancake.

His hesitation lasted a moment too long.

I lifted my gaze from my plate. His jaw was tight. His eye slid away from mine.

"What?" I asked. "What happened?"

"I'm going to tell you something because I think you deserve to know. But I want you to understand that whatever you decide, I'm going to support you. And if you don't want to make a decision right now, that's fine too." He wrung a kitchen towel between his hands, but before I could ask him what he was talking about, he spoke again. "He came by. This morning." And then, in a rush, "While you were getting the tree."

"What? Who?" But that was a bad joke, so I immediately asked, "H?"

Dad nodded. "He…he left you something. A gift. I told him no. And I didn't let him in the house like I promised. But he left the gift on the porch, and I didn't want you to find it like that, and—"

"But—but you were asleep."

Rolling his eyes, Dad said, "My only son is going through some bad stuff. Please give me a little credit; when I heard you sneak out, I got up to make sure you weren't going to do anything you'd regret."

I couldn't handle that, whatever it meant. Not right then. I didn't know what to say. I didn't know if I could say anything.

"I guess what I'm asking," Dad said, "is do you want the gift? Do you want me to throw it away? Do you want to decide later?" More words burst free. "He was—he looked really bad, Jack. Whatever happened between the two of you, it's tearing him up." Dad snapped the towel against his thigh. "I shouldn't have said that."

I stared at him. I shook my head.

"Ok," he said. "That's ok. Maybe I shouldn't have said anything—"

"I want it." I pushed my plate away; it skittered across the countertop. "I changed my mind. I want it."

"Jack."

"I want it."

Dad studied me. Then, drawing the towel taut between his hands, he took off toward his bedroom. When he came back a moment later, he was carrying a small package wrapped in red buffalo-plaid paper. The expensive stuff; I could tell as soon as I touched it. It had a small golden bow in the right corner. I knew what his hands would have looked like, pressing it there. The incredible attention to detail. All the immense focus that he could bring to bear dedicated, in that instant, to this. For me.

"If you want to wait," Dad said.

But I slid my finger under the tape, and the wrapping popped open. I pulled out a black notebook, the kind Holmes loved. Which he carried everywhere. Where he wrote everything.

A note had been taped to the front cover. *Jack, I know you will never forgive me, but I want to explain—*

I dropped the notebook on the counter.

Two pieces of paper fell out.

One was the sticky note I'd left on Holmes's desk back in September, the one with the happy janitor blowing a kiss. The one he'd kept. The one I'd seen that night in the athletic center. The one that had made me start to hope.

The second was Holmes's answer to my sketch. It was obvious at first glance that he was both much more technically adept than I was and had some amount of artistic training. Of course he did; he was a Holmes. I recognized us from the night I'd spent in his room. Me propping myself up on one elbow. Holmes's mouth near my own. I knew that moment. No one had to tell me. It was that heartbeat after his first, uncertain kiss. Before I had reached for him. It was the moment Holmes had been most vulnerable in his life, and he had given it to me. And now here he was, giving it to me again.

I scrambled off the stool.

"Jack—"

Stan Smith's. Keys. Phone. I tore open the door.

"Son, wait!"

I raced out into the morning. Across campus. The sky wide and bright overhead, a dome of light cupping me. The cold cutting me to ribbons because I'd forgotten my coat. I didn't care. Even that felt good, like I was coming apart—the pain that had weighed me down was gone, and I felt light. My feet didn't seem to touch the ground.

As I ran, I placed the call to his phone. An automatic message picked up and told me that number was no longer in service. I placed the call again, phone dropping to my side, and kept running.

Baker House was dark when I reached it. In the lobby, as I sprinted toward the stairs, the air that met me felt so hot that my skin wanted to crack, even though part of me knew we'd kept the temperature low, at sixty, while the students were away. Up the stairs, my steps hammering echoes back at me. And then out into the second-floor hall.

Room 221.

Maybe it was the cold, that it had pushed me beyond shivering and into somewhere else. Maybe it was the unrelenting lightness buoying me up. I should have been shaking, but the key slid into the door smoothly.

I stopped just inside.

The bed had been stripped.

The closet door stood open, the hangers bare.

Every drawer in the desk and dresser was open and empty.

I raised my phone. The automated message was still telling me, over and over again, that the number was no longer in service.

He wasn't here.

He was gone.

And I knew, in that moment, he wasn't coming back. Not ever. The notebook, the message, the drawing, they hadn't been an apology. They hadn't been an explanation. They had been goodbye.

WHERE ALL PATHS MEET

Keep reading for a sneak preview of *Where All Paths Meet,* the final volume of The Adventures of Holloway Holmes.

Chapter 1

The Incredible Growing Boy

I stared at myself in the mirror. "I'm going to do the mature thing."

Dad didn't exactly sigh, but he did rub his forehead.

"I'm going to do the only sensible thing," I said.

"They don't give out enough good parenting awards, you know that? And they never give them out for moments like this."

"I'm going to skip prom, spend the rest of my life single, and die alone, at home, a virgin."

"A little late for that," Dad muttered.

I broke away from the mirror and rounded on him. "Excuse me?"

"It's not that bad," Dad said in a soothing voice. "You look very handsome."

"That's what parents say. Because they're legally obligated." I held out my arm, so he could see the tux's sleeve sliding up past my wrist. I showed him the trousers hitting me above the ankle. I crossed my arms for emphasis, and in the silence, you could hear the seams in the shoulders straining. When I'd asked about renting a tux, he'd produced this abomination from under his bed. He probably thought I didn't know about what else he kept down there. The gun safe, for one. That was new.

"Ok," Dad said. "You're a little bigger than I was when Mom and I got married. God knows you've been working out enough."

"I look like Frankenstein."

"I thought Frankenstein had cut-offs."

"Dad!"

"We'll figure it out, buddy. We'll get it tailored."

"Tailored? No. This thing needs to be burned. And then somebody needs to perform an exorcism on the ashes. And then I can die at home, alone—"

"A 'virgin.' Yeah, I heard you."

Proof of bad fathering: he even drew the air quotes with his fingers.

"I'm glad this is funny. I'm never going on a date again. I'm never going to fall in love. I'm never going to move out. I'm going to die alone, in your basement—"

"We don't have a basement."

I drew myself up—which, ok, was kind of hard because the jacket was so snug—and glared at him.

Dad was rubbing his chin suspiciously and refusing to look at me. "What about Glo? You two are cute together. Oh, wait—what about Rowe?"

"Don't do that."

"He's a nice-looking guy."

"You are not going to weasel out of this by pretending to be supportive of my bisexuality."

"Hey, hold on, I am supportive—"

"Glo is dating Rowe!"

"Oh." Dad rubbed his chin. Vigorously. "Well, how was I supposed to know that?"

"They sit on your couch and suck each other's faces off!"

"What about Emma? You're always hanging out with Emma."

"Emma is going with Rowe and Glo. They're together."

"Why—

"If you ask me why I don't go with them, I'm going to Hulk out!"

"You're halfway out of the tux already."

I was still trying to Hulk my way out of the tux when the knock came at the door.

"It's not even that I'm mad," Dad said as he headed down the hall. "I'm just disappointed."

"That's not how you're supposed to use that!" I shouted after him.

"Perfect timing," Dad said at the other end of the cottage. "Will you please be a gentleman and ask my son to prom?"

I couldn't stop my squawk of "Dad!"

"Sorry, Mr. Moreno," Rowe said, his voice moving toward me. "I'm going with Glo and Emma."

"Can he go with you?"

"Stop embarrassing me!"

Rowe appeared in my doorway. He was one of those obnoxiously masculine guys: he had a few inches on me, as well as probably fifty pounds of muscle, and he had that Minnesota-Scandinavian look of perpetually ruddy cheeks. Combined with puppy-dog brown eyes, an annoyingly full beard, and disheveled blond bangs, he pretty much had the whole package going. So, if he'd asked, I probably would have said yes. To prom, I mean. Not that he was bi. And not that he would have asked me if he was. Not that I even thought about him like that.

He took one look at me and burst out laughing. "Holy cow, man. That's hilarious!"

"It's not a joke," I snapped. I tried to squirm out of the jacket, but I couldn't. "For fuck's sake, help me!'

"Jack," Dad bellowed from the front of the house.

Rowe was still laughing as he tugged off the jacket. When it came loose, I said, "Knock it off. It's my dad's fault."

"Rowe, please tell him to be polite to his elderly parents."

"Stay out of this," I shouted back. "You're the whole reason I'm in this mess."

"Dude," Rowe said with a smile.

I glowered at him too because Rowe was like a teddy bear, and he could take pretty much any amount of glowering and it didn't have any effect on him. I shucked the tuxedo pants, found a pair of shorts and one of Dad's old Nirvana tees, and pulled them on. It might have been my imagination, but the shorts seemed to hit me higher on the thigh than I remembered, and the shirt might—might—have been a tiny bit too small. I considered changing again. But what if it wasn't my imagination? And by then, Rowe was straddling my chair backward, waiting. He was already geared up: running shoes, mesh shorts, a *Sin City* t-shirt in a bro cut.

"Ready?" Rowe asked.

"Yeah, almost, hold on. Let me finish of dying from parental neglect and internalized humiliation."

Rowe worked a finger in his ear.

"Rowe's not going to want to date you if you treat your father like that," Dad called back.

"Everybody's a comedian," I said.

I flipped off the lights, and Rowe trailed after me. "So," he said, "I was thinking we'd change things up. We'll finish with sprints this time."

I groaned. "No. I changed my mind. I'm not going."

He bumped me, and I stumbled into a half-jog and caught myself on the counter. I stopped when I saw the envelope there—the kind of reinforced cardboard mailer that official documents might come in. Lord knows I'd seen enough of those in the year after the accident. Only instead of Dad's name, it had mine, and there was no return address.

"What's this?" I asked.

"Rowe brought it in," Dad said from his recliner, where he was flipping channels.

"I found it on the porch."

"What is it?" I asked.

"Well, son, there's this thing called an envelope—"

"I'm going to run away," I said as I grabbed the mailer. "I'm going to join the circus."

"The incredible growing boy," Rowe said. "No clothes in the world will fit him."

Dad sounded like he was choking, but he managed to say, "It's probably a college packet."

"Yeah," I said as I opened the envelope. "With my grades."

Two pieces of paper lay inside. The first looked like a greeting card, but when I touched it, it was different—heavier, with a feel and texture that said it was seriously expensive. I pulled it out and gave it a closer look. It wasn't a greeting card; it was an invitation.

You are invited to the Zodiac "Fabulous Five" Anniversary Party. Below that, it gave details—the party was Saturday, tomorrow, and I was allowed to bring a guest. The only people I knew at Zodiac, the tech conglomerate located at the north end of Utah Valley, were Maggie Moriarty and Blackfriar Holmes. Both of them, I was pretty sure, had tried to kill me. So, all things considered, that was a pass.

I shoved the invitation back in the mailer and took out the smaller piece of paper. It felt different from the invitation—cheap, like copy paper. On it was printed a single sentence: *Come if you want to know the truth about your mother*.

"Well?" Dad asked. "What is it?"

Giving Rowe a warning look, I dropped the paper back into the mailer. "Like you said. College stuff."

"What college?"

"BYU."

Dad snorted a laugh.

I took the mailer to my room and shoved it under the mattress. When I rejoined Rowe, he was giving me a look, which I chose to ignore.

"All right," I said. "We're leaving."

"Go easy on the sprints," Dad said. "If you puke on my porch, you're cleaning it up."

"See?" I asked Rowe as I ushered him out of the house. "See what kind of love I get?"

The May evening was soft in the twilight, the air sweet with the smell of the water from the sprinklers, the new growth of grass. Rowe was giving me that look again.

"We're not going to talk about it," I said. "And you'd better not say anything to my dad."

"If you need to—"

"I don't," I said. And then, because I couldn't help myself, "I'm not getting caught up in that mess again."

Rowe made a face. Then he said, "Race you to the athletic center?"

"Are you stupid? We're doing sprints—God damn it, Rowe!"

I tore off after him.

But as I ran, words thundered in time with my steps.

Come if you want to know the truth about your mother.

Come. Come. Come.

And the answer rose inside me: You'd better believe I fucking will.

Acknowledgments

My deepest thanks go out to the following people (in alphabetical order):

Justene Adamec, for pointing out plot holes that needed patching, and for her kind words about Jack and Holmes.

Savannah Cordle, for all her excellent questions that needed answers, for catching my missing commas, and for making me laugh through my tears with her final comment.

Fritz, for catching so many of my typos, for all his help with continuity, and most of all, for helping me with Ariana and how the truth about Aston comes out.

Austin Gwin, for spotting missing words, for asking about Emma and the blackmail, and most importantly, for everything about Jack and Holmes and what's going on in Jack's head.

Steve Leonard, for help with official Fleshlights, for helping me again with my In-N-Out references (Double-Double!), and for taking time to talk with me about Jack and Holmes (especially about Jack being an idiot).

Raj Mangat, for fixing my lip balm blunder, for catching so many continuity errors, and for her wonderful recommendation about the kiss (and for being so understanding about the final version)

Cheryl Oakley, for helping me fix Kazen's phone and video; for reminding me that Jack is way past curfew; and, among so many things, nudging me to give a little refresher about Olin Campbell.

Pepe, for sending me corrections for my mistakes, for asking so many good questions about this book (some of which, I'm afraid, I have left unanswered), and for asking so many more excellent questions that will be answered in the next one!

Nichole Reeder, for, among other things, keeping track of what Aston actually said, locating Mr. Patrick in the vestibule, and giving me Inifiniti (not, sigh, Infinity).

Tray Stephenson, for catching my many typos, including the ones that were so close to being right, and for his helpful feedback on the next stage in Jack and H's relationship!

Mark Wallace, for catching my many typos, for sharing his reader brain and his personal connections to the story, and for being spot on about my reaction to my mistakes (i.e., "I can't believe I did that").

Jo Wegstein, for help with an abundance of errors, and for special help with Roblox Robux, with trivia about the Ivys, and for her thorough recalculating of the timeline.

About the Author

For advanced access, exclusive content, limited-time promotions, and insider information, please sign up for my mailing list at **www.gregoryashe.com**.

www.ingramcontent.com/pod-product-compliance
Lightning Source LLC
Chambersburg PA
CBHW051955240626
47153CB00005B/1771